MW00355541

THE WRANGLER AND THE ORPHAN

ALSO BY JACKIE NORTH

The Farthingdale Ranch Series

The Foreman and the Drifter

The Blacksmith and the Ex-Con

The Ranch Hand and the Single Dad

The Wrangler and the Orphan

The Cook and the Gangster

The Trail Boss and the Brat

The Love Across Time Series

Heroes for Ghosts

Honey From the Lion

Wild as the West Texas Wind

Ride the Whirlwind

Hemingway's Notebook

For the Love of a Ghost

Love Across Time Sequels

Heroes Across Time - Sequel to Heroes for Ghosts

The Oliver & Jack Series

Fagin's Boy

At Lodgings in Lyme

In Axminster Workhouse

Out in the World

On the Isle of Dogs

In London Towne

THE WRANGLER AND THE ORPHAN

A GAY M/M COWBOY ROMANCE

JACKIE NORTH

Jackie North

MM Romance Author

For all those who know that love is love...
...and to all those orphans out there.
You know who you are.

"There are things that a horse did for me that a human couldn't have done."

~~ Buck Brannaman

CONTENTS

BRODY

$\mathcal{D}$oing favors for other people wasn't really Brody's thing, but Jasper, the ranch's blacksmith, had asked so nicely, so Brody had said yes. Evidently, the owner of the Latham Street Laundromat was about to charge Jasper rent on the pile of clothes Ellis, Jasper's partner and assistant at the forge, had left in the machine.

It was an easy errand, as Brody had been on his way back from dropping off a horse that Jasper had shod for a client. And now that he had the large bag of laundry in his hand, nicely finished by the owner of the laundromat, he could leave the downtown of Farthing, where a Greyhound bus was currently churning out clouds of diesel fumes at the bus station catty corner to the laundromat. He could go back to the ranch, and re-enter his world of blue sky and green grass and herds of horses he looked upon as being his own.

He didn't own those horses, not a one. They belonged to the ranch, but from the top of their eager, sharp-pointed ears, to heir big liquid eyes, down their manes to their withers, and along their fetlocks to their well-tended hooves, they were his. He knew their names, could tell their moods by the swish of their tails or the lift or fall of their sweet heads. It didn't matter if it was the elegant Big Red or the more modest Dusty, they were all lovable to him and, in his heart, they were his.

He was theirs, as well, though this would have been harder to explain than he cared to think about explaining to anyone, should anyone care to ask. Those horses nickered when they saw him coming, trotted up to the long, barbed wire fence line, and it didn't matter if he had carrots in his pockets or not.

They caught his scent with their sensitive noses, and scented him right back as they curved their necks toward him for pets and scratches, leaving his hand traced with their fur, their smell, their warmth. Out in the world, such as he was, that place, his world, seemed far away, like a locked-off kingdom with huge doors standing barrier to the outside world that he mustn't lose the keys for.

Those keys he kept locked tight in his heart, and as long as he didn't lose them, he was fine. He could go on living the life he'd earned through the years, being the wrangler at Farthingdale Ranch, where guests came during the high summer months and the shoulder season at either end to enjoy the fresh air, to ride horses, to play at being cowboy.

His job was to make sure the horses were healthy and happy and ready to be ridden. He did it with pride. And it wasn't just his job, it was his life. Which made leaving the ranch more of a pain than a pleasure, each and every time.

Whistling low, he tossed the bag of laundry over his shoulder as he made his way across the street from the laundromat to where he'd parked the silver F150 that was currently hauling an empty horse trailer, also silver to match the truck.

At some point, Leland, the ranch's manager, had the truck and trailer detailed with the ranch's logo on the side. It looked nice. It could also attract the wrong kind of attention, which was why Brody had parked in front of the Rusty Nail, on purpose, to bother Eddie Piggot, who owned and ran the bar and hated everything to do with the ranch.

From what Brody could gather, the hatred stemmed from the fact that Eddie felt the ranch was full of fake cowboys, which it was, though why that should matter was anyone's guess. It certainly wasn't that the ranch was competition for the bar, for it was a watering hole for the locals and sometimes when guests would find their way into town, which wasn't often. They seemed to enjoy the rustic air of the place, and took pictures of each other holding frothy frosted mugs of Budweiser for the folks back home.

Brody had been shown some of those photos and reluctantly looked, and pretended more enjoyment than he felt. People who had pictures to share with those at home had families, and loads of friends, and always looked like they were having such a good time they were about to explode.

This was exactly the kind of publicity Leland particularly enjoyed for the ranch, the rich, organic pleasure people shared with their friends and everyone they knew. The ranch was doing better with each passing week, and though Brody was happy for that, he kind of missed the earlier part of the season when he'd gotten to spend more time with horses than people.

Still, what he had now was a damn sight better than the life he'd had before, before Quint, the trail boss on the ranch, had pulled him out of his old life and into his new one on the ranch. There was no looking back from that life, and Brody didn't want to. But still, sometimes he got reminders of how it used to be that left a pang in his heart and a sense of always searching for the memory of what he'd never had.

As Brody reached the truck, he saw a slip of paper shoved beneath the passenger side windshield wiper. He smiled.

Even from this distance, he could see the paper was the back of an order slip and that the angry block lettering was large enough and dark enough to look like a scream. Sure enough, when he pulled the slip out to read, it was from Eddie Piggot who, in no uncertain terms, did not want the ranch's shitbag truck in front of his place.

Brody crumpled the paper in one hand and let it fall to the gutter. Eddie knew as well as anyone that the parking all along every street in town was free to all comers. Nobody owned this particular stretch of sidewalk in front of which Brody was currently parked, not even Eddie.

If Brody took a minute to clean the back of the horse trailer free of manure, it would leave a fine mess in the street in front of the bar and serve Eddie right. But that would be beneath the pettiness Brody wanted to be associated with, so he went around the front of the truck to the driver's side door, thinking he'd throw the laundry in the back and head on home. Home to the ranch and peace and quiet.

Out of the corner of his eye, he saw the flash of sunlight on glass. When he looked, the basement window of the Rusty Nail was being pushed open. The window was an old one, painted brown along the edges, a long rectangle that was flush to the sidewalk.

Pausing, Brody watched as a pair of arms was followed by slender shoulders, and then a body rolled onto the sidewalk. The sidewalk was too hot for much rolling, but the body got to its feet, turning into a young man with his hair askew, his long-sleeved t-shirt grubby, something dark on his face.

From somewhere, perhaps inside the Rusty Nail, a door slammed. Brody could have sworn he heard Eddie Piggot shouting. The moment froze like an unexpected energy had slapped the air, waiting for the ricochet or the next blow.

The young man, dirty dishwater hair sticking to his face, looked at him, and Brody returned the look. They were connected, like a fine wire had been strung between them.

The expression on the young man's face was drawn, he was sheened with sweat, and yes, there was blood on his face. It was so obviously blood. That and the fact that he'd had to crawl out of the basement told Brody more than what he wanted to know.

The kid was the same one Clay, a ranch hand on the ranch, had almost lost his job over, when he'd come to the kid's protection when Eddie had been smacking him around. When Clay mentioned that fight, he typically emphasized that Eddie clearly had lost while Clay had the upper hand. Then he would shake his head, and Brody would leave unvoiced his concerns over what had happened to the kid after Clay had left the bar.

Clay's world was nothing like Brody's. His past, as Brody had heard, when Clay would expound, was a green cornfield in the middle of a peaceful summer's day in Iowa. Even the winters there sounded peaceful, the fields snow-covered, and overhead the sky was always blue.

Brody never took the time to explain to Clay that not everyone came from a loving family, and sometimes blows and slaps were part of an everyday life. Clay was too gentle-hearted for Brody to do that, and besides, Clay would be wounded to realize he might have left behind more destruction in that kid's life than what he'd intended when the rescue had commenced.

More shouting came from the open rectangle-shaped window in the basement of the Rusty Nail. Clearly Eddie had gone downstairs to check on the kid and found him missing and was now taking his ire out on whatever cardboard boxes he could kick.

As to why the kid had been in the basement and why he had considered crawling out a narrow window to a very hot and dusty sidewalk to be his best option, Brody could put all of these ideas and questions together faster than he'd care to think about.

Eddie had been mad and taken it out on the kid. He'd locked him in the basement. And now the kid was on the run, looking at Brody like he was the next obstacle to overcome in a wild, and most likely unsuccessful, bid for freedom.

Eddie would only be a minute. He'd go up those stairs and come tearing through the front door of the Rusty Nail. There the kid would be, unprepared and unable to retain the freedom he'd fought so hard for. A capture at this point would be only the beginning of the kid's new set of troubles, and Brody knew that for a fact.

Brody whistled. A high pitched whistle, a single tone going up at the end, that would call even the most reluctant horse in from the upper fields on the ranch. When the kid's jaw dropped, Brody jerked his head at the truck, and gestured with his hand. He whistled again, then, still holding onto the bag of laundry, got in the driver's side.

The kid ran to Brody and swung open the passenger door and climbed into the truck, obeying directly when Brody pointed to the footwell of the passenger side. The kid curled into it, and Brody threw the bag of laundry on top of him. Then he blew a long breath while he started the truck's engine, casually, as though he was tired of this errand and longed to be back at the ranch and only that.

Eddie came tearing out the front door of the Rusty Nail, as predicted. He raced straight up to the truck, pounding on the window, shouting at Brody to roll it down.

Brody pretended he didn't quite understand what Eddie wanted for a good full minute, then pushed the button and rolled down the window.

"What is it Eddie?" asked Brody in the friendliest of ways. "I hope it's not something I can help with, 'cause I gotta get back to the ranch." Brody pointed westward, his hands on the steering wheel like he was already in motion, an important man with even more important places to be.

"That damn kid broke my window!" The words came at full volume, like they were both in a storm at sea, and only Eddie's shouting would save them.

"Kid?" asked Brody, casually, like his heart wasn't pounding, which it was, a little bit.

Across the street, directly across from the Rusty Nail, the Greyhound bus station filled with a churn of dark greasy smoke. The big bus chuffed its way out of the parking bay, pausing at the opening as the bus driver looked left and then right, up and down the mostly empty street.

The bus only came three times a week, which was plenty for a small town like Farthing. It was always smelly and noisy and Brody sighed, wishing he didn't have to inhale the poison it churned out.

"Yeah, the kid, Kit!" Pounding his fists on the open window frame, Eddie was almost spitting. "He just came out of there. He broke out— his mom owes me money!"

"Broke out, you say?" Brody asked, most innocently. "So that kid I just saw running over to the bus station, like he was going to climb aboard the bus that's about to leave—his mom owes you money?"

"The bus?" shrieked Eddie. He looked at the bus like he'd never

6

considered the fact he lived directly across from the town's one and only Greyhound station.

"Yeah, that bus." Brody pointed to the bus that was turning slowly to the right to head east up Second Street, and from there to the edge of town and the drive to the highway and all points beyond. "The one that's just leaving."

"Fuck it and shit!" Eddie's teeth were bared and his face was red.

Had Brody been the quivering fifteen year old that he used to be, then Eddie would have scared him to death. But he was a man now, fully grown and independent, and he no longer needed to fear men like Eddie.

Old habits died hard, though, and that kind of fear lurked beneath his skin as Eddie raced back inside the Rusty Nail. There, he would no doubt grab his keys, hop in his truck, and race in a mad frenzy after the bus. Which was crazy, as anyone knew, because the bus would stop for no man, as it had a schedule to meet, and only a fool would mess with a Greyhound bus driver.

All of this would keep Eddie good and occupied for a nice long space of time. Meanwhile, Brody made his casual exit and drove back to the ranch like he didn't have a scared kid in his truck hiding beneath a bag of Jasper and Ellis' laundry.

"Stay down," he said as he waited and watched while Eddie's almost-new, solid black Chevy truck skidded from the alley and onto the street, heading east in pursuit of an unstoppable Greyhound bus.

Brody rolled down all of the windows, both front and back, letting the wisp of a breeze from the west float through the cab of the truck. It was warm, but it would be cool once they got moving. Brody hated air conditioned air enough to put up with sweating a little. The smell of real air was always preferable.

"I'm going to take you back to the ranch," said Brody to the curl of body beneath the bag of laundry. "We'll figure it out from there, okay?"

Hearing a sound he decided to take as an affirmative, Brody drove slowly out of town, shaking his head at his own foolishness. Getting involved was not his thing and yet here he'd gone and done that exact thing.

Leland had said time and again to stay upwind of Eddie Piggot and here Brody, the least likely person, had waved his flag and stood on a hill he was not entirely sure he wanted to defend. Brody had his own troubles, and everybody else had theirs, and never the two should meet, that was his motto.

Yet how could he have left the kid—Kit—standing there for Eddie to find? That would have been like cutting out the softest part of his heart to toss it on the sidewalk. There wasn't much softness left in him, and he wanted to keep it for himself. Yet, when the lump stirred beneath the laundry, Brody patted the bag.

"Give it five minutes, Kit, then you can sit up." Brody looked in his rearview mirror, where the small town of Farthing was getting smaller as he drove into the open country along the road that led to the ranch. "I don't want any witnesses who could report seeing you leave with me."

Brody had never taken anyone with him like this in his life. Never rescued anyone, ever. He'd only had the strength to rescue himself and barely that. If it'd not been for Quint McKay, Brody would probably be dead by now.

What would Quint say when he found out that Brody had now become the rescuer? Quint would probably give Brody a silent nod that said Brody had done good. All Brody could feel, though, now that Eddie was tearing up the two-lane blacktop after that bus, going in the opposite direction, was a low sense of dread.

He wasn't good at this, had never tried. Now he had a kid on his hands. A kid who had blood on his face and a terrified look in his pewter blue eyes. And Brody had no idea what to do next.

2

KIT

*W*hat was normal was the fact that after Kit's mom, Katie, ran off, her now-ex boyfriend Eddie Piggot began smacking Kit around. This was both to chastise him for not being able to keep up with the dirty dishes and also to blow off steam. What wasn't normal was that Eddie never reached into his pocket to pull out a twenty or even a five dollar bill like the rest of Katie's men usually did after they hit him.

Most of Katie's men just wanted Kit out of the room where it happened, and so would pay him to go away. They would pay him extra to stay out late and swim in the motel's swimming pool, or the trailer park's swimming pool. If there wasn't a pool, they'd pay him to head on down to the local Stop n' Go or 7-Eleven or whatever all-night convenience store was within walking distance of the motel. The late-night treats of beef jerky and a soda, or off-brand pop tarts, along with the leftover money in his pocket made the bruises worthwhile, sometimes.

The summer when he turned twelve and before he'd started junior high, he'd begun saving up those twenties and tens in a paper bag in the bottom of his backpack. He'd been intending to sign up for the school lunch program for once so he wouldn't have to resort to eating off trays that had been left in the bussing area, or picking up that sandwich, still wrapped in a plastic baggie, that some kid had run over with his bicycle.

No, that year, he'd wanted to eat with the other kids. He wanted to drink fresh cartons of milk and eat off plastic trays with little squares full of food, like corn niblets and carrot slices and those decadent square-cut slices of doughy pizza. Maybe then he could be like one of those kids he saw in the movies and on TV, who had a hot lunch every single day. He was going to be quite casual about it as he carried his tray to one of the long tables in the lunchroom and sat down like he belonged, like it was a given, a done deal.

The other thing he'd wanted that semester was to buy one of those four-colored retractable Bic pens, which had suddenly become all the rage the first week after school started. They were thick, sturdy pens, and wrote in blue, black, green, and red ink.

They clicked really loud and before the school principal determined they were off limits to students, Kit wanted to be part of the fun. Maybe he'd even get two of those pens, after all they were only two bucks each at the local Target.

His secret wish, which he shared with no one, not even Katie, was to be one of those cool kids whose parents got them new spiral notebooks at the beginning of each school year, along with packs of blue and red and black pens, and new yellow pencils and packs of Pink Pearl erasers. Kids who had a separate pair of sneakers for gym. Kids who had new coats for school and whose blue jeans did not have patches on them.

Just once, just one time, he wanted to be like those kids, so he'd saved his money in preparation for his first semester in junior high. Only to discover that Katie had found his stash of money and taken it to buy what she insisted were things she needed.

"That was my money," he told Katie, his cheek hot and stinging from her slap. "I was going to buy stuff with it."

"No kid needs that much money," she said, flinging her hair over her shoulder, like she was still twenty and cute and this was her siren song to draw men to her. "And I needed more vodka for when Toby comes over."

Toby was not a big tipper, but he had been coming around for two solid weeks, so maybe luck would be with Kit and that would change, and Toby would stick around and Kit could sign up for lunches and get one of those cool pens.

When Toby left, which he would, the next man in line would have the same kind of name, short, to the point. He'd be called something like Brad, or Dan, or Craig, like there was no sense in him pretending he was with Katie for any other reason other than the real reason. They all had the same kind of background, and job, and manner, and smell, too. After a few years of this, Kit figured out that their personas were what fit the situation: they were the men who could take Katie to bed, have a little fun, and leave her high and dry.

Katie never figured this out, but Kit had. And so what if some of them got awfully rough with his mom? They got rough with him, too.

The only question had been where he could hide that money so Katie couldn't find it again. The only answer had been in his pocket and then to spend it as he went. No point saving it, no point at all.

As for the four-color retractable Bic pen, Kit filched the one sitting on Greg's desk in English class. Greg had big ears he'd not quite grown into and a sweet face with soft brown eyes to match. He was upset when he found the pen was gone and was just about crying when the teacher pulled him to the front of the classroom to plea for the pen's safe return.

All the while Kit had clicked and un-clicked the pen in his pocket, softly. With each click the pen became more and more his, until it didn't quite matter that he'd stolen it. And since a lot of kids had the same pen, nobody could point the finger at him and he only had to wait an hour before pulling it out to use it on a pop quiz in history class.

The pen broke after only two weeks with all the clicking he did to it. Instead of buying a new one with the change in his pocket, Kit made a practice of grabbing whatever pen and notebook, chewing gum and candy bar, or whatever had been left out unattended for even a minute. He needed those things, whereas all the other kids had parents who could afford to replace them, who would even *care* to replace them. His constant five-fingered discount kept him stocked with school supplies, making him a little more like a regular kid, and nobody ever suspected him.

Meanwhile, just before Thanksgiving that year, his first semester of Junior High, Katie decided she'd had enough of Denver. She made them pack in the middle of the night so they could take the Greyhound bus to Las Vegas. There, Katie did her best to get a job as a cocktail waitress in one of the casinos. But since all those ladies were high class, well-trained, and professional, not to mention they could make change in their heads, all Katie could manage was a night cleaner.

Kit would go with her to work from ten at night till six in the morning, scrounging along the wildly patterned carpets for change that had dropped from pockets. Katie would find odd tokens, too, and when she cashed them in after she got off her shift, they would head to Denny's for a hot breakfast, or if there wasn't enough, they would buy knock-off blueberry Pop Tarts at the 7-11, which never tasted as good as the real thing, even if they were the frosted kind. Then they would lollygag in the motel room until it was time for Katie to go back to work.

Kit had to wait two whole months before he could register for school again, but even that stint in Vegas lasted only three months before Katie headed back to Denver, dragging Kit behind her as she made her way up and down the Front Range.

It was likely that this time, after Katie left him in the hands of Eddie Piggot, a man she had only known a month, she'd headed back to Vegas once more. This had happened before, so Kit's plan had been to hang out with Eddie till Katie came back.

Which might be a while, as the pickings in Vegas were thick on the ground and, as Katie had often told Kit in a much-familiar drunken slur, there was a man she needed to meet there. Some man. Any man. A man who would take care of her, and take her to his castle far away, where Kit could even have his own room!

This was a promise Kit had heard for the last nine years, ever since he'd been ten, when Katie felt she could not survive the boring suburban life of the man she'd had a baby with, and left that man high and dry.

Kit's memory of his father was a sepia-toned thumbprint over a face. All he knew was Katie. All he knew was him and Katie constantly on the move from motel to trailer park to a basement apartment.

Once and only once, Katie had hooked up with a decent guy, a bronc rider in the rodeo circuit. When the circuit had come to Vegas, Katie had met this handsome cowboy in a bar, cooed over the bandage over his eye, and the other bandage around his wrist. Then she'd cooed her way into his pants.

She'd been just about on the verge of cooing her way into his wallet when the bronc rider, a nice fellow, all things considered, who'd given Kit a fifty-dollar bill one time without hitting him first, had figured out what Katie's racket was and began blocking her on his phone.

Katie's cell phone number never changed. Kit knew it by heart, but though he'd called it every day since she left Eddie and Kit behind, she never picked up. Her voicemail box was full so he couldn't tell her how badly it was going and ask her to please come and get him.

When Eddie had figured out that Kit called Katie every day, he began badgering Kit about it, and would hit him until Kit agreed to include in the message the very pointed fact that Katie had taken five thousand dollars of Eddie's money and she needed to bring it back right away.

The money was important, as it had something to do with taxes Eddie owed, but Kit didn't care about that. He just wanted Katie to come get him and take him away from this hellhole in the middle of fucking nowhere.

He could never figure out why she'd hooked up with Eddie, who was on the ugly side of handsome. He had straw-colored hair that always stuck out from his head like he'd just gotten out of bed, and a pair of pale blue eyes that always looked like he was searching for ghosts on the other side of you. He had a pot belly, and a backhanded slap that always found its mark. Always, always, always.

"I *just* called her," said Kit, rubbing his cheek as he stood at the back door of the bar's kitchen. The door had a screen, and he was trying to gulp in some fresh air to offset the fug of old beer, rancid soap, and some undercurrent that might have been the smell of a rat who had died in the drain in the floor, unable to get out.

He felt a whole lot like that rat right about now because Eddie was blocking the fresh air with his body. His hands were on his hips so his elbow was blocking the way to the front of the kitchen. In back of Kit was the doorway to the cellar, where cardboard boxes were kept, as well as untaxed bottles of booze, maraschino cherries way past their sell-by date, and a host of supplies for the bar.

At one point, early on in their relationship, Eddie had told Kit to go down and clean up the cellar. When Kit told Eddie to fuck himself, that's when Kit had first found out how accurate Eddie's aim was. As for Katie, she'd helped Kit off the floor and told him he ought to be nicer to Eddie, since they were living under his roof.

Now Katie had left them to each other's company, like she simply didn't care that Eddie would get mad about his missing money—no, make that *furious*—and that Kit would pay the price for the theft. Maybe if it had been a hundred bucks or so, the amount Katie had sometimes taken in the past, Eddie wouldn't be so pissed. But she had stolen five thousand dollars, and so here he was.

Someone came up behind Eddie, one of the kitchen workers, and tapped him on the shoulder.

"Boss," said the guy. "Truck from that ranch is parked out front." He jerked his thumb, like he was pointing at the street. "It's towing a trailer and taking up half the block. You said you wanted to know."

"Fucking shit," said Eddie. "That stupid shit ranch and their damn stupid—" Eddie stopped and grabbed Kit by his upper arm, squeezing hard. "You go out there and write a note. Tell them to keep their stinking damn vehicles out of my sight."

Kit knew all about the ranch and how much Eddie hated it. Everyone who worked for him knew. Hell, probably the whole world knew, since Eddie hardly drew a breath without complaining about it, day and night.

As to why Eddie hated the ranch, Kit could never figure out. The way Eddie described it, really, it was just a guest ranch where people came to play at being cowboy and what was wrong with that? Nothing as far as Kit could see.

"I guess if you actually knew how to read and write," said Kit, his mouth running away with him, easy as could be. "Then you could write that note your own self. In the meantime, I'm leaving. I'm getting my stuff an' I'm out of here. I don't need you. I'll go to Vegas and find Katie."

"The hell you are."

Normally, Eddie got red faced and hauled back and lashed out. Sometimes Kit could duck, most times he couldn't. There'd only been one time when Eddie'd hit him so hard he'd blacked out and walked around with a headache for three days, but he could always sense when Eddie had reached that one particular point when using his backhanded slap seemed the best solution.

Not this time. Eddie went white, and he grabbed Kit even harder, yanked open the door to the cellar, and pulled Kit down those stairs. When he got to the bottom, he threw Kit on the cold and dusty cement floor.

Kit's body rolled, scattering cardboard boxes before he bumped into the case of maraschino cherries. As he looked up, palms spread on the gritty cement, he realized with a hard stab of dismay that Eddie was taking off his belt. No, he *hauled* it off, going so fast that the end of the belt snapped in the air with a hard, quick pop.

"Fuck you." Kit tried to get up, but his knees were shaking and he knew he had nowhere to run, no escape out of the cellar except the stairs they'd just come down. "J-just fuck you."

When Eddie stepped forward, the belt folded in two, Kit could only be grateful that Eddie was holding the buckle end and the tail of the belt in his hand. The folded end wouldn't hurt so much as the other way around, and there was no way not to remember how he knew that, or how many times he'd been in exactly this position.

The only thing to do was to curl small and stay still for the whipping to come. If you ran or fought back, and the other guy was bigger, like Eddie was? It got worse. Hurt worse. Left scars and marks that simply couldn't be explained away in the locker room at school after gym class.

Kit had missed a lot of gym class that way. And now, even if there wasn't school and counselors and teachers to be gotten around, he was going to miss a few days on his feet, that was for sure.

It was going to be bad. Eddie was mad and the belt came down just like Kit knew it would. Like a knife made of leather, whistling through the air, accompanied by Eddie's grunts of effort, regular, measured, alternating tempo with the sing of the belt, which found every tender spot, every bit of thin skin above bone, the backs of his thighs, the front of his chest when Eddie kicked him to get better access.

Eddie seemed to know all of Kit's usual ways to avoid the more solid dense blows. Seemed to hit harder to make up for the fact that after the beating was over, there would be no Katie to help Kit to his feet.

Kit didn't cry out, though maybe that would have helped Eddie be more satisfied with what he was dishing out. He went numb before Eddie was finished, the unfolded belt hanging from one hand as he breathed hard and fast.

At least now Eddie's face went red, which meant that the worst was over. White-faced anger was worse, for some reason. Red-faced anger was easily spent. Easily borne.

"You're going to clean up this cellar like I told you," said Eddie, swallowing a mouthful of spit from his efforts. "I'm going to deal with that stupid fucking truck and then I'll be back and you better be working. Elbows and assholes, understood?"

Forming his mouth around the words *fuck you*, Kit considered his options. That kind of response would be considered backtalk and would get him another whipping, he was sure of it. It was better to appear cowed and to find another way to get the hell out of Dodge. He needed to be outside of Eddie's reach, even if it meant leaving everything he owned behind.

He didn't let himself look at the high windows in the cellar that were at street level. He didn't let it show in his eyes that the boxes of beer were stacked just about to the windows. No, he looked down and shuddered.

The shudder was real, and the only thing he could see was the floor, covered with drops of Eddie's sweat. Drops of his own, and no, he wasn't crying. No way, no how.

"You say yes, sir when I tell you to do something, got it?" Eddie screamed the words and advanced, hand raised, belt rippling like a snake in the air.

Two options. There were always two options. One led to more pain. The other led to a hideous amount of self-loathing that was also life-preserving. If he cowered, he would live to run another day.

"Yes, sir," said Kit, low, licking the corner of his mouth, tasting blood. The belt had hit him in the face, but only a little bit. That would soon heal, as would the rest of him. He could get away if only Eddie would leave the cellar. "Yes, sir," he said again, nodding for good measure.

"That's better."

With a grunt, several grunts, Eddie put the belt back on, one hole too tight, which made him look like a fool, but Kit didn't laugh. Just stayed half-curled on the cold cement floor, smelling his own sweat, acid from pain, and watched Eddie march up those stairs to slam the cellar door behind him.

Kit didn't know for sure, but he maybe had five minutes for his getaway. His exit from this hellhole was one window at the top of a row of boxes that already looked ajar. The others looked like they'd been painted shut.

Kit was skinny. He would fit. It wouldn't feel good but he would fit. After that? The wide world awaited. Vegas awaited. Katie. He would find her and then they could go on as they always did. That's what he was used to, what he knew.

3

BRODY

*B*rody paused the truck at the gate to the ranch, gently, so the horse trailer's brakes would have plenty of time to kick in.

Normally, at this point, the person in the passenger seat would leap out to open the gate and then to shut it when the vehicle had gone through. Normally, however, Brody wouldn't have a passenger who was only now sliding out from beneath the bag of clean laundry, kicking it out of the way of his feet with dirty sneakers.

"Hey, now," said Brody, the way he might with a horse who was startled into aggressive behavior. "I'm Brody." He touched his own chest. "And, first things first, Eddie Piggot is a shithead. Whatever else happens, let's be clear about that."

"He sure is," said Kit in a clear, strong voice. Like he wasn't trying to hold himself still against a case of the shakes. Like he didn't have blood on his mouth. Like his eyes weren't wide with the shine of shock. "I'm Kit, by the way. Kit Foster."

"Brody Calhoun," said Brody in response to that, as it seemed the natural, civilized thing to do. Exchange names like one of them had not just rescued the other from a stupendously huge beating from

Eddie Piggot, possibly second one of the day. Who knew how many others there had been before.

"Look," he said. "I don't know what I'm doing, but I figure I'll get you something to eat and you can clean up. Then, in the morning, we'll figure this all out."

"I need to get to Vegas," said Kit, the tip of his tongue touching the corner of his bloodied mouth, like he was trying to figure out where the taste of copper pennies was coming from. "That's where Katie's gone, I'm sure of it."

"Katie?" asked Brody.

"That's my mom," said Kit. When he shrugged, the neck of his long-sleeved t-shirt moved up and down, like it was simply too big for his neck. "That's where she went."

"Vegas," said Brody. He'd been through Vegas a few times, though he'd never stopped.

Daddy Frank used to say Vegas was too big for the likes of them, and Quint simply didn't like the bright lights and the noise. That someone would go there on purpose was beyond Brody to figure out.

"She likes it there." Another shrug, and a small wince as a thin line of sweat lingered on Kit's neck. "I figure that's the only place she'd go after cleaning Eddie out."

"Yeah, he mentioned that."

Brody tapped his fingers on the wheel, gently, like he was softly playing notes on a piano, and looked through the gate to the ranch beyond.

The wooden fencing on either side of the gate was for decoration. Beyond a few feet, the fence was barbed wire. Neither of which, not the gate or the fence, mattered to the land at all, as it retained its sense of wildness, summer-brown tipped grasses waving in the warm breeze, the sun in the blue sky baking the ground to hardness.

In August, or thereabouts, they'd get heavy rains, which would sometimes not soak into the earth fast enough and cause flooding. At the ranch, all the buildings, except Jasper's blacksmith forge and cabin where he and Ellis lived, were high enough above the Horse Creek River to be out of danger. But even Jasper's cabin had been designed to be just above a high waterline. The ranch would be safe, and the earth would be grateful, and it was hard now, with the sun shining, the air sparkling with heat, to ever imagine it could ever rain that hard.

Hard, as well, for him to imagine how he was going to manage this. Somewhere, written on some unknown page of a book he'd never read, was a straightforward description of what he should do. He'd take Kit to his room, get some food from the dining hall for him, give Kit the privacy he needed to take a shower, and then make the kid a bed out of blankets on the floor.

In the morning, he'd give the kid a hundred bucks or so and drive him to Cheyenne to catch the next Greyhound to Vegas or wherever he decided he needed to go. Maybe he'd give Kit two hundred bucks, after all, he had the money.

He never bought anything, never needed anything. His one weakness was good-quality cowboy boots, and he had three pairs in his closet already. Even if he'd recently been eying another pair of Tecovas cowboy boots, he could spare the cash. He could take the time to drive to Cheyenne.

Beneath that commonsense list of what to do, beneath his own stillness, echoed by Kit's stillness, as he and Kit sat together as the truck's engine idled, lurked something more wild and worked up. It would have been easier had Kit asked why they were not going through the gate. Asked why they were not driving on, or any other question, which would have distracted Brody, given him something to focus on, rather than having no defense against the sudden swamp of memories he'd worked so hard to bury. Had stomped on to keep them trapped beneath a black blanket of forgetting.

Now the memories lunged up, *all* of them, dancing like yesterday's ghosts set free by a careless hand. Him at the age of ten on the plywood stage of a small town country fair, swirling his lasso just above stage level, while his older brother, Bryson, swirled his lasso around the both of them.

It had been early June evening, with a fine mist swamping the stage, hazing the audience beyond the footlights to grey. The music had been jaunty and the little show they'd practiced for days and days had been going well.

The mistake had come when the dampness had caused Brody's hand to slip on the hard-braided end of the rope. His rope had swirled up before he could catch it, knocking into Bryson's rope, which tugged the hard-braided end of Bryson's rope clean out of his hand.

The audience had laughed and clapped as Bryson scrambled for his rope again and, counting out the beats, the two of them had managed to continue on, finishing with a bow. All the while Daddy Frank watched from the sidelines, his jaw working beneath the shade of his dark blue felt cowboy hat, trimmed with a hat band of glittering silver diamonds.

The diamonds weren't real silver, of course, just aluminum and glass polished to shine. Daddy Frank's outfit was designed to be part of the spectacle. Just like the matching hats they wore, and the matching bolo ties, black leather, tipped with aluminum, with a large chunk of blue glass at the neck. Their white-stitched blue jeans had matched along with the cowboy belts and their cheap K-Mart plastic cowboy boots matched.

All of this looked real good from the audience's perspective, but the boots gave Brody and Bryson blisters. The bright blue polyester shirts itched under their arms and along their necks. None of that mattered to Daddy Frank, though, just as long as they looked the part.

And, as long as they played their parts, doing the rope tricks Daddy Frank made them do, then everything was fine. If they made a mistake and Daddy Frank was in a good mood, then everything was fine. But if Daddy Frank had been drinking, or if Mama had said something he didn't like, then nothing was fine.

That night, after the show, Daddy Frank drove them both back to their elderly trailer in the campground in back of the fairgrounds. In the darkness, lit by a single light atop a wooden pole in the middle of the campground, before they'd even gone into the trailer, Daddy Frank made them take off their jeans and their boots and their hats and shirts and bolo ties so they wouldn't get ruined. Then he bent them over the hard metal tailgate of his truck and took off his fancy aluminum-tipped fancy belt and whipped them with it.

You couldn't move or the whipping would start all over again. You couldn't kick your feet, and even heaven couldn't help you if your bare feet slipped on the wet grass.

Brody could remember with more clarity than he cared to how he'd dug his toes into that grass, into the mud beneath, and how he'd fallen off the tailgate, knocking his chin. And how Daddy Frank had stood over him and, without a word, whipped him all over, shoulder to ankle, until he was out of breath, chest heaving, the aluminum diamonds on his hat band glittering in the rain-dappled light.

At least this had distracted Daddy Frank from whipping Bryson anymore. At least it had stopped. Though, as they dressed in silence and limped in the growing mist to the trailer carrying their socks and boots, the middle toes on Brody's left foot ached and complained.

He didn't say anything, though, just smiled when Mama kissed them both and told them to change out of their stage clothes and into their regular clothes so they could have the dinner she made for them.

In the morning, those toes were swollen, puffy and red. Daddy Frank had Mama tape them together so the break would heal straight. Brody's sneakers would barely fit, and he hobbled around till Daddy Frank cuffed him on the back of his head and told him to cut out the drama.

That was just one county fair, just one night. On other nights, if Daddy Frank didn't outright beat them, he would slap them for looking at him wrong, and threaten them with worse if they didn't get their asses in gear and practice. He would lay out a pair of plywood planks so they could practice on wood, rather than in mud. Sometimes the plywood planks would slip apart, and they'd have to be plenty on their toes to not fall and mess up.

Some nights, if Daddy Frank had been drinking a bit, he'd get all riled and smack at their legs with the practice rope, harder and harder till they were jumping up and down, which wasn't easy in the small confines of the old camper. *Now Frank,* was all Mama would say, upset that the meal she'd prepared was getting interrupted.

23

Daddy Frank had dreams of hitting the big circuit, the bigger county fairs, the nicer rodeos. Once, when Brody was twelve years old, they'd gotten a slot in the Iowa County Fair in Tipton, Iowa. It had been a night of sparkling goodness. They'd done so well performing their rope tricks that Daddy Frank had given them enough money to stroll the fair with and buy cotton candy and corn dogs and whatever they wanted.

Afterward, Brody's stomach had ached all night, but Mama had said it was his own fault and that he needed to learn his lesson, so she wouldn't let him have any baking soda in water, like she sometimes did.

When Brody had turned thirteen and Bryson was fifteen, Daddy Frank had met a horseman in a bar who convinced Daddy Frank that rope tricks were a thing of the past and that the new thing was riding a trick horse, doing stunts. Which might have been a whole lot scarier than learning rope tricks and failing, except the horseman, a rough but steady fellow by the name of Milt Coogan, was the one to teach them.

Milt was a good horseman, a good teacher. Brody and his brother learned how to stand up while galloping, to face backward in the saddle and smile as the horse raced around the arena. When Bryson learned how to hang off the saddle, holding on with only his feet, arms wide, smiling to the applause, Brody wanted to learn that, too.

Milt taught them everything. Daddy Frank rented the horses from Milt, and they split the proceeds, which earned them a lot more than they'd gotten with simple rope tricks and they travelled from little county fair to little county fair.

Then Daddy Frank and Milt had cooked up a scheme to have the boys do rope tricks *while* doing trick riding. This took more coordination, more training. When Milt was done with his lesson for the day, Daddy Frank made Brody and Bryson practice while on top of a tall stool set on those two wooden planks. Then he'd wobble the planks and holler at them if they fell off, and he'd whip them if they lost track of the rope or dropped it. Later, under Milt's direction, they'd work the same tricks while on horseback, over and over, until they could do it galloping.

During the school year, everything was mostly not as bad. Some mornings, though after a beating from Daddy Frank the night before for looking at him sideways, Brody struggled with his studies, with staying awake.

Daddy Frank would take both boys out of school if he wanted them home, and after Daddy Frank started drinking because Mama had run off with some man she'd met behind the Tilt-a-Whirl, those were always bad days. The smack would come out of nowhere. The belt would come off for no reason. Daddy Frank would beat them for breathing wrong.

4

BRODY

*W*hen Brody had been fifteen and Bryson had been seventeen, Bryson had run off, leaving Brody alone with Daddy Frank. Who, oddly, was quite kind to Brody for a good long while. He would buy him things like a pair of real leather cowboy boots, and mostly wouldn't whip him when he screwed up.

Brody privately thought Daddy Frank was being nice because Daddy Frank was afraid of Brody leaving him, like the others had. Besides, Brody was Daddy Frank's meal ticket. Without him, how would he make a living?

Brody didn't rightly care, but it was nice to sleep in his own bunk bed without having to fight over how much space on the mattress was his, and have a good hot breakfast before practicing in the arena. To screw up without getting smacked around.

All of this was a novelty that soon wore off, and everything went back to normal. And then Milt decided to bug out, taking all the horses, and the horse trailer. The ropes and costumes were in the trailer, and though Daddy Frank was wild to get those things back, Milt simply never answered his phone.

That's when Daddy Frank started picking up odd jobs at the

county fairs, and he made Brody stay out of school to do odd jobs, too, so they could save up to buy new outfits for Brody, new rope. Maybe they'd buy a horse of their own so Brody could ride it and do amazing tricks for the audience.

Usually, in the evening, after a hard day of shoveling horse shit or moving hay bales or setting up tents and booths, Daddy Frank would drink and smack Brody around, or sometimes he would drink and fall asleep. Either was as likely, and Brody began to wonder if this was going to be the rest of his life.

Why didn't he run off? He'd stuck it two more years after Bryson'd run away because Daddy Frank had promised him a horse of his own that he could name and train and take care of. Daddy Frank would drive the camper, and Brody could get a fake driver's license and drive the trailer.

Maybe off the profits they could get a nicer camper. Real leather boots for Brody, as he'd quickly outgrown the original leather pair. Maybe Bryson would come back and the three of them could go on the road together. Maybe, maybe.

One night Daddy Frank had gotten drunk, yelling about Milt running off like it was Brody's fault. Daddy Frank was mad enough to smack Brody around and tie him to the narrow metal step of the camper in the rain. That was the night Brody had met Quint McKay. And that was the night his life had changed forever.

In the bleakness of the backlot that was the camping area for a mid-level county fair, rain had strung Brody's hair in his face, blinding him. The rope hurt, cutting into his upper arms, growing tighter, it seemed, as it soaked up water.

He shouldn't move but he did, shifting to get comfortable, biting his lip so he didn't make a sound. Sound would bring Daddy Frank out of the trailer, and if that happened, it would escalate beyond Brody's ability to bear.

Then, amidst the sheets of rain, came a man. A large, broad shouldered man, who looked at Brody without a word from beneath the brim of his cowboy hat, then pulled out his knife and sliced through the rope.

"You can't do that," said Brody, though his body sighed as the pressure of the rope fell, snakelike, around his feet. "Daddy Frank's going to be pissed."

"Been watching you," said the man. "Saw you at the last fair. You put on a good show, kid, and the audience loved your performance. But, after the show, your daddy didn't seem to agree. Passed by your trailer that night, just to see what was what. He whipped you. That weren't right, so I figured out where you'd gone to and followed."

Brody had gone silent, unable to answer this or respond to it or say anything. Nobody was supposed to know what Daddy Frank did. Brody and Bryson had learned not to tell their teachers at school, or to tell any friends they might happen to make along the way. If they did tell, Daddy Frank would lash out, and yank them out of school, or yell at those kids, creating a rather solid, impenetrable bubble around their private hell.

His skin felt hot all over in spite of the rain because someone knew how it was, knew what had happened. In another minute, the man was going to ask why he hadn't already left Daddy Frank high and dry. Brody knew the question would leave him burning with shame because he was too scared to try and make it on his own.

Maybe if Bryson had called or reached out, sent a postcard even, then Brody would have known what was possible. All he knew was Daddy Frank and this life. Beyond that was a great big blank of unknowns.

His only happiness came when he rode those horses, full speed, standing in the saddle, arms wide as the crowd roared and the horse's hooves thundered beneath the thunder of his own heart. That was life.

Nowhere else in the world could he ride horses like that. Except now there were no horses because Milt Coogan had taken everything from Daddy Frank. There was only shoveling horse shit and pounding nails into wood for temporary structures that would be dismantled upon the close of the county fair. All of which would start up again as soon as they reached the next fair.

"What's your name?" asked the man. He moved closer in the rain, his voice low, his touch to Brody's shoulder making him flinch. "I'm not going to hurt you. My name is Quint McKay. I manage livestock at various rodeos and sometimes I help with the animal judging at these little county fairs. So I'll ask again. What's your name?"

"Brody," said Brody, swallowing hard, his fingers laced over the cuts in his arm. Maybe the rain would wash them clean. Maybe they wouldn't get infected. "Brody Calhoun."

"Well, Brody Calhoun, how old are you?"

Not included with this question was the normal hand-shaking ceremony everybody did at these fairs, like a ticket of admittance into a secret brotherhood. No, Quint just stood there waiting for his answer, like everything else was nonsense and a waste of time.

"Seventeen," said Brody. "Just this last May."

"You finish school?" asked Quint, his voice still low, like this was a very private conversation even though the questions seemed ordinary to Brody.

"No." Brody swallowed hard because the questions seemed like a test he was sure to fail. When he did, Quint would lash out and it would get loud and then Daddy Frank would come out of the camper and then things would get worse from there, especially since Quint had sliced through the rope Daddy Frank had tied very carefully to teach Brody a lesson.

"Shame."

It *was* a shame as it left Brody without any way to make a living, to make his way in the world. He knew horses and he knew rope and that was just about it. The county fair circuit was the only way he knew to make a living, and he had to do it, marching in time with Daddy Frank.

Brody squinted into the rain up at Quint McKay, waiting for him to smack him or leave. What else could he be planning as he tilted his head until the brim of his cowboy hat dripped rain onto his face?

Now that Quint was standing still, blocking the single light atop a wooden pole, Brody could see the dark, crisp-edged outline of him. Could see he was dressed like someone who would work the rodeo circuit more than a county fair, with a dark hat, a long-sleeved shirt, jeans, and what was probably cowboy boots.

All of this was just a dark shape, but Brody had seen so many cowboys, so many cowboy wannabes, that the staple outfit of a cowboy was hard to miss, even in the dark.

Quint turned to Brody, and Brody thought he heard Quint sigh, soft and low, like he'd made a decision, in spite of himself. Brody almost jumped back to slam against the door of the trailer when Quint held out his hand. All around them in that silent moment, the rain fell, pattering softly against the mud and bits of straw and old cotton candy cones left to drown.

"What say you come with me?" asked Quint.

"What?" asked Brody.

"Come with me," said Quint. "Work for me. I'll pay you. I'll feed you and house you. You might not get to do any trick riding, but you won't get whipped for messing up either."

"Not ride?" asked Brody, his heart reaching for the one thing he loved in the whole wide world.

"Didn't say that." Quint nodded, rain glittering in the lamplight on the brim of his dark cowboy hat. "Plenty of opportunity for riding in this business. I figure I got a few more years before I settle on a job that don't require driving from pillar to post all season, but wherever I land, there will be horses and there will be riding."

"I can't leave." Brody's jaw worked as his mind tried to figure out exactly why that was. At the same time, his heart hammered that Daddy Frank would hear them talking and open the door, shoving Brody right into the mud, which would be the least of his worries.

"Why not?"

"I just can't." The energy in this short response to Quint's question faded like dew in the morning. Why couldn't he? Why shouldn't he go with this man? And if he did, how long would it be before Daddy Frank caught up to them and killed them both? "Daddy Frank," he said, finally, lifting his shoulders in a slight shrug that made his arms hurt.

"Daddy Frank has taught you tricks, that's for certain." Quint took off his hat to shake the rain from the brim, then replaced it, looking straight down at Brody. His eyes were in shadow, though Brody could see the strong line of his jaw. "I'll teach you horses."

"Horses," said Brody, unwilling even in the depths of himself to admit what a draw that was.

"You come with me, I'll patch you up. I'll feed you and give you a dry place to sleep. Teach you a trade." Quint lifted his head to look over at the main part of the arena, where safety lights dotted the top of the stadium. "I'm pulling out in the morning."

Brody's whole body jerked, like he'd been startled into wakefulness.

"You can wait till morning to think about it," said Quint, quite gently. "Or you can walk away from this life and into another'n. Right now."

Again Quint held out his hand and this time Brody took it. Quint pulled Brody to his feet, and then let go, somehow knowing that Brody's pride would insist that he limp on his own away from his camper to follow Quint into the rain, to a different camper, headed to parts unknown.

Quint's camper was much like Daddy Frank's except it was newer and better cared for and there wasn't that dratted blood stain in the linoleum floor that could never be scrubbed up. Quint sat Brody down on the bench seat of the dining table, brought him a towel to dry off with, and then, very gently, cleaned the rope burns.

"That might leave scars," said Quint as he looped tape around the wide gauze squares on Brody's upper arms. "But maybe the mystery will draw the ladies closer, eh?"

Blinking, Brody thought about this question and how he didn't quite know the answer to it. The more immediate item of interest was the bowl of instant Ramen noodle soup Quint was heating up in his little camper-sized microwave oven.

Quint handed the cup and a metal spoon to Brody, and placed one out for himself and, sitting opposite Brody, the two of them ate, slurping the noodles and the broth. Afterward, Quint gave Brody a dry t-shirt to wear, and pointed to the upper bunk.

"It's late. You get some sleep, and we'll head out early, as soon as it's light. Daddy Frank won't have any idea which way we went, because nobody but the admin at this fair knows me, and nobody here knows my route."

Stripping to the skin, unabashed, shivering, Brody changed into the dry t-shirt before clambering up to the upper bunk at the back of the trailer. As he slid between clean sheets, he looked at Quint.

Quint was shaking his head. Probably not because he'd just seen Brody's naked ass, but because, more likely, he'd seen the scars from all the whippings Daddy Frank had delivered. Some of the thin white lines had disappeared over time, others had stayed, bold, a permanent reminder that Brody better watch his step or else.

"You're safe with me," said Quint as he went about shutting the camper down, turning off the lights, putting their spoons in the small sink, the paper cups in the trash. "Sleep good."

"You too."

The camper went dark and still. A small, cool rain-scented breeze came in through the screens over the rectangular-shaped windows. As Quint undressed and settled in the larger bunk below, Brody drew the sheet to his chin and stared at the ceiling which he knew was only half a foot away but, in the darkness, seemed to dissolve into an eternity of blackness.

What the hell had he just done? He'd run away like Bryson had, only—only he'd gone with a man he didn't even know. But even if that was true, it was by far the better option than another day with Daddy Frank and his unpredictable and violent temper, his insane rules, his drive to make Brody the best trick rider in the world, even if he had to beat Brody to a standstill to achieve it.

Before dawn the next morning, in the darkness, Quint woke Brody up with a gentle touch to his arm. He made him wash and get dressed in the clothes Quint had hung up to dry the night before.

"We'll leave quick as we can," said Quint. "We'll get breakfast on the road and I'll change those bandages before noon."

"Where are we going?" asked Brody as he scrambled out of bed, eager to be obedient and avoid Quint's displeasure.

Dressing quickly, he looked up as he slipped his own t-shirt over his head, and realized that Quint was watching him with hard eyes. Shivering, he backed up.

"The hell away from here," said Quint, rubbing his jaw as if thinking about a shave and how long that would take. "Here's the problem." Quint looked around the trailer, like a man determining what he could carry on his back if he had to leave in a hurry. "You're underage, at least here in Oregon. Daddy Frank finds out you spent the night under my roof, he could have me arrested."

"I'll get a fake license," said Brody. He was confident he could because Daddy Frank had talked about it with him when they had discussed their future plans. There was always a guy in every town who knew how to fake a license, sometimes even passports. "I don't care. Please take me with you."

He started shaking, then. He didn't think Quint was going to back out and leave Brody behind when he pulled out of the campground with his truck and camper. It was just he was shook by the idea of how long a reach Daddy Frank would have for years to come. He'd be so mad, he'd even get the cops involved, be on the phone screaming to the FBI or whoever he thought would bring his meal ticket back. Not his son, his meal ticket.

"Oh, I'm taking you." Quint's scowl was hard as he began securing things in the camper, looking out the red and white cafe curtains from time to time, as if scanning for an enemy who might appear out of the predawn darkness.

"Why?" Brody asked. He moved closer, close as he dared to this near stranger who could squash him flat, but who moved with purpose and strength, and didn't seem to mind Brody's question. The same kind of question Daddy Frank would have smacked him to the floor for. "Why are you taking me?"

"Because." Now Quint stopped moving, looming over Brody, looking at him with dark eyes, a hard color like something dug out of the earth. All of this would have scared the hell out of Brody, enough to make him pee his pants, except Quint moved slowly, breathed slowly. "I don't like cruelty and I need a change, something to shake

34

me up while I'm looking for the next horizon." With a quiet breath, Quint added, "We'll help each other."

5

BRODY

*T*hey were on the road within the hour, Quint driving them slowly out of the campground just as the sun was peeking through the trees, with Brody curled up in the passenger seat of the well-kept truck, blinking against the coming dawn, light on the inside, his limbs leaden.

True to his word, Quint got them a hot breakfast at a little eatery along a secondary road. Then they drove and drove, each mile a blur, each turn in the road a quick, brisk step into an unknown future.

At some point that first day, Quint got better bandages for Brody's arms, though Brody couldn't have cared less about that. As long as there were no new bruises or scars, he could bear the ones he had.

That first night, when they camped in a little KOA off the main highway, deep in the woods of Northern California, Brody slept like a bug in a rug for the first time in years.

They made the circuit of the western states, or Quint's idea of it, a rough-edged circle down the west coast, across the Arizona desert, stopping a whole bunch of times in Texas before heading north to Kansas, up to Idaho, and across to Oregon again. He took them to big county fairs and small ones, to big rodeos, and little ones.

Quint knew the admins of the arenas, made handshake deals, got them both jobs, insisting each time that Brody was his right hand man and he couldn't do without him. Quint managed the care and feeding of livestock, cattle and horses, both, and feed and grain supplies, handled invoices and receipts, dealt with drunk cowboys and the younger ones who just missed their moms, this being their first time out from home.

He told people who asked that Brody was his nephew, and that seemed good enough for everyone they met. Brody stuck close to Quint's side and learned everything he could about fairs and rodeos and animals.

Quint made Brody study to get his GED, tutoring him each night, helping him with math and science. When Brody joked that Quint had missed his calling, Quint just smiled and changed the subject.

Quint also bought books off Amazon, making sure the deliveries caught up with them at each fair, each rodeo ground. The books were about history, and food, and art, and mostly they were about horses. How to ride, how to take care of them, how to watch for the condition of their hooves. How to whisper in their ears and make them love you.

Brody could spend hours reading in the evening without Quint saying a thing, but sometimes Quint wanted Brody to play cards with him. He'd say, *A man's gotta know how to control his poker face*, even though they mostly played gin rummy or crazy eights or slap jack.

Sometimes Quint would pull out an ancient Yahtzee set. Then, by the yellow kerosene light set on the narrow camp table in front of the camper, they would play. They used dice so old they had cracks and chips, tiny pencils with no erasers, and pads of paper that were soft around the edges, as if they'd once gotten wet.

Sometimes folks from other campers, horse wranglers, rodeo clowns, cooks, and the guy who ran the cotton candy stand, would join them for a short while, bringing beer and chips and sour pickles. Moths would flutter to the kerosene light, and the warm air would sift around them like a shawl laid on your shoulders by someone who cared that you might feel chilly when the sun went down.

When that first summer was over and the winds in Montana began to taste of winter, and the season began to wind down, Quint pulled out an atlas of crackling paper and taped-up spine and spread it on the little dining table in the camper. Laying his hands on the two page spread that encompassed the entirety of the United States, he looked at Brody with eyes the color of dark spinel.

"Where shall we go?" he asked. "Where shall we go for the winter?"

Brody had been on the verge of taking that exam for his GED so he knew his geography by now. Still, Quint turned the map toward him, so he could read everything right side up. Up to that point, though Brody had been all over the place, following Daddy Frank's mad plan, he'd never been anywhere special, at least not anywhere he could name or remember.

"Where would you go?" asked Brody.

"I prefer a beach," said Quint. "Someplace warm, that's all I ask. You pick."

The only place Brody wanted to go was wherever Quint was. That's all he asked, all he would ever ask. Quint was patient with him and kind, looked after him when he was sick.

Sometimes Quint asked Brody to take a walk when he wanted to entertain a visitor, but he never ever hit him. Never got irritated or impatient, never exploded into rage. Quint didn't like it when Brody didn't tell him about a blister or a wrecked boot heel, or even a splinter. From Quint, Brody learned how it could be when you truly cared for another person.

"Go on, kid," said Quint, pushing the wide map of the country toward him. "Pick someplace nice."

"I don't want to screw up," said Brody.

"You can't," said Quint. "Not when any beach in the whole wide world is heaven in the wintertime."

Brody, swallowing his nerves, picked Port Aransas, Texas, which was where they parked two days later when the winds started to howl in Montana.

The RV park had a heated pool and plenty of clean showers, a laundry room, a little coffee shop, and even a clubhouse, where they could practice their game of pool, or darts. They were on vacation.

Brody spent hours at the pool, and studied for and took his GED test there, using a laptop Quint had gotten for him.

They celebrated when his certificate came in, and went to a nearby steakhouse for rare meat and cold beer. Which yes, Brody could drink because he'd gotten that fake driver's license after all, due to the fact that working with animals meant sometimes driving trailers or flatbeds full of hay. Both he and Quint agreed that they didn't want any county fair or rodeo to get busted when they found out Brody was underage, hence the fake license.

In his mind, he was already twenty one like the card said, instead of the most of the way to eighteen that he really was. This idea was constantly with him, and it made him feel like a man, to walk tall and do the right thing and to focus on the future, on the good things to come.

Sometimes, when it was cold and the sand skittered across the beach in flat, angry lines driven by the winter wind, Brody would feel the darkness come down, like someone had shoved him into a barrel before kicking him over a cliff. Quint would dose him with CBD oil and chicken noodle soup and chocolate and would read out loud to him till he calmed down.

Brody's nightmares would come and go, and mostly they were of Daddy Frank finding him and killing him by cutting him into tiny bits with an aluminum and glass diamond from his hatband. Only sleeping with Quint, curled in Quint's arms in the lower bunk, would ever help him with those nightmares.

Quint was always on the lookout and said that one time he saw a notice that Daddy Frank had gotten arrested for drunk driving outside of Boulder, Colorado. But whether he'd been released on bail or kept locked up for three months, the notice didn't say.

"We'll steer clear of Colorado for a season or two," Quint said, to which Brody readily agreed.

He looked different now, his hair cut short, like Quint's. He acted different, too, more confident, more able to give his opinion without shrinking down into himself to avoid what he always expected would be a violent reaction.

Being in Quint's shadow when they were working, it never got violent because nobody dared to cross Quint. Not that he was mean or rude or grouchy, it was just the way he stood, the way he held himself, the way he spoke. The cowboys obeyed him, the arena admins adored him for the efficient way he brought them receipts and invoices and knew the way they liked horse trailers to be arranged in the far parking lot.

One time they were working a county fair and rodeo in Broken Bow, Nebraska, where they tended to the pens of prize-winning sheep and barn stalls full of blue-ribbon-worthy draft horses. It was then things shifted between them, but in a good way that built the trust between them even stronger.

Quint had asked if Brody would meander over to the KOA building that evening and give Quint some privacy for one of his visitors. Brody had said yes, and figured he'd first take a short bit of shut-eye before playing some pool, or working the pinball machine.

Except that's not how it had gone. Brody had fallen asleep and Quint and his visitor must have thought he was gone, for they'd gotten right to it, stripping off their clothes before falling into the lower bunk.

Brody knew he'd slept through some of this, but he'd figured out what was happening when he woke to the sounds, low thuds, gasps for air, of two people fucking. Or, to be more clear, two men fucking, because the gasps were masculine and definitely not all Quint's.

Quint had been whispering roughly, *Take it, take it,* and the other man was definitely taking it, for the trailer shifted on its stabilizers, just a fraction, with each hard thrust.

It had been clear, early on, that Quint liked to sleep with men as well as women. He'd made it clear to Brody that word got around and sometimes people lined up for what Quint liked to dish out. But not until that moment had Brody a taste of what that meant.

The man sounded like he was in pain, but in a delicious way, and Brody could tell by the hard sharp edge in the air that Quint was totally focused on dishing it out.

All up and down his body, Brody felt that edge dig inside of him, making his muscles taut, making him hard, his cock flat and heavy against his belly. All of him quivered, a sheen of need lacing his skin, crawling up the back of his skull.

He licked his palm, and curled his fingers around his erection, and slowly, quietly, matched Quint's thrusts, stroking himself. Blending into the background of the passion below, thrusting into his own palm in time, an echo. The scent of their sweat rose up in the small confines of the camper, salt and heat and desire, all in one breath.

Cool air came in through the narrow window he'd propped open before he'd fallen asleep, bringing the scent of summer night, the faraway hint of rain, the labor of dirt trod flat. The wet hay, the sweet tang of sugared almonds. All the smells he knew.

He knew Quint's scent as well, powerful, dark, full of energy. Energy which he now matched with his own as he jacked off, slowly, quietly, letting the passion simmer in his veins like a low promise until it rose, and he came when Quint and his partner came, hiding his gasping breaths as Quint's partner gasped and sputtered his thanks.

There was almost no response from Quint, save a low grunt, Quint's acknowledgment. The question then became whether Brody would announce his presence or lay low and pretend he'd been in the KOA building the entire time.

The thing was, he and Quint were always honest and up front with each other. Quint didn't like liars, and Brody had learned and internalized that trait from him.

So while he did wait while Quint's fuckbuddy got dressed and left, when Quint stood up, Brody rolled to look over the edge of the upper bunk.

Quint was in his boxer-briefs, his spent passion a sheen on his naked shoulders and chest, glinting on his wiry chest hair, the single light over the stove casting shadows across his muscles.

Quint, ever attentive, sensed Brody there and paused while drinking water from a coffee mug. His eyebrows went up, but he didn't stop or act like anything was unusual, even though it was, a little.

"Well," said Quint in a matter-of-fact way. "I *did* think you were gone."

"I was going to be, but I fell asleep." Brody yawed, partly for effect. He scratched his belly, and pulled up the waist of his briefs, tucking himself inside. And thought about whether or not Quint wanted to go get cheeseburgers with him. "He seemed to like it rough."

"They all do," said Quint. "And I like to give it to 'em rough."

Brody's eyebrows rose as a question, formless and uncertain, began to take shape.

"And no, I'm not giving it to you," said Quint. He smiled, a small curve to his mouth, and dumped the water from the china mug into the small sink. "You're far too gentle for the likes of me."

"I'm not *that* gentle," said Brody in protest as the idea of it raced around inside of him like a squirrel on the loose. Not that Quint had considered the idea of them fucking and had decided against it, but because of the reason.

Brody was a rough, tough man and did not need coddling, or so he'd always thought. Now Quint had shown him a different reflection in a mirror he'd not known had existed.

He believed Quint in this, he truly did, and now, as he considered the idea of it, he knew Quint was right. There was a huge part of him still wounded even after all this time, even after hours and hours in Quint's company.

He'd also spent time in the company of good, decent people who did not resort to violence, did not ever act like a thwarted three year old when things didn't go their way. Who were not Daddy Frank. Not one of them.

"Can we go get cheeseburgers, d'you think?" asked Brody as he grabbed the wooden edge of the upper bunk and kipped over the edge to the floor.

"Good idea," said Quint.

The cheeseburgers had been delicious, and after that evening, they went on as they always had, except sometimes Brody simply didn't head off to the pool or the clubhouse or the bank of showers when Quint said he had a visitor coming. He simply stayed in the upper bunk, vicariously tuning in to the hard-edged fucking below. Quint, of course, knew he was there, and that didn't slow him down, at all.

Though Quint seemed to enjoy men and women equally, the men were always the more interesting ones, to Brody, at least. Sometimes Brody asked if he could have a visitor and although Quint always accommodated Brody, heading off into the darkness when Brody'd brought someone home from the fair or the 7-11, mostly Brody slept alone. Alone was better. Alone was safer. Alone was alone.

And now he was not alone. He had a passenger sitting next to him on a sunny, mid-summer day, looking at him with pewter blue eyes so full of anxiety and questions, which seemed to spill out of him with every breath.

"I'm going to get the gate," said Brody because it was always a good habit to constantly talk to a nervous horse, to give it all of your attention so it would always know where you were, which would calm it, minute by minute. "Then we're going to drop off this bag of laundry at Jasper's cabin. I'm thinking you should duck down till I park this truck next to the supply shed."

If he'd been Kit, Brody knew that, at this moment, he'd be wondering whether he'd signed on with a madman, or jumped into the truck belonging to someone on the FBI's most wanted list.

Kit slid down into the wheel well, and stayed there through Brody's quick chat with Jasper, and all through the trundling drive along the main road through the ranch to the barn. There, Brody parked the trailer in its spot, unhitched it, pulled around to park the truck, and turned off the engine. He checked in the rearview mirror to make sure nobody was looking and sighed, taking in a lungful of clean mountain air.

Kit pulled himself into the passenger seat once more, and looked at Brody, shoulders stiff, blood in the corner of his mouth. The drive hadn't settled him, but then, as Brody knew quite well, beneath the face Kit was showing him was a pile of emotions stacked as deep as the unseen part of an iceberg below the surface of the dark ocean.

"I don't quite know what I'm doing," said Brody, being honest, as Quint had always been with him. "But we're going to walk to my room in the staff quarters like nobody's watching, and we'll get you fed and cleaned up, and—"

"And then I'm going to Vegas," said Kit. "That's where Katie is."

"I can give you some money for the bus," said Brody, thinking about the amount in his wallet, and in the dresser in his room.

Brody restrained himself from asking how old Kit was, and from asking about his obsession with his mom. But then, Brody had never really had a mom, and sometimes kids who did actually loved them and wanted to be with them. So who was he to question that Kit wanted to join Katie in Sin City?

"Sounds like a plan," said Brody. He had to turn on the power to the truck to roll up the windows all the way to keep insects and varmints out of the cab, then nodded to Kit. "Let's go. Just follow me."

6

BRODY

*K*it followed Brody along the dirt service road between the storage building and the staff quarters, exactly in the manner of a cat walking along a fence line between two yards, both with equally vicious dogs in them.

Brody knew that walk, knew the tension in Kit's body that echoed inside of his own, memories and years of doing that exact same walk to keep from falling. To keep from getting eaten alive.

It was with a kind of blind trust, or super-focused tunnel vision that Kit followed Brody up the wooden stairs to his room on the second floor, at the very end of the hallway. There, Brody unlocked the door, thinking how he never actually needed to lock it, and ushered Kit inside.

Whether anybody had seen them was anybody's guess. As to why he was hiding Kit was another question. In the meantime, there Kit stood in the middle of his small room, with the sunshine streaming in through the parted curtains in the window to the west. It was late afternoon. Smells from the dining hall soaked through the air.

"You hungry?" asked Brody. "Why don't I bring us something to eat from the dining hall while you take a shower. I'll bring some ice for your mouth."

"Why?" asked Kit, the question blunt, almost like he felt he was doing Brody a favor by being there.

"Why food?" asked Brody. "Because it's just about dinnertime, that's why."

"No, why the ice?"

Ah. Another puzzle solved. Another emotion heard from.

Until Quint had taken Brody in, nobody had hardly ever offered him an ice cloth for his sore face, or mentioned bandages or healing salve for his bruised back. Kit, it seemed, was cut from the same life, the same trail of untended bruises, unacknowledged suffering. Which made Brody wonder if there was more damage currently hiding underneath Kit's clothes.

There was time for that later. First dinner and a shower, then the tending, which he hoped Kit would allow him to actually do.

Maybe Kit would just take off while Brody was gone. But, as Quint had always told him, *You can't tie a hurt horse. You have to trust it to trust you till it stands still.* Well, that's exactly what Brody was going to do. Trust Kit and do his best.

"I'll be back in ten minutes," said Brody, opening the door. "Time enough for a shower."

He left Kit in his room, not really worried about it because there was nothing worth stealing except his small collection of cowboy boots, which would be too big for Kit anyway.

Walking along the maintenance road past the staff quarters helped his body relax. Inhaling huge lungfuls of crisp, rain-scented air, relaxed him even further. As did the acting-as-if behavior of nodding to guests as he mounted the steps to the dining hall, and made his way to the back kitchen. There, he found Levi amidst the pre-dinner bustle, aproned from neck to waist, guiding the kitchen staff, a cleaning cloth in his hand, always moving.

"Hello, Brody," said Levi in his slightly formal way. "What can I help you with?"

"Couple of sandwiches in a bag, an apple and some cookies. Couple of cartons of milk." Brody nodded like the transaction was already a done deal. "I have a guest who doesn't feel like he wants to eat in the dining hall."

That much was true. It wasn't a lie. Kit probably didn't feel like eating with strangers looking at him. Brody well knew the feeling, back in the day, not wanting looks of pity or sympathy for his bangs and bruises.

"Sure," said Levi, with a graceful nod. "Let me fix you something."

Brody only had to wait about five minutes before Levi came over to him with a large paper bag, neatly folded at the top, sealed with a sticker with the ranch's new logo on it.

As Brody took the bag, he already knew there weren't just two sandwiches in there, there were two *delicious* sandwiches wrapped neatly in waxed paper. Not just two apples, but two shiny Honey Crisp apples. Not just two cartons of milk, but organic milk. Two homemade chocolate chip cookies. A thin white paper box of in-house kettle chips, liberal on the salt. Napkins.

Levi did not stint on service, and he was well known for that. Brody just hoped Levi wouldn't be pissed when he found out who the food was for.

"Thanks," said Brody.

"You're welcome," said Levi.

Carrying the paper bag in both hands, Brody made his way beneath the green-leafed trees to his room in the staff quarters, acting like this was something he did every now and then, and today was just another day. Nothing to see here.

All the while, beneath the surface, he wondered why he was hiding like this. He'd not had to hide in years, and pulling on this cloak of pretend invisibility was taking him way back into memories he'd long determined he had no use for.

The door to his room was unlocked. He opened it quietly, balancing the bag in one hand, which, being heavy, was not easily balanced. He put the bag on the top of his dresser, and was about to open it up to reveal the goodness inside, when he paused.

Kit was asleep on Brody's bed, the bedclothes half-shoved back, sheets rumpled, streaked with dirt. Kit slept on, oblivious to Brody's presence, but that didn't surprise Brody. Sometimes, after Daddy Frank had delivered one of his hard whippings, it was all Brody could do to keep his eyes open.

What was discouraging was that though there was a rumpled towel on the bathroom floor, and the tale-tell *plink-plink* of the shower-head dripping, the sheen of water on the linoleum floor and the edge of the sink, Kit's bare feet were not only grimy, they were perfectly dry to Brody's touch. Kit's dishwater blond hair was streaked with dampness at the edges, but everything else was bone dry.

The fake taking of a shower was a mere tableaux, a demonstration for Brody's benefit. Kit was his own man and would shower or not, as he pleased, and nobody, not even Brody and his kindness, was going to change that.

Brody had met a horse or two this stubborn. He was willing to put in the work if Kit would meet him somewhere near the middle, but currently the middle was a long way off.

More disturbing was the fact that at the collar of Kit's long-sleeve t-shirt, gapped away from his neck, and at his waist, where the shirt had ridden up, were not just bruises, but ladders of them, green and black-blue, looking hard and sore and dark against Kit's pale skin. The bruises even went beneath the loose waist of his thin blue jeans.

Kit was not just beaten up, he was covered with the leavings of Eddie Piggot's temper. This wasn't just Brody rescuing a scared kid. This was Brody stepping into a hornet's nest.

He didn't need to call Quint on his cell phone to ask what to do, to ask for advice to help him as he staggered beneath the weight of responsibility for what he'd just done, though he wanted to. Quint had taught him enough over the years.

Brody needed to reach out to Leland, and Leland was most assuredly going to call the sheriff, and Brody needed to be ready for Kit's sense of betrayal. The trust between them was unspoken, a tenuous connection between two people who had only just met, but who had both dragged behind them the weight of their own almost unlivable lives.

If Leland didn't contact the sheriff, which he most assuredly would, then Brody would have to do that himself. Nobody, as Quint had taught him, deserved to be treated this way. And nobody should get away with treating someone this way.

Kit was going to be pissed at him, but Brody would rather betray that trust, unspoken, undeveloped, then let this go unanswered. Besides, it was about time Eddie Piggot got his comeuppance.

So he didn't wake Kit up and confront him over the fake shower, didn't ask him about the map of bruises and how they had happened. He knew the story Kit was telling, for he'd told it himself, time and again. To teachers, and school counselors. To fair ground staff and waitresses. To anybody he'd encountered when he'd lived with Daddy Frank, though living wasn't exactly the right word.

He'd been existing with Daddy Frank, just like Kit had been existing with Eddie Piggot, and given Kit's response, how he'd been existing with Katie. The story was an old one, well worn, and though better forgotten, well remembered.

Quietly, he left the room, shutting the door softly behind him. Typically, Leland, the ranch's manager, made an event of showing up at the dining hall for most meals, there to circulate and visit with guests and staff alike, spreading his energy like a welcoming blanket, making everybody feel special.

The force of his energy was hard to resist, and who would want to? Not Brody, that was for sure. He especially appreciated the way Leland didn't dig at you, trying to get to know you his own way. No, he let you come to him, in your own time, which was, as Quint had often remarked, the sign of a genuine horseman.

So Brody knew that if Leland wasn't already at the dining hall with that celebration of energy and joy in full swing, he was still at his office in the barn, on the phone or meeting with heads of staff, clearing up issues, solving problems, delegating as he went.

It was in his office Brody found him, finishing up a phone call as he stood at his desk, the cell phone tucked beneath his chin, his straw cowboy hat being twirled slowly, slowly, around between his hands.

"Yes, that's fine," said Leland to the caller at the other end of the line, jerking his chin up in greeting as he saw Brody at his open door-way. "I don't care which day you come for those interviews, but I'd rather you film when the sky is blue. Check the weather. Understand?"

Leland paused, raising his eyebrows at Brody to indicate he wanted the phone call to end, also, so he could find out what Brody needed and help him.

"Yes, it's fine if there's a clip of a rainy day, to capture the mood of that. It's pretty up here all the time, even in bad weather. But I want to give your viewers a sense of the energy up here, and a day with clear skies is better for that. Sure, yes. Two weeks out. Sounds good. Goodbye."

"Well," said Brody by way of greeting. "That the YouTube guy?"

"Indeed, it was," said Leland. He gestured to his spare chair as he sat down and grabbed himself a cold locally brewed root beer from his small red electric fridge. "Sure, come up and film, I told him when he asked. Had no idea there'd be so many small details."

Leland smiled as he swallowed some root beer, but Brody wasn't fooled. If there was a man good at the myriad small details involved in getting the world to notice Farthingdale Guest Ranch, it was Leland Tate, and he was not only good at it, he loved doing it.

"What's up?" asked Leland, also not fooled, for Brody seldom stopped by Leland's office, and mostly took care of the horses on the ranch the way he saw fit, without asking permission first.

"I've done something today that I've never done before, and I'm not quite sure what to do next." Brody said the words clearly and slowly, making sure the explanation prepared Leland for the serious-ness of it.

He'd never before given Leland any indication he was unsure what his job called for, and now he had. Leland, in response, put the root beer on his desk, and leaned forward, all of his attention on Brody.

"Okay," said Leland. "What happened? How can I help?"

Brody told him about parking in front of the Rusty Nail, just to see Eddie rage. Leland did not smile when he learned Eddie *had* raged, though he didn't chide Brody for this, either.

Then Brody described how Kit had crawled out through a cellar window, and how he'd decided to get Kit out of there, almost without a second thought. And how, after he'd returned with Kit's dinner, he'd seen the display of the untaken shower, and the display of abuse all over Kit's body.

"This the same kid Clay stood up for a while back?" asked Leland, though Brody knew Leland already knew the answer to that.

"Yes," said Brody. "I'd like to say I did it to get back at Eddie, but honestly, I don't care about that now. I only care about this kid. He wants to go to his mom, Katie, who he thinks is in Vegas."

"Thinks?" asked Leland, his eyebrows going up.

"Exactly," said Brody.

Leland knew what was up as well as Brody did. As well, beneath Brody's own words, he knew he cared about this kid, cared what happened to him beyond anything to do with Eddie Piggot.

Sure, revenge would be sweet, even if it sometimes wasn't, but more importantly, Kit would be safe. Leland would help him make sure of that.

"Think we should call the sheriff," said Leland, and it was not a question.

"I wish I was enjoying the idea of this more," said Brody, admitting it beyond his ability to be shocked that he was sharing this much. Leland was a good man, and a good boss, but Brody's life was private and not for sharing.

"The situation with Eddie Piggot has gone on way too long." Leland stood up and dialed 911 on his cell phone. "I should have stepped in way before this."

Leland's conversation with Sheriff Fletcher Lamont was short, with Leland conveying the facts in crisp to-the-point sentences. If he had any pleasure in the fact that the sheriff would soon be questioning Eddie and very likely arresting him, he showed none of it. Leland was not a man to gloat or to do anything out of spite. Leland was a man who got things done for the right reasons.

"He'll be here in ten minutes, no lights or sirens," said Leland as he clicked off the call. "Think your new friend will take off or will he be here?"

"He's so tired, he's not going anywhere soon."

Brody didn't want to explain how he knew that after a beating your body felt like it had leaden weights attached to it, and the only thing you could feel was the sensation of sinking into dark water as the weights pulled you lower and lower into the depths.

7

KIT

The room was warm when Kit woke up, a slight breeze moving the cotton curtains in a sluggish, almost uninterested way as though they wanted to retain the afternoon's stillness. He sat up and looked at the black streaks his bare feet had made on the white sheets.

His neck ached, and his back ached, and frankly, he hurt all over. That happened sometimes, after one of Katie's men would knock him around. The bruises seemed to grow with time, the hurts and the sore places blossomed beneath his skin until it was easier to figure out what didn't hurt than what did.

None of Katie's men had ever whipped him like Eddie had, and though a few had tossed him about, none of them had dragged him down the stairs like that. Part of him, some deep part, still quivered with the memory of holding himself upright while Eddie pulled him down those stairs, like an echo of falling his body was simply unwilling to forget.

He was alone in the room.

The light coming through the windows was a soft gold-drenched blue, and between the curtains he could see puffy white clouds floating along, like they didn't have a care in the world. Which of course they didn't. Nobody would ever raise a hand to a cloud.

Brody was gone, though his presence still lingered, the flash of his gaze, the shifting colors of his eyes, the soft sound of his voice. The way he said things, like he'd practiced for a good long while to say them just the way he wanted to say them.

He was a good looking guy, sharp-jawed, with a straight nose and a sweetly curved mouth, dark hair spilling over his temples and his ears. He was the kind of guy Katie would have sidled up to the second she clapped eyes on him. The kind of guy who would have given her the once-over and turned away.

Brody reminded Kit of the bronc rider, in a way, slow to voice his thoughts, slow to move, careful with his hands. And maybe like the bronc rider, Brody would be one of those guys whose first reaction when Kit screwed up wouldn't be to hit him.

He didn't know if he wanted to wait around long enough to find out if he was right. He should put his socks and sneakers back on and walk right out of the room. There was nobody to stop him, after all, and he had places to be. But as he stood up, his legs protested, bruises pulsing to life just beneath the skin. A three-day bus ride to Vegas would be hell right about now. And didn't Brody say he'd give Kit some money for the ticket? Maybe he should wait for that money.

Across the room on the tall dresser was a large white paper bag taped shut with a circular white sticker. Getting up, Kit padded barefoot across to it and tore it open, inhaling the smells of sweet apples, touching the dapple of beaded moisture on one of the milk cartons.

That Brody had left this for him to eat was obvious, so the food was his. He inhaled the funny-shaped potato chips, and the cookies, both of them chocolate chip, and ignored the apples and the milk and the napkin while he nibbled on one of the roast beef sandwiches. Maybe he'd save some of the food for his bus ride to Vegas.

Rolling the sandwich back up, he let the ripped paper bag fall to the floor and poked around in the dresser, pulling out fifty bucks and a lovely buck knife that he snapped and unsnapped in his hand. Both went into his pockets. Both were his now.

Maybe there was more money around the room? Lots of people, Katie always said, kept money in multiple places. So he looked in the books, most of which were about horses, some of which were about the stars. Boring stuff. No money showed up, but he did his best to neaten the mess he'd made in Brody's underwear drawer when he finished searching there.

Next, he rifled in the bathroom medicine cabinet for throat lozenges, which were always a good stand-in for candy, especially Luden's Wild Cherry ones. Brody didn't have any of those, only boring Ricola. There was also a bottle of CBD oil, but Kit didn't touch that, as Katie always said it was a gateway drug.

All in all Brody had a very boring room. It was peaceful, yes, but there was nothing much to look at, no TV or anything, though Kit did spot an older model laptop on the bottom shelf of the bookshelf. It was dusty and didn't look like it got used much and probably didn't even work.

He straightened up, wincing as his back complained. He had fifty bucks so why was he sticking around? He wasn't a prisoner or anything. Except he needed his cell phone so he could call Katie, and then he needed to get the hell out of Dodge before Eddie figured out where he'd gone. If Eddie found Kit on the ranch he hated so damn much, he'd not just kill Kit, he'd tear him apart.

There was a knock on the door and then it opened. Brody came striding into the room, all glory and light, making Kit's heart skip, just for a second. But then he was followed by man Kit didn't know, and Sheriff Lamont, whom Kit recognized from Lamont's visits to the Rusty Nail.

"What the fuck." Kit spat the words. Of course Brody had let him down, of *course* he had. And just when Kit was thinking Brody was a nice guy, one of the good ones. There was no reason to ever trust anybody again. Ever, ever, *ever*.

"You can't arrest me," said Kit, almost spitting the words as he backed up until his legs hit the bed. "The food was for me, I know it was. And besides, I'm leaving. Gonna catch a Greyhound out of town."

"The Greyhound already left today," said Brody in that calm way of his. "The next one's not till Friday."

"Don't care." Kit jutted out his chin, keeping an eye on Brody while at the same time trying to keep his eye on the other two men. "I'll hitchhike."

"All we want, Kit," said Sheriff Lamont. "Is to get your statement about how and why Eddie Piggot assaulted you."

"Assaulted?" Kit laughed, doing his best scoff. Katie had always told him never to involve the law, no matter what. "Sure he got a little rough, but he didn't assault me."

"Brody says the physical evidence says otherwise," said Sheriff Lamont. "If you'll lift your shirt, I can take pictures, and then you can sign this form."

"You're a fucking *prick* and I'm not taking off my clothes for nobody."

If there'd only been Brody in the room, or Brody and one other guy, Kit could have made a break for it. But there were three of them and they blocked the door. They were all taller than him, more broad-shouldered. More intent on getting him to tell a truth he simply did not want to share. Well, he knew what to do with that.

"Doesn't matter," Kit said, crossing his arms over his chest. "Doesn't matter what he did. I'm not pressing charges and you can't make me."

Besides, Katie would kill him if he got Eddie in trouble, and never mind that Eddie was well and truly pissed at her for stealing his money. He didn't want Katie so mad at him that she stayed away longer than she normally did.

"How old are you, Kit?" asked Sheriff Lamont.

"Nineteen, not that it's any of your fucking business."

"He's of age," said Sheriff Lamont with a slow shake of his head. "I can't force him to sign a complaint and I can't make an arrest without that."

"Fine," said the other man, his blue eyes snapping. He was a tall man with long legs and a focused air that, had they been alone, would have had Kit running for the hills. "I'd like to make a formal complaint myself, then. This is the third time Eddie's expressed his temper with his fists. Third time he's attacked someone who lives on ranch property. I want you to talk to him and tell him he's on your radar."

"That'll work," said Sheriff Lamont. "I'll keep my eye on him, Leland."

"Thank you," said Leland. He straightened up and looked at Brody and then at Kit. "I'll get Stella's team to bring a cot because nobody sleeps on the floor under my watch. And I'll see the both of you in my office, after the meeting in the morning. Understood?"

"Yes, sir," said Brody without a hint of sarcasm.

The two men left and in their wake a bell of silence settled over the room.

"Who the fuck was that?" asked Kit. "The Lord God Almighty?"

"That," said Brody with a small, wry smile. "That was the manager of Farthingdale Ranch, and a man you do not want to cross."

"The fuck do I care." Kit flung his arm like he meant to fend off Brody's advice. "I'm outta here anyway cause there's no way I'd stick around with someone who'd call the freaking sheriff on me."

"I had to," said Brody, simply.

"But why?"

Brody made that little gesture with his head, the same one he'd done before when Kit had asked why, as in why Brody felt he needed to bring Kit some ice. He looked to the side, like he was looking at someone standing there, waiting for the answer to an unasked question. Like he was taking notes so maybe he could translate to someone, Kit maybe, as to what had been said, what had been listened to.

"Because." Brody bent to pick up the paper bag and toss it in the trash can next to the desk. Then he unwrapped the second beef sandwich and started eating it, standing there. "Man, this is good. Anyway, you don't deserve to be treated like Eddie treated you and Eddie doesn't deserve to get away with it." With a swallow, Brody licked the mayonnaise from the corner of his mouth, and sighed. "I could eat five more of these."

Kit felt a little bad about eating all the good stuff and leaving the yucky stuff, but Brody seemed content with the two cartons of milk and the apples and the other sandwich. In the midst of this eating, Brody sat on the chair he'd pulled out from the desk.

Kit was watching him carefully from the other end of the room, when the door opened yet again. In walked a blousy older woman with wild carrot-colored hair and a map of freckles on her face. Following behind her were two sturdy looking young men carrying a cot between them.

"Stella, my dear," said Brody, getting up as he dusted his hands together.

"Don't you my dear me, young man," said Stella, and though her words were cross, she seemed to have a small smile meant only for Brody. "Here's your cot, with clean sheets, a set of towels, and so on. Why Leland thinks I have time for this, I have no idea."

"Because it's for me, dear Stella," said Brody.

"Bah," she said, waving her hands at him. "C'mon boys, let's finish up and we all can go home."

"Thank you, Stella," said Brody. "Thank you, guys."

"I'm not staying here," said Kit as he eyed the cot, which looked nice and comfortable. Certainly no worse than any he'd slept on before and from the looks of the thickness of the mattress, maybe a damn sight better.

"You don't actually have to," said Brody. He appraised Kit with eyes that shifted color so quickly, Kit wanted to reach out and hold onto the sensation that rippled through him when Brody looked at him that way. "You don't have to do anything you don't want to do. You can go, or you can stay and see what the morning brings."

"I need to get to Vegas," said Kit, shifting on his feet, looking around to see where he'd tossed his sneakers and socks. "I need to get my stuff from Eddie before I go."

"Not a good idea." Brody shook his head, irritation flaring in Kit that this near-stranger was telling him what he could and couldn't do. "Let's send the sheriff. He'll bring back your things and then you can go."

"Is this a trick?" asked Kit. Of course it had to be, for who would be nice to Kit this way if they didn't have a plan to mess him up?

With a shake of his head, Brody stepped to the side. The door was open. The way was clear.

"You can leave right now, or at any time. But see the sense in getting a good night's sleep and eating a hot breakfast in the morning."

"When that Leland guy is going to yell at us."

"Maybe," said Brody. He smiled as if at some private memory. "If he does, it'll be Leland-style, so be ready."

If there was one thing Kit was used to, it was getting yelled at. Maybe he'd already seen the worst Leland had to offer, though, so whatever the boss man might hand out in the morning, he'd be able to bear it.

It was the cot that drew his eye, now. The idea of it, somewhere safe to sleep that wasn't above a noisy bar whose patrons simply didn't want to leave at two in the morning, pulled at him, hard. And Brody didn't seem the type to wake Kit up at odd hours to get him more ice for his drink, the way Katie sometimes did.

"Listen," said Brody. "I'm going to take a shower and then you can take one, okay?"

"Don't need a shower," said Kit. "I already took one."

"Sure you did." Brody took off his cowboy boots to set them neatly side by side next to his bed. Then he bent to pull out a cardboard box, his dark hair falling across his cheek. "You faked a shower before and believe me, I know the signs. I'd also prefer it if you didn't leave any more black streaks on the sheets, as it makes Stella quite cross."

"I'll think about it," said Kit, which he often had said to Katie, trusting that her mind would wander off to other things and she'd soon forget what she'd wanted Kit to do for her.

As he watched Brody disrobe most of the way, sliding out of worn blue jeans, pulling off his long sleeved shirt and then his t-shirt to stand there in his socks and underwear, it occurred to Kit to wonder why Brody seemed so casually to accept Kit's presence in the small room. Why arranging it so that Kit wouldn't have to go back to the Rusty Nail seemed a given, a no brainer. And to wonder why the hell Brody was helping him in the first place.

The rescue, only a while ago, with Kit panting on a hot sidewalk wondering which way to run, knowing he had no money in his pockets for a ticket on the Greyhound bus chuffing away in the bus station, let alone anything else, had been a miracle. He'd heard that whistle, and like a trained dog he'd responded and looked up.

There Brody had stood, with the door to a bright silver truck open, his straw cowboy hat shading his face from the hard afternoon sun, expectant and still, as if it had been a foregone conclusion that Kit would take Brody up on his offer and follow a stranger home. And follow he had.

Going with Brody had been his only option. And now here he stood in a room with a half-naked stranger. He had fifty bucks in his pocket, sure, and a buck knife he could pawn, if he could get to a pawn shop. But that still netted him less than the price of a bus ticket to Vegas.

Maybe while Brody was in the shower, he could rifle around a little more. Or, as he watched Brody peel the socks from his ankles and place them on the bed neatly, with his other clothes, he could just sink onto the comfortable cot and eat the other half of his roast beef sandwich.

8

—————

KIT

*B*rody came out of the shower in a small cloud of steam, dressed only in his underwear, his skin still damp, bits of dark hair sticking to his tan cheeks. He was muscles all up and down, ribbed abs, long thighs. His arms were corded with muscles, and he had odd scars along his biceps, and lighter white ones on the backs of his legs.

"It's rude to stare," said Brody as he finished toweling off.

"Well you're a freak for taking a shower so early," said Kit.

"I'm covered with dust from the day. I like to be clean, so I can relax in the evenings."

As Brody pulled on his blue jeans and a clean t-shirt from the dresser, he didn't seem to care that Kit had been rude to him. Didn't lash out or threaten to hit him or try to make Kit cower in any way.

Maybe Kit didn't have to be so much on guard with this guy, didn't have to push and shove, at least for a minute. He'd get a good night's sleep and in the morning he'd head out for Vegas, like he'd planned.

"You need to take a shower." Brody sat on the bed with the cardboard box and pulled out a small tin of something and a little white bit of cloth.

"No, I don't."

"Yes, you do." Brody picked up one of his cowboy boots and began wiping it down with the cloth. "I already told you. Rules of the house. I don't want Stella cross with me."

"Why do you care?" Kit kicked the roll of plastic wrap that had dropped from the rest of his sandwich. "She's just a housekeeper."

"She's not *just* an anything," said Brody, and now his tone was stern, like it hadn't been before. "She helps keep this place running, and she gave me a new cardboard box for my polishing kit when my old box fell apart."

"You like her because she gave you a cardboard box?" Any more of this and Kit was going to go out of his mind. "Jeez, you're easy."

"No, I'm hard," said Brody. "Stella is good to me and I want to keep it that way. She brings me fresh towels when I need them, which is a lot, since I'm out with the horses all day long and take a lot of showers." With a little flip of his wrist, Brody opened a small tin of what looked like lard and used the small cloth to dab it on the boot before smoothing it in with the cloth and sometimes his fingers. "And I want her to stay happy, which means you're going to take a shower before you get in that bed."

Kit debated arguing about it, and thought about how his ribs were throbbing and how something was rubbing along the waistband of his jeans. And how, if he kept resisting, Brody would know something was up.

The one rule he always followed was to never let on how much it hurt. Guys like Eddie and Bob and Mac and whoever else Katie had shacked up with always lunged for the kill when they smelled blood in the water.

Brody seemed pretty clever, and smart enough to figure out that if Kit kept not taking a shower, there was a reason he didn't want to. Maybe Kit should give in and just get it over with so Brody would quit hammering on him.

"Fine."

Plowing into the bathroom like he was struggling through six feet of snow, Kit figured he'd done enough to let Brody know he didn't much like the idea of it but he was going to do it anyway, just to get

Brody off his back. He was going to have to take a shower this time, rather than faking it, as Kit had seen the way Brody was watching him, and figured those strange color-shifting eyes wouldn't miss a thing. Besides, he liked showers just fine when he wasn't covered with bruises. Sometimes he liked to sit down and let the water stream over his head like it was raining.

He closed the door, and stood inside the pale yellow walls of the small bathroom before he started getting undressed. His underwear snagged on his hip and tore, the last of the elastic giving up the ghost, and his jeans were dirty enough that they could stand by themselves in the corner.

What of it? That was how it usually went, as Katie never seemed to have enough quarters when *he* needed clean clothes to wear, so he was used to it by now. Peeling off his long-sleeved t-shirt was the hardest part, as his ribs were sore and his shoulders ached when he lifted them over his head.

Hissing, he tossed the t-shirt on the pile, and turned on the shower. There didn't seem to be a way to make the stream of water gentle, it came out full force, though he did turn the temperature down and waited a minute, grabbed a clean washcloth from the pile on the back of the toilet and gritted his teeth and stepped in.

It hurt as much as he figured it would, so he'd make it quick. The soap, lavender-scented liquid soap in a bottle, of all things, stung when it hit his bruises. He made light work of cleaning himself where he stunk the most, and skimmed everywhere else.

Except his feet. Brody seemed obsessed with how clean his feet were, so he scrubbed those extra good, balancing with one hand against the side of the shower stall while he used the washcloth and plenty of soap on the bottom of each one. Finally he washed his hair and rinsed, standing under the spray, getting used to the pressure by now and thinking maybe the shower had been a good idea, as he was starting to feel better. Not that he'd tell Brody that, no way.

Turning off the water, he stepped out and rubbed his hair lightly with the towel before wrapping it around his waist, wincing as the roughness of the cloth caught along his back. Then he looked in the semi-fogged up mirror, rubbing his chin while he wondered if it had been long enough so he could shave again.

No, no luck. The down on his face was fair and faint and besides Brody would probably get pissed if Kit borrowed his shaving things without asking. So he'd ask in the morning, and see how that went. Besides, he didn't want to look at his own face for too long, a flash glance was all he needed and he didn't like seeing the memories in his own eyes.

When he adjusted the towel on his waist, his foot skidded a bit in water on the floor, and he looked down. A curl of red blood had ribboned its way down his leg, and now coyly slithered across his ankle, ending with a blot on his big toe.

In the same instant his mind realized that Eddie had cut the skin with his belt, some other part of him, vulnerable and hurt, spilled upward, racing and mad, crowding his chest with a darkness he could not control. He was far from everywhere, in the middle of nowhere, Katie had been gone too long, much longer than normal, and he was *bleeding*.

Whimpering, he pulled the towel away from his waist and peeked at it, and yes, there was a jagged stain of blood, and his lower back stung like something was biting it. Staggering, he grabbed onto the sink's edge and held onto the towel just as there was a knock on the door.

"Kit?" asked Brody. The door opened a little way and Brody's shadow, his presence, eased into the room. "You okay?"

"Go away." The words trembled and Kit struggled for breath. There was now blood on the floor, and the towel was ruined, and Brody was going to hate him forever for pissing off Stella. "I mean it, go *away*."

"No."

Now the door opened all the way and Brody came in, barefoot and ready. In one glance he seemed to assess the state of the floor, and the towel, but his attention was focused on Kit. Kit staggered back beneath the force of that gaze.

"You cut?"

There was no hiding this. No running away. The window above the toilet was narrow and too small and he was two floors up, so there was no leaping out of that window even if it had been big enough. The other two windows were on the other side of Brody, as was the door. Besides, the evidence was there, and Brody wasn't stupid.

"Eddie's belt did it," said Kit, barely managing the words. "I just need a minute."

"You need help," said Brody. "And hopefully not stitches."

Kit whimpered again, unable to swallow the sound, unable to stop himself from shrinking back as Brody advanced.

"Keep the towel," said Brody. "But let me see."

Kit was all the way backed up now, his legs touching the cold porcelain edge of the toilet. The dampness in the room hampered his breathing and he knew he was going to pass out. Which would be the worst because he'd be unconscious on the floor and Brody could do anything he liked—

"Let me open that window," said Brody, reaching past Kit to raise the sash on the window above the toilet. "And turn just a bit."

Helplessly, Kit did as he was told, his knees knocking together, shoulders shaking. He felt a tug on the towel, and loosened his fingers, which had a death grip on the edge of the towel. He felt the sweep of Brody's fingers across his hip, his back, and he tensed for it, tensed for the moment when Brody would dig into where it hurt and declare that it would need stitches, lots of them.

"Hey, now." The words were soft, like Brody was attempting to gentle the air with them. "It's not a cut, just a deep abrasion. We can clean this and bandage it up. It'll heal. Okay?"

The only sounds Kit could make were low, panting grunts as he grabbed on hard to the sink, holding onto that towel with all of his might. He didn't want a near-stranger looking at his ass, and longed, very hard, to be very far from where he was.

"Let me get the first aid kit."

Brody bent down behind Kit and stood up with something in his hands, which he plonked in the sink.

"Another gift from Stella," said Brody. "My very own first aid kit."

"Wh-wh—why do you need your very own?" asked Kit, his voice high, throat tight as he did his best to distract himself.

"Gates bite. Horses bite sometimes, though not very often. Nails are rusty, and sometimes buckles on bridles catch on your knuckles."

All of this made sense in a weird kind of way, a distant way, the words swimming around as Brody touched him and cleaned him and taped a large bandage over a hand-sized area on his back above his right hip.

"I'll get you something clean to wear."

Brody left the room and when he came back, he tossed a t-shirt and some cotton boxers onto the closed toilet lid. Then he wet a washcloth and knelt at Kit's feet to clean his ankle, his calf, his thigh. When he stood up, he handed Kit the washcloth.

"Clean the rest of you," he said. "Then get dressed. There's Advil in the medicine cabinet, so you might take that. And if you're still hungry, I have peanut butter crackers."

"In another cardboard box?" asked Kit with a croak.

"Actually it's in a plastic bin," said Brody, and the smile in his voice floated over Kit's shoulder as Brody left the bathroom, shutting the door very quietly behind him.

Kit dropped the towel and used the cloth to clean between his thighs, like he imagined some girl on her period might. Then he wiped the back of his thigh and, with a sigh, tossed the stained washcloth on top of the stained towel. And wondered how he'd ever come to this, where he was worried about what a cleaning lady would make of those stains. Why should he care? He didn't care. Never did. Never should. Never.

By the time he'd pulled on the t-shirt and boxers, both of which were soft and shifted over his skin like a gentle caress, his head was throbbing. He took three Advil, and because there was no glass, he had to cup his hand for water beneath the faucet. But he was used to doing that, because there wasn't always a glass in the bathroom that didn't look like it had been stored at the bottom of a sewer pipe for years and years.

When Kit straightened up, chin dripping with water, he looked at himself in the mirror again. His face was pale, which was no surprise, and he looked like he'd been smacked around, which wasn't a surprise either.

Why did he always look like he was lost and didn't know where he was going? Was that the face Brody saw? Well, Kit wasn't lost because even if he didn't know where he was right at that moment, he was headed to Vegas, just as soon as he could manage it.

Thinking quickly, he gathered up his long-sleeve t-shirt and his jeans, feeling inside the jean's pocket for the money and the knife. The clothes were filthy against his newly-cleaned skin, and he wondered how he could hide the money if Brody took it in his head to throw Kit's clothes into a laundry bin or, even worse, throw them away.

Brody seemed like that kind of guy. In the end, Kit decided to cause a fuss if Brody so much as touched his clothes. He'd store them under the pillow on the cot, and in the morning, he'd figure everything else out.

9

BRODY

*B*rody remembered always being hungry. Daddy Frank always told Brody he needed to stay skinny so that when he stood in the saddle as a horse galloped wildly around the ring, it would be more effective for the audience.

Daddy Frank's reason for this was something about looking fragile like a girl. Brody would have liked to argue that point, as many girls and women, both, did barrel racing and dressage and stunts, and rode cutting horses, and all of them had arms with steel muscles inside of them, legs like iron. Constitutions like a mountain of granite.

But he didn't argue the point with Daddy Frank about that, then or ever. Instead, he constantly struggled with his growling stomach and the ache of his growing legs, his shoulders pushing out of the shoulders of his shirts long before Daddy Frank broke down and got him a different size. *Quit growing*, Daddy Frank would growl just before he cuffed the back of Brody's head. Brody had disobeyed Daddy Frank in this, and had paid the price many times over.

The windows were open as he lay in the bed. A dark, cool breeze sifted between the cotton curtains, both through the window over the desk, and the one above the bed, and the one in the bathroom. The air was fresh and damp, and smelled like pine trees giving off their baked scent as the night grew still.

Brody's bare feet had already shoved down the sheets and single woven cotton blanket, letting the coolness take him, hoping it would take him into sleep. But maybe it was the events of the day, or maybe it was the stranger lying in the cot along the wall in front of his bookcase and dresser that kept him awake.

Maybe it was the combination of the two. That and the memory, strong with each pulse of his heart, of Daddy Frank standing over Brody while he lay on the floor, bleeding from his mouth, telling Brody to *get up, damn it, get the fuck up and get back to practicing.* The voice echoed in his head even now.

Sometimes, the body needed to stop. Brody was aware of the signs in his own body, the tightness along his back, the quiver in his thighs. Now that there was nobody to whip him to keep going, he could stop. He knew when to rest. To take a drink of water. To sit in the shade, perhaps, and nod to Leland as the boss man walked by.

Leland trusted that the people who worked for him knew their own limits and would rest when they needed to. This kind of attitude was much like the one Quint had. You did your best and you stopped every now and then to take a breath, and then you re-hefted your grip around whatever you were working on and got on with it.

But watching Kit struggle today, both with his escape from the basement of the Rusty Nail, and with confronting Sheriff Lamont and Leland together, watching Kit bluster and fumble with his resistance —all of this told Brody a lot about what Kit had been through, maybe even more than Brody wanted to know or remember. And that Kit had no idea how to take a break.

Brody knew what it felt like to be backed in a corner so hard, there was no way out but down. He knew the feelings you got when a school counselor or other responsible person pointed out that maybe you having dirty clothes was cause for alarm, and never mind the bruises hiding underneath them. Bruises that must be hidden from all eyes at all costs.

Watching Kit today told Brody loud and clear that Kit had no idea of his own limits and, worse, had never been told to give himself a break. Kit would probably go down fighting and snarling, never realizing how ill-used he'd been.

Eddie Piggot had roughed Kit up and then some. Brody trusted that Eddie's cruelty and temper had gotten the best of him pretty much most of the time, and Kit had been standing right *there*, such a tempting target.

The worst of it, the very worst, was Katie, who'd dumped Kit off like he was an unwanted parcel. Who knew if she was really in Vegas, but Brody could bet that if she came back for her kid, if she ever did, she'd be full of breezy excuses.

He could predict what Katie would do because he'd been witness to the one time, the only time, Social Services had been called to the county fair to investigate after Brody had fallen from his horse during a difficult upside-down maneuver.

The horse, nimble-footed, had barely stepped on him, and had slowed down so Brody could leap aboard again and finish the ride. But someone, perhaps someone in the crowd, or one of the decent rodeo guys, had figured Brody was too young to be doing what he was doing, too skinny, too, yes, *fragile*, and called it in.

Daddy Frank's response to the pair of suited Social Service workers, had been that way, the way Brody figured Katie would be when confronted with the evidence of Kit's appearance. Friendly, helpful, answering all the questions with energy and concern.

The excuse Daddy Frank had given was that Brody missed his brother, Bryson, who'd gone off to New York to study to be an accountant, and Daddy Frank, unable to resist Brody's woebegone face, had agreed to the extra-difficult riding trick. Had agreed to the late night, as a treat, and golly, as a father, he should not be so softhearted, should he.

Daddy Frank's song and dance had been worthy of an award. The Social Service workers' thanks and apologies to Daddy Frank for taking up so much of his time, had been worth another award. Paperwork was duly signed off on, and the kindly do-gooders had gone on their way. Whoever had reported Brody to the do-gooders had gone *their* way, as well.

And, for one night, and one night only, this one time, Daddy Frank had told Brody to take off his clothes in the trailer and patched him up instead of whipping him. Luckily, nothing had needed stitches, or Daddy Frank would probably have taken it upon himself to tend to that personally, as well, most likely without anything to numb the pain.

Brody had used a good topical first aid cream, the best he had in the box, the kind that numbed the pain. The abrasion along Kit's lower back had been longer than the length of Brody's palm from his fingertips to the heel, and he'd only had one bandage big enough.

There was nothing worse than having a bandage too small, and the only thing covering the hurt place was part of the bandage and half the tape, which would be agony to pull off when it came time to change the bandage. So Brody had made sure, very sure, that the bandage covered the abrasion, and that the tape was far at the edge.

To his surprise Kit had stood still through all of this, and though a fine quiver raced through his body with every other breath, Kit's expression had been neutral. Like this happened every day, and as far as Brody could figure, it probably had.

Kit didn't know how messed up his life was, and, as Brody had often done himself, was perhaps pretending it simply wasn't as bad as it was.

That would only get you so far because after a point, everything would break and you'd find yourself standing in the rain looking up at a man with a buck knife in his hand and the ropes your father tied you with in a snake-like puddle at your feet. At that point, you either stayed where you were or you got up and walked away with the man.

The trouble was, Brody didn't know if Kit would realize that he'd reached that point. That he needed to walk away from Katie and Eddie, or whatever man she might feel the need to leave her kid with next. Needed to walk away and start anew. And, perhaps, he needed someone to point him in the right direction.

Was that person Brody? He didn't know. But he did know that Kit was better off with him, even for a little while, than on a bus to pretty much anywhere, at that moment.

Beneath this, the night memories lurked, as they tended to do when he let them go galloping off instead of reining them in hard and fast. Kit had been the distraction, but Brody couldn't blame Kit when the memories roamed free. That was all on him.

It was late, and there was no help for it, so Brody got up and slithered out of bed. Though he did his best not to wake Kit, not turning any lights on, tip toeing, Kit sat up with a rustle and a slight squeak of the metal frame of the cot.

"What are you doing?" asked Kit in a voice clear enough to tell Brody that Kit had been awake this whole time.

"Getting something to help me sleep."

The answer was not enough. Kit got out of bed and padded behind Brody, softly, following him like a soft grey shadow. Kit blinked at Brody when he turned on the light over the medicine cabinet, like he was a sentry standing guard and needed to be sure of Brody's every movement.

Only a guy who'd lived through several hells would be that edgy. Brody's heart went out to Kit, an impulse he couldn't still, didn't want to.

"What's that?" asked Kit. "Is that the drug oil?"

It occurred to Brody, then, that Kit had seen everything in his medicine cabinet when he'd gotten the Advil. Normally, nobody went through Brody's things, not since Brody had gone with Quint, anyway. Now he had someone right there, watching him.

"It's CBD," said Brody. He pulled the stopper to put a few drops under his tongue, letting the filmy earth-tasting oil sit there a few seconds before swallowing. "I should have taken it earlier."

He tightened the lid, put the small brown bottle back in the medicine cabinet, and closed the glass door before looking at Kit.

It was just the two of them in the half-circle of bright light that reflected off the mirror and into the room. Just the two of them, dressed for sleep, their legs and arms bare. Hair messed from their pillows. Night air gleaming on their skins.

Kit's bruises were swamp-dark, and his eyes were wide, the anxiety pulsing out of them like warning signals. He was like a nervous colt standing there in need of a guiding hand. And who was better with horses than Brody? Nobody, that's who.

"Want some cheese and crackers now?" asked Brody. "I think I've got peanut butter crackers, too. And gorp."

"Okay." Kit nodded. "What's gorp?"

"You're in for a treat, my friend."

Brody went to his bed and reached beneath for the small plastic bin where he kept his snacks. Most, like the cheese crackers and peanut butter crackers, he'd bought at the ranch's store, but Levi was kind enough to save back some of the gorp he made for trail rides, which he put in plastic baggies for anyone who wanted some.

"Gorp is raisins and almonds and peanuts and peanut M & Ms. All the good stuff. Here."

Pulling the box with him, Brody slithered onto the bed till he could lean his back against the wall. He held the plastic box on his bare legs and patted the space beside him.

"C'mon then, Kit," he said. "We'll have a little midnight feast."

"Is it midnight?" asked Kit as he clambered on the bed, hands and knees, till he was at Brody's side, his posture an echo of Brody's.

"I could check my phone," said Brody as he glanced over at the little alcove where his desk was. "But it's all the way over there and besides, who cares." He peeled off the blue plastic lid and put the plastic box on Kit's thighs. "Check this out."

Kit made a sound, a sigh, like he'd not seen food in years instead of hours. Maybe a single sandwich and some chips and cookies wasn't enough for someone who was still growing, so Brody needed to make sure that Kit's meals were regular and hearty. In the meantime, though, he was pleased to see Kit's eyes glowing in the single light from the bathroom, his fingers diving into the pile of little packets labelled Ritz and Keebler, like he'd found gold.

"These are brand name ones," said Kit, looking up at Brody with amazement. Which made Brody sad, as it meant that Katie and whoever else had been haphazardly feeding this kid had been doing it with generic, store-bought foods always.

Kit tore open a packet of peanut butter crackers and shoved the whole thing in his mouth. Brody followed suit with a cheese cracker, and they crunched through the crackers, contentedly, followed by a handful of gorp, though Kit seemed to favor the M & M's over the raisins.

"I like pop tarts," said Kit, his mouth full, crumbs scattering. "Can we put pop tarts in there?"

"Sure," said Brody. He licked his lips clean of salt, and watched Kit watching him. "What flavor do you like?"

"Blueberry, always blueberry," said Kit, and his smile almost reached his eyes. "Though I never can figure whether I like frosted or plain, better."

If there was one thing Brody knew, knew better than perhaps anything else in the world, was the point at which a fractious or anxious horse had turned a corner in its own life. When a horse nickered as you approached it, or turned its head to watch you fill its feed bin. When it took a carrot from your hand, however cautiously. When it leaned into the petting it had previously shied away from.

All these actions, or any of them, meant that the horse wanted to trust you. Was perhaps *desperate* to trust you. This was that moment with Kit, and Brody was going to make the most of it.

"Oh, I don't know," said Brody, with only a small tease in his voice. "I don't know that I've ever done a side by side comparison. Have you?"

Kit shook his head, his mouth full of crackers.

"Well, maybe I should order one of each so we can do a taste test." Brody pretended to consider the notion extra hard.

Of course the truth of it was Levi wouldn't have a real pop tart on the ranch if you paid him all the money in the world. The dining hall's breakfast always included popovers, made in-house, with real raspberry or cherries or apples inside. Levi also made scones with blueberries that melted in your mouth.

Kit didn't know that, but Brody would make sure he tasted those scones. In the meantime, they would get some blueberry pop tarts to put in the eats and treats box.

"They only carry off-brand in the bodega in Farthing, but the grocery store in Chugwater might have them. Or we might have to order from Amazon."

Kit's mouth was in a small round shape of surprise. As though nobody in his life had ever considered doing this for him. As though nobody had bothered to simply order for him exactly what he wanted on Amazon.

"But we can't tell Levi," said Brody. "He's the head chef for the ranch, and he'd blow a gasket if he knew we were eating those when he's got homemade scones with blueberries in them."

"Homemade?"

Brody wanted to cry, just then, like he'd not cried in years, for a kid who said the word *homemade* like a prayer or a mad hope for something he'd never had.

Brody had tasted homemade goods plenty of times over the years, but that was because Daddy Frank was tight-fisted and figured he could save money by making their meals himself. The result had been edible but boring, but at least Levi's notion of homemade was miles away from Daddy Frank's idea.

As for Kit, he'd missed out on a lot of good things, and however this turned out, Brody was going to do his best to make sure he had what he needed, ate what he wanted, and didn't get smacked around anymore.

"Yeah," said Brody. "It's good stuff. Maybe better than pop tarts from a box." He shrugged. "We'll have to taste all of it just to make sure."

"Okay." Pleasure seemed to simmer beneath Kit's skin, or maybe that was the CBD oil finally kicking in for Brody. Maybe Brody could sleep now, and maybe Kit could as well, and stop standing sentinel at his own gate.

The ranch was a good place, a safe place, where nobody got slapped for walking too slow, or knocked to the ground for breathing wrong. When you messed up on the ranch, somebody helped you to your feet, and you were able to get on with things rather than looking over your shoulder in fear. Brody wanted to make sure Kit knew all of this.

He couldn't make Kit stay, just like he could walk a horse to water but not be able to make him drink. He could coax Kit to experience all the ranch was, all the goodness it contained, even if in the end it would be Kit's choice to go or to stay.

And Brody found, beneath it all, that he wanted Kit to stay. But why should he want this, when he'd pretty much figured out that being alone was the way he wanted to be?

If he'd not just taken CBD oil, and if he did not have a guest in the room that he'd pretty much signed up to be responsible for, he would have gotten dressed, put on his boots, and snuck out beneath the moonlit-drenched night. He'd have gone up to the barn to grab a hackamore bridle and then eased into the lower fields, where the horses were kept.

There, he'd have petted his way through the herd, cupping soft noses, petting arched necks, leaning against warm withers as he whispered his apologies for waking anyone. Then, boldly and against all the rules of the ranch, he would have slipped that hack-amore over the ears of the closest horse, and then, once astride, he would have raced across the fields bareback, up along the hills, feeling the wind in his hair, fresh air in his lungs, the power of the horse beneath him.

After a ride like that, his troubles always seemed to shrink into something he could handle on his own, or, after a bit of confirmation from Quint, he could go and do whatever needed doing, knowing it was the right thing to do.

After a ride like that, his heart would be able to tell him how he felt about Kit and why he had taken Kit in, thinking all the while about how Quint had taken him in.

In Kit, Brody saw himself, the lost young animal he used to be. If anyone knew what Kit needed, it was him, perhaps better than anyone in the world.

Below this awareness, though, like a low, pulling tide, surged other questions, a tugging need, a dark ocean of something he could not name. If he could ride beneath the moonlight, he would be able to name it, he was sure. And maybe, just maybe, he'd ask Kit to go with him.

10

BRODY

*I*n the morning, with the crisp air coming through all three open windows, Brody had to hustle himself out of bed. He had to hustle Kit out of his cot, as well, so they could wash up and get dressed. The morning meetings that Leland ran pretty much every day came directly after breakfast, and all staff who needed to attend were expected to eat an early breakfast so they wouldn't be late and wouldn't be hungry when Leland was going over the duty roster.

For a good long minute sitting up, Kit seemed to forget where he was, but when he saw Brody getting dressed, he got dressed, and though he was fresh from his shower the night before, his clothes were filthy and his sneakers were on their last legs.

"We'll get you some new clothes," said Brody as he sat on his bed to tug on his cowboy boots. "And then we need to wash the ones you have."

"My clothes are fine," said Kit as he fingered a tear in the sleeve of his long-sleeved t-shirt. Then he slipped his hand in his pocket, where the buck knife and money were. "Besides I have other clothes at Eddie's place."

"We'll get those picked up," said Brody. He stood and pressed his heels down into the cowboy boots, enjoying their snug feel. "Remind me to call the sheriff. In the meantime, we have guests who pay a lot of money to be here, and Leland won't want you walking around looking like a ragamuffin street kid."

Kit's response was a mulish look, his lower lip pooched out like he was about to start up with his angry backtalk. In response, Brody petted Kit's arm while he made sure the treat box was stowed away, like he would a horse whose morning routine has been interrupted.

"Not to worry, eh?" he said as he ushered Kit out the door and closed it behind them. "You don't have to wear the new clothes if you don't want to."

This was an easy promise to make because Brody didn't know anyone on the ranch who didn't want to start wearing blue jeans and cowboy hats and cowboy boots within five minutes of arrival. It went with the territory, and no matter how much resistance to the idea Kit thought he had, he was going to find out he was very wrong. Besides, guests loved it when members of staff dressed the part.

Once outside the staff quarters, Brody led the way beneath the morning-damp green-leafed trees to the dining hall where, as always, good strong smells of frying bacon and toasted bread, along with the sweetness of sugar on top of those scones, dragged him inside, almost helpless to resist.

Kit stayed right at his side. He was like a scared foal in a new field, but seemed to enjoy the smells and the bustle of the dining hall, filled with happy chatter, folks having a cup of coffee before getting in the buffet line.

As always, Leland was there, walking around, bright and chipper with that broad smile of his, and a gesture that seemed to encompass all the joy in the morning that he wanted to share.

"It's like a cafeteria," Brody explained as they picked up their trays and utensils. "Take as much of whatever you want, but remember, you can always go for seconds or thirds, so don't overfill your plate. Okay?"

Nodding, his eyes wide at the abundance of the buffet offerings, Kit was Brody's shadow, taking whatever Brody took.

When Brody realized this, he made sure to get the cheesiest scrambled eggs, the most evenly fried bacon, the most perfectly golden blueberry scone. Milk. Little squares of butter. Orange juice, which he normally didn't get as it made his tongue hurt. A serving of hash browns fried with onions. All the good things to fill Kit's belly. To make him content. For who could resist eating like this every single day? Not Brody, that's who.

"No pop tarts," Kit mock whispered as they sat down at one of the tables along the wall. Then Kit winced as if he wasn't sure the small joke would be appreciated or if maybe Brody thought he was making fun of all this.

"Just don't let Levi know you want them," said Brody, mock-whispering right back as he dug into his eggs. "We'll order them today, for sure. Both kinds. Frosted and unfrosted."

The shy smile Kit gave him was the reward Brody had not known he'd wanted, though it made him a little angry, deep inside, that a kid who loved pop tarts, such a simple thing, had been treated the way he had. Had been knocked around most of his life, like Brody had.

All of this was so wrong. His impulse was to flood Kit with pop tarts, though he knew that he needed to do more. Wanted to do more. Was going to do more in all the ways he could.

After breakfast, they bussed their trays, and Brody hustled them out of the dining hall, down the wooden steps, and up the dirt road to the barn, where the morning meetings were held.

There, he kept Kit by his side, which might have seemed like he didn't trust that Kit wouldn't run off. But, more, Kit seemed to want to stay close, and everything wasn't yet settled with Leland about all of this.

"Morning," said Clay with a wave as Brody and Kit joined the assembly near the open doors of the barn. "Who's this?"

As always, Clay's dimples were in evidence, and his blue eyes shone as deep and as rich as the sky above.

Clay was a morning person, but he was always cheerful like this, happy to be where he was, spreading his joy much like Leland did. They were a lot alike, though they might be surprised that Brody thought so. Then again, Clay's ambition was to be as much like Leland as he possibly could be, up to and including running a ranch of his own one day.

"Clay, this is Kit, a friend of mine," said Brody, waving between the two of them. "And Kit, this is Clay. He's a ranch hand and a damn good one. You guys might remember each other from the Rusty Nail a while back, when Clay got into a punch-out with good old Eddie Piggot."

"Holy cow," said Clay, his grin even wider. "I didn't recognize you as I only got a glimpse of you that night. Eddie sure is an asshat, isn't he?"

"Uh, hi," said Kit, perhaps overwhelmed by Clay and his bright energy. "And, uh, thanks. For trying to help me, I mean."

"How did you end up here?" asked Clay, but before Brody could tell him it was a long story, Leland stepped to the front of the assembled gathering of staff, and held up his clipboard. Maddy, the ranch's admin, was at his side, and they quickly conferred with each other before Leland cleared his throat, which was the signal for silence.

"Tell you later," Brody whispered.

Clay nodded and they turned their attention to the front, to Leland.

The meeting went quickly, even though there was a lot to talk about. Brody was pleased to learn that today was the day he and Quint would get to move the herd from the north field to the south field, which was always a treat. Another announcement included the construction of a new, smaller arena next to the service road, as well as the fact that in the coming weeks, they'd all be interviewed for a short documentary on western living and guest ranches.

"You won't all be asked," said Leland in a tone Brody assumed was meant to reassure. "But if you are, there's a reason for it, and I'd like it if you'd step up and answer a few questions while being filmed."

Which, in Leland-speak, meant he expected their full cooperation.

"Thanks everyone, and have a good day." Leland waved them off and then gestured to Brody and Kit. "I'll see you two in my office now."

Leland's office was a cool oasis amidst the early morning bustle of the barn, where Clay and other staff were getting a string of horses ready for an early-morning ride. Normally, Brody would have jumped right in to help, but he had a different responsibility now.

"Have a seat," said Leland, throwing himself into his creaky wooden chair on rollers. He waited till Brody had sat down in the other wooden chair on rollers, and Kit sat in the stiff wooden chair that was a leftover from the dining hall. "So. I get why you did what you did, Brody, and I believe I would have done the same, so let's get that straight right up front."

Brody nodded to show he was listening, just as Kit shifted in his seat, fidgeting. Out of nerves, probably.

"The question is, what are we going to do moving forward? What are we going to do with Kit?"

"Keep him here if he wants to stay," said Brody without hesitation. "Put him to work."

"Kit, do you know anything about horses?" asked Leland, his voice stern and clear.

"No," said Kit. He swallowed loudly. "No, sir."

"So how's this going to work, Brody?" asked Leland, leaning back in his chair. "This is not an island for lost boys."

"I beg to differ with you, Leland." Though Kit looked at him a bit shocked, Brody didn't have any fear of speaking his mind to Leland. Quint had taught him how to test people and how to hang on to the ones who responded without anger, without malice, regardless. Leland was one of those people.

"You beg to differ?" Leland's smile told Brody he knew where Brody was going with this but wanted to hear it just the same.

"Well," said Brody with a smile that echoed Leland's. "We could talk about a certain drifter, if you wanted to. Or we could talk about a certain ex-con, too, who is a permanent resident and member of staff. Or maybe it would be more appropriate to talk about Dorothy. Remember the widow? She might not be a boy, but she came here lost, and when she left on Sunday, she was a whole lot less lost."

Brody waited while Leland thought all of this over, but as always, he knew Leland expected him, as he did all of his staff, to point him in the right direction. Leland would help make things happen, but he wanted his people involved in the decision, even if it meant letting his staff fumble for a little while before they figured it out.

Brody did not want to fumble. All he had was his own instinct as to what might help Kit best, and his experience, from when Quint had stepped in and taken care of him.

"I don't know *anything* about horses," said Kit, as though desperate to remind them of this. "I just need to get to Vegas."

"Kit," said Brody, turning the focus of the conversation onto Kit, which made him fidget again. "Humor me for a minute, here. Without deciding whether or not you'll leave or stay, what's one thing you could do on a ranch like this to earn your keep? Just one thing."

"Uh." Kit stared at his hands in his lap, idly touched his finger to his tongue before picking up a bit of hash brown that had made the journey all the way from the dining hall. "I could work in the kitchen, like I did at the bar. I can bus and mop and sweep. And I know how to use a Hobart."

"What's a Hobart?" asked Brody, confused.

"That's the silver machine that can clean dishes in a heartbeat," said Leland. "It's got a track that goes through the machine, pulling racks of dishes under hot water and soap."

"Oh." Brody was seldom aware of anything outside of his own world, but perhaps it was time to open that gate a little wider. "What about working with horses. You ever ride?"

"Oh, no," said Kit with a shake of his head. "Horses'll kill you as soon as look at you. I don't like 'em."

"Kill you?" Brody drew back. He knew that sometimes guests were anxious around horses, and that timid new riders had a hard time during their first lessons, but to be so afraid of a horse? It just didn't make sense.

"It's up to you, Brody," said Leland, his words considered and slow. "And you, Kit. I'm sure Levi could use more help in the kitchen, as we get high turnover there. He's a tad picky. But you'll have to learn to work around horses too, learn the basics, learn to ride, like everybody on the ranch. Otherwise—"

For a moment, Brody was shocked that Leland would draw the line so firmly in the sand. If Kit didn't agree, then Kit would have to go. And Brody would have to watch him go, and feel a bit of his heart tearing away at Kit's retreat.

Yet, he could see the sense of it, what Leland was trying to do. If Kit could adapt to the ranch, he could adapt anywhere. It'd be good for him, right alongside regular meals and kind treatment. Sometimes, even with horses, a firm line needed to be drawn. And at least Kit hadn't continued to insist that his only choice was to leave for Vegas.

"That's right," said Brody. "Sure you can wash dishes, but you also need to clean stalls, and clean tack, and groom horses after they're ridden. You have to know how to work around horses, otherwise—" Brody felt his throat tighten. He didn't want Kit to balk at this, didn't want Kit to leave. Kit needed to be strong, and for that to happen, Brody needed to be tough. "Otherwise, I can give you some money for the bus tomorrow and wish you well on your travels."

"Oh."

For a long minute, Kit looked at his hands, at his knuckles, his fingers, as if he might find the answer there.

As Brody well knew, when you sat that still, if you had bruises like Kit had, they thumped beneath your skin in tune with your heartbeat. Sometimes they could be loud enough to mask all other sounds, like those of a school counselor whose poking and prodding questions were better lost beneath the ocean of heartbeat and pain and the memory of feeling so small, so unable to fight back, that any answer you might give simply didn't matter.

Brody almost held his breath as he waited, and saw Leland looking at him, an odd expression in his eyes.

"There's work to be done here, Kit. Good, honest work," said Leland. "We'll pay you well and feed and house you, so what do you say?"

"Okay, I guess," said Kit, worry washing over his features that maybe he'd made the wrong choice, picked the wrong direction. It was up to Brody to reassure him.

"Good," said Brody, firmly, with all the confidence he had. "You'll be a big help around here."

"Speaking of around here," said Leland as he got up, grabbing his hat from the hook. "There's no other beds available, so if you two don't mind bunking up for a while longer, that'll add less stress to Stella and her team."

"Sure, boss." Brody stood up too, and gestured to Kit. "We're fine as we are. Right?"

"Right." Kit's answer had strength behind it, like there was no doubt in his mind that sleeping on a cot was the best thing that had ever happened to him. And, maybe it was, which was the saddest thing of all.

"We need Kit's things," said Brody, as they all stood up in the little office. "I was going to call Sheriff Lamont to get them."

"I'll do that," said Leland. "I need to make sure he's talked to Eddie anyway." Leland picked up his hat from the desk and tossed it around his fingers, as though thinking. "Eddie's not welcome on the ranch, Kit. I just want you to know that."

With a nod, Leland put his straw cowboy hat on his head, and strode out of the office.

"Let's put you to work," said Brody, tugging gently on Kit's sleeve. "Later we'll get you set up, but for now, let's show Leland what a good idea this is."

"Okay," said Kit, a little dubious, but there was a small smile on his face as though he felt he'd done the right thing in agreeing to stay.

KIT

*K*it's body felt the fear, but Kit made his face hide it as Brody dropped him off at the dining hall, introduced him to Levi, the head cook, and said something about horses and fields and moving things around before leaving.

When he was gone, though there were people all around, there was an empty space around Kit, a Brody-less space. Kit tied on his apron, with the string around the front of his waist, and tried to feel normal.

Of course, Eddie at the Rusty Nail hadn't given a rat's fart in a high wind about his staff wearing aprons or washing their hands ever, but here, Kit could see the difference in the way things were done.

It was easier to look up at Levi, who was tall, and carried himself tall, and listen to the drill about the Hobart and the soap, and where the brooms and mops and suchlike were kept, than to think about what he'd gotten himself into.

Sure, he could work in a kitchen. Sure, he could bus tables and pick up the tips any guests left, but he sure as hell wasn't going to turn those over. Only an idiot would do that, and he wasn't an idiot. And sure, all of this was the easy part.

At some point, evidently, they were going to expect him to shovel horse shit, and groom horses, and do all kinds of stuff with an animal

Kit had no experience with whatsoever. It made his stomach ache to think of it.

Katie didn't like horses, which was funny, as she seemed to enjoy the company of rodeo men, bronc riders especially, and so Kit had no experience around them. All he knew was what he'd gleaned from overheard horror stories about getting bucked off and getting kicked in the head and stuff.

There was no way he wanted any of that. And yet, there was Brody. Who was good with horses, it seemed, knew all about them. At least Kit figured he did, given the amount of books about horses on his little bookshelf, and the fact that the morning's task of moving a whole herd of horses between fields had lit Brody up like a firecracker, like he would have glowed with the anticipation of it even in the darkest night.

Kit had never met anybody like Brody before, and yet, everybody on the ranch seemed to be a little like Brody, from Leland with his bossy ways, to that guy named Clay, who had a smile like a sunrise, to Levi, who looked down his nose at Kit, but who seemed to be willing to give him a chance. All of them were gung ho about their lives on the ranch, and seemed happy to be where they were, which was a damn sight different than anyplace Kit had ever worked.

"We've got AC going in the kitchen to keep down the heat from the stoves and ovens, so don't leave the door open when you take out the trash, please. And wear your hat at all times you're on duty."

Please, yet. This guy had some manners on him, and a way of carrying himself like he came from far away and had somehow found himself as a cook on a ranch.

"Sure," said Kit, pulling his paper hat out of his back pocket to put it on, at a rakish angle, of course. He knew how much he could get away with and in a few days, he'd know all the ways to skip out on work, or at least skip out on working very hard. "What do you want me to do first?"

"Here's the roster." Levi pointed with an elegant hand to a list on a clipboard on a hook attached to the wall. The list was laminated, and someone with very neat handwriting had written the names in grease pencil next to tasks and times. "It rotates. As you can see here, you'll be bussing first, then cleaning the floor in the dining hall, then you'll come back and do dishes. Tomorrow, you'll be on vegetables, then floor, then stocking, and so on. If you ever have a free moment, make sure the vertical surfaces around you are clean."

"That's a lot of floor," said Kit, thinking of how achingly boring it would be to sweep and mop so often.

"It's a big dining hall and it gets a lot of traffic," said Levi. "It's important to keep it to a high standard of cleanliness. We're getting busier, but that doesn't mean we don't attend to the small details."

"Sure," said Kit again.

He did his best to not roll his eyes. But even as he grabbed a grey plastic bussing tub and headed out to the main dining area where some guests were lingering over coffee while others excitedly left their dishes in a heap, headed off to tons more fun than Kit was about to have, he thought about Brody. About what Brody might do if he was asked to bus a table or sweep and mop an enormous floor filled with tables and chairs.

Brody would look at the disarray with those eyes of his shifting gold and blue. Then he'd nod, shrug his broad shoulders, look to the side, and then he'd get to work. He wouldn't balk or complain, he'd just do it.

Already the other kitchen staff were at it, elbows and assholes, as Eddie would say. But they weren't grousing or complaining or lolly-gagging, they were actually working, calling out to each other to answer questions or explain something.

In order not to stand out, Kit put his bussing tub down on the nearest table and started in. Half eaten congealed scrambled eggs were gross. Maple syrup that dripped over the edge of the plate was gross. But at least there were no cigarette butts smashed in the food.

And there wasn't that edge-of-midnight beer smell all around him, either. Instead, fresh air came in from the open double doors, and there was a hum from the kitchen, a comforting low sound of clanking dishes, the sound of a pot hitting the edge of the metal sink.

The churn of the Hobart, a sound that, in its own way, made things around him feel more familiar.

He did his best has he bussed tables, cleaned the floor in the dining hall with the others, but mostly he enjoyed working with the loud, clanking steamy Hobart, which took dirty dishes and polished them clean without a finger being lifted. After, of course, the dishes were hot as he stacked them on the metal shelves along the wall. And yes, he had to clean out the sink trap, and yeah, he had to take many loads of garbage and compost out to the huge metal bins behind the dining hall, which was gross. But, in spite of himself, for no reason he could figure, it had been a good morning.

"Well done," said Levi, to a small group of white-aproned staff, Kit included. "Everybody get some lunch but be sure to wash up and take off your aprons first. And Kit, you did a good job keeping up, thank you. I'll turn you over to the stables for the afternoon and will expect to see you again after breakfast tomorrow."

"Okay." That's what he'd usually say to a speech like that, but he rose on his toes a little, pride at the praise flashing through him like an unexpected gift. Which was different, way different, than it had been at the Rusty Nail.

Kit washed up, doffed his apron and his paper hat, and went through the double doors from the kitchen to the dining hall where guests were already lining up for the lunch buffet. Kit got in line, looking around for Brody, but was disappointed at not finding him.

He piled his plate high with baked spaghetti casserole, extra slices of bread and butter, two helpings of chocolate cake, and trundled out fully loaded to find somewhere to sit. He didn't recognize anybody, so found an empty spot at a table he'd bussed only a little while ago, and sighed with happiness at the amount of food before him.

"Mind if I join you?"

Kit looked up. A tall, broad shouldered man with greying short hair and a grim look about him stood there with his tray in two meaty hands. Normally, Kit would have told the joker to buzz off, but this guy, without being asked, sat across from Kit, and smiled a low smile at him.

"I'm Quint, Brody's friend," said Quint as he rearranged his plates on the table, taking them from the tray. "And you're the orphan Clay told me about, right?"

"Don't call me that," said Kit with a snap. "I've got a mom, so I'm not an orphan."

"Ah," said Quint, nodding, like Kit had just told him all of his secrets. "Well, it's nice to meet you, Kit."

Scowling, half the pleasure of the anticipated meal leaving him, Kit started to eat like it didn't matter that this rough-looking rude guy was taking up half the table with all his plates and rearranging and stuff. But Quint was such a presence as he sat there, silently eating what looked like all healthy stuff, that he was hard to ignore.

"Why are you dressed like that?" asked Kit, when he noticed other guests looking their way, mostly at Quint, who was wearing a leather vest and had long, leather leggings on over his blue jeans.

"Like this?" Quint gestured to the folded gloves he'd neatly placed on the table. They were made of thick leather, creased and sunburned, like they'd been used a lot, exposed to a lot. "I'm dressed for herding horses over on BLM land, which is land the government owns that we use for grazing. When you ride for hours, doing that kind of work, the chaps and the gloves protect you."

A guest came over and wanted her picture taken with Quint, so interrupting his own lunch, Kit stood up, took her phone and clicked a few images as she swung her arm around Quint's shoulders, and didn't seem to mind his sweaty neck or the dust on his chin.

Levi had been so specific about washing up before eating, and Brody, too, that Kit couldn't imagine how Quint's sweaty and dusty state wasn't against the rules. Not that Kit was a rule follower, no, but everybody else seemed to be, so why was Quint allowed to do this?

The guest went away, but two others came up, also wanting photographs with Quint. They stood on either side of him, their arms around his sunburned neck, and Quint grinned as Kit scowled and took a few more snaps. When they went away, Kit sat down with a huff.

"Finally," he said, digging into his baked spaghetti. "What the fuck was that all about?"

"Language," said Quint sternly, like he fully expected Kit to stop swearing then and there for the rest of his life. "It's a story we're telling, you see?"

"No I don't see." Kit wanted to say *No I don't fucking see*, but Quint was too close and could have clouted him from across the table, easy.

"Guests come to the ranch to experience what I call cowboy play-acting." Quint's eyes focused on Kit as though to make sure he was listening. "It's a nice clean place, easy to be in, nothing going on to cause strife. Well." Quint wiped his mouth with his napkin, and looked over his shoulder as if to include everyone in the room in his explanation. "There's a level of veritas Leland likes to put into the experience, which is why, after Brody and I herd those horses from one field to another, we stay in our outfits, including chaps and gloves, and come join the guests. We come in gritty and dusty from the field, and guests act like it's amazing. They respond like a cowboy rock star has stepped into their midst."

Kit had no idea what *veritas* meant, but he got the rest of it. Quint was telling a story, he and Brody both. To make the story more real, they stepped off the stage still wearing their costumes, and guests ate it up.

"That is to say," said Quint with a wry grin. "They're impressed with me and want photos and suchlike, but wait till Brody enters the room, still dressed for work. He's the *real* rock star in these parts. You watch. You'll see."

"Where is he?" Kit looked around, still not seeing Brody.

"Grooming the horses we rode," said Quint, eating steadily. "It's his turn this time. Next time, it'll be mine."

Kit couldn't imagine that Brody would look any different wearing the dumb chaps that Quint had on. Brody'd look the same as he always did no matter what he was wearing, right?

He was wrong. Dead wrong.

Just as the crowd thinned and most guests were sitting and eating, chatting away happily, the low din in the dining hall fell even lower.

People in the line for the buffet stepped aside and Brody walked through.

All eyes were on Brody. He didn't stop to get in line, but looked around the dining hall. When he spotted Kit, he brightened, and that was saying something, as he was pretty bright already.

Half the guests were staring at Brody. The other half dug out their phones and took pictures of Brody as he walked slowly through the dining hall. His legs were long, his stride insouciant. The fringed chaps he wore hugged his legs, cupped his backside, and emphasized, by contrast, the curve of his groin.

His hair was disheveled and wild, like he'd been riding the wind, and his face was bright with sunshine, his eyes snapping and bright with pleasure. There was a line of sweat down the side of his face, and the neck of his snap-button shirt was open halfway down his chest, which gleamed with sweat. He was glowing, all over, and Kit felt like his own chest had opened, like it wanted to take all of this energy radiating from Brody and absorb it into his own self.

Brody was the coolest kid in school, and though he might have been very aware of this fact, he seemed nonchalant as he stopped and put his arm around a guest, or two guests, one on each side, and smiled as his picture was taken and answered questions with his chin tucked down, absorbed in the guest he was speaking to. He did this for a good ten minutes, pleasant and calm all the way through, even laughing with the three young women who giggled and tittered and simpered around him, like he was an animal on display.

"See what I mean?" asked Quint, but there was no jealousy in his voice or in his eyes, as he turned in his chair to look at Brody. Instead there seemed to be a calm pride, and maybe a little bit of pleasure that it wasn't him having to wait and wait to have lunch.

"I guess I do," said Kit, the words faint in his own ears.

Maybe he ought to re-think this whole horse thing. If he had to learn, if he had to be around them, maybe he'd get to be around Brody when he looked like this. Maybe because he was Brody's roommate, he'd get special treatment and Leland would go, *Of course, you will work with Brody all day!* That'd be the life. Then he could look at Brody and soak him in and maybe that sparkling energy in Brody's eyes would be inside of him.

"Hey," said Brody as he came up to the table. Pausing, he pulled the fringed gloves from the waistband of his jeans and chaps and placed them, folded, on the table, along with the straw cowboy hat he'd been carrying. "Think I can eat yet?" he asked, his smile low, and maybe a little abashed, as if the way the guests had responded to him was a surprise to him.

"Here comes Levi," said Quint.

As if understanding that having Brody stand in line might create more of a ruckus than him simply walking into the dining hall, Levi strode over with a tray full of food for Brody. He placed it with care in front of Brody as he sat across from Kit.

"Can I get you anything else?" asked Levi.

"No, thank you," said Brody, looking up to smile at Levi. "This is perfect."

Levi strode off, seeming to ignore the crowd around him as he went. Brody picked up his napkin and laid it in his lap, and smiled at Kit.

His shifting blue-gold eyes made Kit want to fall into them, and the sweat along the muscles of his neck made Kit want to run around and do hard stuff, like shoveling dirt or whatever, so he'd glow like that, look handsome like that. To be one of the cool kids like Brody would be a dream life, and suddenly, he wanted that dream. Wanted to be like Brody so hard, it was hard to swallow his mouthful of food.

"Kit's going to want your autograph soon," said Quint, pointing to Kit with his fork.

"No, I don't," said Kit, scowling. He needed to do a better job of faking it so Quint didn't notice so much. But he wanted Brody to notice him, wanted Brody to like him. The only way to do that was to work with the horses, because working with the horses that morning had buffed Brody to a high shine, like he was floating on happiness and wasn't ever coming down.

"So," said Kit, and found both Quint and Brody's attention fully focused on him. "Uh." Kit swallowed hard. "Leland said I should work with you and the horses in the afternoon?"

The smile Brody gave him lit up the already-bright dining hall, as though Kit had given Brody a present he'd very much wanted but also feared he'd never get.

"We'll get you started, right after lunch," said Brody, smiling with his white teeth. "You'll be with me."

Kit gave a little hop in his chair, and looked down to hide his smile of pleasure. But then he looked up, and while Quint was smirking, Brody looked as happy as a kid on Christmas morning. Kit decided to do his best to make sure Brody stayed that happy with him, because, oddly, and all of a sudden, Kit didn't want to be someone who took that smile away.

BRODY

*T*he morning, with its bright sun and open fields, the backs of the horses shining like polished metal as they raced across the prairie grass, had been perfect.

Some days, when Brody and Quint would move horses from one field to another, or bring field horses down to the arena to be groomed, others to be put in box stalls for the vet to visit later, it would be raining. Or the sky would be gloomy with smoke from forest fires to the west, deep inside the mountain range. Or the wind would be sharp, and the horses would balk at being moved.

Sometimes it was a struggle to get the horses to go where they needed to go, though he loved working with the herd in spite of that.

Riding the open range was the best part of his job. There wasn't an audience, there weren't any guests around, just Quint and him, and maybe sometimes a few others. That morning it had been Quint and him, and though the slight breeze had brought the smell of smoke from a faraway forest, the sky above had been clear and the scent of sun-warmed pine had been strong.

The horses had galloped, skittish at first to see the pair of them approach on horseback. Maybe they liked to pretend they'd forgotten the smell of man and leather and oil and sweat. Maybe they liked to pretend they were still fully wild, not tamed at all, free to run where they would. But the pretending only lasted as long as it did, until the horses had their fun and allowed themselves to be herded up and moved from a faraway field to a closer one.

Sometimes moving the herd meant spending a lot of time in the saddle beneath the hot sun, dust kicking up from the horses' hooves, catching flecks of horse sweat on his arm, glimpsing the dance of bees in the air along the small no-name creek that jagged its way along the edge of the upper field.

The scent of grass and hot pine twirled around Brody's head as he slapped his own thigh with his gloved hand and whistled and kept Old Blue pointed where he needed him to be pointed. Though Old Blue was still all dance and anxiety after having been stung by a wasp beneath his saddle blanket, the horse knew what he was doing, like maybe he had quarter horse blood in him, even a memory of it from somewhere that made him fast on the cut and turn when some horse decided it didn't like being herded.

Across the field from him, riding the well-trained and powerful Diablo, a gelding with splotches on its coat and an uncertain back-ground, having been rescued from the animal food factory, was Quint.

Diablo wasn't for guests, even the most experienced ones, and only the best riders on the ranch rode him, as Diablo had a mind of his own. He wasn't mean, he just knew more about herding than his rider did, even Quint, who had to work to keep up with the choices Diablo was making.

Unsaddled, Diablo could be trusted with the smallest child, as he was a sleepy, calm horse who only wanted a bit of shade, a bit of water and food. Diablo was not a pretty horse and though on the ranch he always got more, and plenty of everything, this seemed to surprise Diablo each and every day.

Brody made sure Diablo had sliced apples, his favorite, and would stop to pet him when he was in the barn or the lower paddock. Saddled, though, Diablo was best left to do as he saw fit, and Quint knew this as he whistled and slapped his thigh, and gestured to Brody that one of the horses in the herd had decided to turn around and go back the way it had come.

The furthest field had to be emptied of horses first, with the herd brought to the field closest to the ranch, where they could easily be caught and groomed and checked over so they were ready to ride. Then the horses in the barn were rotated out to the upper fields, the faraway ones along the high ridge.

Brody could always tell that some of the horses, and it didn't matter whether they were older or younger, remembered the upper field and were eager to race all the way up there. It was Brody and Quint's job to guide them safely through the gates and along the barbed wire to the green, green field, bordered by rocks and cliffs on one side, and miles of high-grass prairie on the other, which was probably the most free they would ever feel.

An errant wind blew Brody's straw cowboy hat off and, as it danced along the grasses, stopping to pose along the creek's banks, or on top of a small jag of stones, Brody smiled. He needed that hat, he *loved* that hat, and there was one way to retrieve it. He pointed Old Blue at the hat and leaned low in the saddle.

"Let's get it, boy," he said to Old Blue, and Old Blue, a horse with an ancient soul and a need for sport, took off like he was chasing a prize bull.

His long, nimble legs carried Brody across the high grasses, dashed to the left when the wind took the hat, swung to the right as the wind tried to trick him. Then, as a long gust pulled the hat along like it was on a string, Brody kicked Old Blue into high gallop, held the horse's reins loosely as he clung tight to the saddle horn, and with a snap, hefted his weight into the left stirrup while hanging off the saddle.

His fingers combed the grasses at high speed and the wind rushed through his hair in a spray of light as Old Blue galloped toward the hat. The saddle was not a trick saddle, was not meant for a rider to hang off it the way Brody was, but he tightened his leg muscles and hung on and remembered the exhilaration of galloping at speed around an arena with the crowd gasping in pleasure at his dare-devil derring-do, the speed and his slight body a flame of energy and skill.

At the last minute, before Old Blue would have to go down into a gully if he went straight, the hat paused. Brody snatched it up, and righted himself in the saddle, laughing as he let Old Blue gallop in a wide circle before he slowed the horse to a canter. As he plonked his hat on his head, smiling, Quint cantered up on Diablo.

"Boy," he said, tugging Diablo to a stop. "You pull a fool stunt like that again I will haul you across my lap and wallop you good."

"No, you won't," said Brody, still smiling.

Quint might seem like the meanest man, might have nighttime partners that liked it rough, but when he came into contact with Brody, it was with the gentlest of hands, the most caring of gestures. Quint wouldn't let so much as a fly harm Brody, and both of them knew it, so the smile Quint returned to Brody was a teasing one. Maybe Quint missed having rough sex in the night, and maybe Quint just liked saying the words, so Brody would let him say them and not be worried about it.

"Let's take this last lot down before lunch," said Quint, and Brody agreed, and sat up in the saddle while beneath him Old Blue collected himself for more fun.

Leland came up to check on their progress, riding Big Red, a tall, fast, long legged horse with thoroughbred blood in his veins. He was accompanied, as he often was, by Jamie, the ranch's groundskeeper as well as Leland's partner, at his side, riding Dusty, who was calm and sturdy and dependable.

"Looks good, fellows," said Leland, reining Big Red in. Big Red liked to run, and Leland would let him, but first they were tending to business. "Well done there." He patted Big Red's neck to calm him. "Will you show Kit the ropes this afternoon, Brody?" asked Leland. "Make sure he knows his way around a horse, knows where things are in the barn?"

"Yes, sir," said Brody, then he added, "I'll be happy to."

Inside of himself, Brody had to bite down his irritation. Leland Tate was a good boss, and a good manager for the ranch, but sometimes. Sometimes he had it in his head that people working for him wouldn't know their asses from their elbows unless he pointed it out to them.

He was always checking up on Brody, doing a bed check, as Quint liked to call it, like Brody didn't have the sense of a newt and didn't know that he not only had to clean the horse's hoof but check the shoes and iron nails as well. Brody knew what he had to do, he'd been working in rodeos and county fairs since he was five, and had been riding horses longer than Leland had.

But he bit his tongue not just because Quint had advised him to, but because, really, Leland was just doing his job. Doing his best as he expected everyone working for him would do their best. Brody couldn't fault Leland for that and privately thought that maybe he was acting a bit spoiled, like a horse chafing beneath a new harness it wasn't quite used to.

For years, he'd cowered beneath the heavy-handed guidance of Daddy Frank. Then for years it had been him and Quint, alone on the road together, deciding together how things should be done. To have Leland striding around on his long legs pointing and gesturing and telling Brody to do this and this and this was like a harness too heavy to bear, sometimes.

On the other hand, there was now a cot in Brody's bedroom, courtesy of Stella, and he had a new roommate, one who needed looking after, and, it seemed, other than telling Brody to show Kit the ropes, Leland was going to leave the how and the where and the what up to Brody. That's how Leland usually liked to do things, and Brody supposed he could be glad about that.

When the last of the horses were brought down to the barn, tucked into box stalls or left in the upper paddock, and watered and fed, Quint strode off to lunch while Brody unsaddled and groomed Diablo and Old Blue. When he entered the dining hall, still grubby from work, the lunchtime adulation rolled off him, which it usually did, as he was used to it and didn't much care for strangers who felt they knew him.

It always took more than someone might think to not wash up before sitting down to lunch. The sweat along the back of his neck had itched, and the chaps were not lightweight leather just for show, but were the heavy, thick kind, made for long rides.

But then he'd seen Kit's face light up when Brody had come up to the table with his best saunter. And then there'd been the pleasure, the newness, of Kit watching him. He'd stared at Brody like he'd seen the moon shining across the rocks of Iron Mountain.

When he'd sat down to lunch and thanked Levi for the tray of food, he wondered at his life, where he wore clothes that some folks took as costumes. But that was part of the job, too, just as looking after Kit was.

13

BRODY

*K*it showed up at the barn soon after lunch, sporting different clothes that under close examination very much resembled the clothes he had been wearing that morning, except the shirt was a different color. The sneakers, limp as old socks, barely clung to his feet, and his jeans, older, more worn than the other pair, hung off his hips like they were a suggestion away from slipping to his ankles. His shirt, a short-sleeved one, had holes in the armpits and a tear at the hem.

In spite of his grubby attire, Kit jumped into the doorway with a *ta-da* gesture like he was the opening act for some big show. Brody sighed and realized he'd missed fully assessing and responding to Kit's needs.

"New clothes?" Brody asked, pulling items from the tack room shelf, a couple of body brushes, some hoof picks, hoof oil and cloths, a pair of rubber curries, a flexible thin metal sweat scraper, and fly ointment and a sponge.

"They sure are," said Kit, smiling wide. "Someone must have dropped my stuff off during lunch, because all my things were on my cot. And my phone too. I plugged it in and left a message for Katie. If I do that every day, she'll probably call me back, right?"

In Brody's mind, if Katie was going to return Kit's calls, she already would have. In other regards, Brody had neglected to realize that Kit's clothes weren't going to be of much use to him in about five minutes, as they wouldn't protect him from the sun, let alone horse slobber. As well, sometimes horses, unintentionally for the most part, stepped on you, so wearing boots was a must.

Typically, a ranch hand or a cook or anyone who worked on the ranch, could get clothes and supplies at a discount at the ranch's store. The cost of those things would be taken out of their pay, sometimes over a period of weeks. This was Kit's first day, but should he do without what he needed simply because he hadn't yet received a paycheck?

Brody knew what it was like to have blisters on your heels because you had holes in your socks and your plastic boots just wouldn't stop rubbing. He knew what it was like to have a thin coat in the winter, and no hat or gloves, which meant you couldn't feel your fingers as you trained and twirled that rope, which meant you would mess up and Daddy Frank would be pissed.

When Quint had taken him in, Quint had paid for Brody's keep out of his own pockets, and never counted the cost. Never asked Brody to pay him back. Brody should pay it forward, then, and get Kit what he needed, from head to toe.

Clay came into the barn, looking shiny and sturdy, his dimples on full view as he waved a greeting to them both.

"I'm here to help," he said to Brody, then turned to Kit. "Hi, Kit. We're glad to have you join the team."

For one brief moment, Kit scowled at Clay, as though not sure what to do with such cheerfulness.

Brody could understand this response completely because, though he would only ever admit it to Quint, he found Clay overwhelming, especially on his own gloomy days.

Clay was well liked by one and all, though, and his can-do attitude and his willingness to be wherever and do whatever anybody wanted him to had helped pull the ranch through the lean times in the early part of the season. Now the ranch was fully booked for the rest of the summer, it looked like, and though Leland had been able to hire extra staff, Clay seemed to think he was fully responsible for leaving no stone unturned when it came to work that needed doing.

He was like a mini-Leland sometimes, though he wasn't as bossy, merely way too happy. Still, Brody needed to focus on Kit, even though they had a group of twenty field-fresh horses that needed grooming before that evening's sunset trail ride.

"Thank you," said Brody. "Here's this box, and I'll grab another sweat scraper. We'll be out in a little bit. I'll need to show Kit how to do it, so we might go a bit slow."

"I can get ten, easy," said Clay. He grabbed the box and walked out of the barn, whistling, for crying out loud. But that was Clay, and Brody preferred him over some grumpy asshole. Not that Leland would hire anyone like that.

"Thank you," said Brody. "Now then, Kit," he said to Kit. "We'll go through this slowly, here in the barn."

"You just brush them, right?" asked Kit.

He looked at the horse Brody was cross-tying between the poles near the front of the bar, a nice mare named Chiquita, who had big brown eyes and looked at Brody like she wanted him to pet her before he did anything else. Obliging her, Brody scratched the muscled curve of her neck with his fingers, going back and forth, loosening flakes of dirt and mud she'd picked up from her time in the field.

"There are a couple of steps," said Brody. "But first, I just want you to come and pet her neck. Her name's Chiquita."

Kit scowled like a three-year-old on the verge of a tantrum.

Brody knew enough to just let him simmer for a minute. After all, Kit had agreed to the parts of the job as Leland had laid them out.

If Kit wanted to back out now, Brody was going to have to let him. He'd help Kit pack, and from there drive him to the Greyhound station in Cheyenne. As Leland would probably say, were he there, *you can bring a fellow to the ranch, but you can't make him stay.*

Brody's feeling was strong on this, that Kit would benefit if he only gave the ranch a chance.

"Come here, Kit," said Brody. "Come and try."

Visibly shaking, Kit came close to Chiquita, moving fast, too fast, perhaps in an effort to overcome his own fear. He stuck his hand out and when Chiquita blew out a breath from her soft nostrils, Kit made a high pitched sound and stumbled back, tumbling to the concrete floor of the barn.

"Hey, now," said Brody to Chiquita as she threw her head, tugging on the lead. "He didn't mean any harm, did you, Kit. Kit?"

Softly, leaving the mare where she was, Brody crouched down close to Kit's curled-up body, pressed close to the open wooden door to the tack room. He didn't touch Kit, but he made his presence known, made his closeness sift over Kit like a soft blanket. That's how he did it with horses, this slow process of connection and reconnection.

He wanted Kit to unfold himself, to lift his face and look Brody in the eyes. At the same time, that'd be like forcing a horse's head, making it do something it didn't want to do, rather than guiding it.

"Look at my hands, Kit," said Brody. He reached out and laid both his hands along Kit's thigh, and left them there for a long, still moment, letting the warmth of his fingers soak through Kit's thin blue jeans. "Please?" he asked to get Kit to do this simple act.

Like a shy thing, Kit dipped one shoulder, looking over at Brody through his lowered eyelashes, arms folded across his chest, ankles tucked close, one knee up, one knee down.

Brody knew exactly what Kit was doing, making himself small, making his body a harder target. Trying to be invisible, trying not to be in the way. He'd been on a floor like Kit was now so many times there was no point counting, and he wanted more than anything to get Kit back on his feet, in more ways than one.

"These hands won't hurt you," he said. "Not ever. And see, there are scars. The long one on my forefinger is from my buck knife, the one Quint gave me. I was trying to carve little wooden animals like he does, only I've not the talent for it. The bumpy scar along the back of two fingers is when I was trying to feed a horse some carrots, only instead of holding my hand flat, I stuck my fingers in the horse's mouth. The horse didn't mean to bite me, of course, but it bled pretty bad."

Brody stroked his fingers along Kit's leg, gently, gently.

"You see, horses don't want to bite you or me or anyone. All they really want is to munch on some hay, maybe roll in the dust, and to have everything be calm around them. That's how horses like it. Calm. Slow."

Nodding, Brody watched Kit relax a little.

"Did you know horses can hear your heartbeat?" he asked.

"They can?" asked Kit in a whisper, looking down at his knees.

"Well, they can sense it in a way that's just about like hearing it." Slowly, Brody stood up, bringing Kit with him. "They know if you're scared, your heart races, just like theirs do. And if you're scared, they think there's something that they should also be scared of. So the trick is, don't be scared of them. They're looking to you to be brave."

Brody watched Kit blink, and let him be for a minute to think it over at his own pace. Behind him, Chiquita was getting restless, and was probably wondering if they were ever going to finish so she could get back to her stall, her feed, her quiet time.

"Can you stand up?" asked Brody. "I'll be right behind you if you'd like to try again."

Kit stood up, keeping one hand on the tack room door as he looked at Brody out of the corner of his eyes.

"Will she bite me if I pet her?" Kit asked.

"No," said Brody. "She wants to be groomed and then she wants some lunch. Can you help me give that to her? Come here, now."

Kit came close and, on impulse, Brody tucked Kit in the curve of his shoulder, warm and close and slow. The top of Kit's dishwater blond head came to just below Brody's chin, so it was a close fit.

Kit's body was lean, supple in the way of young men, like a biddable ribbon that didn't quite know where it wanted to go. He could smell the sweetness of Kit's hair, feel the curve of Kit's breath across his collarbones as he walked them both slowly over to the mare.

Chiquita blinked sleepily at them both, inhaled their scent, and then settled on three long legs, one back hoof cocked on its edge like a lady showing off a new shoe.

"Here," said Brody. "I'll show you."

He curved his arm around Kit's arm and cupped Kit's hand in his. Then slowly, more slowly still, he guided Kit's hand to the mare's neck. The mare sighed and leaned into the light stroke, as though she wanted it deepened, wanted more pressure, demanding it with a snort and a slight shake of her mane.

Kit stiffened but Brody didn't let him pull back. They'd come too far for that now, and besides, petting a horse was one of the most relaxing things on the planet. Touching a horse, being around them, had the power to soothe all the nerves in Brody's body, when he was rattled, when he was fraught with memories, when the night was too dark and he couldn't sleep.

Almost gasping, Kit let Brody guide the stroke of his hand across the soft, warm slowly-breathing side of the horse. A touch, a stroke, their palms firm, Kit's fingertips drifting across the brown fur.

Kit was still and calm beneath the pressure of Brody's fingers, almost seeming to let himself be absorbed into the moment, where his fears had no sway. Where his mind was bestilled by the quietness of the barn, the low sound of the wind in the trees through the open doorway.

Kit was leaning back against Brody's body, Kit's bottom against Brody's hips, Kit's back to Brody's front like they were slow dancing. He was connected to Brody in that moment, in that peaceful, sweet echoless quiet, their joined hands sliding along Chiquita's mountain-dusty coat.

Brody could feel Kit breathe in and out. And, somewhere inside of him, his own breath slowed down to match Kit's, so the rise and fall of their chests were together in the hay-sparkled barn with dust motes flickered with captured light rising and falling lazily around them.

When Kit looked up, the top of his head brushed the bottom of Brody's chin, and there was a trust in those pewter blue eyes, low and hesitant, but it was there.

How many times had Kit looked at one of Katie's men that way, wanting to believe that they would be kind to him? And how long had it been before a careless word or a hard gesture had sent that trust skittering for a safe dark place to hide? Brody found he wanted to be the protector now, rather than the protected, wanted to make sure the growing trust never vanished from Kit's eyes.

"Well done," he said, low, conscious of his dry lips, of the hair tickling his temples, of Kit's wide eyes, the softening of his mouth, perhaps in surprise at the praise. "We've no biters on the ranch, you know," he said. "And I would never put you with a horse that'd be more'n you can handle. I promise." Wanting a response, he asked, "Okay?"

"Okay." Kit breathed the word as if astonished to find himself where he was.

Brody dipped down to grab a body brush out of the grooming box. He let go of Kit's hand, but stayed curved around him.

"Hold out your hand," he said.

Kit did as he was told.

"Now, feel the pressure of this brush." He pressed the brush's bristles into the palm of Kit's hand. "Can you feel it?"

Kit nodded.

"That's how hard you should brush. Firm, but not rough."

Brody handed the brush to Kit.

"Now, take this brush in your other hand, and press the brush against your palm. Feel how much pressure you're giving and receiving. Never press too hard. You're getting the dirt off the horse, you're making the blood flow beneath their skin. If you do it right, it feels nice to them. It's like a massage." He moved behind Kit, staying close, his hips tucked to Kit's bottom. "You try. Brush her, slowly neck to tail, neck to tail."

Kit seemed to be breathing a little fast. This might upset Chiquita, so Brody wrapped his arms around Kit's waist as though to stabilize him, and leaned into each stroke of the brush, as though he was brushing Chiquita right along with Kit.

He could have moved away. Could have separated himself from the line of warmth between their bodies. Could have decided that Kit was well on his way and that Brody needed to step back and let him get on with it. He didn't.

To move away would be like disconnecting himself from a small spark that needed him to shield it. If he stepped away, the spark might go out, mightn't it? He couldn't let that happen and besides, the line of Kit's bottom fit right into the dip of his thigh—but when Kit looked up at him over his shoulder, looked at Brody with big round eyes that seemed a little shocked to find him so close, Brody blinked and stepped back.

"You've got it now, I think," he said, almost gasping. "Just keep on with it, steady as you go."

That was something Quint said to him from time to time, back in the day, or some other words to calm him when he was trying too hard, wanted too much to not be who he was, a troubled young man raised by a father with a violent temper and unreasonable standards. Now he was grown, still a few years from thirty, with a steady head and broad shoulders that carried a lot of responsibility at the ranch.

Mostly that responsibility included looking out for the horses, for their health and welfare, for their happiness. He read their moods as often as he groomed them, cleaned their hooves, checked their glossy coats.

He thought again, how when it was late, or if he'd had a long day, he'd soothe himself by picking a horse at random, and then he'd step up to them in their box stall or maybe they'd be in the field, and he'd tuck himself close and wrap his arms around their necks.

Usually the horses, knowing his scent, his touch, would bend their heads, forelocks falling over their big, tender eyes, and they'd tuck him close with their jawbones along his back. That was their way of hugging him back.

Some horses didn't like that so much and preferred it if he just stood sloped along their shoulders, maybe with an arm across their warm withers. Brody didn't care either way, the closeness in whatever shape it came was their gift to him. And in return he took care of them.

It would be sweet if he could take Kit with him on one of his late evening visits to the barn or the field, or to take Kit with him on a moonlight ride, so he could show Kit the magic of it all and help him get over his fears.

And now, as Kit brushed Chiquita's coat, Brody knew he had to take care of Kit. That he needed to be on top of what Kit was going through so he didn't push him too hard.

Yes, hard enough, but not over the edge. Nobody needed that. But Kit needed boots, sturdier clothes, new shirts, and a whole host of things that Brody took for granted at being available whenever he needed them. Maybe Kit could get good enough with the horses so he wouldn't have to work in the kitchens, for who wanted to be indoors all day? Not him, that's who. Maybe not Kit, either.

Together they groomed Chiquita, with Brody showing Kit how to use the scraper, the curry, the comb on the mare's mane and tail. Kit watched, close and wide eyed, while Brody cleaned Chiquita's hooves with the hoof pick, and then showed Kit how to kneel down with a metal bottle of hoof oil and a small cloth.

"We don't always oil their hooves, but if they've been out in the field a while, it's nice to give them a dash of shine."

Kit seemed to like this part of the task, and also seemed to forget where he was, for he crawled around on the cement barn floor close to Chiquita's legs, like he hadn't been afraid only moments before that she'd bite him. Scrambling around like he'd been around horses forever.

As they finished up with the mare, and Brody was unhitching her from the cross-ties, Clay strolled in carrying a broken body brush.

"Dang it, these plastic ones," said Clay as he casually tossed the brush in the recycle bin. "I'm going to hear it again from everybody, aren't I."

"Those yellow ones are so pretty," said Brody, teasing. "Well, they were. That's the last one to break, isn't it?"

"Sure is," said Clay. "How you fellows getting along in here? The wind's kicking up a bit, so I'm hustling to get done before it rains."

"We'll catch up, never fear," said Brody to Clay's departing back as he strode out of the barn. "And we'll be out to help you soon."

113

"We're behind because of me," said Kit in a hard whisper when Brody went out and brought a gelding back into the barn.

"You're learning," said Brody, firmly. "And that takes time. Clay knows that. Besides, he'll love to brag about how many he did by himself."

"Don't you like him?" asked Kit. "When he's around, you act like you don't like him."

They started grooming the gelding, with Brody standing close behind Kit as he used the body brush, and Brody had to think about this idea. He liked Clay plenty fine, liked his dimples, liked his smile.

There'd been that one time Clay had come on to him. Brody didn't exactly remember how it had gone, but if there'd been a kiss between them, it'd been less than satisfactory, for there'd not been another to follow it. Clay hadn't acted like he held any grudges, and Brody figured it was a one-off and they'd both put it behind them.

"Of course I like him," said Brody slowly, rubbing his mouth with his fingers, enjoying the stillness of the barn as the wind started up outside. "He reminds me of a Haflinger."

"A what?" Kit stopped, mid stroke, and turned to look at him. "What's that?"

"Oh, it's a cute horse with a blond mane and tail. Looks like a palomino, only smaller. More juicy."

Kit laughed and got back to brushing the gelding. His body was still stiff and he still held the body brush like his hand was a claw, but they were getting there.

"What is Quint?" asked Kit, when Brody picked up the curry comb and started following Kit around the horse, pausing to pull out a snag in the horse's tail.

"Quint's the trail boss," answered Brody, a little confused. He looked at Kit over the horse's back, hands splayed, the curry comb resting on a well-formed rump. "But you knew that, right?"

"No, I mean if he was a horse. What horse is he?"

While Kit finished up with the curry comb, Brody cleaned the gelding's hooves and thought about this.

"I don't know," he said, straightening up, giving the horse a pat on its behind as it lifted its tail and farted gently in his face. "I guess to be fair—I should compare everybody."

"Right," said Kit, excited now, almost jumping toward Brody, until Brody held up both hands, palm out. "Everybody's a horse."

"Let's get the next horse to groom and I'll think about it."

They took the horse to a box stall, and hurried in the rain-dotted wind to help Clay bring all the horses under shelter. They were behind in the grooming task, and would soon have to go for dinner, but the rain, if it kept up, would forestall any trail ride that evening, so it almost didn't matter. The rest of the horses could be groomed in the morning. Together with Clay, they brushed and curried and cleaned, and got most of the horses ready to go.

"You've got a good assistant here," said Clay, in that way he had, flinging praise all around, raising people's spirits for no reason at all. Which was fine by Brody.

"Thanks," said Kit, rising on his toes.

"I have to get cleaned up," said Clay, tugging on his rolled up shirt sleeves. "See you at dinner?"

"Sure, but where's Austin?" asked Brody. He dusted his hands on a cloth, but it was hopeless. Hoof oil and horse dander simply didn't brush off.

"He had to drive Bea to summer camp today." Clay smiled. "I'll miss the little mite, but it'll be nice to have a break, too. I'm not used to being a co-parent yet! Anyway, see you at dinner."

With a wave, Clay strode off with long strides, strong legs, and a happy whistle.

"Who's Austin? Who's Bea?" asked Kit, tugging on Brody's arm. "I don't know everybody."

The last statement came out as an almost-wail, as though Kit imagined he should have memorized everybody's name before he met them. Which was, as Brody well knew, another sad signal as to how Kit had moved through the world. Brody had been in that spot himself, many times, with Daddy Frank.

"Austin is the ranch's accountant," said Brody as they headed back to the staff quarters to wash for dinner. "Bea is his daughter. She's little and *very* cute." Brody rolled his eyes, because of course she was cute. She was the darling of the ranch, and pretty much had the run of the place. "Austin and Clay fell in love, and I think they're going to get married, but right now they're shacking up. Over there. In that third cabin along."

As they followed the path beneath the trees that dripped every now and then with cold dots of rain, he pointed to the third manager cabin. Brody was of the opinion that there should be more cabins like that, so people could have privacy and quiet, and the coziness of a little space all on their own.

That sense of coziness, of separateness, was something Brody had grown up with, sharing a little trailer with Daddy Frank and Bryson, and then later with Quint. He was used to living all tumbled with someone else, and though he enjoyed his little bedsit on the second floor, sometimes he missed those days of waking up next to his brother on the upper bunk, or waking up to hear Quint fucking his latest date in the lower bunk. At least now, come to think of it, he had a neighbor in the room, in a cot against the wall, and he could get used to that mighty quick.

14

BRODY

*B*ack in the room, they washed at the sink, getting water pretty much everywhere. Kit acted like washing before eating was something new, a lark, and Brody considered that yes, before Quint came into his life, there were a lot of things he'd not known other people did.

"Want to borrow one of my shirts?" asked Brody, as he peeled off his horse-scented one and grabbed a nice snap-button shirt from his closet. "How about this one?"

He handed Kit a blue and green-hued snap button shirt that was sure to hang off his slender frame. It was too small for Brody and anyhow, it set off Kit's eyes, making them an even deeper pewter blue.

"Looks good on you," he said as he rolled up his sleeves, noting that Kit was doing it the same, with the same rolling and folding motions. "Why don't you keep it? We can get you other ones later."

"Keep it?" asked Kit, his eyebrows going up, looking at Brody like he was playing a trick on him. "You mean it?"

"Sure," said Brody. "It doesn't fit me."

"It's soft."

Brushing the sleeve of his shirt with one hand, Kit looked up at Brody like Brody had just given Kit the keys to a kingdom he'd not known existed. As though a second-hand shirt, properly broken in and looked after, was a pile of gold and the best thing since sliced bread, combined.

Brody could see it. How Kit had managed with shirts with holes in them for a good long time, and being so used to it, never gave it a second thought. But then, were shirts with holes in them better or worse than plastic boots that caused not only holes in thin socks but blisters as well?

Never mind that now. It wasn't good to linger on these thoughts, not when Kit's stomach was grumbling and Brody could smell fried potatoes lingering on the rain-fresh air as they made their way down the steps and along the path to the dining hall.

Once inside the dining hall, a gathering of ladies was waiting for Brody. With their cell phones held high, going *click click click,* they cooed to him as they asked to have their picture taken with them. He obliged them all, though it meant Kit had to wait and the line to the buffet moved on without them.

This was part of his job, and he was fine with it, though he never really understood what they got excited about. Sure, he was easy on the eye, Quint had told him that much once or twice. And maybe his face was interesting, though he personally thought his nose was too sharp, his face too angled.

Levi, the ranch's cook, was the good looking one, the handsomest man on the ranch, should anyone have asked Brody. But Levi, the lucky fuck, got to be in the kitchen all the time, unseen, hidden. Even if guests happened to see him, they saw the cook's apron, and bibbed white shirt, and that darned paper hat, and their eyes just skidded over them to the roast beef he was slicing at the carver station.

These ladies were ignoring Kit that way too, now, so finally, when he saw Leland nod at him from across the room, Brody knew he could step down from his adoring fans and get in line and get something to eat.

"Thank you, ladies," he said, gesturing to Kit, who'd waited patiently with barely any hopping up and down. "We're going to eat now. I hope you all have a wonderful rest of your week."

Amidst the genial din of the high-ceilinged dining hall, Kit stuck close to Brody's side, like he had before, as they made their way through the line. He was taking onto his plate everything Brody was, so Brody made a point of getting a few more spears of asparagus, and a slice of cherry pie rather than chocolate cake because fruit was better for you, right? Maybe not after Levi had doctored the cherries up with sugar, though.

With trays in hand, Brody and his shadow made their way to a long table, where Clay and his partner Austin were already ensconced, side by side, looking at each other like they were shy lovers newly met, rather than the shacked up and practically-married couple they actually were. Brody had a feeling that their air of young love was going to last them for the rest of their lives.

"That's going to be me one day," said Clay as Brody and Kit took places across the table from Clay and Austin.

"What's that, then?" asked Brody. He settled himself in his chair, arranging his cutlery the way he liked it before looking up at Clay.

"Them taking pictures of me like they do you." Clay made a pout with his pink mouth, like he was really upset about this, though Brody knew full and well it was a compliment, or meant to be.

"I'm plenty sure there are guests who prefer your butter-sweet face to mine," said Brody.

"Are you saying my face is like butter?" asked Clay, mock-affronted.

"I *like* butter," said Austin, low, in a voice meant only for Clay to hear, but of course, Brody heard it and Kit did, too. "Sweet butter."

"See?" said Brody. "He likes butter, the same way guests do. It's just —" He stalled, unable to explain why he was the one they took pictures of, and generally not anyone else. Except sometimes they took photos of Leland, who was tall and carried the authority of responsibility with him at all times, wrapped around him like a noble cloak of midnight blue.

"You've got striking features," said Austin, pointing at Brody with a fork. "That's what it is. You look like you stepped out of a classic Italian painting."

"What?" Brody shook his head as he started eating. "Calhoun is an Irish name."

"Well," said Austin, with that gentle smile of his. "There's no saying somebody from Italy didn't connect with someone in Ireland, ages ago."

"True," said Brody. He didn't bring up Levi for comparison's sake, because he didn't want the discussion to continue, didn't want to keep talking about how he looked, for crying out loud.

"Say," said Clay, almost abruptly as if he realized how desperately Brody wanted to change the subject. "Austin and I are going out in Ladybelle to look at the stars later. Want to come?"

"No, but thanks," said Brody before he realized that the offer had made Kit sit up in his chair, like he would have wanted to go. What Kit didn't realize was that if you went out with Clay and Austin, you'd get a big eyeful of the two men billing and cooing like lovebirds. And while Brody generally enjoyed seeing romance in the air, when Clay was your ride home, there was no escape from it. "Maybe another time," he said, gently, looking at Kit, nodding.

"Who's Ladybelle?" asked Kit, his voice wobbling with worry that he'd get points taken off for not already knowing.

"That's my truck," said Clay with pride. "My old yellow truck, tried and true and faithful."

"It's hard to keep track of who everyone is," said Austin, also looking at Kit. "It took me ages and ages, and thank goodness, Clay knows everyone and can whisper their names in my ear if I forget who I'm talking to."

Kit's mouth fell open a little bit like he was shocked someone was saying something nice to him for no reason at all.

"That's a joke," said Clay. He nudged Austin with his elbow, and yes, let the billing and cooing begin, but Brody stifled the impulse to roll his eyes. "You're the one with the brains under all that red hair. Brains and sense."

Austin blushed a soft red and, chuckling, dipped his chin and focused on his meal. Meanwhile, Kit was looking at Brody with wide eyes, as though checking his response to every word, every gesture.

Brody knew that feeling well. Knew how he used to respond in strange, new situations when he didn't know who was going to do what, or whether Daddy Frank was going to lash out over a misspoken word, or even, merely, get angry over the expression on Brody's face.

If you weren't sure, you stayed still. You watched, carefully taking notes, to see how other people did things, and all the while anxiety was building in case you messed up. Like how Kit was eating, the position of his hands an echo of Brody's hands, which food he was eating, how he was drinking milk, though, truth be told, Kit had a milk mustache that looked rather adorable.

Brody wiped his mouth with his napkin and gestured to Kit, who followed suit and wiped the milk mustache away, sweet and trusting that this was the right way to behave. When Kit flicked his asparagus off his plate, making a face, Brody looked at him.

"Hey, now," said Brody. "Enough of that."

"They smell like cat's piss," said Kit, rubbing his fingers on his jeans.

"Then don't eat them," said Brody, staying calm. "But don't flick them on the table like that, either. Okay?"

"Okay."

Kit's face fell like he felt he'd screwed up beyond redemption, and Brody knew that feeling, too. His body shifted in sympathy, echoes of Kit's distress rippling through him.

Daddy Frank always made him eat everything on his plate, even if it was simply too horrible to swallow. Now that Brody was older, he didn't have to eat anything he didn't want to, and sometimes would get lima beans or green peas and just let them sit there on his plate till they grew cool. Then he'd smile to himself and scrape them into the trash. Sure it was wasting food, but such a little amount wouldn't matter. Kit needed to learn this.

"Yeah, just leave 'em," Brody said now. "Don't worry about it. You want green beans instead?"

"Yuck," said Kit, sticking his tongue out.

"Levi's green beans are really good," said Clay, doing his best to help, as was his nature. "He uses garlic and butter when he cooks them."

"I'll get you some," said Brody, getting up without waiting for an answer. When he came back with a small dish of green beans, Kit looked at him like Brody'd just asked him to walk across fire barefooted.

"Just try them," said Brody as he put the bowl in front of Kit.

It was all very well to have a passionate love for pop tarts, but it was important, especially for someone still growing—Brody's throat felt thick, like someone had reminded him, yet again, that other kids had mothers who pushed veggies and teeth brushing and who didn't smack their kids around for breathing wrong.

Kit's life had been the same as Brody's, it seemed, at least in a lot of ways. Quint had encouraged good food and exposed Brody to the wonders of a nicely-grilled medium rare steak, so Brody would do the same with Kit.

And, like a horse who perhaps wanted to please more than it realized, Kit stabbed a bit of green bean with a fork and shoved it in his mouth. And then chewed *hard* to show that he was chewing and to demonstrate how utterly painful it all was to do as he was told. But, after a minute, probably right as the garlic and butter hit his taste buds, Kit nodded, looking down, maybe to relieve the pressure of having to give in, to admit that Brody was right.

"How are they?" asked Brody, sitting down and taking up his fork again.

"They're okay," came the casual reply, though the green beans were disappearing at a fast rate.

Sometimes the care and feeding of a youngling took some tweaking.

"Gosh, I could do with some ice cream," announced Clay as he scraped his plate clean with his fork and looked at Kit, smiling. "Levi makes it in house and man, is it good. All kinds of flavors. I like strawberry best. Want me to get you some?"

Kit had to know this was his reward for eating his vegetables, and if it made him feel like a five year old who must be coaxed to do what was good for him, he didn't show it. Instead, he looked at Brody like he was asking permission, and Brody's heart broke all over again into little pieces. Who had treated Kit so badly over the years that he thought that maybe the ice cream wasn't meant for the likes of him? And why had Katie been such a horrible mother?

"Let's all go," said Brody. "We'll get huge bowls of it."

Together they bussed their places, taking their used crockery and cutlery up to the bussing area, then they got back into the buffet line, grabbing bowls and spoons and heading straight for the dessert area.

Levi and his team had made fresh batches of ice cream that day, something they didn't do every day, so it was special. The tubs were half empty, frosted at the edges of the round plastic containers from being in the freezer, but there was enough to go around. Brody got strawberry, as did Clay, while Austin got peach. Kit, he noted, got a little bit of everything, as if overwhelmed by the choices before him.

As the dining hall cleared out, and everyone finished their ice cream, Brody sensed that Austin and Clay were ready for their evening lovebird session beneath the stars. He never liked being the one to cramp anyone's style, so he stood up, with his bowl in his hands, and looked at Kit with a jerk of his chin as if to signal their imminent departure.

Kit, for his part, brightened and stood up too, like he was in on a secret, and was pleased to be trusted with it.

"We'll see you guys in the morning," said Brody.

"In the morning," echoed Kit.

They took their bowls to the bussing area and went out of the dining hall and into the soft light of sunset, where the shadows lengthened beneath the trees and the dusky smell of horse and hay and damp dirt stirred all around. Beside him, as they walked, Kit slumped, shoulders low, and Brody knew why. Kit had put in a full day's work, and perhaps he didn't realize this as he walked along, but he had.

"Tired?" Brody asked as they climbed the stairs of the staff quarters.

"No," said Kit, visibly straightening as he waited for Brody to open the door to their room. "Are there any evening activities? I could go for one of those."

Bluster was always a good way to cover the truth, as Brody well knew. But he didn't say anything as he unbuttoned his snap-button shirt and sat down to tug off his boots so he could clean them.

"If you take a shower, I can look at those bruises again," said Brody. He reached for the cardboard box beneath his bed, and pulled out his cloth and his little tin of polish and began working on his boots. The scent of leather oil filled the room, a bit of a breeze coming in through the partly opened windows to stir the curtains. "Or I can take a shower first. It doesn't matter to me."

To him, it didn't matter who went first, only that Kit understood that not taking a shower was not an option. Brody waited for Kit's response, like he would wait on a horse who has been shown the way out of a barn, patiently, as if nothing were amiss, and nothing was at stake. No pressure, none at all.

"I'm not dirty."

Brody paused, one boot tucked between his thighs, the other at his feet. He could, of course, explain to Kit how much sweat he'd worked up while working in the kitchen and then in the barn, with the horses. That, yes, Kit was dirty and sweaty and a shower would feel nice. But sometimes more explanation did not equal results.

"You go first," said Brody, returning his attention to his boot cleaning, like it was a done deal. "You'll have plenty of hot water if you go first."

What Kit didn't know, and Brody wouldn't tell him, was that the water in the staff quarters had on-demand heating and would never run out. He waited, head bent over his task, body relaxing at the tail end of the day, nothing before him but the ease of evening and then sleep in his own bed.

"Okay, I guess," said Kit, firmly, as if giving in was his choice and his alone, and he was doing Brody a favor by going first.

Brody listened to the shower, attentive for details that would tell him a shower was actually being taken. He finished cleaning his boots, then placed them carefully away, eyeing the three pairs of very nice boots, all in a row, as he considered how and when he was going to get new gear for Kit. Then he stripped to his underwear and t-shirt while wondering if Kit was going to get water everywhere when he stepped out of the shower.

All of this distracted him in a pleasant way, as it was nice, for a change, to have someone else to worry about, rather than being with his own troubled thoughts in the evening.

Of course, he could have gone to visit Jasper and Ellis in their cabin along the river, or he could have joined Quint on the porch of his small cabin and coaxed him into a game of gin rummy or even Yahtzee. Either of which would be a good distraction, but as he knew, having learned over the years, sometimes you had to walk through the memories rather than ignoring them.

When the shower went off, it was only a moment or two before Kit stepped out of the bathroom in a cloud of steam. His hair had been half-dried. A slightly-damp towel was wrapped around his waist as before, and though he held his shoulders straight, the fist at the knot in the towel was white from being clenched, and his worried eyes tracked Brody's movements as he went past Kit to grab the first aid kit from beneath the sink.

"Everything's fine," said Kit. "Nothing hurts. I mean, maybe a little, but not much. I'm fine. I don't need you to look."

The words were said so fast, so rushed, Brody knew that in the past someone had wanted to see the state of Kit's body and then had done nothing. Or they'd seen and overreacted, and scared Kit and got Katie pissed at him because someone had found out. The truth was, most of the bruises on Kit's body had darkened, as though to show how deep they'd gone, how much they hurt. A few bruises were still blossoming, their colors a mix of green and yellow with traces of blue.

Like artwork, all of this was layered across Kit's back, his side, like someone had been painting a sign that told the world what a bad kid Kit was. Which wasn't true, Brody could tell, inside his heart. Kit had a ragged background, that was all. He needed tender touches and care, that was all.

"Here," said Brody. He reached for the bottle of Advil. "Take some of those and then let me look."

Kit tucked the towel tighter at his waist and then bent to cup some water in his palm to swallow the Advil down with. Brody didn't really wonder that Kit had not remarked on the lack of a drinking glass, but then, that was the kind of world he knew. You didn't question what you didn't have, even if everyone in the world had it. You simply didn't question.

Maybe Brody needed to get a drinking glass, just the same. Maybe Kit would like one.

"Come here, then," said Brody. He sat on the bed. He'd be lower than Kit that way, lower and less scary, and like an apprehensive horse, Kit approached. "Turn the other way and just let the towel fall a little."

Kit hesitated, then turned, his shoulders hitched up, back stiff. But he lowered the towel on his waist, baring himself to the overhead light, to the room, to Brody.

The bruises along his back and side layered his skin in stripes, and it was easy to tell that Eddie Piggot was right-handed. Beneath the wide bandage, the abrasion along Kit's lower right back was scabbing over, though the scabs were soft from the shower, so Brody didn't touch them, only replaced the broad bandage over the scabs to protect them while they healed fully. Then he snapped open the cap of the tube of analgesic cream, and spread it gently wherever he could reach.

At one point, Brody tugged on the towel and Kit, his head bent, let the towel fall to swag low on his hips.

He paused.

Sometimes a horse had been so abused it fully trusted the first human who was kind to it. That could be dangerous, because what if that human was simply the next in the line of abusers?

The horse didn't know, and yet it trusted. It had to. And so, it seemed, Kit felt he had to.

Way down someplace deep inside of him, Kit must know he had to trust Brody, otherwise he'd not be mostly naked in front of Brody like this. Bare head to toe, dampness glistening on his shoulders and the backs of his slender thighs. The jut of his hipbone stark beneath the overhead light. The slope of his bent neck, the tender shallow between his shoulder blades. The soft curve of his buttocks above the edge of the white towel.

All at once Brody knew he held in his hands something precious and rare, this trust between them, the ability of Kit's young soul to try just one more time in the hope that someone would help him.

Maybe he thought he only needed a hand up, a quick, hard yank out of a deep hole he was inside of through no fault of his own. Or maybe he realized he needed more than that. Sure, maybe he knew he needed a roof over his head, three hot meals a day, hot water to clean himself with. And maybe Brody needed—

"Everything okay?" asked Kit, looking over his shoulder, his eyebrows high in his forehead as though he was afraid Brody was about to deliver some amazingly bad news. "It doesn't hurt, at least not much."

A lie on top of everything else. And whether it was meant to protect Kit or to protect Brody from the truth, it didn't matter. Kit was doing his best to make this easy on Brody.

"Oh," said Brody casually as he finished applying the cream, then pulled the towel up so Kit could tug it tight to his waist, so he'd know the first aid was done. "I'm not so sure about that. I've seen bruises like that a time or two when Quint or I have fallen off a horse."

"Yeah?" asked Kit. He turned to face Brody, apprehension tightening his body all up and down, beads of dampness quivering on his bare shoulders, his naked chest.

"Yeah," said Brody. He nodded. "Bruises hurt and anybody who tells you different is a liar."

"Oh." Kit's expression softened, like Brody had given him a gift. A little gift of affirmation and acknowledgment all at once.

"I'll take a shower now," said Brody, standing up, gratified that while Kit backed up, he didn't back up all the way across the room. "We'll get your clothes washed tomorrow, and buy you some boots and other stuff. But tomorrow, 'cause I'm bushed."

"Okay." Some of the tenseness left Kit's face to be replaced by, it seemed, an impulse for more bluster, more coverup. Like Kit wanted to say *I'm not tired, not at all*, when the opposite was so clearly true. Kit had put in a full day's work, a man's day, hours and hours of tasks that were new and probably so out of his realm of experience his brain was still processing everything. "If you want," said Kit, the words short, as if the acknowledgement cost him.

"Yeah, I want."

Brody went into the bathroom and hurried through his shower, part of him afraid, somehow, that if he turned his back on Kit for an instant, Kit would light out for Vegas and Brody would never see him again. But then, if Kit could trust Brody enough to strip almost all the way naked, then perhaps Brody needed to trust Kit in return.

Kit was waiting on a phone call from Katie, anyway, as he only suspected she'd gone to Vegas. To meet up with her, he needed to know where she was.

Kit didn't have any money to go anywhere, otherwise he already would have gone. So maybe Brody's instincts were right. Kit needed a break, a stop off point. In other words, Kit needed someone like Brody. So he'd be staying, though for how long was another matter.

Showering in the most perfunctory way possible, Brody figured he'd beat his record by a good two minutes by the time he stepped out of the shower in his own cloud of steam. The hastily wiped mirror told him he needed to shave, but that could wait. And he needed a haircut, as his dark hair was falling into his eyes, but that could also wait.

He buffed himself dry, pulled on soft boxers and an even softer t-shirt and stepped out of the bathroom to find Kit already in bed, sleepy eyed and ready for Brody to switch off the overhead light.

Brody went over to the desk to pull the window open wider and checked the time on his cell phone. It was barely nine o'clock, but some days were like that. He got up pretty early and since Kit was sharing his room, Kit would be getting up early, too.

"Do you need anything?" Brody asked as he walked to the door where the light switch was.

"A bedtime story?" asked Kit, smiling and yawning hugely.

"Ha ha," said Brody, smiling, pleased to see that Kit's sense of humor was intact.

Between the two of them they had a ways to go, and beyond Brody's own fear that Kit would take off before he was ready, was the deeper question. Just how much was all of this affecting him?

He'd never had anyone to care for like this. Sure, he'd cared for dozens of horses, perhaps hundreds over the years, but horses were different in that they sensed a need to stick with the herd, stick with what was known to them. Yet Kit had been flung into the world by his own mother, and had no herd to go to. Or maybe Brody was his herd now. Maybe they were each other's herd.

"I'll turn off the light in a minute," he said, and went back into the bathroom to dose himself with CBD oil.

The bottle was almost empty, but he didn't like asking Quint to get him more, even though Quint would go to Colorado in a heartbeat. CBD oil was illegal in Wyoming, so Quint insisted on doing this for Brody, perhaps because he felt he was the better smuggler.

The only thing was, Leland could never find out or he'd fire both of them on the spot. Or maybe he'd deliver a small, gentle lecture on getting the proper kind of help rather than using illegal substances, and *then* he'd fire them. In either case, both Quint and Brody would be out of a job, when right now Brody knew the ranch was the place for him, just as it was the place for Kit.

"Taking your drugs?" asked Kit as Brody clicked off the light and climbed into bed.

"Helps me sleep sometimes," said Brody.

He sighed and clasped his hands behind his head on the pillow and listened to the night as it came through the screens on the open windows. There was the soft murmur of grasses bending to each other to whisper goodnight, and there was the high scratching sound of pine needles shifting against each other. He couldn't hear the river but he could imagine the low rippling sound it made, and he could scent the dampness in the air.

There was no place like the ranch, and Kit would learn that in time. And in time, perhaps he would decide to stay.

15

KIT

*B*rody got up early and that was just a fact.

Kit burrowed his head beneath the pillow as Brody padded barefoot around the room, peeing in the toilet, doing this and that. The low sounds were comforting in a way, but a little scary, too. Brody had been nice, but that was up till now. When would he turn mean? Surely at some point he would.

Or would he? Eddie Piggot had sure hated the ranch, and maybe the reason was because there was nobody on the ranch who was like Eddie, or like any of the men Katie had dated. At least not so far. Maybe they were in hiding and would jump out to scare the hell out of Kit when he least expected it, so he needed to be on his guard.

Still. While the bruises thumped below Kit's skin, he felt better so maybe standing half-naked in the bathroom, all of his hurts on display, had been worth it. Besides, never once had Brody lost his temper, and his hands had always been gentle. Katie, on the other hand, had never even so much as handed Kit a bandage, let alone tended to him like Brody had.

"Hey, now," said Brody with a gentle touch to Kit's blanketed shoulder. "Time to get up now. Let's go get some breakfast."

Kit made a sound that he used to scare people away, to let them know he was as mean as they were. Except the gentle touch remained and seemed like it would remain forever, or until hell froze, so Kit pulled down the sheet and light blanket and blinked up at Brody. The bathroom light was on, but the overhead light was not, and it was kind of nice not to be blinded by that.

"Do you need to shave?" asked Brody. "I've got a spare razor, if you do."

"Maybe tomorrow."

Kit spread his fingers along his jaw where a fine mist of hair could be felt. He knew other guys his age were already shaving daily, and they had lots of hair around their balls, and they all were very manly. Kit was not manly, and while he wouldn't have admitted this fact to anyone, the fact that Brody had offered meant that he thought, sure, Kit needed to shave just like any other guy. As though he considered that Kit was already a man, fully grown.

"No problem," said Brody. "Get dressed then."

Crawling out of bed, leaving the sheets and light blanket any old how, Kit crawled into yesterday's clothes and blinked as Brody tidied up his bed and then Kit's. Like that was what you did. Like people on TV did.

He didn't say anything about that either, because he didn't want Brody to think that what was going on around him was so unusual, even if it was. He didn't want Brody to think that he was weird.

Slowly, the idea that the ranch was its own place was growing inside of him. It wasn't like anywhere else. People made their beds and washed up before eating and were polite at mealtimes *just like the people on TV.*

He wanted to tell Katie about all of it, though maybe she would respond like the last time he told her, years ago, when she told Kit that TV shows like that weren't real, they were fake. Kit was old enough to know she was right. But still.

He left a message for her while Brody was snapping the buttons on his shirt and thumping his heels into his boots, then he was hustling Kit out of the room when they were both dressed and ready, like it mattered that they might be late. They walked beneath the night-damp trees to the dining hall and got in line amidst the cheerful chatter as people waited their turn.

Kit could smell coffee and frying potatoes and something sweet, like honey, floated in the air. People in line smiled at him for no reason, and when he got up to where the trays were, someone handed him a bright yellow one, and Brody placed a rolled packet of silverware inside of a napkin on his tray for him.

"I didn't notice yesterday," said Brody as they stopped in front of the drinks station. "But do you drink coffee?"

Kit shrugged. He had drunk coffee in the past, when one of Katie's men had taken them to a coffee shop in Colorado Springs, and insisted they all get something called pour-over coffee. It had been black and bitter and powerful and when Katie elbowed him to finish his cup, he'd finished it, almost choking.

"Let's get milk, then," said Brody. He gestured to someone behind the counter at a blank space in the buffet. "Can I get two glasses of milk please?" He looked at Kit with a smile in his eyes. "Levi orders the good stuff, which doesn't keep well in the regular dispenser, so you have to ask for it, special."

Brody was making a fuss about the milk like the guy had been making a fuss about the pour-over coffee, but maybe this would be different just like everything else had been different. The pancakes looked golden and the little bowls of fruit were pretty and bright, so Kit piled his tray with those, and smiled to himself when Brody got exactly the same things.

When they took their places at a small table, the first thing Brody did was take a long swallow of milk. Kit did the same and was surprised when it tasted good and rich and creamy.

"That's organic A2 milk right there," said Brody, smiling at Kit's delight.

"A2?" asked Kit. He'd never heard of such a thing, though he knew what organic was. Super expensive and silly, Katie had always said.

"Special cows who are never injected with growth hormone," said Brody. "In other words, no additives, and more butterfat. Yum."

They were running behind, so they ate breakfast quickly, and, bellies full, hustled out of the dining hall while all the guests got to linger over their plates and laugh and chat, like they'd no place to be for a while.

Kit stuck to Brody's side as they went to the meeting outside the barn. They had to stand while Leland and Maddy yammered on. The meeting was boring, just like it had been the day before, but Brody was attentive to every word. When Leland dismissed them with a wave, Brody turned to him.

"You're with Levi again this morning," said Brody with a gentle touch to Kit's shoulder. "Okay? Then after lunch, I'll take you to the shop to get some different clothes. We'll do laundry after dinner."

"I don't need no clothes."

In Kit's life, it had always come down to the clothes, like they mattered. School counselors, teachers, the one rodeo guy, even, had remarked upon what Kit wore, and suggested that he get something different, like he could afford that. Every bit of money he made, he bought food with to keep his belly quiet. If Brody thought he wanted to spend money on new jeans when he already had two pairs he was crazy.

"I got clothes already. I'm wearing 'em."

Someone stood behind Brody, but the sun was bright through the trees, so Kit couldn't see who it was for a minute. The air was sharp and clear and cool, like the first day of school, when Katie would get excited for a day or two and actually take time to drive Kit to where he needed to go. Then she would lose interest, or she would get fired and want Kit to hang out with her so she wouldn't get bored.

All of these memories crowded him so hard, so quickly, that he almost didn't hear the conversation going on between Brody and the other guy who, when he stepped into the shadow of the barn, turned out to be Quint.

"How's it going, orphan?" asked Quint.

"Don't call him that," said Brody, as though completely unafraid of Quint's bulk and power. "His name is Kit."

The way Brody said Kit's name sounded crisp, like Brody enjoyed the movement his mouth made when he said it. Like he liked the shape of it on his tongue. Like maybe he liked Kit, after all.

"Kit, then," said Quint, backing down with an easy smile, like it was all the same to him. "Drop him off wherever he needs to be, then you and I need to saddle up to check those fence lines this morning."

"I don't need dropping off," said Kit stoutly. All he needed to do was head back to the dining hall where Levi was, and this asshole was acting like Kit was in the first grade. "So fuck off."

"Boy, that kid's got a mouth on him," said Quint. His smile was still easy, but there was something in his eyes, like he was testing Kit.

"Back off, Quint," said Brody, like he was unafraid of Quint, never had been, never would be.

"Sure, sure. But shake that ass, if you would. I don't want to risk Leland's wrath."

Without saying goodbye, Kit stalked off in the direction of the main lodge, where the dining hall was. When he went around a curve, he was in a clump of trees, and suddenly felt he'd lost his way somehow, even though he was on the same dirt road they'd followed before.

Feeling a little lost, he turned around, wondering how he was going to find his way to the main lodge. Then someone came walking past him, striding on with a cheery hello and no care at all in the world. Kit followed the man, who was dressed like a guest, and came to the main lodge and clomped on inside, almost whistling, like he'd not been scared he was lost, and the sweat wasn't cooling on the back of his neck.

In the back of the kitchen, Levi greeted Kit with an absent smile, which was fine. He preferred it when bosses were casual with their attention on him, so he could pretty much do what he liked and get away with it.

Except, even though there were a dozen people working in Levi's kitchen, Levi never seemed to lose track of any of them or what they were doing. Which meant Kit had to scrape vegetables, and sweep floors, and take out trash, all beneath the force of Levi's focus.

Though, in the end, Levi praised him with a quick nod, and

dismissed Kit for lunch like he'd done a good job. And that was different for sure, though Kit was misted with his own sweat and the backs of his legs felt trembly.

Brody met him in the buffet line for lunch.

"So," said Brody as they helped themselves to fried chicken and mashed potatoes for lunch, and found a place to sit. "We'll go down after lunch and get you some new gear, okay?"

"I told you." Kit chomped into the fried chicken which he himself had bathed earlier in vinegar and helped to coat with egg and flour. "I don't need no clothes. I got plenty."

He didn't ask when he was going to get paid because the ranch seemed like the kind of place that would be honest about that, about how many hours he'd worked and all.

"I beg to differ." Brody chewed for a minute, and then looked at Kit. His lips were shiny with chicken grease, and when he licked them, it mesmerized Kit to the point where he almost forgot to be angry about the fact that Brody was pretty much treating him like he was a charity case. "Everybody on the ranch has to dress to a standard. You are currently not dressed to that standard."

Kit scraped crumbs of fried chicken bits from his mouth with the back of his hand, completely forgetting his napkin, which he'd laid in his lap just like Brody had done. The conversation was one of those that was going to go on and on unless he gave in or bit back.

"Look, I can't afford it, okay? So just shut up about it." With a snarl, Kit waited for Brody to get mad and lash back at him, which would nicely distract the conversation away from clothes.

"Oh, is that it?" Digging into his mashed potatoes, Brody seemed to be willing to let the crackling air between them die its own death. "Typically, your first set of gear is on the ranch, so there's nothing to afford."

"You're lying."

"No, I'm not," said Brody. "Ask anyone and they'll tell you. The first set of gear is on the ranch and after that, you can charge it to the ranch's store and they'll take it out of your paycheck."

"I ain't signed nothing," said Kit, blinking hard at how quickly the conversation was out of his control. "I ain't signed for a W-2 or anything, so how can they take it out of my paycheck?"

"Well, Levi's keeping track of your hours, and I'm keeping track." Brody nodded. "We'll get the paperwork sorted with Maddy before we go to the store."

"What if I leave tomorrow?" Kit wanted to stand up and shout this and then march out of the dining hall. "Will I get my pay anyhow?"

"We'd get your money to you," said Brody and the look on his face told Kit he meant it. Then Brody dipped his head and did that thing where he looked sideways, like he was looking for someone to prompt him as to what to say. "If you wanted to leave."

Brody's voice wobbled on that last word and inside of those first few seconds, Kit's heart sped up. It sounded like Brody didn't want him to leave. Like it actually mattered to him that Kit stayed. And like before, when Brody had said his name to Quint, the feeling rose like a ribbon on a shy wind that maybe Brody liked him.

Just like the bronc rider Katie had dated for five whole minutes, Brody seemed sincere in everything he said or did, so maybe he really meant it. It was up to Kit as to what he wanted to do, but sometimes, it paid to stick around, and maybe something good would happen if he did.

"I guess I'll stay," said Kit as casually as he could, as though it was no never mind to him whether he stayed or went. Like he couldn't care less that Brody's smile at Kit's response became a warm blossom of sweetness that galloped into his heart like Brody had guided it there. "Until Katie calls."

He'd left three messages for her already, and the messages had gone through so her voice mailbox wasn't full. But as to why she'd not yet called him back, well, it was too early to be worried. Sometimes Katie could take a whole week to give a damn that Kit had called her.

When lunch was over, they headed down the dirt road to the main parking lot, which Kit had never seen, since he'd been hiding in the passenger well of Brody's truck. Now he saw the broad stretch of gravel and the two wooden buildings with two flagpoles between them. Around the parking lot were white-painted rocks, and stretches of rough wooden fencing, which added to the rustic atmosphere.

"Let's do paperwork with Maddy, first," said Brody, leading the way up the wooden steps to the first wooden structure.

Inside, it was cool and dark and still, and though Maddy *tut-tutted* at Kit's lack of a bank account, she told him she could hold his pay until he had that set up.

"Do you have a driver's license?" she asked.

"Yeah," said Kit. He pulled it out and slapped it on her desk, and then realized that Brody probably wouldn't want him being so mean about it. "Sorry," he said, reaching to adjust the plastic card. "It slipped."

After that was done, they headed over to the other building, which was the ranch's store. Inside, everything was cool and organized. And while it was easy to wait as Brody told the clerk to pull down boots and a straw hat, and other things that began to grow in a pile on the glass countertop, Kit had to hold onto the idea that he'd agreed to this.

He'd said yes to the free gear, and there was no backing out now. Not that he wanted to, especially when Brody opened the lid of a very long shoebox to expose a pair of dark brown cowboy boots. The leather gleamed like a low promise and the pattern along the side reminded him of the pair Brody currently wore.

"Those are nice," said the clerk, like it wasn't already a done deal that Kit wanted them. He toed off his sneakers and yanked the boots over his thin socks and sighed as the classy weight of them settled around his calves. They were a little loose but that was because his socks were thin. He'd never owned a pair of boots like this, never in his life, and he fell in love with them, then and there.

"We'll need work boots, too," said Brody. "Same size, as it looks like those cowboy boots fit."

Between the two of them, the nice clerk and Brody, they amassed a pile of gear that surely, *surely* was outside the scope of the ranch's policy. But no, the clerk had Kit sign the receipt to show he'd gotten two pairs of boots, a straw cowboy hat, two pairs of new blue jeans, and several different colors and patterns of snap-button shirts, not to mention new socks, and underwear, and t-shirts, and clearly there were only zeros at the bottom of the receipt.

It was almost too much. Kit should refuse everything and walk out, as he had his pride to think of after all. On the other hand, a rush of excitement was building inside of him, like a signal that the new clothes might represent the start of something new and good.

"Try on the work boots with the new socks, so we can check the fit," said Brody.

Pretending to be more grumpy than he was, Kit sat down in the narrow chair next to the boot rack, and did as he was told. The contrast between his thin hole-ridden socks and his worn-out sneakers and the thick socks that came all the way up to his knee and the leather work boots with their thick waffle-patterned sole was like night and day. Night and *fucking* day.

It was a toss-up as to whether his feet preferred the cowboy boots or the work boots, and that was not anything he'd ever expected to feel.

He looked up at Brody, his heart thumping in his chest. This was the kind of thing that happened to other people, other kids, when their parents would say, *Oh, sweet child, it looks like you need new shoes, so here you go.* Which had never, ever, *ever* happened to him.

He never remembered going to Katie very often for anything he needed. When he had, her response was usually along the lines of, *Sorry, kiddo, can't afford it,* when all along she was showing him the new dress she'd bought and a new purse to match. He'd look down at the holes in his one pair of sneakers and sigh. Katie never even noticed.

Brody noticed, though. His smile was warm and his hand was on the large plastic bag the clerk had loaded everything into. Beneath his arm, he had tucked the long shoe box that held the precious new cowboy boots in that mouth-wateringly delicious brown leather.

What would Kit's life be like if he fit into the ranch like his feet fit into the work boots he was wearing? What would every day be like if he had enough to eat and his clothes didn't have holes in them and nobody looked at him like they pitied him? What would his life be like if he had Brody looking at him like he was now, sort of sweet and hopeful, like it mattered to him that Kit was happy?

To his everlasting horror, hot tears filled his eyes and threatened to spill over. He was overworked, that's what it was, and exhausted, and he scrubbed at his eyes furiously and was startled when Brody knelt in front of him, his hands on Kit's knees.

"Hey, now," said Brody, quite gently, and low, as though he didn't want the clerk to hear. But the clerk was moving away, giving them their privacy, and it was only Kit and Brody now inside a little bubble built for two.

"No, no, no, no." Kit choked out the word over and over, hardly knowing what he meant. He wasn't a charity child, he could work for his keep, and now this guy, this cowboy guy, was looking at him, dark brows drawn over his ever-shifting eyes, concerned, bending close.

"Yes," said Brody. "If you're going to be my assistant, you need to look the part. Besides." With his long, steady fingers, Brody cupped the breadth of Kit's knees, and tightened those fingers like a small hug. "I *want* you to stay. I think there's a place for you here, on the ranch, I truly do, and I don't say that lightly. But really, I want you to stay."

The tears escaped Kit, then, streaking down his cheeks like hot mercury. And when Brody took his hands off Kit's knees and seemed to lean forward, his hands lifted as though he wanted to catch Kit, with a blubbery sigh, he leaned right back and let himself be caught.

Brody's arms were warm, and Kit tucked himself into the curve of those arms, and hid his face against Brody's neck, and cried. He didn't cry for very long, as Katie's voice was in his head, *Stop crying. Get up and stop crying*, and he desperately didn't want Brody to think he was a fool.

But when he lifted himself up and wiped his face with the stretched length of his long-sleeve t-shirt, Brody wasn't looking at him like he thought Kit was a fool. He was looking at Kit with a wise, solemn expression that seemed to state he knew exactly what Kit was feeling, just then. Knew and understood and didn't blame Kit for reacting the way he had at all.

"Our first stop," said Brody, ever-practical. "Is to get all of this back to the room and then we need to get to work in the barn. We don't want Clay doing all the work, do we?"

"No." The word came out thick with the tears Kit had just shed, but his heart felt full, and a strange sensation was running through him that maybe everything was going to work out, maybe just for a little while, but it was going to work out, maybe. If he gave it a chance.

16

KIT

As they carried Brody's blue Ikea bag full of Kit's new socks, and underwear, and t-shirts, and blue jeans, and plaid snap-button shirts down to the laundry room in the staff quarters, the weight of the buck knife and the fifty dollars in his pocket seemed heavier than it ought to. He'd managed to hide them both, keeping them on him at all times, but he imagined that at some point Brody would look in the top drawer of his dresser and find out they were missing and then what?

"We'll wash all your new things," said Brody as he opened the door to the laundry room at the bottom of the stairs. "And then tomorrow, when they're nice and soft and broken in, you can wear them."

"What about—?"

"I've got your old clothes in there, too," said Brody. "And we can wash what you have on next week."

It all sounded so very organized and regular and wholesome, and though what Brody wanted him to do was exactly what the people on TV did, being locked in to such a regular schedule was a little more constraining than he imagined it would be.

The laundry room was a long space, with the walls painted pale yellow, and large white-trimmed windows on one side, looking out into the darkness of early evening. The floor was a shiny brown linoleum, and overhead were squares of fluorescent lights in a white ceiling.

It was no better than, no newer than any laundromat Kit had ever been to, and that wasn't many, but somehow, with the red glow of the soda machine at the far end and the low hum of someone's clothes flipping around in one of the front-load dryers, it was cozy.

Along one wall was a row of front load washing machines that looked quite new, or at least well taken care of. In the middle of the room was a row of six front load dryers, which faced the washing machines. Behind that were two long tables, and behind the tables were the three tall, wide windows, only half covered by blinds.

"Go get some quarters," said Brody as he hefted the laundry bag and dumped it on the nearest table.

"Some *what?*" asked Kit, looking around.

"Over there, near the soda machine." Brody pointed with his chin, busy sorting lights from darks. "Get yourself a soda and get me one too, please."

Instinctively, Kit reached into his pocket, though he knew what was in there. Fifty bucks and a buck knife, both stolen, and no quarters. Except on the end of the far table, close to the soda machine that sold all the good stuff and nothing generic, was an opaque plastic bin without a lid.

It was filled nearly to the brim with quarters, both shiny and dirty, new and worn. The coins glinted in the overhead lights, nearly begging Kit to take handfuls and shove them into his pockets, and in his new work boots, and then make a run for it.

"How many?" asked Kit, completely unsure of what to do, his eyes glued to the pile of money just sitting there. The door to the laundry room had not been locked, and though Brody had told him the outside doors were locked at night, during the day, anyone could come in and take the whole thing. And yet there the bin sat, dripping with money.

"Two for now," said Brody, humming a little. "We'll use two

washers and then two dryers, I think, just to get this all done in one go."

"Okay." Kit brought over two quarters that felt slippery and cool in his palm. When he handed the quarters to Brody, Brody went to the machine nearest the door and opened the lid. Then he put the quarter in the slot and pushed the metal lip, but it wouldn't budge.

"Dang," said Brody. "This is full. Can you empty it?"

Wide-eyed, Kit watched as Brody pulled out the metal tray that was full to the brim with quarters.

"Empty it?" asked Kit.

"Into the bin with the rest of the quarters," said Brody. Calmly, as though he wasn't handing over a metal box with a pile of money. "We'll save Stella's team a step, eh?" Brody looked at Kit, brows drawn together as though he was confused at Kit's open mouth and wide eyes. "While you're over there, get some detergent from the cupboard, and I'll get these machines going."

With numb fingers, Kit carried the metal box to the far table, and dumped it into the plastic bin. There were so many quarters, some slid onto the table or rolled onto the floor.

"Just stack the extras," said Brody. "And hurry with that detergent." Turning, Brody wiped his hands on his jeans to look at Kit. "What kind of soda you want? I don't usually drink any but sometimes when I do laundry, I treat myself."

Nodding, like a boss who has just hit the mother lode, Brody sauntered over and grabbed two quarters from the bin, while the two washing machines filled up with hot water. Bending at the waist, Brody slid a quarter into the slot and then shook his head.

"This'n's full too," he said, pulling open the door to the machine to grab the coin box at the bottom. "Oh, pennies. Take those out and stack them on the windowsill, would you? People might need them, and Stella doesn't like them in the machine."

"Uh."

Kit watched as Brody emptied out the metal box onto the table, a dragon's hoard of dimes and nickels and quarters that shone dully in the overhead lights, along with a handful of copper pennies.

"Sort these, would you?" asked Brody. "What kind of soda?" he asked as he went back to the soda machine and returned the coin box and closed the door with a snap.

"Orange," said Kit, as he'd seen there were plenty of those.

"One for me too."

Brody handed Kit his soda, then opened his and bustled about, getting out a bottle of detergent from a cupboard along the wall next to the soda machine. There was no coin slot for this, no way to pay, which meant that the use of the detergent and bleach and dryer sheets was, amazingly, simply, free. Everything was free. *Everything.*

It occurred to Kit that while he'd been upstairs stealing fifty bucks from Brody, down in the laundry room in the basement of the staff quarters had been probably about sixty or so bucks in coins. Coins were harder to carry, noisier, even, but—if he'd known, he could have left days ago with one hundred and ten dollars, which would have been enough for a bus ticket to Vegas.

He could leave right now. Today. He could just take all this money, grab a couple sodas for the road, and, wearing his new boots, march right out of Farthingdale Ranch, a wealthy man.

Except—

Hands shaking, Kit pulled out all the pennies and stacked them in little piles of five along the nearest wide windowsill, beyond which, the evening had darkened, with the pine-needle strewn ground lit up by rectangular patches of light from the laundry room. After he did that, he did his best to make stacks on the table of the overflow of quarters and shiny dimes and rugged round nickels, so that Stella wouldn't have to bend down to get any coins off the floor, and so she could easily see that, perhaps, some money might be taken to the bank or secured away somewhere.

Who the hell set up a laundry room like this? And why was his stomach squirreling in knots as he picked up his orange soda and went over to where Brody was just finishing loading two washers with Kit's clothes, one with lighter colors, and the other with the new blue jeans and the two snap-button plaid shirts.

"Does everybody do their laundry here?" asked Kit.

Brody was humming to himself, and he smiled as Kit came up.

"Well, mostly," said Brody. "Jasper likes to take his into town so he has an excuse to go to Dairy Queen, but everybody else uses these machines."

Brody closed the lids on the washing machines.

"That'll take forty-five minutes," said Brody. "We'll wait, and then transfer everything to dryers, which we can leave overnight, and pick up in the morning. In the meantime," said Brody with a warm smile. "This is what I like to do."

Going over to the door, Brody flipped off all the lights, which cast the room in dark shadows lit only by the glow of the soda machine. Then he pulled on the strings to pull up the blinds on the middle window, and appeared to pull himself up to sit on the edge of it.

"C'mon," said Brody as he patted the table. "Stella doesn't exactly like it when I sit on the table, but as long as we're not dancing on it, I figure it'll be okay."

Startled, perhaps beyond his capacity to understand why, Kit placed his half-drunk soda on the table, then took his place beside Brody. They were sitting quite close in the dark, and ahead of them, like a wide-screen TV that looked out into the shadowed darkness, the frame of the window encompassed the outlines of pine trees, the soft movement of leafed trees in the evening wind. The flicker of stars, silver dots in a carpet of black, began to show, and Kit sat quite still, hardly breathing.

This was a new world. A totally new world. Rather than bring his old laptop with him, or a tablet, or anything, Brody seemed content to look out at the growing evening, drinking a soda that had been free, waiting till Kit's two free loads of laundry were done before putting the damp clothes into two dryers that would dry the clothes for free. Using free dryer sheets.

Everything was free, and here Kit sat with stolen money in his pocket, a stolen buck knife. The taste of the orange soda became sour in his mouth as the weight of the knife grew heavier, the fold of money more dense.

Here on the ranch was abundance so natural, so easy, that

everyone had what they needed. The idea of it made him feel different inside, like someone had taken off the locks inside of him and opened the doors, opened them wide to feel the summer breeze, see the bright sunshine.

People lived like this, all around him, and though he'd known that, he'd not really known it, and had certainly never experienced it.

Behind them, the two washing machines churned in a low, almost comforting way, and the single dryer went thump-thump, as if it wanted to announce what a good job it was doing. Ahead of them was the night, the simple, clear-skied night filled with air so pure that the smell of warm pine needles cooling down in the dark dusk had seeped into the cleanest laundry room Kit had ever seen.

The worst part was sitting next to Brody, hip to hip, Brody's knee brushing Kit's as Brody swung his leg idly, back and forth, back and forth. Brody thought Kit was worth a pair of shiny new cowboy boots, worth spending a Friday evening doing laundry so that Kit's clothes would be soft rather than scratchy when he put them on in the morning.

Brody probably thought Kit was honest like he was and simply wasn't worried that Kit might take anything that didn't belong to him. After all, nobody on the ranch stole anything. Nobody locked their doors. There was plenty of food to eat and tons of hot water for showers, and in this laundry room were piles of money that nobody could be bothered to take.

Unable to take it anymore, the weight of the buck knife and the fold of money in Kit's pocket was suddenly too heavy to bear.

"Uh, Brody?"

"Yeah, Kit?" asked Brody in that way he had, his voice warm, his mouth probably moving over Kit's name in the way that Kit adored, though he couldn't really say why. "What is it?"

"Uh," said Kit, swallowing hard. "I didn't know it was wrong—I mean I did know, right? But. Anyway. Here. These belong to you."

Before he could stop himself, Kit pulled out the buck knife and the fold of money, and laid both on Brody's thigh. Brody had to put down his soda to catch the items before they rolled to the floor, and Kit reached out to help him, because he wouldn't be able to stand it if Brody had to get up and turn on the overhead lights to retrieve what Kit had stolen from him.

Better it happened in the dark, so the wash of heat across Kit's face could go unnoticed. Better the look of surprise on Brody's face should remain unseen.

Kit felt the weight of Brody's gaze just the same, in that silent moment as Kit took his hand from Brody's thigh and the crinkle of paper money could just about be heard over the low churn of the two washing machines, the industrious thump-thump of the single dryer doing its job.

"This is my buck knife," said Brody, and if there was a hard edge to his voice, Kit didn't blame him. "And my—my mad money."

Kit had come from a world where people didn't have money just to go crazy with on a whim. Katie and he had lived day to day, scrounging on casino floors for coins and tokens, taking what they wanted from the 7-11 when the cashier's back was turned. They regularly paid in torn-edged bills for rooms at the cheapest motel in town and when there weren't enough of those, Katie would do favors in return for rent.

"Do you need the money?" asked Brody. "I'm glad for the return of the knife, as it's very important to me, but if you need money, you can have it."

Kit sensed that Brody was holding out the fifty bucks. His hand would be steady. The offer was in earnest, and Kit realized that not only were his eyes hot, his cheeks aflame, his stomach all wound up, he wanted to shove Brody's hand away and run from the room. Run all the way to Vegas, rather than accept such kindness.

It was like the ranch's store all over again, only this time he wasn't going to let himself cry. He had to swallow hard and then swallow hard again, and all the while the lump in his throat refused to go down.

"I thought I needed the money, the knife," said Kit, and to his horror he knew he sounded like was going to cry. But he wouldn't. He wouldn't. He scrubbed his mouth, fierce and hard, and tried again. "But I don't anymore and I'm sorry I took them."

His nose was running in spite of himself, and his eyes sparked, the tears still threatening. He'd never ever said sorry for stealing before, and now he had, and what was he supposed to do with that? And, more importantly, what was Brody thinking? In the dark, he couldn't tell, only that Brody's leg had stopped swinging and the whine as the washer went on high spin seemed to pierce his skull.

"Here," said Brody.

Something brushed the back of Kit's hand. It was his half-drunk orange soda.

"Wait," said Brody. "Let me get us both cold ones."

Brody hopped off the table and came back to hand Kit a cold can.

"I reached blind," said Brody with a little laugh as he re-seated himself on the table next to Kit and popped open his soda. "So you just don't know what you have. A grape Nehi maybe? Or a Diet Coke? Who knows?"

Kit could barely feel the coldness of the metal soda can beneath his fingers.

"Are you mad?"

"No," said Brody, swallowing. "Ah, a regular Coke. Perfect."

"You're not?"

"No, I'm not," said Brody. He was still for a minute, and Kit sensed him looking forward, looking out the window into the night. "But I'm disappointed you didn't know that if you needed anything, all you had to do was ask. I should have told you, should have made it clear."

That Kit could have anything he wanted or needed just by asking was as though Brody was speaking in a totally new language. One that Kit knew, at least his heart, but had never heard before.

Oh, sweet child, it looks like you need new shoes, so here you go.

"I don't need anything," he said, hardly believing what he was saying, even though he knew it was true for perhaps the first time in his life. "Got everything I need."

"Keep it that way," said Brody, sounding a bit stern for the first time that evening. "And I'm serious. Just ask. Ask instead of stealing."

"Okay."

Kit took a sip of his soda, which turned out to be something grape that swirled around in his mouth, thick flavored, unctuous.

He could spit it out. He could get another soda easily, grabbing from the row right inside the soda machine, where the orange sodas were, rather than finishing something that tasted more like medicine than soda.

But. That would be rude, in the face of Brody's kindness. In the face of his first taste of true abundance, he was going to finish that soda, swallow every drop. To be polite and appreciative in a way he'd never been before. And for Brody. Just for Brody. For Brody, he found, he would do just about anything.

"Thanks," said Kit, meaning it with his whole heart. "And, uh. Could you swing your leg again?"

"Swing my leg?" The surprise was clear in Brody's voice.

"Yeah, like you were doing before. In time with the machine." Kit took a huge swallow of the grape Nehi, wincing. "It was nice. Soothing."

"Ah."

Kit sensed that Brody nodded, and gently, quite gently, his leg began to swing, slowly, slowly, in time with the rhythm of the washing machines. The night settled around them, and Kit's heartbeat began to slow, though he felt sore all over and especially inside his chest, as though he'd hurt himself bad, only he'd not noticed it till now.

In Brody's presence, the hurt would heal, he knew that. He just needed to trust where he'd found himself. Trust that things might be good after all. And, as long as he was near Brody, perhaps they would be.

17

BRODY

*W*hen the laundry was done, they moved all the damp clothes to two dryers, put in the quarters and, recycling their soda cans, went upstairs to their room. Kit took his shower first, and by the time Brody was done with his, Kit was fast asleep.

A fine mist from the bathroom eased into the room, giving the single shaft of light a sparkly look, as though Brody had intentionally spread fairy dust in the air. Kit's hair, still dishwater blond, curled against his forehead, and his cheeks were flushed, dark lashes across his cheek.

Kit had only been at the ranch a few days, but he looked so much better, at least to Brody's eyes. Maybe the impulse to care for another person had been inside of Brody all along, only he never knew it. Not until now.

Pulling on his softest boxers and t-shirt he turned off the bathroom light and made his way to Kit's cot. There, he hunkered down and waited till his eyes adjusted to the darkness in the room, to where he could see the curve of Kit's cheek, hear his soft breathing. Feel the warm summer air through the open windows swirl around them both, an invisible embrace.

On impulse, Brody reached out to trace his fingers across Kit's forehead, pushing his blond forelock away, softly, slowly.

Part of him was still stung by the fact that Kit had taken the buck knife Quint had freed him with and then given to him all those years ago.

Brody had been looking through the drawers in the trailer for a half teaspoon measuring spoon, as Quint was mighty particular about the amount of pepper flakes that went into his chili. He came upon the buck knife, neatly folded closed, the same one Quint had cut the ropes that Daddy Frank had tied around him.

Oh look, he'd said. *I found this.*

He remembered Quint looking at him with serious eyes, the wooden spoon halfway to his mouth so he could taste how the chili was coming along.

You want it? Quint had asked, in his most giving tone, as if Brody only had to ask for the moon, and Quint would get it for him. There could be a love no more pure than that, though Quint had to know that all Brody wanted was to be with Quint.

Can I have it? Brody had asked.

Sure.

Quint had pulled Brody to him and hugged him, patted his back to let him know the hug was finished, then returned to his chili. That night they'd feasted on chili with sour cream and cheese on top, hunks of buttered cornbread, and bottles of cheap beer.

Brody couldn't remember what kind of beer it had been, but the tart bubbles had been perfect with the chili. And, as far as he knew, Quint had only ever shared that chili recipe with one person, and that person was Levi Walker, the ranch's head chef. Guests were always raving and asking for the recipe, and Brody had seen Levi shake his head time and again, saying, *I made a promise I wouldn't share.*

Just like Quint had made a promise to look after Brody.

And just like Brody had made the same kind of promise to Kit, in spite of the stolen buck knife.

The money was nothing, just mad money for the bar or pizza ordered in, just for the fun of it. The buck knife was something else, though, its smooth wooden handle soaked with Quint's essence, the butt and the bolster, tipped in brass, glamoured with that rainy night of rescue and freedom, and the first step into a new life. A better one.

Yes, it stung that Kit had taken it. But, perhaps more importantly, he'd given it back and apologized. And this from a young man who'd evidently been raised to steal, which explained how he'd managed all these years without a stable home life, a bank account, or an allowance.

There must have been many things Kit had taken over the years because he wanted or thought he needed them, but Brody would bet good money that this buck knife, the blade thin from wear and sharpening, the handle worn from gripping, had been the first thing Kit had handed back to its rightful owner.

It must have taken a lot for Kit to return it and apologize. Though at the same time, Brody had seen how wide-eyed Kit had been over the laundry room. It was a simple place to do laundry, nothing fancy, not even a TV to watch while your clothes spun around and around.

Most members of staff left their laundry and came back when it was ready. Personally, Brody liked to sit on the table in the half darkness on a Friday night and think about the hills and the horses and the wind in the grasses.

It was a peaceful place that, that Brody knew as he watched Kit walking around, his mouth open in a kind of shock, wasn't like other places. Just like the ranch wasn't like other places.

There were piles of quarters, just *piles* of them, so many they fell on the floor. There were nickels and dimes and copper pennies all over the place. The sodas, the laundry detergent, basically everything in the room was free for staff to use as needed.

In Kit's eyes, the room must have been a veritable gold mine and, thinking back, Brody realized that Kit's stiff body as he'd carried the metal box of quarters from the washer to the plastic bin, was an indication as to how hard he'd been thinking about taking some—no, actually taking a *great many* quarters and just lighting out, like Huck Finn lighting out for the territory ahead of the rest. To become the man Katie must have raised him to be, the kind who only wanted to get good at the big shill and the little con. The kind of man who would be content with holes in his long sleeved t-shirt, just as long as he didn't have to work too hard or pay for anything with good money, honestly earned.

Except now, a corner had been turned, and Katie's hopes and dreams that her little man, if she ever came looking for him, was now well on his way to becoming a different person. Not a better person, for Kit had a goodness in his heart that had just been waiting to get out.

Tonight, in the yellow-walled, white-trimmed laundry room, something had changed. If allowed another wager, Brody would have stated that the number of quarters when they left the laundry room was exactly the same number of quarters as when they'd entered, and there was nothing Katie could do about that, should she ever decide to call Kit back. Brody hoped she never would, for Kit deserved all the goodness in the world, and Brody wanted to give it to him. Wanted to teach him that the high standards of the ranch, though they might seem difficult to achieve for Kit right now, were good standards and would serve him well all the days of his life.

And as for the tender places inside of Brody that he'd wanted to protect—he now wanted to expand them and open them to Kit.

Brody stood up, his heart beating a little fast. What he needed was fresh air and wild, dark nighttime skies. He needed the warmth of a horse's neck, the arched muscles, the soft down behind a horse's perked ear.

Getting dressed in his softest blue jeans, his oldest cowboy boots that hugged his feet in all the right places, Brody slid on a t-shirt and very quietly left the room to go down the stairs to the front door. He left it unlocked behind him, but that would be all right as he would be back just as soon as he'd eased his soul in the best way he knew how.

Slipping beneath the trees, Brody avoided the auto-lights as best he could, sly enough to avoid triggering most of them except the big one on the near side of the barn. But even that light went back off after he grabbed a hackamore from the tack room and went steadily up the road. Going past the arena, he slipped through the barbed wire to the lower field, where horses moved in the darkness, alerting each other to a stranger in their midst.

"Hey, now," said Brody low, his eyes adjusting to the starlit dark, the moon just a yellow sliver over the horizon. It was better this way anyhow, as he reached out his hand and made clucking noises with his tongue and breathed out his breath to see which horse would smell him and come closer of their own free will.

The herd in this field was just on the verge of being moved to the barn, where they would easily be accessible for lessons and trail rides. They were several days from the upper field and being well-seasoned, knew the drill as well as Brody did. To be ridden, they would need to be groomed, and since they'd not been groomed, they weren't about to be ridden.

But all of the horses knew Brody and many moved close, brushing against him, scenting him with their cool nighttime coats, flicking their tails, welcoming him into the center of the herd where he'd be safe from mountain lions and other predators. To be welcomed so, accepted like this, warmed him through, and calmed him. With his hand outstretched, he treated each and every horse that came close, the dark-coated ones, the spotted ones, the painted ones, the buckskins, touching their noses, scratching their muscled necks, planting kisses on their planed cheeks.

Up came Old Blue, with a nicker and a half trot, the greeting stirring inside Brody as though Old Blue had turned human and hugged him, then turned back into a horse again. Sometimes, beneath the starry skies, the wind from Iron Mountain flickering through the mountain grasses at his feet, it was like this, when reality would bend itself into a softer unreality, a magic created by the night, the air, and Brody himself.

"Want to gallop, Old Blue?" asked Brody, politely, for nighttime gallops were not part of any horse's job description. And, indeed, nighttime gallops with or without a saddle or iron-bit bridle were strictly forbidden, for safety's sake. And yet. Yet. There was no horse Brody couldn't ride, and while it'd be him astride Old Blue, all the horses were welcome to gallop at their side. The horses and Brody knew the trails along the hills, over the ride, down in the flats beside the sleek and glassy river.

Old Blue came close, dipping his head, snuffling at Brody's blue jeans as if smelling Kit's essence there.

"Yeah," said Brody, half to himself and half to Old Blue as he eased the simple and softly braided hackamore over Old Blue's ears and nose, then looped the reins over his black-maned neck. "That's Kit. He lives with me now. He makes me feel—"

There were so many things Kit made him feel it was hard to list them all, to keep track of them as they raced around inside of his heart. So Brody focused on what he did know, and that was how to mount a horse without a saddle by simply springing on his toes and jumping up to throw his leg over Old Blue's back.

Old Blue, who was not, actually, old, tensed to attention, shifting beneath Brody's weight, testing the length of the reins and the pressure of the hackamore upon his nose. Brody held the reins loose in his hand as he patted Old Blue's neck, enjoying the feel of him, the warmth of his hide, the strength of Old Blue's body between his legs.

"Down and back again," said Brody, leaning forward to whisper into Old Blue's pointed ears that swiveled back to listen. "Just a mile or so, down along the river and back again. Okay?"

He nudged Old Blue forward with his heels, lightly, very lightly, and Old Blue straightened his head like he'd been asked to run a long distance race with a bag of sliced carrots as the prize. Well, Old Blue would get those carrots and then some, in the morning as guests were leaving. As would any horse that went with them, and any horse who didn't.

Clucking, Brody urged Old Blue to a trot, using his nighttime vision to guide them to the wide dusty path that guests used on gentle trail rides. Beside him, gathering around Brody and Old Blue as they rode, trotting in the darkness, came the herd, joining them for this dark ride, this unauthorized outing, this starlit romp, this nighttime dance.

The only tricky part was going over the ridge, where it was sensible, whether riding bareback or with a saddle, to go at a walk. You had to lean back while going down into the valley, and while some guests freaked out, the horses always knew the right pace, so Brody wasn't worried as they topped the ridge and went down the other side of it in the darkness that was slowly turning into almost-darkness, as his eyes adjusted.

As for the horses, they had better nighttime vision than he did, and knew their own limits, knew the curves and slant of the trail, and went down at a walk, all of them, kicking up dust as they went, snorting as they maneuvered the slant, the rocks, and went down into the valley, guiding Brody and Old Blue.

At the bottom of the trail from the ridge, the valley spread out, miles and miles of inky velvet grass shifting in the starlight as though reaching up to the sky. The river, Horse Creek, glinted as it moved slowly within its banks, and beside it was the trail, a dusty wide track that curved where the river curved.

All around him, the herd shifted, flicking their tails, waiting for the signal. Not one of them would go if he did not, and if he turned back around at that moment, they would go with him, their heads nodding as if it was of no never mind to them, they just wanted to be where he was. Just like he wanted to be where Kit was

Maybe he'd bring Kit one day, to show him the magic and the moonlight on the horses' backs, their flanks, shining off their big eyes, starlight limning their manes and tails. But this time, this was for him, and for Old Blue who, truth be told, was usually the first horse who stepped up at Brody's unasked ask.

"Let's go," he said, and clucking beneath his breath, gave Old Blue a slight squeeze to his side.

Old Blue took off like he'd been waiting for the signal, and Brody leaned close, keeping his body tight, so the herd could come close to them, as they might if they were wild and galloped free across the high prairies together. As if Brody was not there at all and they ran beneath the moonlight because they wanted to.

In the starlit dark, the wind whipped Brody's hair and the ground was almost unseen beneath the horse's churning feet. It was as though they were racing along a black velvet road rather than one of dust and gravel. As if they galloped above it and the road dipped away and they were flying, flying like a herd of winged horses, racing because they loved it, taking Brody with them because they loved him, because he was one of them.

At the speed of the horses' gallop, the nighttime air was chill, edged with the dampness of the river, stark in the air, scented with dust and the perfume from horses' manes, from Brody's own sweat of excitement—all of this churned in his lungs, a heady mix, and he lifted his arms from the braided loop of rein and tipped his head back and let the wind race over his skin, a blessing, like a cool kiss.

The horses slowed as they reached the mile marker. From there, the valley wound its way up into the hills, the dusty track a ribbon inside of it, the river dipping low while the track went upwards. With a few half trots and a few feints of kicks, the horses milled about as though waiting for Brody to decide. Forward or back to the ranch. Into the night, or return to the field to munch on grass and doze standing up until the sun rose over the eastern horizon bathing every-thing in rose and gold strands of light.

Some nights, Brody would stay out for hours, staying on Old Blue's back, or Dusty, or whichever horse had volunteered. Gwen, the buckskin mare, had a nice broad back, and while astride her, Brody would lean back to rest his head on her croup, his legs dangling against her legs as she dipped her head and grazed, while the herd dipped their heads and grazed around them. And stare at the stars and the moon, if it was out, and let the wind whisper over him.

But tonight, Kit was sleeping in his cot, and if he were to wake up and find Brody gone, he might grow anxious or worried, and Brody didn't want that. Kit needed his rest to be ready for the busy activity on Saturday, when guests checked out and staff set the ranch to rights in preparation for the new group of guests who would arrive on Sunday.

"Let's go back," said Brody. He gathered the reins, tugging a little, and whistled to the horses, who all turned to go the way they'd come. And at a slow canter, easing them along the road, rather than rushing them, for he didn't want them to feel ill used or tired come morning, they headed back to the ranch. Up the trail, up over the ridge, and back down to the first field they went. When they arrived, Brody slid off Old Blue and removed the hackamore, which was Old Blue's signal that the night's adventure was at an end.

"Thank you, Old Blue," he said, giving Old Blue gentle pats along his neck and a kiss on his soft nose. "Extra carrots for everyone tomorrow, I promise."

Old Blue nickered as Brody walked away to slip through the gap in the barbed wire, then returned to eating the wild grasses, and the herd followed Old Blue's example. If they were thirsty after their run, the water trough was full, Brody made sure, dipping his fingers in the trough as he passed it.

Then he strode back to the barn to return the hackamore to its place in the flicker of the auto-light. In the morning, he'd wipe it down, but as for now, he trotted along the service road to the staff quarters, and took his boots off before racing up the stairs to the room where Kit slept.

Opening the door, he slipped inside, putting his boots beside the door, rather than risk waking Kit up by opening the closet, whose hinges were loud. Kit slept on as Brody approached his cot and hunkered down as he had before. Only now his skin was laced with the night's perfume, with the sweat of horses, the dust of the road.

Kit stirred in the cot as if sensing Brody was near. Brody reached out his hand to trace the curve of Kit's cheek and then drew his hand away. He did not want Kit to waken and ask why Brody was dressed and why his hair was so wild. One day, if Kit stayed, Brody would share the magic of nighttime rides, and maybe that would allay Kit's fear of horses. If Kit stayed. If.

The only thing now was for Brody to change clothes and get into bed and hope to get a few hours of sleep until morning came. And hope that he could figure out what he was feeling and why he'd touched Kit the way he had. Softly, gently, as though Kit was precious to him.

18

KIT

*W*earing his new clothes, his work boots, and a crisp-edged brand new yellow straw hat, Kit marched down to the main parking lot after helping out in the kitchen that morning, as he was on Leland's list to help guests get their suitcases hefted from the various cabins and rooms in the main lodge to the parking lot, where cars and busses were waiting to take them home. He felt sparkling new, shining like a diamond beneath the blue sky, like he was well on his way to stepping up into the good kind of life the ranch seemed to offer.

Maddy was on the porch with her clipboard, already, directing members of staff and the various ranch hands as to how they could best help. Brody was at the barn, grooming horses, working with tack, so Kit was on his own. Except there was Clay, smiling as he waved Kit close.

"Hey," said Clay in a way that felt like he was happy to see Kit. "I like the new duds. Can you go over there and help those two ladies lift their suitcases into the van?"

Kit looked around until he saw them, two grey-haired ladies, the kind who would have drawn to the side should they happen to meet Katie and Kit on their way to work. But something told him this would be different, so he marched over to the dark blue minivan, where the two ladies were discussing their luggage, while two men gabbed, their hands on their hips, and three teenagers stood and waited, rolling their eyes like they were bored out of their minds.

Kit knew that feeling, but even though he did, he could see it from the other side, too, now, even though he was a teenager himself. The bored teenagers were coming to pick up their moms or their aunts or whatever, and hadn't experienced the ranch the way Kit had. He pretended he was Brody and, just as cool as anything, marched right up to the van.

"Hey, there," he said, waving at all of them. "How can I help today?"

"Oh, hello," said one of the ladies. She was wearing cowboy gear, and looked sad. "I don't want to leave, but they're all booked up for the next three weeks."

"We thought about having them stay," said one of the men, and now that he was up close, Kit could see that both men had their phones out, like they'd just made calls. "We got the big fat no."

"Ah," said Kit, not quite sure what to say, only that had Brody been there, he would have said something nice. "Did you get on the waiting list?" He wasn't even sure that there was one, but there might be.

"That's a good idea," said the second man.

"We can't afford it, honey," said the second woman.

"We can," said both men in unison, and then the first man added, "If you want it, you can have it."

The three teenagers still looked bored, leaving Kit floundering as to what to do next, as the two older women were between him and the luggage, and he didn't quite think that shoving his way through was going to be the right thing to do. All at once he was out of his depth and the morning didn't feel as shiny anymore.

"Hi," said Clay, coming up from behind Kit, and when he turned, Clay was touching his finger to his hat in greeting. "What's up? How can I help?"

"They want to stay," said Kit, pointing in a general way, lost as to what he could do about it. "There's a waiting list they could get on, right?"

"There sure is," said Clay. He put an arm around Kit's shoulders. "Just call the booking number, and tell them what you want. Sometimes, toward the end of the season, things open up a little bit, and it sure is pretty around here, when the leaves start to turn. Though it does rain sometimes, that time of year."

"Oh, don't you two look cute together," said the first woman. She pulled out her cell phone, and held it out, as though to show her intentions. "Can I get your picture?"

To Kit's amazement, Clay moved close, his arm around Kit's shoulder.

"Tip your hat back so they can see your face," said Clay, dipping his chin, so the words could be heard by Kit only. "And smile."

Kit did as he was asked, and then Clay dropped his arm, with a smile, and one of the husbands, who'd been on the phone, waved the phone in the air.

"You're on the list, honey," he said. "Both of you. First week in September, so you'll have plenty of time to get ready. We'll keep our fingers crossed and save our pennies."

September was six weeks away. But as the women hugged their husbands, and the three teenagers still looked bored, there was excitement in the women's eyes. Kit hoped they were able to get a real reservation come September.

Clay helped Kit get the luggage in the van, and then gave him a cart and asked him to go back up to the lodge to see if anyone needed help getting their luggage down the stairs or out to the parking lot. But before Kit was able to go, another group of ladies came up and wanted their picture together. Again, he and Clay stood side by side with their best smiles, their hats on the backs of their heads, posing for the guests.

"If Brody was here," said Clay with a wry smile. "We'd be nobody."

"Oh, I don't know," said Kit, a little uncomfortable, though he wasn't sure why, that Clay thought himself second rate compared to Brody. And he knew Brody wouldn't want Clay to feel that way. "Can we see?" he asked the closest woman.

Happily, three camera phones were held out to him, and the

pictures of the two of them were arrayed before them. In all of them, Clay looked solid and dependable, his dimples on display, his golden hair shining in the sun. Beside him, Kit looked narrow-faced and maybe a bit sallow. But even though his hair was in his eyes, he was smiling just as widely as Clay was.

"Oh, those are nice," said Clay, his face going pink. "You made me look handsome."

"Do you want a copy?" asked one of the women.

"Sure," said Clay, then he gave them the ranch's email address. "We can put this on the website."

After that, Clay sent Kit off with the cart to the main lodge, and though it was busy, Clay seemed to be checking in on Kit, and though this might have irritated him in the past, he appreciated Clay's advice, and direction. And when Kit got a twenty-dollar tip from one of the guests, he held the bill out and marched to Maddy's office to give it to her, making sure everyone saw him do this by strutting a bit and walking slow.

"Hey, Maddy," he said, as he stomped into her office, which was calm and cool in the midst of the bustle outside. "I got a tip here." He held out the bill to her.

"Oh my," she said, taking it, and as she stuffed it in one of her drawers, she smiled at him. "It's going to be a mighty fine end-of-year party this season, for sure."

"Great," he said, thinking of how only days ago he would have squirreled the money in his own pocket and not told anyone that he'd gotten a tip. Now, it was different. Now everything felt different. "Well, I'm off," he said, and went out to thump down the wooden steps to see what else he could do, who else he could help.

He missed working with Brody all Sunday morning, missed him at lunch when he helped Stella's team carry bags of trash to the dumpster behind the supply shed, and piles of laundry from the laundry room in the staff quarters, where the quarters flew from the box in the machines to the plastic bin and back again.

He was just about to ask if he could take a break, and maybe he'd lie about how tired he was, when Stella told him he could go.

"Nice job today, Kit," said Stella. "Thanks for the extra pair of hands."

Kit went upstairs to wash for dinner and all he could think about was Brody, where Brody was, and whether they'd get to eat dinner together. They almost didn't, and Kit had been halfway through his bowl of terrific chili when Brody walked in, Quint at his side. That they'd been working together all day was obvious from the way their faces were turned toward each other as they walked, the way their bodies were in sync as they moved.

He shouldn't be jealous. He knew that, but it was hard not to jump up and shout at Quint and say that Brody belonged to him. That was how he used to feel with Katie when he was young and would run up to her current boyfriend and want to punch him and tell him to stay away. The impulse was a strong one, except what was different this time was that as Quint and Brody came over with their trays, Quint went off with Leland, and Brody came up to where Kit was sitting, shaking his head.

"He's working hard on that pitch of his," said Brody as he sat down. "Oh, I love this chili, just love it."

"Pitch?" asked Kit, his shoulders relaxing as he realized he had Brody all to himself, at least for a little while.

"Yeah," said Brody with a shrug, looking across the dining hall to where Quint and Leland were earnestly talking. "He's got this adventure ride idea. You know, where you go off on a trail ride, up in the canyon, and survive in the wilderness on a handful of salt and three matches."

"That doesn't sound like fun to me," said Kit, happily shoving his chili into his mouth with his eye on the sticky bun that waited patiently for him on its plate.

"Me either, youngling," said Brody. "But Quint's got this idea that things need to be hard to be truly enjoyed, so. Anyway." His smile at Kit, his eyes glinting as though he was truly pleased to see Kit and maybe had missed Kit as much as Kit had missed him. "Don't eat more than one of those," said Brody, pointing at the sticky bun.

"Why not?" asked Kit, for that had been the very thing he'd planned to do, go up and get seconds of everything.

"I've got a present for you in the room," said Brody. "It came today."

Kit's jaw dropped. Brody had already given him so much and hadn't been mad about the things Kit had taken without permission, it was hard to imagine that Brody would deem him worthy of a present. A surprise.

"What is it?" Kit asked, sitting up in his chair.

"Eat your chili," said Brody, mock-stern, which made Kit feel warm inside, and when Clay and Austin came by to invite them out to a nearby bar, Brody shook his head. "Thanks, but we've got plans. Next time though. Maybe next weekend."

"Just you an' me?" asked Kit as Clay and Austin walked away, a slow warmth spreading through him when Brody solemnly nodded yes, that it was so, all the while concentrating on his dinner, enjoying every mouthful of the chili, licking his lips absently, as though he was fully unaware of how much a draw that was to Kit.

When they finished with dinner and bussed their trays, they stepped out onto the porch of the main lodge. Rain was coming down in whispery sheets, the wind dashing the tops of the trees about. A group of guests were standing on the porch with mugs of coffee, talking in low tones, as though appraising the weather and their ability to go out into it.

"Wait here," said Brody. "I'll be right back."

Which left Kit alone on the porch with the guests. He went to stand by the last pole on the porch, so as to be on the edge of things, to not be in anybody's way. But one of the men came up to him, and pointed at him with his mug of coffee.

"Do you work here?" the man asked.

"Of course he does, Grant," said a second man, joining the conversation as though he'd been invited. "He's dressed like a real cowboy, except for the hat. Where's your hat, kid?"

"It's in the room," said Kit. "We don't usually wear our hats in the dining hall."

"When's it going to stop raining, kid?" asked Grant, and if his tone was gruff and somewhat accusing, Kit tried to shake it off. "We paid good money for this trip, more than enough, to have it ruined by rain."

"Grant—" said the second man in a chiding tone. "It's not his fault."

Up came Brody with a box curled in one arm. He slung his other arm around Kit's shoulders, and pulled him close.

"That's right, Grant," said Brody, the words polite but edged with chill. "Nobody human is in charge of the weather up here, but the flanks of Iron Mountain can tell you what's coming. All day the edges of that mountain have been greyed with damp, and if you'd taken the time to look, you'd know better than to accuse Kit here of making it rain. Besides, he's my new assistant and he's got more important things to do than listen to you bitch."

"Sorry," said the second man, while Grant sputtered, looking like he wanted to fume and rant a bit more. But Brody pulled Kit off the porch and into the drizzle, like he didn't give a damn what Leland might have to say about his behavior with guests. That was the kind of bravery Kit wanted to have, to be able to stand up for himself and others, rather than lashing out or running away.

"Thanks, Brody," said Kit, enjoying the taste of Brody's name on his tongue.

They walked along the path, beneath the dripping trees, hurrying to get to the staff quarters and out of the rain. Kit's long-sleeved shirt was dotted with rain, and Brody's dark hair glistened with it, and he was smiling as he opened the door to their room and bowed to Kit to enter.

On the bed was a small cardboard box with the smiling Amazon logo on the side.

"Can we open it now?" asked Kit, going over to it, fingers sliding over the seam. There was no telling what was inside.

"Shower first, youngling," said Brody. He put the box he'd been carrying on top of the dresser. "Then dry clothes, as I don't want either of us catching cold."

Kit raced to shower, smiling the whole while. When he looked

169

down at himself, the bruises hardly showed at all, and his body didn't ache, and he simply didn't know what to do with all the happiness that bubbled inside of him. Drying off, he hung his towel on the rack, and dressed in soft sleep boxers and t-shirt and marched out into the room with a ta-da gesture to show Brody he was ready.

"Now me," said Brody. He shook his finger at Kit. "No peeking, okay?"

"Okay," said Kit with a solemn nod.

Kit did not peek, but he did shake the box on the bed a little, just to test it. The box was mostly light, with a bit of weight at one end, which told Kit exactly nothing about the contents. The box on the dresser was sealed with only a round sticker with the ranch's logo on it, and though Kit picked at the edges of the sticker, he didn't open it.

"That's enough now," said Brody as he came out of the bathroom on a cloud of steam, smiling, dressed for bed. "Get that box and come sit on the bed with me."

Doing as he was told, eager, he carried the box to the bed and clambered to sit next to Brody.

"Now," said Brody as they sat side by side, their bare thighs touching as the rain pelted the window over the bed. "Which box first?"

"This one," said Kit, shaking the box he held. At Brody's nod, Kit peeled back the sticker and opened the loosely closed box. From inside he pulled out a tall thermos, a battered two-slice toaster, and two short brown plastic cups. "What is this?" asked Kit as he picked up one of the plastic cups.

"Now open this," said Brody. He took the box from Kit and handed him the Amazon one. "Open it."

Kit knew how to open an Amazon box, so he tore through the webbed tape and popped the box open. Inside, amidst way too much bubble wrap were two smaller boxes, and even before Kit turned them over, he knew that they were boxes of Pop Tarts. Blueberry flavored, one frosted, one not. Beneath that was a package of beef jerky, a can of Pringles potato chips, and a little bag of chocolate covered macadamia nuts.

"I know you know by now how good Levi's blueberry scones are," said Brody. "But this will be for when we're jonesing for junk food."

"Junk food," said Kit as he tried the idea of it on for size, that the food he was used to eating to live on was considered by Brody, and probably by Levi, too, as junk, food to eat for fun, not to survive. "I do like those scones," he added. "But look at this. *Look* at it!" He held up both boxes like he was showing Brody bowls of gold.

"The idea is to heat one of each kind, frosted and unfrosted," said Brody. "And then we can drink the milk in the thermos to go with it. Levi wants the toaster back, but he says we can keep the plastic glasses, as the dining hall has plenty."

Kit turned the glass in his hand, recognizing it now. Sometimes when they got orange juice, they drank out of those little glasses, but mostly they didn't because Brody didn't seem to like orange juice. And now they would have something to keep in the bathroom when they needed water.

"Thank you," said Kit, his mouth watering to taste that frosting. "Seriously. Thank you."

"You toast and I'll pour."

Kit scrambled off the bed to plug in the toaster, which he placed on top of the dresser, and while Brody poured two glasses of milk from the thermos, Kit opened the boxes and the silver packets inside, and popped one of each kind in the toaster. Frosted on the left, and unfrosted on the right.

When the toaster dinged and popped the Pop Tarts up, Kit hurriedly placed half of a slice of each on the paper plates and blew on his fingers. He'd forgotten how volcanic hot Pop Tarts were. Then, standing, they savored several bites of each kind, and when Kit watched Brody lick his lips, he licked his own in sympathy.

"There's something pure about the unfrosted kind," said Brody, as serious as could be. "But the frosting just takes it over the top, you know?"

"Pow," said Kit, smiling as he gobbled down the rest of his two-half slices. The flavor went bland on his tongue as the Pop Tarts cooled and he washed that away with a swallow of milk. "Frosted for sure," he said.

"Yeah, frosted." Brody shook his head. "But gah, the aftertaste."

"Yeah," said Kit. "I didn't realize it before, but it's there."

Standing there, barefooted, bare legged, feeling the chill of rain come in through the single open window over the desk, Kit knew there were a lot of things he'd not realized before now, before he'd come to the ranch. And the biggest was this: that the simplest things could be enjoyed without a lot of fanfare, and that his favorite thing in the whole world was when Brody looked at him like he was looking now. Kind of out of the corner of his eye, as if he'd been looking at something else, but had been paying attention to Kit all along. And that what he saw, Kit in his clothes for sleeping, his hair messy, probably, was exactly what he wanted to see, and that he wanted for nothing different.

"Let's finish the milk and rinse out the thermos so we can take it back to Levi in the morning," said Brody. "And the toaster too. And we'll be sure to tell Levi that his scones win over the Pop Tarts."

"Yes," said Kit, hardly believing how much he agreed.

After they finished the milk, they rinsed the thermos and their new plastic glasses, and put everything in the box to take to Levi in the morning. Then they brushed their teeth, and Kit's body relaxed as the evening ritual continued. The only difference was, Brody closed all the windows so the rain wouldn't get in while they slept and ruin the wooden floors.

"I'd hate for Stella to have to deal with that," said Brody. "And here, I promised you this."

Brody turned off all the lights except the one on the nightstand, and grabbed a book from the little bookshelf. He climbed on the bed and patted the space beside him, and Kit was never so happy to oblige.

"What're we doing?" asked Kit, as Brody flipped through the pages of the book. It was one of Brody's horse books, with large drawings of horses, fully colored and looking almost alive.

"We're going to compare horses to people," said Brody. He pointed to a picture of a tall, long legged copper colored horse. "Here. This one is Leland."

"It looks like the horse he rides," said Kit.

"Big Red," said Brody, nodding. He turned the pages and pointed out horses that he thought resembled people on the ranch. "This is a Haflinger, which is Clay, and this red roan is Austin, and this is a grey-spotted Percheron, which is Jasper, and this sleek looking chestnut Pony of America is Jamie—"

"And what am I?" asked Kit, reaching to grab the book, but then he pulled back, almost warm from the idea of it, that there'd be a horse that Brody would look at and think of him. "Which one am I?"

"Oh," said Brody. "Yes, I've picked you out." Turning through the pages, Brody opened the book wider at the image of a creamy-white pony with pert ears and sweet, dark eyes. "This is you. It's a Welsh pony, so sweet, graceful. Even-tempered."

"I'm even tempered?" asked Kit, thinking that it couldn't be so.

"Well you are," said Brody. "Most of the time, and you *are* sweet, and are just looking for someone to be nice to you."

"You're nice to me," said Kit, the words breathy and heartfelt.

"Well then," said Brody, and it seemed like he was blushing as he tried to close the book. "I don't know what horse Levi is and I've never been able to figure out which one Quint is—"

"But what about you?" asked Kit. He tugged the book to him and licked his fingers to shuffle through the pages so fast, they threatened to tear. "Which one are you?"

"Don't know," said Brody. He leaned back against the wall, chin tilted up like he was contemplating the rain in the half dark, lit only by the lamp on the nightstand. "Never thought about it."

"This one." Kit played the book on Brody's lap, the pages opened to a horse that looked like Gwen, with a golden-tan coat and a black mane and tail. "It's a buckskin. You remind me of a buckskin, like Gwen is. She's different from the others, but beautiful. Like you."

Brody's face softened as he looked at Kit, as if he was realizing in that moment that Kit had given him something he'd not known he was looking for.

"I love buckskin horses," said Brody. He rubbed his thumb along his lower lip, and seemed to look to the side as though searching for a memory. "I always thought they were the prettiest, smartest horses."

"Well, they are," said Kit, bumping his shoulder against Brody's. "Just like you."

With a smile, Brody tousled Kit's hair, and closed the book, making all the gestures that it was bedtime. Kit didn't want to sleep in his own cot that night but since he didn't know how to ask for anything else, he crawled between the sheets, pulling the light blanket up to his chin.

"It's chilly with the rain," said Brody. He was reaching for something in the upper shelf of the closet, and when he came over to Kit, he had a blanket. This he laid over Kit, gently, and bent to fold the top sheet over the blanket, tucking it beneath Kit's chin. "Sleep well."

"You too," said Kit as Brody turned out the light at his bedside, and the room went dark. Leaving Kit with feelings, good feelings that seemed to swirl out of him, reaching toward Brody, in bed, curled on his side, facing the wall. It wouldn't be right to bother Brody with questions Kit wasn't sure the shape of, so they would wait until morning.

KIT

*W*hen Kit walked with Brody up to the main arena, where the riding lesson was to be held, he felt like he was ten feet tall and covered with hair. Neither of those were true, of course, but he had a cowboy hat on and a snap-button shirt in the prettiest gentle plaid pattern of grey-blue and rust, which Brody had picked out for him.

The new blue jeans fairly crackled their newness around him, and as for the cowboy boots on his feet? They made him feel ten and a *half* feet tall. The dust from the road barely seemed to dim their glamour, and it was hard to pretend he wasn't looking at his feet as he walked.

Brody went right up to the arena, where ten guests waited inside, already holding the reins to their horses. Clay was in the arena, too, and everybody was looking at Brody, and not at Kit at all, which was fine. Except then Brody introduced him.

"Thank you everyone, for joining us today," said Brody as he stepped between the fence rails to stand inside the sandy arena. "And to Clay who is going to lead the lesson. Also, I'd like to introduce my assistant, Kit, who is learning the ropes, and will be joining the lesson."

Everybody waved at Kit as Clay led a horse over to Kit, and

handed him the reins, like he fully expected Kit would know what to do with them. The horse was Chiquita, who he had already met, and while Kit wanted to reach and pet her, he didn't. His whole body felt frozen. They were going to make him ride a horse, after all.

He could leave. That was one choice. He could steal a bunch of coins from the laundry room, and he had a whole stack of new clothes. He could make it to Vegas by bus in three days if he left right now.

But Brody was looking at him, smiling that smile, soft and low, and almost expectant that Kit would somehow magically grow wings and be able to not only get on the horse but ride it. It was hard to walk away from that smile, and tomorrow it would be even harder, as that smile seemed to be sinking its hooks into him, and Brody had already said he wanted Kit to stay.

So he was going to stay, for now. Just for now. Until Katie called.

The lesson started easily enough. Clay explained the parts of a horse, the parts of the saddle, and demonstrated how to mount with a little hop-hop motion before he pulled himself astride.

All the guests were eager learners and laughed as they tried to mount, and Clay and Brody hurried to help them lift their legs over the saddles.

When Brody came to help Kit, Kit wanted to shout at him to go away, he didn't need help, he never needed help. But Brody's strong hands were around his hips, guiding him, and a touch of Brody's fingers to the back of his knee helped him bend his knee so he could fit his foot in the stirrup.

His new cowboy boot slid into the stirrup like it was made for it, like it was greased with butter, and then, as his heel caught the stirrup, the boot seemed locked into place. Which was so cool, Kit was able to lift himself up and swing his leg over to land in Chiquita's saddle with a bit of a thump. Now he was tall, and Brody looked up at him, his hand resting on Kit's bright blue-jeaned thigh.

"Nice," said Brody, from the shadow of his straw cowboy hat. "You'll get the hang of it."

The lesson continued from there, with Clay giving them instructions to gently squeeze the sides of their mount, and maybe to click encouragement as they lifted the reins from their horses' necks. While Brody monitored the horses from the middle of the arena, several feet away from Clay, the horses walked sedately around the arena, their noses brushing the butt of the horse in front of it.

Kit rode at the back of the line of horses, which made sense, as he was part of the ranch staff, amazingly enough, and everybody else was a guest. He sat up straight in the saddle as Chiquita ambled along beneath him, and the sensation of being quite high off the ground settled into that walk, the gentle rhythm of it.

The leather saddle was hard beneath him, and slippery, and there was a bit of dark horse mane caught in his reins, so he leaned forward to untangle it. His legs slid back, still in the stirrups, and—bam, Chiquita shied beneath him—fast—and Kit went over the horse's head and landed with his ass in the dirt.

Chiquita loomed above him, dancing on her feet like he was a live snake about to bite him. Kit rolled, the sand gritting into his skin through his shirt, and crouched beneath the fence rails, watching Chiquita's iron-shod hooves move closer and closer and he tensed, waiting for the moment when the mare would kick him in the head.

"Hey, now," said Brody as he came up, and all Kit wanted to do was curl into a ball so Brody couldn't find him. Which was ridiculous. The sun was shining in the sky and there wasn't a cloud to be had. Brody could see him, plain enough, which meant that inside of a moment, Brody was crouched down, Kit's new straw cowboy hat in his hand. "Easy," he said. "I was watching. You leaned forward and kicked her flank, which is very sensitive."

"Fuck this," said Kit, tasting sand and dust. He bit his lip before he could say anything more because even he knew, even without Quint's warnings, that you couldn't say stuff like that when there were guests around. "Fuck it," he said anyway, low, grinding it out.

"Do me a favor," said Brody, drawing Kit's gaze to him, to the worried expression in his shifting-colored blue-gold eyes, his dark hair sticking to his temple in the warmth of the day. "All these guests are beginners just like you, but there's something to be gained here.

Show them. Get up on that horse and show them how it's done. *Be* the example. Otherwise, they all might get scared and quit."

"You kiddin' me?" Kit spat out and of course, Brody wasn't kidding. Brody seemed like the kind of guy who took his job very seriously, kind of like the bronc rider Katie had dated, and now he wanted Kit to do the impossible.

"Please, Kit?" asked Brody. He dipped his chin and looked at Kit like he was his last hope. "It'd mean a lot to the ranch. To me. And to yourself."

Kit didn't give a damn what it would mean, only that Brody had asked him. Had said *please* in that soft voice, had said Kit's name in that way that reached inside of Kit and tugged at him, all of his attention focused on Kit.

When Brody reached out his hand, Kit took it and let Brody help him to his feet. With deft, warm hands, Brody brushed the sand from Kit's new blue jeans and handed him his new straw cowboy hat.

"It's all you, Kit," said Brody, his mouth making that shape like it enjoyed the feel of Kit's name on his tongue. "Up you get, then."

Brody drew Chiquita close as he petted her neck and whispered in her ear. She flicked her tail at both of them, but seemed content to stand there and let Kit fumble with the stirrup, which seemed higher than it had the first time, and scramble aboard her back, heart thumping, sweat breaking out beneath his armpits. At least Brody stood there with the mare's reins in his hands, looking like he wasn't going to let go and hand the reins over to Kit until he was good and ready.

"Wave," said Brody, low. "Wave to the guests."

Kit did as he was told, lifting his arm high and waving like he was the king of the parade. The guests laughed and clapped, and suddenly Kit felt a rush move through him. It might have been pride or joy, he didn't know, only that it made his fear seem like a distant memory.

"Play into it," said Brody. He looped the reins around Chiquita's neck and handed them to Kit. "That's your audience."

Mouth dry, heart pounding, Kit nodded at Brody and touched his finger to his hat before looking up. All the guests were looking at him with wide eyes.

"I'm ready," he said loudly, so everyone could hear him.

Everyone clapped again, and Clay stepped up and took over the lesson. Kit rode slowly at the back of the line, kept his hands on his reins and didn't get bucked off again. But he was covered in his own sweat and horse hair and dust by the time the lesson was over and he hurt everywhere.

As he dismounted, Brody and Clay were talking to the guests, totally absorbed in chatting and smiling, like everything was okay. Only Kit's hip hurt bad, and he didn't think Brody would appreciate the interruption, so he loosely tied Chiquita any old how to a post, and walked off, or tried to.

Nobody saw him leave, nobody noticed, and maybe that was a good thing. The stab in his hip caused him to limp and his new boots with their slick soles made him slip and the stairs were steep and it was ages till he got to the room at the end of the hall.

It had been too much, just too much. He wasn't cut out for this, not at all, and not all the fancy slick cowboy boots in the world was going to make one bit of difference. He'd fallen off during his first lesson. They were going to shove him into the kitchen to work full time there, that was a given.

As for his fear, nobody gave a damn. Brody had *made* him step into the limelight, like almost getting kicked by a horse or stepped on or bit was nothing. Like he should shake it off and just keep going. Which was what Katie would do when Kit had gotten smacked around by his teammates after a football game in gym class for simply not being able to catch the ball or stumbling over his own feet when he tried to run with it.

You're fine, Katie would always say. *You're fine, stop being a baby and get your mom some ice down at the 7-11 cause the damn ice machine's broken at the motel.*

Fumbling, Kit took off the cowboy boots and tossed them hard against the wall, leaving a mark and a dent in the plaster, and stripped off all his clothes. Left them in a pile and went into the bathroom to turn on the shower. He made the temperature just the way he liked it, the perfect shade of rain-warm, and stepped in and sat down beneath the spray.

His hip ached, but nobody would care if he told them, so he wasn't going to. He'd just have to get through this on his own, just like he had to with everything else. Like getting yelled at by the gym teacher for only having one pair of sneakers. Or getting detention for failing yet another math test and being a clown about it by putting the test with the F in red pencil on it on his head so he could pretend it didn't matter. Or when the kids made fun of him because he smelled because the motel he and Katie were staying at was out of soap, and she'd used what little there had been.

You just punch those kids, Katie would say when he told her. *Just punch 'em. That'll shut them up.*

Only when he had tried punching, those kids had older brothers and sisters, and Kit's ability to do anything about that vanished after he'd gotten slammed into the brick wall outside the cafeteria, over and over and over. After that, he stopped telling Katie, and did his best on his own.

You're not hurt. You're fine. Walk it off.

But what was he supposed to do when he could barely walk? His leg was stiffening even as the warm water spilled over it.

Sometimes, when Katie had gone out late, he'd do this in the motel shower, sit at the bottom of the stall and pretend it was raining. That he was in the tropics, naked except for maybe a loincloth. He carried a knife made out of bone or shell or something and he was barefoot and brave and utterly fearless.

Then Katie would come home and holler for him to get out because she'd ordered pizza or brought home tacos. And then he'd have to get out of the shower, dripping wet, the game of pretend in his head at an end.

Head bowed, Kit pressed his forehead against his bent knee, rubbing his hip, licking the water that slid into his mouth. Eyes shut tight, the sense of rain all around him.

When he heard the door open, he froze.

"Kit?" he heard Brody call. "Are you in the shower?"

Of course he was in the shower, there was no place else for him to be. What did Brody care anyhow?

"Are you okay?"

His body tightening, Kit raced over his options. He could get up, or try to, and hop out of the shower to grab a towel and go about the business of drying off, like anybody would. That seemed the best route to take. Only when he braced himself to stand, his hand slipped against the side of the stall, and he thudded against the side of the shower, water in his eyes, the back of his head thumping, his hip screaming at him.

"Kit."

That sound. Of his name. The way Brody said it went straight into Kit's heart and he wanted to cry. He was going to lose this because he was a stupid stupid idiot who didn't know how to not kick a horse in the flanks. And who didn't deserve new cowboy boots. Or anything. Not *anything*.

"Kit, I'm coming in."

Brody opened the door and stepped into the bathroom and reached into the shower to turn it off.

"There's water all over the floor, what're you—"

Brody stopped. Crouched down, moisture beading his forehead, sticking his dark hair to his temples. Kit was naked and wet and stuck, everything on display, his cock limp against his thigh, his sparse pubic hair, splayed around by the water. His hip cramped and he tried to rub it, but it didn't help, and Brody was still *looking* at him—

"Let me help you up."

As though completely unconcerned that Kit was wet and naked, Brody leaned close and slipped his arm around Kit's shoulders, beneath his arms, and hauled him to his feet in one strong, steady move.

Brody didn't seem to care that he was now soaked to the skin, that Kit's bare hip was rubbing against Brody's bejeaned groin, though he hissed as if in sympathy when Kit's hip cramped again and he had to balance on one foot while trying to rub his hip.

"You got banged up bad," said Brody. "You're already black and blue where you landed. I'm sorry, I didn't—"

"Shut up," spat Kit. "Just shut up. You don't care, so don't pretend you do."

Normally, any of Katie's men would have taken offense to Kit snarling at them and smacked him or tripped him. Brody, instead, grabbed a towel from the rack and gently wrapped it around Kit's shoulders. Then he reached up into the medicine cabinet for the single tube of numbing cream in there and, still supporting Kit with one arm beneath his shoulders, popped the cap with his thumb. The click was loud in the small bathroom, almost bouncing off the damp tiles.

Kit shuddered a breath, tried to stop it. Failed. When Brody's fingers touched his hip, Brody's grip shifted and Kit was flat against him, hip to hip, his belly damp against Brody's belt buckle. Heartfelt, his sigh was almost a sob as he buried his face into Brody's neck, and let Brody stroke the medicine cream into his hip, his naked, damp behind.

Bits of warmth soaked into him from Brody's fingertips, from the steady way he smoothed the cream into Kit's skin. More warmth surrounded him from Brody's arm around his shoulders, holding him close, Brody's breath as it eased past his face, down his neck.

The towel dropped away, slithering to the floor between them. And for a moment, Brody's hand paused, fingers curled around Kit's bottom.

Kit's cock pushed against his belly, forcing its way between them, and when he looked up, Brody blinked at him, like he was surprised by this but not repelled. Not repulsed. But rather as though Kit's body's desires were natural, just part of the day.

Then Kit sensed that Brody was hard too, his cock an iron bar, but whether Brody really wanted him or this was just how his body was reacting to a naked Kit in his arms, Kit didn't want to find out the truth for sure.

"I'm okay," Kit said, breathing the words against Brody's neck as he ducked his head once more. "I'm fine."

"Sure you are," said Brody as though bemused by Kit's lie. "Let the cream soak in and then dry off. Take some Advil. Better make it four. Then get dressed in clean clothes. And next time, when you're hurt, you tell me. Understand?"

Kit shrugged Brody's arm off him, and stepped back, half stumbling on the towel but holding his hand out for Brody to leave him be.

"I said understand?"

"Sure," said Kit, fighting it. Fighting the care and concern in Brody's expression, the way he held his hands out like he was totally ready to catch Kit if he fell. Like he had all the patience in the world for whatever Kit needed.

When Brody stepped away, it was like having part of him sliced off. As though the moment between them had connected them somehow, only Brody was denying it had ever happened. Except the look in his eyes told Kit in no uncertain terms that it *had* happened, only Brody didn't know what to do with it any more than Kit did.

"I need to get back and help Clay groom the horses from the lesson," said Brody, half whispering. "Want to join me?"

Of course, Brody was ever-responsible, just like everyone on the ranch seemed to be. But as hard as Kit tried to rouse his anger, to reject everything that Brody was, tall and strong and just way too cool for the likes of Kit, he couldn't manage it. Didn't know if he wanted to, even if it would be hard as hell to keep that moment close to his heart and nurse it into a fuller bloom.

To Brody, getting back to work was the order of things. But he'd taken care of Kit, made sure he had what he needed, like it mattered to him how Kit felt. And, rather than being told to walk it off, as would have happened with Katie, he was being offered a place at Brody's side.

"Sure," he said. "I just need a clean shirt."

"I'll get you one," said Brody. Then he stepped out of the bathroom and closed the door behind him.

Leaving Kit with his cock still against his belly, his face flushed from the total awareness that Brody had seen him this way. And his heart full of a very small fire, low and timidly flickering, that maybe this would be different. This time. This place.

20

BRODY

*T*he beginning of a new week was always a busy time, and Brody was still adjusting to the energy growing between him and Kit, Kit who stuck to his side at every possible chance, and who seemed to value Brody's opinion over all others. And who was such a comfortable presence that when Stella told Brody that someone from the kitchens had quit and there was a room available on the first floor, Brody had told her, thanks but no thanks, and never mentioned it to Kit.

Maybe he should asked Kit about this because maybe Kit would want his own room, where he could have his own space, a bit of privacy. It nagged him to the point that even as he was waiting outside of Maddy's office for his turn to be interviewed for the documentary about Wyoming and guest ranches, he whistled to Kit to come close.

Kit was dressed for the interview in his newest jeans, polished boots, his straw cowboy hat carefully dusted. The hat seemed a little big for him, but maybe that was simply because he was still growing into his shoulders, still figuring out how far back to set the hat on his head.

He seemed to want to be interviewed because it all seemed so exciting to him. Even as Brody wanted to warn him how draining it could be, he kept his mouth shut about that and let Kit enjoy the excitement swirling around them both.

"What is it?" asked Kit, practically skipping up the steps, eager, looking to Brody, almost pushing people aside to get to him.

"Stella mentioned there was a room that opened up," said Brody. He tugged on the tassels on his cream-colored suede vest, making sure they were untangled, looking for dust spots on his cream-colored suede chaps. The bits of silver and turquoise that bound each tassel on the vest sparkled like daytime stars, and the fringes on the chaps moved like sea foam across his thighs. "I told her we were fine, but I thought I'd let you know, in case you thought different."

"Yes," said Kit, his face brightening, rising up on his toes, hands in his back pockets as though to keep him still. "I mean, no, or whatever. The cot's fine. Besides, I like sharing a room with you."

There was Kit's heart, right there on his sleeve, plain as anything. He was like a newly bloomed flower, standing there in the shade of the porch of Maddy's office. Inside, Bill was finishing up, talking to the cameraman and the interviewer who was making the documentary about Wyoming. He was also talking about Old Joe and his little red fox, in spite of Leland's hasty gesture that Bill should just shut the hell up about it. Bill firmly ignored Leland, finished answering the questions, and stood up and strode out of the office and past Brody and Kit and into the bright sunshine.

"That'll show him," said Bill, seemingly to himself. Bill was his own man, and when he nodded at Brody and tipped his hat at Kit, Brody tipped his hat in return, careful not to smudge the cream-colored suede.

Next up for being interviewed was Levi, who came dressed in a new set of cook's whites, his apron carefully tied about his waist, his chestnut hair as glossy as could be. The only thing out of place was his expression, which was grim, his eyes dark.

Levi had made it plain he did not want to be filmed, did not want to be on camera, but as head chef, director of dining services, Leland had made it equally plain that Levi needed to allow himself to be interviewed.

But that was Levi, all over the place. He was from back east, so maybe that was why he didn't want to be seen, kept himself to himself for the most part, and answered the questions with short answers, his face tight, no warmth in his voice at all, and he hastened away as soon as he could.

"I'm next," said Brody to Kit as the cameraman gestured to him that it was his turn.

"Will I be interviewed after that?" asked Kit, hope shining in his eyes.

"You're on the list, right?" asked Brody. "Check with Maddy, okay? Make sure."

Taking a breath to still his nerves, Brody touched Kit on the shoulder, as if for good luck, and marched into the display area of Maddy's office. This was where she kept old journals and books and silver spoons and all the trinkets and things she'd collected while researching the history of the ranch. Everything was in a glass case, neatly described on small cards in front of each item. Sometimes she rotated out what she kept in boxes, but mostly she didn't, and the display stayed the same.

The bright lights on stands that the cameraman had placed around gleamed on the sepia-toned photographs arranged on the wall. Some of the photos were of John Henton's cabin in various stages of disrepair. Others were of the hills around the ranch before all the trees were planted, and also of Jasper's cabin by the river, how it used to look before it was expanded to include plumbing and modern electricity.

Brody did his best to focus on the things that he knew, fists clenched as he sat down. It wasn't that he was shy, or timid about answering questions on camera. More, it was that he was too experienced with being in the limelight, dressed for rope tricks.

If he let it, the image of Daddy Frank would appear right next to the cameraman, or maybe on the other side of the interviewer, who was currently comfortably ensconced in an old leather chair. When he'd been on the circuit with Bryson and Daddy Frank, sometimes they got interviewed to publicize their act or whatever county fair they were in, and Daddy Frank would school them as to what to say. *Always be positive, never complain.*

If they answered the questions wrong, after the interview was over, Daddy Frank would haul them off and whip them. And then, aching and sore, he'd make them do the interview over, with Daddy Frank acting as the man behind the microphone.

Most days, pretty much, Brody could go on like all of this was behind him, because it was. But now the memories came back hard and fast even as the interviewer started chatting, making Brody comfortable before the real interview began.

"Hey, Brody, thanks for being here with us today," said the interviewer. "I'm Finn Keating and this is Artie Larkin, my cameraman and all around right-hand man."

"Hey," said Brody, using his fringed cream-colored suede gloves as a kind of welcome flag.

"Normally I do videos about ghost hunting, but sometimes I like to take a break from that." Finn smiled and then chatted on, doing that thing good interviewers did, which was talk and smile and make like the person being interviewed wasn't going to be in a hard, glaring spotlight in about a minute and a half. They acted like they had all the time in the world, and that nothing scary was going to happen.

Brody was not scared, not of Finn anyway, He did his best to be distracted by what Finn was telling him, that Finn also did ghost tours in Harlin, Colorado, and wrote ghost stories, had a ghost blog, and about how doing interviews about life in Wyoming was a kind of side gig, a second stream of income. And could Brody tell Finn anything more about Old Joe, the ranch's famous ghost, according to Bill?

Leland appeared right where Brody had imagined Daddy Frank was standing. He shook his head at Brody as he pointed his finger at the door, as if to summon Bill back into the room, like he wanted him to renounce everything he'd said about Old Joe and his fox friend.

"Let's skip that one," said Brody. "I don't know much about it."

He actually did, since he always had time for Bill and his stories, and felt there was something fey about it that only Bill remembered telling that particular story around the campfire on cookout night.

But his heart was hammering now as Leland stood there, watching over the proceedings, making sure Brody answered all the questions in just the way he should.

Leland was not Daddy Frank, not by any stretch of the imagination, but with Brody dressed up like he was, answering questions like he was, the bright lights shining in his face, it was all coming back to him like a rising swamp of confusion and fear that Daddy Frank was simply not going to tolerate any foolishness, and any boy unwise enough to disobey was going to get his ass blistered.

Searching the collection of people behind the bright lights, Brody wanted to imagine that Kit was there, watching wide eyed and hopeful, waiting for his turn to be in the spotlight. Brody would have given up his place, that very minute, to Kit, and he would have stood close by to make sure that Finn, the interviewer, didn't badger Kit with too many questions he simply couldn't answer, like how much hay horses ate during a season, and whether Brody went around dressed in cream-colored suede all the time—

"No," said Brody, putting on a smile he simply didn't feel while his breath caught in his throat and his lungs seemed to be simply unable to inhale. "It's for the interview."

"And later you'll do a demo for us, right?" asked Finn, pleasant and kind and totally unaware that Brody was feeling like he was about to slip off his stool and collapse to the floor while he begged Daddy Frank not to whip him, he didn't mean to screw up, *please, please, please*—

"Sure will," said Brody, the words ghosts on his tongue.

"We'll look forward to that," said Finn. "And we really appreciate your time today, so thank you."

"You're welcome," said Brody, remembering his manners as he stood up and stumbled past Finn and his cameraman and assistant, Artie, looking for Kit the whole time as someone stepped up to be interviewed next, the brightness of the day outside contrasting with the shadows and harsh lights of the display area.

Nobody was paying him any mind, which was fine by him. He'd

stumble out and get himself a drink of cool water and pretend that none of this had ever happened.

Someone came up to him and clasped his hand and stuck something cool into his palm.

"Here, Brody," said Kit from faraway. "I brought you this."

Doing his best to focus, Brody blinked at what was in his hand. It was a small brown bottle, mostly empty, that held his CBD oil.

"Take it," said Kit. "You don't look right."

Brody focused on Kit who, as he stood there in the low shadow of the porch, was sweating, his temples dappled with it, his hat in his hands, hair plastered to his forehead, breathing hard.

By all evidence, Kit had raced to their room and grabbed the oil, and not only was it killing Brody that Kit had seen Brody falling apart, but that Kit had risked losing his spot to be interviewed. And all because he cared. All because he was now Brody's rescuer.

"Okay."

Brody uncapped the small bottle and tipped the contents into his mouth, being careful not to get any on the suede because it would simply not come out. Not that the CBD oil would do him much good. The point of it was to take it ahead of time, like half an hour before he went to bed. It wasn't good at instantly blotting out the horror his memories had marched up and down in front of him.

But maybe that didn't matter. Taking the medicine that Kit had brought him was the point, and the gesture, the effort, was medicine in and of itself.

"What's going on?"

Quint came up the steps to the porch, as steady as could be, and created a shield between them and everyone else on the porch. The space for the three of them was small, but it was in the shade, and Brody had no hesitation showing Quint what was in his palm.

"Looks like you're almost out," said Quint, as he took the small bottle in his fingers and shoved it in his pocket. "Why didn't you say?"

"He took a lot because he couldn't sleep with me in the room," said Kit, scowling and fierce, looking up at Quint like he wanted to get rid of him somehow.

"That's not it," said Brody. "Not it at all."

"I'll go fetch you more," said Quint, looking at Kit in much the way an older, wiser dog will be bemused by a rascal of a young pup.

"No." Brody shook his head and took a deep breath. "I don't want you going to Colorado. It'd take too long. You'll be missed."

"I know a guy in Cheyenne," said Quint. "It'll take an hour tops. And next time, you tell me when you're running low. Hear?"

"I hear."

Having Quint scold him like that was helping, helping so much, but Quint probably knew that because he was still glowering at Brody like he was going to take Brody across his knee and give him a sound spanking, or whatever mock-threat he might come up with.

It took Brody back to their days in the trailer, in Port Aransas, where the world was made up of Quint carving his wooden animals and Brody studying for his GED, and nothing was scary except maybe the condition of the bottoms of the shower stalls in the KOA building after a long holiday weekend. An easier time. A sweet time.

Maddy came up to them with a clipboard in her hand and whether she was oblivious to what had just happened or was politely ignoring it, Brody didn't know. She was all business. Behind her, Brody sensed Artie focusing the camera on them, perhaps for some candid footage.

"You're up, Kit," she said. "Quint here has stoutly refused to be interviewed, and they need one more. Are you ready?"

Quint smiled at Brody and winked at Kit, and Brody's throat filled up with gratitude. Only Quint could get away with disobeying Leland's request so boldly, but also, he might know how desperately Kit wanted to be interviewed, to be on camera for a documentary. Though it was doubtful Katie would be even the least bit interested in the little film, it might also be the way for him to reach her, or so Kit must be hoping.

"Is it okay if I go, Brody?" asked Kit, looking up at Brody with wide eyes. "It'll be so cool—but I want to be sure. Is it okay?"

It was clear that if Brody indicated, even slightly, that he needed Kit to stay with him, Kit would forego the interview. Oh, sure, he'd stomp and pout, but he'd do it, holding onto Brody's hand, staying close.

But while you could rescue a fledgling bird and hold it in your cupped hands, the point was to lift your hands so the bird could fly. And Kit needed to fly. Needed to enjoy the excitement and be the most important person in the room for a good five minutes, which was how long Finn kept each person in the hot seat.

"Sure," said Brody. "You go on. You show 'em. I'll be here when you're done."

"You want to talk about it?" asked Quint as they both watched Kit race off, boot heels thumping on the wooden floor as he made his way through the small crowd to where Finn was.

"Later," said Brody.

"Okay then," said Quint with a warm hand to Brody's suede-covered shoulder. "I'll be here when you need me."

Quint was always there for him, and he did his best to be there for Quint in return, not that Quint seemed to need much from him. And now Quint wanted to make sure of Brody and Kit, as though that was the natural direction to take, the best next step.

Brody had a sudden impulse to ask Quint if they could buy back the old trailer from the young DIY couple Quint had sold it to. They could bundle together in blankets on the lower bunk, the way they used to do when summer was ending and the spot where the trailer was parked was due to be empty soon for the next person to rent it.

You couldn't go back to the old days and mostly Brody didn't want to. But it would have been nice to have that comfort, Quint's warm body next to his in the bunk, and the feeling that nothing and nobody could get at him.

Quint would do it if Brody asked him to. But while Brody wanted it, that sense of comfort, he knew the trailer was long gone and that Quint now had a shiny Airstream, and that Quint, as always, looked forward, looked to the future, the next step, the next stopover point. Quint didn't wallow in memories, he made new ones.

From the first moment of meeting Quint, Brody wanted to be like him. They were so different in many ways, but Brody wanted to look forward to the future, too.

"Let's watch the youngling," said Brody. "He'll ask, *didja see me?* And I want to be able to say yes, I did."

With a nod, Quint followed Brody back into the bustle of the small crowd as they made their way to where they could see Kit being interviewed.

With the spotlights on him, Kit sat forward in the old leather chair, his hands on his knees. His eyes were bright blue, polished pewter, his cheeks flushed. He'd scraped his damp hair back from his forehead, and his straw cowboy hat was adorably propped on the back of his head.

"I'm his assistant," said Kit, with all the joy, all the pleasure in the words so obvious to Brody it made his heart ache. "I'm still learning, and yeah, I miss my mom, so Katie, if you're out there, hi, from me."

Kit made a little wave at the camera, and Brody wanted to vow that if Katie didn't call her son back, Brody was going to head to Vegas and hunt her down himself. Who did that to their kid? Katie, that's who.

"What's the hardest thing you've had to do on the ranch?" asked Finn, now.

"Getting on a horse," said Kit. "Riding a horse."

"Really?" asked Finn, in a way that was obvious to Brody, because if you were scared of horses, why on earth would you work on a guest ranch?

"It's a fear I need to get over," said Kit. "Brody says some guests are scared of horses too, but they're here anyway. Same with me. I'm going to learn as much as I can to help them."

Brody hadn't said that exactly, but when he'd insisted Kit get back on Chiquita after being bucked off, that must have been what Kit had taken to heart.

"It's a big chance for me, and I'm lucky." Kit was nodding and while his eyes were still shining, his expression was solemn, the smile gone. "Lucky to be here. Lucky to be working for Brody."

Kit worked for the ranch, not for Brody, but as Kit got up and came over to where Quint and Brody were standing, working his way through the crowd, Brody didn't want to tell him that.

What he wanted to tell Kit was what he knew about horses. That a nervous horse became less nervous the more you talked to it, the more you paid attention to it. That a scared horse became calm the more you loved on it. And that was what he knew. That love could heal, if given time. That Kit had turned from a scared horse into a hopeful one was proof of that.

The only trouble was, when Katie did call, Kit would be on his way. Brody didn't know, wouldn't know, any other response that Kit could have to her crooking her finger at Kit to get him to come with her.

Brody couldn't hide Kit's phone or anything like that. He had to let Kit keep making those calls and leaving those messages. And then he'd have to let Kit go, which would break his heart.

But in the meantime, he could keep on the way he had been, doing what he was doing now which was, with his hat in his hands, carefully held by the edges so as not to mar the suede, to give Kit his biggest smile, hiding all his own worries and letting Kit have his moment.

"You were good," he said.

"Real good," added Quint. "Thanks for taking my place, there, Kit, cause there's nothing I hate worse than being interviewed. Nothing."

"Oh." Kit looked up at Quint like he'd just considered that maybe Quint was friend rather than foe. "Glad to," he said. "Any time."

"Are we done here?" asked Quint to no one in particular. "Could you eat?" he asked Kit, then he looked up at Brody. "You could eat, right? But you'll have to change out of that garb first."

Quint had bought that garb for Brody one summer when they'd signed on to a circuit of fairs that specifically asked for Brody's trick rope talents. It had been a good summer with lots of cash, but the sheen had worn thin quickly, and the circuit wasn't anything they signed up for again.

But now, as they headed up the dirt road beneath the green trees to the staff quarters so Brody could change, it felt like Quint was gently folding his wing over them both, like a Mama plover protecting her nestlings. And beneath that, Brody was spreading his wing over Kit, just Kit, drawing him close. Keeping a watchful eye.

It felt good, felt defining, to be the protector now, rather than the protected. Felt good to have Kit look up at him with shining eyes, his mouth shaped in a smile that seemed like it still felt new and unfamiliar.

Kit's hair was in his eyes. Brody reached up and shifted the forelock out of the way and Kit's smile deepened into warmth, into pleasure.

"I'm famous now, right?" asked Kit, though it was easy to see he was joking, playing around with the feeling of celebrity but willing to toss it away in the very next moment.

"You sure are," said Brody.

"Can I have your autograph?" asked Quint.

Quint laughed to show he didn't mean it, and Kit laughed with him, and Brody's heart was so full, it was about to burst.

Artie had taken photographs of each person both before and after their interviews. Maybe Brody could get a copy of a photograph of Kit, so he'd have something to look at when Kit left. In the meantime, he was hungry, which meant Kit was hungry, so they needed to hurry before they all starved to death. Which they wouldn't. There was never any fear of that, not on the ranch.

BRODY

*a*fter dinner, Brody had to get back in his suede outfit to do a demonstration on the dance floor that the staff assembled each week in front of the dining hall.

Most weeks there was a dance, outdoors, beneath the stars, with the night coming down like a dark purple cloak. But most weeks Brody didn't have to demo his trick roping skills, only this week he did because Finn and Artie had set up their camera, and the band was tuning up, and all the guests were waiting to see what he could do.

Trick roping had some standard basics, and the tricks weren't all that hard. The beauty of the display came with the pageantry, the costume, the right kind of western music, and the combination from simple flat loop tricks to the more sophisticated vertical tricks and back again in a kind of dance.

He wasn't nervous, now that the CBD oil had kicked in, and once everyone who was watching was on the other side of the lights, leaving Brody alone on the dance floor with only the shadows to watch him, he could imagine he was the only one present, him, and Kit watching.

He couldn't see Kit because of the lights, but he was there, Brody could feel his energy.

With a nod to the band to start up, and the three-two-one count from Finn, Brody began, the feeling familiar, the muscle memory slipping into gear.

He ran through the basics, which to him was a warm up, but which to the audience seemed like something amazing, first the flat spin to show them how fluid the rope was, then he tightened it around his body to show them how he was in control of the rope. He did a little crow step, then spun the rope behind his body, bringing it to the fore.

The band had to rush keep up with his pace, and that was just fine, it made everything he was doing more exciting to watch as he did a few Texas skips to gasps of astonishment and pleasure, and then, for the big finale, he did ocean waves on each side, and finished with a full-body wedding ring maneuver, the rope spinning outside his body, with him inside the loop.

Then he drew the wedding ring up and down several times, as it was pretty spectacular to watch, and then ended with the rope high up above his head, and then whipped the rope loose so it'd spin itself and wrap around his waist like a snake.

Then the applause came and he bowed, sweat dripping from his forehead. He whipped off his cream-colored suede hat to save it from stains, and gasped as someone barreled into him, arms around his waist. Through the gleam of Finn's camera lights, he saw it was Kit, who'd barged through the crowd, it seemed, unable to contain himself.

"You were great," said Kit, gasping and smiling, looking up at Brody. "You were so great. I wanna do that. I wanna be like you."

Brody considered that the last thing he wanted was for Kit to be like him as trick roping was no way to live a life. But what Kit meant was probably something different. Still, the glamour of being in the spotlight burned bright and fast, and after the audience was gone, it was all over and all you were left with was darkness.

"I'll teach you sometime," said Brody. There was a flash of light, maybe from a camera, as he flung his arm around Kit's shoulders and hugged him close and felt the warmth of the moment and wanted to hold it to him forever.

Guests and staff were moving around them both, putting up the fairy lights and turning them on, removing the camera, moving onto the dance floor for the next part of the evening's festivities.

He didn't want to stay and dance, was quite ready to be done being the center of attention, and if he stayed, especially wearing his trick roping outfit, he surely would be. But maybe Kit wanted to dance? It was a big deal with Leland that staff participate and mingle to make the evening a lively success, but it wasn't always required.

"Are we done?" asked Kit. "Can we go home now?"

Brody hugged him harder. Home for Kit was somewhere in Vegas, with Katie, but for now, his home was with Brody.

"Let's go," he said to Kit. "Hey, Leland," he called out to the boss who was hurrying by with a crate full of locally brewed root beer. "I think I'm done for the night."

"You did good," said Leland, giving Brody his nod of dismissal. "See you in the morning."

With quick steps, they walked together off the dance floor and onto the road that would lead them to the path to the staff quarters. With each step, the night grew cooler, and the silence swirled around them, the leaves shifting overhead in the dark-edged wind. With each step, Brody relaxed, his hat and gloves in his hands, Kit at his side.

"How'd you learn to do that?" asked Kit as Brody opened the door to their room and began peeling himself out of the cream-colored suede. "Did you learn online or something?"

"No."

Brody, stripped to his sweaty t-shirt and boxers, carefully brushed the suede outfit and hung it in its bag in the closet. He only wore it a few times a year, at Leland's special request, and typically on the first week and the last week of the season, to mark the passage of time. The rest of the time he forgot he even had it, as his trick rope days were far, far behind him.

"Daddy Frank taught me."

That was an understatement. Daddy Frank had beaten into him how to perform rope tricks and hadn't let up until Brody's level of skill had met his unreasonable expectations.

"I need to shower," he said, grabbing a clean pair of boxers and t-shirt for sleep. "You can go next, okay?"

"Okay."

Kit looked a little lost as Brody gently shut the bathroom door behind him, but he needed to get the sweat off his body, needed to cut the connection between him and the past, where he didn't want to be. He always said yes when Leland asked him to do a demo, but sometimes it was harder after the performance than during it.

Showering quickly, he came out in a waft of steam to find Kit, propped on the edge of his cot and hard at work wiping his new brown cowboy boots down, using the soft rag to remove any traces of dust.

The boots were still too new to need any polish, but when Kit looked up at Brody, eyebrows raised, Brody felt as though he was leaving traces of himself all over Kit, so when Katie next saw him, she'd hardly recognize him. Which might not be fair, but Katie was the one who'd left Kit behind so maybe she deserved it.

"Go ahead and shower," said Brody with a nod to the bathroom. "Then we can finish up our boots together."

That Kit was willing to have such a quiet evening with him when there was dancing and festivities at the dining hall spoke to Brody's heart. That Kit would rather be with him than having fun with everyone else—the idea of it—soaked into him like a balm, easing the jagged edges leftover from the demo.

He made sure the windows were open to catch the breeze, pulled out the bag of gorp from beneath the bed and got the boot polish and the cloths, the little brush for the boots' seams, and arranged everything on his bed. Then he sat on his bed with his back against the wall. All the while he listened to the sounds of another human being in the shower. Connected with that sound, and wondered how empty he would feel when Kit left. And how he would manage that emptiness.

When Kit danced into the room, still drying his hair with a towel, Brody knew it would hurt and hurt bad when Kit left, but for now he had this. Kit and him side by side on his bed in their soft sleep boxers and t-shirts, both of them serious and intent on cleaning their boots, and maybe Kit's boots could use a little polish on the toe, an extra wiping along the boot heel.

When they were done, the two pairs of boots sat side by side in the narrow closet with the rest of Brody's boots, and Brody held out the bag of gorp before placing it between them on the bed.

"Where's Daddy Frank now?" asked Kit as he reached into the bag to pull out a big handful of gorp, as though Daddy Frank had just stepped out or left on an errand and would soon be back. The question didn't hurt, though it did leave its trace. "And why do you call him Daddy Frank? Is he your dad or your uncle—?"

"He's dead," said Brody as he popped a handful of gorp into his mouth, enjoying the contrast between salty and sweet. "And I call him that because—" Brody stopped as the memories started up like a badly-spotted and aged old time eight millimeter film, with him so little and Bryson not much older and the man they knew as their dad turned into a taskmaster with his hard path to glory and fame. "He wasn't much of a dad," said Brody, licking his lips to taste the salt from the peanuts.

"Was he mean?" asked Kit, leaning close, reaching into the plastic bag of gorp at the same time Brody did. "Was he meaner than Eddie Piggot?"

Brody tangled his fingers with Kit's. He let himself enjoy that contact, just as he was enjoying how Kit's shoulder pressed against his, how the warmth of Kit's body meshed with his own, and how peaceful the moment was with just the two of them and the bag between them. Brody lifted the bag so it rested on his thighs, and so the weight of Kit's body could shift even closer.

"Eddie Piggot's an asshole and he's mean, for sure," said Brody. He licked his fingertips and watched Kit watching him do this. "But Daddy Frank was mean all the time. He wanted us to be trick rope stars—"

"Us?" asked Kit, his eyes wide.

"Me and my brother Bryson and no, before you ask, I don't know where he is."

Bryson had left Brody in Daddy Frank's clutches, though since he'd only been seventeen when he'd left, Brody could hardly have expected him to take his fifteen year old younger brother with him.

What a lot of responsibility that would have been, towing a kid with you when you were on the run. Finding food for two, shelter for two, trying to stay low so Daddy Frank didn't find you.

"Oh," said Kit now, and when he reached into the bag of gorp, Brody could feel the weight of those fingers against his thigh. "I don't have a brother. Just Katie. Maybe it would have been nice to have one. Was it nice?"

"For a while," said Brody.

"How did Daddy Frank die?"

For a moment, the question startled Brody, as part of his mind tended to believe that Daddy Frank was still out there somewhere, looking for his sons, trying to recapture the glory of the old days, when they were on the road, when doing rope tricks was something people who went to a county fair wanted to see. Part of him still believed that if he screwed up, Daddy Frank was going to find out. Which he never would because he was dead.

"It was a car accident," said Brody. "Leastways that's what Quint told me."

"Quint told you?" Now Kit looked worried, because, as it was plain to see, Quint scared the pants off him, and maybe he was a little jealous of the close friendship he sensed between Brody and Quint.

"We used to travel together, Quint and me," said Brody, leaving out all the details of their travels. "He was kind of protective, so when he found out what happened to Daddy Frank, he told me about it but said I could never do a search on it."

With a low sigh, Brody dipped his chin and looked at Kit who was leaning against him, looking down at the red candy, which was now staining his fingers as he rolled the candy over and over.

"He was drunk and went through a red light and smashed into a flatbed semi. Tore his head clean off."

Kit shuddered and moved close, his head leaning on Brody's shoulder.

"I'm sorry," said Kit. "D'you miss him?"

"No."

He would never miss Daddy Frank, had never missed him, didn't even miss not having a dad. Quint had been his dad and his brother and his friend, and that was more than some people had. When Daddy Frank died, that's when Brody started needing more CBD and sometimes even THC oil to help him sleep some nights.

The gorp bag was almost empty, so they finished it off, and Brody planned to make a stop at the dining hall for more, in the morning. In the meantime, the air coming through the screen windows was cool, and edged with the promise of autumn to come, which was how it was in Wyoming. Summer was just fully underway, and already the turn of the seasons was being announced on the breeze.

"Brush your teeth," said Brody. "I'll brush mine too. I'm beat."

Kit was so amiable, he seemed happy to brush his teeth and pee in the toilet with the door open when Brody was flipping off the lights.

The surprise came when Brody was crawling into bed. As he pulled back the sheets, he felt the weight of Kit's body beside him. He looked at Kit's outline, at the darker dark behind him, and the faint trail of light on the side of his face, his soft cheek.

"I just want to be with you," said Kit. "Is that okay?"

Brody could easily have shoved Kit off the bed and told him to go to his cot. But his own skin was burred rough from memories he knew were safe in the past but which had a way of marching in and sticking around. With Kit there, his focus could be on Kit and everything else could be safely hemmed back.

"Sure."

Brody scooted close to the wall and pulled the sheet and light blanket back so Kit could climb in. When Kit settled, Brody let his arm fall over Kit's waist, because really, Kit was so slight and the night air would be cold in the morning, and Kit needed his share of blanket and sheet.

Right away, Kit's warmth joined Brody's warmth and he sighed, and closed his eyes, and curled his fingers up to trail around the curve of Kit's neck.

"Do you miss him?" asked Kit, nighttime low.

"Who? Daddy Frank?"

"No, your brother. Do you miss him?"

"Sometimes," said Brody. "Not now, though." He didn't add that the reason he didn't miss Bryson was because he had Quint and the ranch —and he had Kit, who shifted in the bed like he wanted to snuggle closer and when he did, the curve of his bottom matched the hollow of Brody's hips. When Kit sighed, Brody sighed, each in tandem with the other.

"Do you miss it, the trick roping?" asked Kit, and then he yawned and tipped his head back so his hair brushed Brody's chin.

"No."

"But why?" Kit's question rose in the darkness of the room. "You're so good at it."

"Because," said Brody. He eased forward and gently, secretly, pressed a kiss to the top of Kit's head. "Those days are long ago. Sleep now. Morning comes early."

22

KIT

$\mathcal{M}$orning found Kit tucked into Brody's arms, pressed against him, with Brody's elbow hooked around Kit's neck kind of like he'd fallen asleep mid-hug. The most amazing part was that when Brody opened his eyes, and Kit had been waiting ages, it seemed, for this to happen, Brody didn't shove him away or act pissed that Kit was hogging the bed, the pillow, not even that maybe Kit's breath smelled sour from sleep.

Instead, Brody merely shook his head in a sleepy way, like he didn't know how Kit had gotten in his bed, and that, also, he didn't mind that Kit was there. His eyes, half-lidded, were warm shades of blue and gold, a treasure unearthed as the sun streamed at an angle through the window over the little desk. The morning air smelled fresh and clean and between them the warmth of their bodies locked in their scent from the night.

Kit had never slept with anybody this way before. Never woken up needing to shift to his hips so the other person didn't know he had an erection. Which was too obvious to hide and really, Brody had one, too. That's what happened to *men* in the morning. It was totally normal and he watched Brody reach down to shift himself, too.

Sure, he and Katie sometimes shared a queen-sized bed in a motel off the interstate, but then, she kept to her side and he to his. Sometimes she wanted the whole bed and made him sleep on the floor, but mostly they shared.

"I'm going to call Katie before breakfast," he said. "See if I can catch her. Maybe she's just getting off the late shift."

Brody turned his head away, and the message was clear. Brody thought Kit was wasting his time, but he wasn't going to stop him. So Kit, focusing on this one task, got out of the bed and padded over to the desk where his cell phone was plugged in, and scrolled for and tapped Katie's number. Once more, she didn't answer, but he left a quick message and asked her to call him back and did she want him to join her in Vegas?

When he clicked off the call and turned around, Brody was already half dressed, bending to lace up his work boots even before he'd done up his snap-button shirt.

"No cowboy boots?" asked Kit, hurrying to get dressed so Brody wouldn't leave him behind.

"Not today, youngling," said Brody in an absent kind of way as he tucked his shirt in. "I've got stuff to do at the barn, and tack to repair. You can help me."

Kit ran the word silently over his tongue. *Youngling.* It didn't sound like an insult like, *hey you, kid,* which Kit had heard a few times before, or *brat,* or anything like what some of Katie's men had called him. There was affection in the word, like Brody meant it in a good way. Like maybe one day, some day, Kit wouldn't be so young and foolish, but maybe now he was, a little bit, and Brody liked him anyway.

"Want to shave real quick?"

Kit looked up from where he was finishing tying the laces on his boots, and stood up. Tested the heels of them by stomping lightly.

"Uh." He felt his chin. There were a few hairs there, coming in hard, and a row of softer ones along his cheeks. "Sure."

"I'll lend you one of my disposables."

Shoulder to shoulder they stood in front of the bathroom mirror, looking at each other rather than themselves, which might have made it hard to shave. Only Brody smiled and handed him the can of shaving cream, like Kit was used to doing this. Like it wasn't something he did every two weeks. Like he was already a man fully grown, one who needed to shave *every* day and had lots of experience doing it.

"Like this." Brody applied the white poofs of shaving cream from the can and layered his face with it, using long, calm strokes. He waited till Kit had done the same and they matched, that way, with smooth white beards. "And like this."

Brody ran the razor under hot water, and Kit did the same, and then Kit watched while Brody shaved. Long, slow strokes with a little flip beneath his ear. Kit could see himself out of the corner of his eyes, in the mirror, his reflection watched Brody shave with something close to awe and a whole bunch of admiration thrown in.

"I want to be like you," he found himself saying.

"Be like yourself," said Brody as he wiped his face with a wet washcloth. "That's better anyhow."

He looked at Kit, who'd not yet started shaving. The shaving cream was starting to melt on his face.

"Need some help?" asked Brody, his dark eyebrows going up.

"Yeah." Kit practically breathed the word when he realized what Brody meant.

In the next second, his heart nearly stopped when Brody took the unused disposable razor from Kit's still hand and ran it under the hot water. Then, with gentle fingers, so gentle, he tipped Kit's face up, touching his chin, smiling at him in a way, relaxed, his blue and gold eyes half-lidded, before they sharpened and focused on his task.

The razor in Brody's hand made smooth silky paths across Kit's face, going down first, and then down again. Each time Brody would rinse the blade and tap the plastic handle on the edge of the sink. Tap, tap, tap. Then he continued on, his tongue in the corner of his mouth as he considered the next path the razor would take, like a sculptor might consider his chisel.

The feel of that blade, controlled by Brody's sure fingers, shivered across Kit's face with each gentle scrape and at one point, Brody used his middle finger against the line of Kit's jaw to turn his head, to expose his throat.

"Gently, now," said Brody, almost as if to himself. "There."

With a satisfied nod, Brody rinsed the blade one last time, then used a warm cloth to wipe Kit's face. Like he was quite young, and totally incapable of doing this himself. Only it felt kind, considerate. Like it mattered to Brody that Kit was clean-shaven, his skin not feeling raw.

"I've got Mennen," said Brody. "It's so old school it's not even funny, but it's what Quint uses, so—"

"What's Mennen?" asked Kit.

"Aftershave." Brody drew a small glass bottle with bright green liquid inside and dappled some in his hands before patting it on his face. "Baby smooth and I smell good, too."

Kit rose on his toes to inhale along the curve of Brody's neck. The aftershave tingled his nose, but he held out his hands so Brody could put a small amount on his palms. Then he patted his face, and made a sound when the aftershave seemed to spark all over his skin.

"Now we're ready," said Brody as he put the Mennen back in the medicine cabinet. "It'll wear off in an hour but—"

"But so what," said Kit, loudly, laughing, his energy rising. He felt like he could take on anything, and he would *do* anything to hear Brody call him youngling again.

They walked together through the early morning sunlight to the dining hall where the buzz and excitement of guests was underlaid with a tinge of sadness that Kit could feel. Everybody would be going home in a few days, everybody but him and Brody and the rest of the people who worked at the ranch.

Kit was one of the lucky ones, for he would get to see the sunset and the sunrise and the next after that. He'd get to sleep with Brody again, too, because surely Brody was okay with it? He'd not kicked Kit out of his bed, and he'd seemed pleased to find Kit there. He'd helped him shave. And he was now, with his hands on Kit's shoulders, moving Kit ahead of him in line.

"Chocolate chip pancake day," said Brody. "I can't stand 'em myself, but Jasper loves them, and Ellis does too. Look, there they are."

Kit waved where Brody was pointing, and he remembered Brody saying something about the bag of Ellis' laundry being dropped off at Jasper's place, but that seemed so long ago now. With a brief wave in the direction Brody had indicated, Kit helped himself to a tall stack of pancakes and a pile of bacon, and laughed when Brody shook his head.

"Other people might like some," Brody said.

"Oh." Kit's laugh died away. "I took too much, didn't I."

"Here," said Brody. "I'll have some of yours instead of the plain ones, and some of your bacon. Levi always makes enough, but it's nice for the guests to feel that there's plenty to go around."

Jutting his jaw to keep his chin from shaking, Kit closed his eyes so he could remember this, remember that nice people, the ones on TV, didn't take more than their fair share before everybody'd had some. When he opened his eyes, Brody was looking at him. Not urging him to move on, that he was holding up the line, but watching him.

"Sorry," said Kit, meaning it. "I didn't think."

"Not a problem," said Brody. "You'll get there."

"Oh, for Pete's sake," said Quint, looming behind them in line. "I'll take those. Brody, get you some plain ones, the kind you like, an' I'll eat these."

Now Kit didn't know what to do. Quint was the kind of friend who would do that. He wasn't Kit, who'd put Brody in the position of having to eat something he didn't like. He kind of hated Quint, in that moment, jealousy stirring below the surface of his skin.

"Quint," said Brody, a warning tone in his voice.

"Don't you fret, none," said Quint. "Brody, you just take those plain pancakes, and I'll take plain too, and Kit will share his chocolate chip ones with Jasper and Ellis, who are pigs about them and will want seconds anyway."

It was all solved. The only thing Kit had to do was go with what Quint had said and somehow bite down on the *fuck you* and the *I don't need your help* that his mouth had all ready to go. And just how had it gotten so complicated so quickly?

"Okay?" asked Brody

When Kit looked at Brody, he could see the question in those eyes, and the unspoken question beneath that. *You okay, youngling?*

The idea of it, the word Brody might say in his sweetly familiar voice, was like a balm. Brody wasn't trying to trip him up and neither was Quint. In fact, Quint was taking two sweet rolls and raising his eyebrows at Kit as if to indicate that one of them was for Kit, and Quint was happy to do this, since Kit's plate was already overflowing with chocolate chip pancakes.

"Yeah, okay," said Kit, taking a deep breath.

Maybe this was how it felt to belong to a family that was like one of those on TV. Maybe emotions rolled around, laughter and dismay, mixing together, because that's just how it was.

And it wasn't a one-way street, because even as Kit felt bad about it, as they walked over to the long table beneath the window where Jasper and Ellis sat, Quint was walking on one side of him and Brody the other, like they planned on blocking anyone who tried to tease Kit about the amount of pancakes he had on his plate and might make a snotty comment about how much bacon he had.

Maybe that's just what friends did.

"Hey," said Quint in greeting as the three of them sat across from Jasper and Ellis. "Look who brought extra to share."

"I took too many," said Kit, a little faintly. He picked his full plate off the tray and put it in the middle of the table. "Guess I got a little greedy."

Without a word, Jasper and Ellis, their eyes bright, took two pancakes each from his plate, which left Kit with three. Which was still a huge stack, so he had plenty for himself. Then he shared his bacon, and Jasper shared the bottle of real maple syrup he'd gotten from somewhere, and silently, Ellis pushed the small dish of gold-foil wrapped butter toward Kit.

"Thank you," said Kit.

"—come," said Ellis as he lifted his chin and Jasper started eating his pancakes like he was starving. "—you."

When Kit looked at Brody, Brody smiled at him like they were sharing a secret.

"He says you're welcome and thank you," said Jasper around a mouthful of food as he sucked the maple syrup off his thumb. "Words come hard for Ellis, sometimes."

"Oh, sure," said Kit, like he knew all about it.

Ellis' expression as he looked away from Kit and began eating, tore at something inside Kit. Like maybe he was worried Kit might make fun of him for not talking like everybody else would.

Well, Kit was the last person in the world to do something like that, especially on the ranch, especially in a place where they were a family. He vowed that the first person to make fun of Ellis would hear about it from him. He could stand up for other people the way Brody had stood up for him. The way Quint had.

Kit wanted to be like that. He wanted to be like them. All he had to do was watch and learn. Watch and learn and repeat over and over until he got it right.

23

KIT

*T*here was no denying how exciting Saturday was, even if this was his second Saturday at the ranch and some of the shine should have worn off, and how important and useful Kit felt as he helped with the luggage in the parking lot. Clay pulled a low hand-cart up and down the dirt road, and Kit helped him load and unload it. Maddy walked around with her clipboard, helping guests who couldn't find the keys to their rooms or their cabins, and while it seemed like a circus, by just after one o'clock, every guest had departed.

Kit kind of missed helping out in the kitchen that morning, but he got to eat with Quint and Clay and Austin at lunch that day, and it felt familiar and right. Like he fit in. Almost like he'd always been there.

"Is the orphan going to pick up trash this afternoon or help you in the barn?" asked Quint to Brody as he dug into his bowl of beef stew.

"I told you not to call him that," said Brody, like he didn't see right away that Quint was teasing him.

Even Kit could see that, and everyone around the table could see it, too. If you knew what to look for, the joke was in Quint's eyes, still and sharp, like a bit of crystal buried in the ground with only a little bit poking up.

"He's going to help me in the barn, right, Kit?" asked Brody.

"Yeah," said Kit. He scrubbed at his milk mustache and tried to keep his elbows off the table, but they kept creeping back. Only then, Quint put his elbows on the table with a loud thump and Clay and Austin followed suit and Brody rolled his eyes and put his elbows on the table, and the laughter rose and swirled around Kit like a good and familiar blanket.

"Why don't we all go to that new brewpub in Chugwater tonight?" asked Clay, waving his sandwich around before chomping down on it. "It's called Outlaw Brewing, or maybe it's Outlaw Brew Pub?" Clay raised his eyebrows at Austin for confirmation.

"Outlaw Brewing," said Austin, nodding, taking a sip of his iced tea.

"I'll drive," said Quint. "Then you kids can drink."

Kit's heart fell. He wasn't old enough to drink at a bar, so he wouldn't get to go. He'd have to hang out at the ranch while everyone else was having fun. Why did it always turn out like this?

"Hey," said Brody. "Kit's not of age—"

"Never mind that." Quint shook his head, scrubbing his hands on his napkin. "I'll say he's my kid. Nobody'll ask to see his ID if I say that, right?" He winked at Kit, and stood up with his tray in his hands and Kit couldn't say thank you because Quint strode off like he had places to be.

"Can he do that?" asked Austin, not like he felt it was wrong, it seemed, but just to be sure of the plan.

"You know anybody gonna question Quint?" asked Clay, laughing. "He'd be a better man than I, Gunga Din."

The afternoon was filled with more activity than Kit would have thought possible, seeing as how there were no guests on the ranch. But he was busy non-stop, helping in the barn, polishing tack, cleaning out stalls, walking with Brody to take a few horses down to Jasper's forge to get them shod, standing in the shaded overhang of the workshop watching the sparks fly from Jasper's anvil.

Beneath it all simmered the excitement of a night out with Brody and everybody. Usually he hung out in motel rooms waiting for Katie to get back, or he'd go over to the 7-Eleven to get some soda and potato chips, if the snack machine at the motel was out, which it always seemed to be. But now, *now* he would get to hang out, he'd get to go to a bar.

He wanted nothing more than to leave a message for Katie to tell her how much fun it was going to be, but somehow he was too busy all afternoon and by the time they went to their room to get ready, he figured he'd call her in the morning.

"This shirt?" asked Brody, holding up two shirts, one a blue and dark blue plaid, the other a soft grey. Both had pearl-snap buttons and either would look very nice, but when Kit pointed to the plaid one, Brody nodded. "You should wear your green plaid shirt," he said.

Kit got dressed, glowing beneath his skin as he did a last minute polish of his boots, standing there rubbing the toe of one boot along the back of his calf as he waited for Brody to check his pockets for his wallet.

"Let's go."

Now Kit's blood hummed as they went down the stairs together and the night air smelled especially sweet, full of crackles of excitement that seemed to echo the faraway silent lightning on the far horizon. They walked along the dirt path to the service building, where staff could park their trucks. Quint stood next to a huge silver truck with the ranch's logo on it.

"Leland said I could take the company car," said Quint. He looked over the assembled group, like he was counting. "Austin, you've got long legs. You're in front, but someone's going to have to sit on someone's lap."

Kit held his breath as Clay shook his head, laughing to himself. Then Brody nodded, touching Kit's shoulder.

"Will you mind?" he asked.

With his belly full of squiggles, his breath racing hard in his throat, Kit nodded, and when Brody had taken his seat in the back seat of the four-door truck, Kit clambered onto his lap. Brody's arm went around his waist, lightly, casually, like it was an everyday thing. His thumb hooked into the belt loop of Kit's jeans.

"You need a belt," said Brody.

"Yeah," said Clay, hanging onto the overhead strap as Quint backed the truck up like they were in a hurry, the truck's wheels jouncing over the bumps in the dirt road. "A cowboy one."

"They have them at the store," said Austin from the front passenger seat.

"I have one," said Kit. "I forgot to put it on."

But it was better this way. If he'd worn his cowboy belt, then maybe Brody wouldn't be hooking his thumb through an empty loop, and maybe Kit wouldn't feel the warmth of Brody's fingers trailing along his ribs. And pretty much nothing was better than the warmth of Brody's thighs beneath his.

"Never mind," said Brody, shaking his head, then pressing his chin against Kit's shoulder. "Belts get in the way when you're playing pool anyhow."

"They got a pool table at this place?" asked Quint, nodding when Austin pointed the direction he should go.

"I think so," said Clay. "All the best brew pubs have them so this one probably does."

The drive to Outlaw Brewing went fast, and Quint drove fast with the windows down. The fresh air rushed into the cab and swirled around as if it too was excited for a night on the town. Even if the town they drove through was on the small side, there was a lot of traffic along the road in front of the brew pub, and Quint had to park the truck halfway into a grassy ditch.

"Guess they didn't figure on it being so popular," said Clay as they all walked across the black-topped road, the evening's darkness set to glimmering in the streetlights, crazy moths batting about, the sound of laughter and chatter in the air.

When they arrived at Outlaw Brewing, it was a long, low building that didn't look big enough to hold as many people as were waiting in front of the door, but Quint spoke to the doorman, handed him a twenty, and they got in. Nobody even asked to see

Kit's ID, not even when they sat down at a high top table, crowding on tall bar stools and looking at the beer offerings on the laminated menu decorated like it was an old wanted poster for outlaws.

Silently, Brody pointed out something called a Badlands IPA, and Kit ordered that when the waitress came around. The beer tasted bitter and then sweet and then bitter again, and Kit drank half his glass in several huge gulps and felt very much the king of his world, right about then.

"Take it slow," said Brody. "Here, have some cheese fries."

The cheese fries were amazing. But what was even more amazing than those, or even drinking beer in a bar, was the fact that he got to sit right next to Brody on those high bar stools, so close that their thighs brushed against each other constantly. So close that when Brody lifted his glass of beer, his elbow brushed Kit's chest.

"Sorry," said Brody, and Kit just shook his head.

The five of them were sitting around a small circle table that was clearly meant for four. Around them, the place was hopping, jukebox music was playing from somewhere, and overhead amidst the wooden cross beams, little fairy lights twinkled like starlight.

"Let's grab a pool table," said Clay, reaching into his pocket to bring out a handful of quarters, wiping sweat from his gleaming temple.

"I suck at pool." Quint drained his beer and signaled to the waitress for another round. "Same thing for everyone, I think," he said to her, and placed a five dollar bill on her tray.

"Sure thing, hon," she said and then sashayed away amidst the crowd.

"You do not suck," said Brody, laughing open mouthed at Quint.

"I suck when it's this crowded," said Quint with a wink at Brody. "I prefer back alley bars that are a little quieter than this."

Clay and Austin found an empty pool table, and as the two of them played, mostly fooling around, the three of them, Quint, Brody, and Kit, watched with their second beers in their hands and then jokingly placed bets to see who would win. It was Austin, quietly bemused and much less drunk than Clay, who won, and Quint dutifully made them pay up their quarters.

"Never bet against a man with such a serious look in his eye," said Quint as he pocketed the money, but then, as they sat at their table, he paid for the next round anyway.

All the while, Kit stuck close to Brody, enjoying the scent of Mennen on his skin, the gleam of sweat along his neck as he rolled up his sleeves, talking to Clay about this horse or that, until Quint begged off shop talk.

Austin ordered onion rings, and Kit was mesmerized by the slow way Brody licked his lower lip free of salt and grease, casually, like he didn't know the sight of this made Kit's belly flip over and over. Or how the touch of Brody's fingers along Kit's thigh, soft and slow, as he offered him the last onion ring, made the bubbles rise in his heart, like sparks were striking and rising and rising, till he was half floating off his bar stool.

It was magical, that feeling, of belonging to this small group, of being at Brody's side. Having Brody check for Kit out of the corner of his eye, as though to make sure of him there. When Quint announced at midnight, that it was time to head back, it seemed the magic might end, but it didn't.

As they all piled into Leland's silver truck, they took their places as before. The windows were open and the dark night air eased into the truck's cab like a velvet cape, still warm with summer, but cold around the edges.

Kit sat gingerly on Brody's lap, his knees banging against the handle on the door, until Brody pulled him close, his hands on Kit's hips, like he was adjusting Kit to suit his thighs, which were warm and strong beneath Kit.

"There," said Brody. He curled his arm around Kit's waist. His thumb again hooked in Kit's empty belt loops, but this time he'd hooked the very front loop, next to the zipper, and his fingers trailed along the creases in Kit's jeans, at the bend at the top of his thigh. "Okay?"

"Okay," said Kit, breathing the word.

His back was to Clay, in the other seat, and he was all focused on making Austin laugh anyway. When Quint drove the truck out of the ditch, Kit was thrown hard against Brody, hard into the curve of his shoulder. Brody grabbed him to keep him steady, pulling Kit close to him, where Kit's bottom was almost between Brody's thighs.

"Up you get," said Brody, hauling Kit upright, but not letting go, for a good long minute as the truck picked up a little more speed, and Quint drove slowly through the midnight-quiet town of Chugwater.

Street lights sped past the open windows, spreading angel wings of bright light followed by capes of darkness, wings and darkness, wings and darkness, until Kit was dizzy with it, excitement building in him until he was hard, his jeans strangling his crotch. Without the belt, the waist of his jeans gapped and when he tried to adjust himself it was so obvious that he felt Brody looking at him.

In the last angel wing of light before Quint went under the bridge to the quiet back road that would take them back to the ranch, he could see Brody's expression. Half-lidded eyes, serious, his gaze on Kit like he was studying him, that brief lift of his dark eyebrow when he placed his hand on Kit's belly to steady him over the bump at the top of the slope that led into the valley.

His palm caught on Kit's erection. Kit thought to shrink back, but Brody's palm pressed hard, not like he wanted to push Kit away, but like he wanted to feel Kit. When his fingers dipped low to stroke the top of Kit's erection where it pushed up against his white underwear, Kit gasped.

They were in darkness, the smoky warm night tinged with the autumn to come, the breeze fresh and wild, scented with the back country where nothing could be tamed. The cool air traced the damp spot there, where Brody's fingers were, where they stroked and petted, like they'd discovered something they liked.

Kit's cock twanged and jumped beneath Brody's slight touches, and he was so glad his back was to Clay, so nobody could hear his small, needy whimper, or hear his hard breaths, or know that when Brody moved close, his warm breath traced Kit's cheek like a caress.

Then, swooping down, Brody eased his fingers inside of Kit's underwear, calloused fingertips warm, soft and then hard, while Kit's breath juddered, and he held onto the handle on the door with such a tight grip he could almost hear the plastic creak.

Quint drove on and on into the darkness on a seemingly never-ending road, the wind rushing as Brody caressed him, drove him half-crazy until finally Kit's whole body tightened and he came, a small jerk of his belly, the warmth and scent of his spend in the cool air. The imagined flicker of Brody's eyelashes against his cheek in the shadows of the back seat of the truck's cab, and his nod, his sigh, the sound in his throat, all of this surrounded Kit like a warm embrace.

When Brody withdrew his hand to wipe it on his own thigh, the truck came to a stop. Everything came to a stop and was still and they'd arrived at the ranch.

Austin hopped out to undo the gate and waited while the truck pulled through. When he got back in, Quint drove slowly along the dirt road, going over the stone bridge and then beneath the canopy of velvet-dark trees. He drove extra slowly through the parking lot in front of Maddy's office and even slower up the dirt road to the service shed, as though he wanted to make the evening linger.

When he parked the truck and turned off the engine, the five of them sat in the silence as the engine ticked to coolness. Then he had to start the engine to roll up the windows, the final marker that their evening out was over.

"Time for bed," said Quint.

Everybody got out of the truck. Kit hurried at Brody's side as they walked beneath the trees, almost not daring to speak. But he had to know, had to.

"Are you mad?"

"No," said Brody, the word whispering across Kit's cheek.

Brody curled his fingers around the back of Kit's neck and stopped them both to kiss him. Brody's mouth tasted like salt and beer and night air, the whispering winds that swirled the tops of the dark trees.

His lips were tender, the feeling pushing inside of Kit so hard, so fast, he almost toppled on his feet, and would have, had Brody not been so close, a support in the half-darkness. That steady hand on Kit's neck, the sigh from Brody's throat.

"Need to get you cleaned up," Brody said. "C'mon."

Kit licked the inside of his lip to catch Brody's taste and hold it and followed Brody up the stairs to their room.

24

BRODY

*B*rody knew he was perhaps more drunk than he ought to be, given what his intentions were. But then, he'd only had three beers. Quint had taken a large swallow of Brody's last one, so as to help a fellow out when he had, perhaps, intentions that went beyond the usual Saturday night hanging out with co-workers at a newly opened brew pub.

From the second Clay had mentioned it, and the ultra second when Brody had seen the hope in Kit's face, a bright beacon of *C'n I come too,* he knew he had to make it happen. He'd also known that when he made his objection about Kit's age, as twenty-one was the drinking age in Wyoming, that Quint would step in and play like he was Kit's dad.

Nobody argued with Quint, not even bouncers at bars. Quint wielded great power, but never abused it, and nothing was more worthy than giving Kit a night out on the town.

Kit had looked sweet in the green plaid snap-button shirt Brody had picked out for him, and pretty adorable as he'd patted Mennen on his cheeks, smiling at Brody like Brody was his world.

How had it come to this, when for Brody being alone was as good as it got, yet now he had his own shadow following him about, looking to him for approval, permission, pretty much everything?

How had it come to this when Quint had announced that someone was going to have to sit on someone's lap, he'd practically grabbed Kit like a second grader who's just been asked to pair up for the class outing. If Clay, whose lap was much sturdier than Brody's, had so much as raised his hand to volunteer, Brody would have shoved him like the meanest playground bully, which totally wasn't how he was.

Even when Kit was on his lap and Quint was barreling down the two-lane road to Chugwater, Brody felt soaked in effervescent wine, a bubbling joy racing through him. The beer at the bar just made it easier to think those thoughts, long buried like a secret treasure, thoughts he'd not known had existed.

He'd never believed that people belonged to other people, but he was finding out, as his hands went about Kit's waist, that some people belonged *with* other people. And once in the bar, sitting at the hightop meant for four people, with Kit at his side, happy just to be there, to be included, his heart expanded like it was welcoming these new feelings, of closeness, of being together, and having Kit by his side always

—He should *not* have toyed with Kit in the car, rather, when he discovered Kit's erection matched his own, he should have moved on. He wasn't the guy to fondle someone in a moving car, and yet—

"Are you mad?" asked Kit, looking up at him with those eyes of his, that young face, sweet with hope.

"No."

When he cupped Kit's neck, the touch was charged with sweetness and light. Kit's nearness surrounded him like a blanket of love. And when he kissed Kit beneath the starlit trees, it felt like a promise.

"C'mon," he said, and hurried up the stairs, Kit at his side.

The beer was still simmering beneath his skin, but the idea of it, of a shower with Kit, seemed like one that was a long time coming.

He always showered alone, though back in the day, when the KOA showers got busy, he and Quint had shared a stall, ignoring the looks of other patrons, hurrying through their ablutions, so used to each other that being naked that way was barely worthy of note. But this idea was different.

In their room, Brody tugged off his boots to throw them on the floor next to the bed, and unsnapped the pearl-snap buttons on his shirt like he wanted to rip the cloth from his body. At Kit's wide eyes, he slowed down and curled his fingers in Kit's belt loops once more to draw him close.

"A shower?" asked Brody, low. "You an' me?"

Kit's response was a sigh that melted into the nighttime summer air that sifted through the open windows, tipping up the edges of the curtains, swirling around them.

Brody's chest was bare beneath the open edges of his shirt. He took Kit's hand and gently laid it on himself, Kit's palm warm against his nipple, the tender edges of Kit's fingers curling through the very faint dusting of dark hair along his breastbone.

"Let me help you," said Brody, and one by one he unsnapped the buttons on Kit's shirt.

The only light came through the window, from some distant auto-light on the barn, perhaps, but it lit the curve of Kit's cheek, and the gleam there told its own story. That Kit wanted this, though maybe, like Brody, he'd not known he'd wanted this until tonight. Until the glasses of brew pub beer had told them what they wanted and set them free.

But it wasn't beer Brody felt in his veins, but, more, a simmer that felt like desire and want all rolled together, swirling around inside of him as he finished unsnapping Kit's buttons, pulled the shirt out from Kit's jeans, and off Kit's shoulders before tossing it on the bed.

Now Kit was half naked and he was half naked. Faraway light skittered across Kit's ribs, the hollow of his belly, which Brody brushed with the backs of his fingers.

When Kit nodded, Brody undid the button and zipper on Kit's jeans, then, with a laugh, he bent to pull off Kit's shiny brown boots, and his socks, and those went on the bed, also, though he thought better of it, and moved everything carefully to the floor.

Kit was breathing hard as Brody tugged off those new blue jeans and then his own. Finally, he pulled off his underwear, standing on one foot as he pulled them all the way off. Which left Kit standing in his white briefs, stock still, arms stiff at his sides.

Which was no way to be, now, was it, so Brody looped his arm around Kit's slender waist, and let the moment settle around them, let the notion, the feel, of their naked thighs brushing, Brody's bare hip brushing Kit's cotton clothed hip. Brody tickled the line of Kit's waist gently.

"Okay?" Brody asked, checking in.

If the beer had worn off and showed beneath that any kind of hesitation or indecisiveness, Brody would have stopped then and there. But the beer was wearing off, leaving glittery zigs and zags all around them in the sweet air, swirling sparks in Brody's belly, all of which reflected in Kit's pewter blue eyes and the way he sighed and tucked his head beneath Brody's chin, his arms coming around Brody's waist.

Warmth grew between them, Brody's erection brushing against Kit's, and a small stillness that was jarred only by the elastic pop of the waistband of Kit's underwear as he tugged at it.

"Let me get that."

"You have more hair than me," said Kit, a kind of panic growing in his voice.

It was easy to see why Kit felt this, as Brody had a dusting of dark hair along his breastbone, below his belly, leading to his groin, and below that, busy dark hair for his cock to nest in. Kit had no hair along his slender chest, and no happy trail along his belly.

When Brody took off Kit's white briefs, and gently cupped Kit's balls, the hair was sparse between his legs. Brody could imagine the hair would be blond and fair. Kit's balls were soft and tucked close, excitement drawing them, making them ready, and his cock was taut against his belly as he shivered while Brody caressed him.

"Some people do," Brody said, mildly, tipping his head to one side. "And some people don't, that's all. A lot of people shave, but I don't, 'cause it itches so when it grows back in."

"You shaved?" asked Kit with a gulp. "Down there?"

"Quint bet me five dollars once that I wouldn't," said Brody with a laugh, enjoying the small moment as his passion pulsed beneath his skin, and Kit's confidence grew. "I had a heck of a time and couldn't get every last hair, but he gave me fifty, just for trying."

"Quint's your friend," said Kit, his voice rising.

"Yeah," said Brody. He dipped his chin and took both hands to clasp Kit's face. "Enough about Quint, now."

He drew his tongue along Kit's lower lip, slowly, letting the feel of it linger, letting Kit respond in his own time. The kiss became deep and when Kit rose on his toes, Brody dropped his hands to slip them around Kit's waist, so slender, he could cup that waist and hold Kit close and feel as though he had something precious and fragile in his hands.

With a small sound, a low grunt, Kit flung his arms around Brody's neck, hugging him tight that way, his erect and warm cock brushing Brody's middle. In response, Brody hugged Kit right back and picked him up around his waist and carried him into the bathroom.

"What?" asked Kit, blinking as Brody turned on the single light above the medicine cabinet.

"A shower," said Brody. He leaned to turn on the water, tested it with his hand, never losing contact with Kit's waist. "It'll be nice, you'll see."

Kit was right behind him when he stepped into the shower, which was longer than it was wide, and not all that large, especially with two men inside of it. With a smile, Brody pulled Kit beneath the spray with him, and carded his fingers through Kit's blond hair, which darkened with the water.

In the shadows of the semi-dark shower stall, he kissed Kit and kissed him again, water slipping past their mouths, like a blessing, curling along Kit's chin as he blinked up at Brody through the spray.

Using the bottle of lavender soap and a dampened washcloth, Brody washed the traces of Kit's excitement, slowing as he circled the cloth around Kit's cock, teasing with the cloth, the slickness of soap. Then he washed Kit all over, and then he washed his hair, and all the while Kit stood perfectly still, as though he imagined that he might startle Brody if he moved.

"Now you do me," said Brody, knowing that if he was Kit he might be anxious about how everything worked. When you taught a horse something new, you did the lesson and then you did the lesson again, gently and slowly. "Here."

He handed Kit the washcloth and tipped his chin up, his hands resting on Kit's hips until Kit started to move. He was hesitant at first, the cloth across Brody's belly light, but then he put more soap on the cloth and seemed to laugh under his breath, and scrubbed Brody from neck to hip, and then bent and scrubbed Brody's thighs, each one.

"You can scrub me anywhere, you know, right?" Brody guided Kit's hands to his groin, where his cock was standing against his belly, patiently waiting till the time was right.

You had to control yourself with a youngling, had to let him know he was safe with you. When Kit's fingers, soapy and slippery, curled around the base of his cock, Brody sighed, and looked at Kit through water speckled lashes and smiled. Kit smiled in return and rose to kiss Brody damply on the mouth.

They rinsed each other off, and Brody turned off the water, grabbed a dry towel, and buffed Kit with it, then stood still when Kit buffed him in return. Brody threw the towel on the floor to save them from slipping in the puddles they'd created.

"Bed," said Brody.

He kept his hand on Kit's silky and slightly damp behind, and flicked off the light over the medicine cabinet, sending the room back into semi-gloom. The air was sweet-scented from the lavender soap, mixed with the deeper chill of the past-midnight hour. It was awkward for only a moment as he guided Kit into the bed, pulling back the sheets, and then clambered in after. Finally, their their two bodies lay side by side, each on their hips, the cotton sheet drifting over their shower-clean skins.

Kit's hair was damp at the ends, the feel of him beneath Brody's hands like a ribbon, a smooth ribbon.

"So," said Brody, biting his lower lip, feeling Kit's gaze on every move he made. "I should have asked before, but kissing you drove it out of my mind—"

"It did?" The pleasure in Kit's eyes shone.

"Yeah, it did." Brody tipped his head down to kiss Kit's nose. "But have you ever been with anybody before?"

"Before you?" asked Kit and when Brody nodded, Kit shook his head. "No, nobody. Just you."

The heartfelt way Kit said this sounded like a vow that lovers made. Though the idea of it, of loving someone, startled him, Brody soothed his heart by kissing Kit and folding his fingers around Kit's shoulders and drawing him close.

"If you get scared," whispered Brody in Kit's ear, softly. "You let me know, okay?"

"Okay." Kit's response was a breath that caressed the line of Brody's neck, sending shivers down his back, his sides.

Brody reached down between their bodies, and curled his fingers around Kit's cock, teasing the slit, drawing moisture down the shaft. He traced the silky hairs around the base of Kit's cock, and then gently drew his fingers back up.

Kit was breathing so hard, his chest rose and fell in sharp jerks, the heated air between their bodies making the places where their skin touched, hips, thighs, all the way down to their toes, hot and slick.

"Easy, now," said Brody, brushing a kiss along Kit's cheek. "I've got you. I'm here."

With damp hands, Kit gripped Brody's shoulders like he was afraid he'd be pulled out to sea, and some unknown terror awaited them. His cock seemed to wilt a bit.

Maybe Brody was going too fast. Maybe he was going about this the wrong way. He eased back on his caresses, and relaxed his head on the pillow, breathing in and out, until Kit did the same, his fair hair on the pillow, his eyes on Brody like a young horse who just wants to be told what the next step is and hopes it's not something scary.

"Let me try somethin' a little different."

"Okay," said Kit, the word jerking out of his mouth.

"Easy does it."

Brody rose on his knees, pushing back the sheet to tumble about Kit's waist, and crawled backward down the bed until he was between

Kit's slender thighs. With one hand, he stroked Kit's thigh, and bent low to breathe warm air across that thigh, to the space between, and sensed Kit's skin shiver beneath his touch.

"Gonna put my mouth on you," he said, whispering a kiss to Kit's groin as he bent low. "It's softer and sweet, you'll see."

He pressed another kiss to the hollow of Kit's hip and waited a heartbeat, waited two heartbeats, until he heard Kit sigh and felt Kit's thighs part, and saw the glisten on the tip of Kit's cock. Sometimes, the body knew what it wanted, even if the head didn't know what to call it.

Brody licked the length of Kit's cock and swirled his tongue around the tip and scooting forward, cupped that length and gripped it gently. He licked and suckled, slow.y, over and over, not shocking or startling, as he might have done with a more experienced man, but quietly, in a predictable way so Kit's body began to rise and fall in anticipation, his hips curling and uncurling, the *lick lick lick* sound weaving between Kit's hard breaths.

When Brody lowered his mouth to cover Kit whole, he sucked hard, cupping Kit's balls, swirling them around his fingers. He lifted and lowered, lifted and lowered, hard and then soft, over and over till Kit's balls tightened, his whole body tightened.

When Kit pulsed he gasped, his head tossed back, and the low grunt that Brody heard told him what he'd hoped for, that Kit loved this. He'd never been with anyone, and Brody was his first, and this, this sucking and licking, was what he loved, and Brody wanted to do it forever and forever.

Only now, Kit was crying, soft low sounds, his face streaked with silver. Brody slithered to his side and held him, wiping away the tears, his heart tearing at itself.

"Was that okay?" he asked, though he sensed the tears were happy ones at having found something you didn't even know you were looking for.

"Yes, yes," said Kit, whispering, his breath coming hard as he threw himself on top of Brody and hugged him tight and tighter still. His face was damp against Brody's neck, and his kisses were many. "That was amazing. Can we do it again? Can I do it to you?"

"Give you five minutes, and sure, yes, I'd love to." Brody smiled into Kit's hair, and twirled his fingers down Kit's spine, tapping his lovely bottom. "And yes, you can. Any time you want."

It was about giving and then giving some more. Kit squirmed on top of him, reaching down to grasp Brody's demanding erection. He didn't pull back at the heft of it, didn't complain that Brody's thigh hair was scratchy and stiff. It was as if with Brody's simple *yes*, all of his fear had left him on wild, happy wings.

Brody spread his thighs so Kit could be between them, and closed his eyes when Kit kissed his belly, tracing the happy trail to Brody's cock with his tongue.

"I'm glad you only shaved the one time," said Kit, tangling his fingers in Brody's pubic hair, playing, experimenting.

"Me too," said Brody, though he'd not thought about it in a long time. When Kit's tongue swirled around the head of Brody's cock, his body jumped and then settled in for the delight that was to come. "Take your time," he said. "And you don't have to swallow, okay?"

"You did so I will."

Kit was looking up at Brody, his eyes wide and shining in the glow of the auto-light through the open windows.

He seemed older in that moment, making a promise that he probably didn't realize he was making, or answering his own earnest call to be like Brody. To do what Brody did.

With that knowledge came the responsibility, feeling long-forged in Brody's heart, that he lead Kit in the right way, with the right intentions. And to let him go when the time came.

25

BRODY

*S*unday mornings were the only lazy time at the ranch. That morning, as Brody woke up with his arms full of Kit, warm and sleepy, pressed close, their limbs tangled, Kit's eyelashes tickling his breastbone, a slow urgency tumbled over the languor and pushed up from his skin.

At any other time, he might have felt that holding Kit and kissing him, loving on him, might have been disastrous. He was alone pretty much all the time, and never felt the need to curl in bed this way, with someone else's body a warm line against his. Now he had it, and all of him was whispering *yes, yes, yes,* a happy energy filling him. A bespoke contentedness surrounding him.

Could this be love? Could this be what he'd not known he'd been searching for?

"Kit," he whispered, low, so as not to startle.

Kit made a sound in his throat, a low sound as he turned his head to kiss whatever bit of skin was closest, which was the curve of Brody's breast, the dark strands of hair.

Below Brody's waist, his cock was all excitement and go and need, and Kit's was too, though Brody kept his hands light as he petted Kit's shoulders, curled fingers behind Kit's ear to tuck the untidy morning hair there.

"It's like a dream," said Kit, also whispering. "Did I dream last night, did I?"

"No," said Brody, low. "But it's like a dream to me, too."

Kit lifted his chin and opened his eyes, the serious pewter blue color drawing all the light in the room, reflecting it back to Brody as the sunlight came through the window over the little desk, and the slanted sunlight over the bed.

There was a shift in Kit's expression, the lines of his face, that was different from the day before. Only hours ago, it seemed, he'd been a young man with a young gaze. A young man with places for experiences to fill within him, to change him, to change his perspective and his outlooks. His fears and his joys. And now all of this was wrapped up in what they'd shared between them the night before.

There was no going back from that, and Brody didn't want to. He just hoped that Kit felt the same.

And it seemed that he did for he tilted his head up and kissed the bottom of Brody's chin and climbed Brody's body as though wrapping himself in Brody's arms, which came about Kit's waist, an embrace that was warm and morning-gentle.

"Can we do it again?" Kit's voice was high and hopeful.

"Yes," said Brody, kissing Kit on the mouth, swiping Kit's lower lip with his tongue so Brody could lick the inside of his mouth and absorb the energy between them. He pulled back and cupped Kit's cheek and swept his thumb below Kit's eye, connecting them. "Any time you like, youngling."

Kit made a sound in his throat that sounded like joy, like hope, and it was all Brody could wish for, though he'd never wished for it before now.

"I'll start," said Brody, his eyebrows going up to let Kit know everything was okay, that it was safe. "And you can follow."

He reached between their bodies, where Kit's morning erection was brushing against his. They were naked beneath the single sheet, which was rolled around them in a comfortable way, as the warmth of their skin, their closeness, was enough in the cool morning air.

Kit's cock was taut against his own belly, warm and silky in Brody's hand, firm and hard, and much more sure of itself than it had been the night before.

"Do this," said Brody.

He took his hand away and licked his palm, nodding to show Kit how it was done. Kit echoed his motion, licking his own palm, his eyes wide and watching Brody's every move.

Kit was like a young horse, again, as he always was in Brody's mind, a yearling, where one wrong move could spoil him forever and make him mean and unruly.

It wasn't that Brody wanted Kit docile in any way. He wanted him strong and sure of himself, his mind quick with excitement, his eyes focused on his own future. Part of that would come from what they were doing now, as Brody wrapped his damp palm around Kit's cock, and curled his fingers up and down the shaft, playing a little, going slow.

"Then this, and a little of this, and some of this." Brody made the motions of his hand smooth and soothing, up and down, swirling, always gentle. There was time enough later, hopefully, maybe, for something more adventurous, pushing the edges of their shared passion, but for now, this was right. It was what Kit needed, and what Brody was happy to give him.

When Kit grasped Brody's cock in his hand, his eyes widened, and the pleasure radiating from them made Brody smile, and he hugged Kit close, squashing him a bit.

"That feels good, right?" he asked, checking to make sure. "When you do it like this, both at once, the brain does something—oh, I dunno—makes a complete loop or something. Short circuits or something. I dunno."

He shook his head, and concentrated on what he was doing, on how it felt to stroke Kit slowly, so slowly, his cock tight in Brody's palm, the slit leaking its pleasure, the pump of Kit's heart almost visible in his throat, pulsing beneath his skin.

As for Kit's hand on him, it was a delicious torture, almost too light, not tight enough, but it was what Kit was ready for, what he was comfortable with. Only when Brody sighed as Kit's thumb did something delicious below the crown of his cock, Kit squeezed and made Brody gasp, his eyes fluttering half-shut, and he had to take a breath to keep from getting dizzy.

"Should I go faster?" asked Kit, panting, his breath warm on Brody's neck.

"Yeah." Brody almost grunted the word. "Yeah."

Kit's hand sped up around Brody, and Brody was the echo now, Brody followed Kit's pace, his movements, curling his fingers along the shaft when Kit did, swiping his thumb across the head when Kit did.

Delirious, delicious shivers rippled up his back and down his thighs, and when Kit came, spilling warmth over Brody's fingers, Brody was close, so close behind, it was like they were one—one body, one soul, tingles following after, gasping breaths tender in the warm sunlight that streamed yellow ribbons across the bed.

Brody's panting slowed while a bit of sweat trailed down his neck, his head on the pillow, Kit curled next to him, his head resting in the hollow of Brody's shoulder.

"There's a meeting in a bit," said Brody, swallowing, thinking about getting up to get some water. Wishing he had a glass so he could bring some back to Kit. "Leland's Sunday morning meeting."

"Are we late?" asked Kit, worry in his voice.

"No." Brody reached to cup Kit's face, to send his hair back from his forehead with gentle fingers. "Remember from last week? It's later on Sundays. And breakfast is first. Mostly baked goods and leftovers from the week that guests didn't eat. But it's still good. Levi's a good cook."

Kit nodded, silent, his cheek warm on Brody's breast, his body becoming still, relaxed, their legs still tangled, the sheet draped about them like a good friend, patiently waiting.

"We can go over to the dining hall," said Brody now. "Get some coffee. Take it slow. Maybe shower first."

"Maybe?" asked Kit, sounding a little confused.

"Maybe no," said Brody. He dipped his chin to look at Kit, fondness and pleasure filling him in unexpected ways, like an unseen, heretofore unknown dam above where his heart resided had suddenly burst forth all of its waters, streaming down, soaking him from head to toe with a kind of almost painful joy. "I want to smell you on me all day."

Kit's smile in response to this was sweet, like Brody had given him a present to take with him and keep close all day long.

"Me too," he said, his mouth rosy, his scent like a perfume to Brody. "Me too."

They washed their faces and necks and got dressed, ready for work the second the meeting ended, long-sleeved shirts to keep the sun from their skins, blue jeans, and sturdy work boots to keep their feet safe. Brody grabbed both of their straw cowboy hats as they went out the door, because sometimes after the meeting, Leland wanted things done and he wanted them done quickly, and there wasn't always time to race back to the room for anything.

The dining hall on a Sunday morning was quiet and almost sleepy, with staff coming in to get a cup of Levi's good coffee, the line to the buffet of leftovers and fresh baked goods short and lazy. They stood together to get coffee and blueberry scones, some freshly fried bacon, cheese and egg and hash brown casserole.

Most Sundays were like this, without the hustle and excitement of the guests, the food tasting more like Levi and his team had made it for him personally, all of his favorites, all the things he liked and none that he didn't. Plenty of carbs and butter and little dishes of honey for the coffee, which Levi didn't normally put out during the week.

They ate unhurriedly. Brody got them second cups of coffee, and slowly stirred his honey in, and smiled as he saw Kit doing the same. Eventually, Kit would develop his own way of doing things, but for now, copying Brody was a good way to learn what he liked and didn't like.

The morning meeting, which took place after breakfast in front of the barn, went like it usually did, with praise for jobs well done, bashful grins at the praise, except for Clay, who always whooped when his name got mentioned, like he was a cheerleader in high school and simply could not let go of the role. Then came the list, usually short, of things that needed improving on, stuff that went not quite as expected.

"We're more than halfway through the season now," said Leland, his eyes serious as he looked at each of them. "It's going well. We've recovered from last year, and are doing well on the profit and loss sheet, according to Austin. More important, guests are having a good time and are telling their friends about us. That organic growth is what we're after. Also, in the next week or so, Finn and Artie will be back to give us a private screening of the documentary they made, so I hope you all will be courteous and attend, as a testament to their hard work and creativity."

Lastly, Leland read the list of tasks for the day. Most Sundays, you might be called on to do something you normally didn't, something that needed extra attention and speed.

That Sunday, when Leland called on Quint and Brody to ride fences, as they'd had a report from the BLM administrator that both cows and horses were somehow ending up in fields where they should not be, Brody groaned inside, even though that was normally a task he liked. Kit could not ride, pretty much at all, had only the one lesson under his belt and thus would have to be left behind. It was a pretty imagination in his head that somehow he'd be assigned to something on the ranch, something local that he and Kit could do together, but he should have known better.

"What about me?" asked Kit, rising on his toes so only Brody would hear the question.

"Wait." Brody pointed up front, where Leland was still reading from his list. "Ah," he said when Kit's name came up. "You're in the kitchen, doing a deep clean with Levi's team. I'll see you at dinner, okay?"

"Okay." Kit looked a bit relieved, and seemed not to mind the basic and unglamorous nature of the assignment.

When Leland dismissed them, they had to go different ways, but before Kit headed off, Brody touched his shoulder to get him to stay a moment longer.

"Maybe we should get you more riding lessons, so you could do different things." He didn't add that he wanted one of those things to be Kit riding at his side, because maybe Kit didn't actually like riding, and maybe Brody's dream was made of empty pipes and fragile bubbles.

"Sure," said Kit, though he didn't seem quite sure.

"Maybe private lessons," said Brody. "Just you and me."

Kit's eyes glowed, his face flushed pink.

"Okay," he said, his smile in his eyes, his body, everywhere.

"Now, off you get." With a quick pat to Kit's bottom, a quick glance to make sure nobody saw, Brody jerked up his chin in a universal guy gesture. "See you."

"See you," said Kit, shadowing the gesture, echoing the words.

As Quint waited in the shadow of the barn, Brody watched Kit stride off, his shoulders relaxed, his chin lifted, the curve of sunlight on his young cheek, the shadow of the straw cowboy hat hiding the joy in his eyes, though Brody knew it was there, strong and sure.

There were moments like this, Quint had told him so, where you captured the image of it in your heart, an indelible marker of time, the passage of which was taking him so swiftly away from his old life and into a new one, it almost made him gasp. But Quint had also taught him that this was the way of life, something to be expected, nothing to be feared. And maybe, with Kit at his side, he would never have to be afraid again.

26

BRODY

*T*he wild mountain grasses on the upper slopes of BLM territory just below where the land grew too rocky for grazing were crisp and taut and green beneath the blazing sun. Quint held Diablo at a fast walk and Brody let Old Blue follow at a trot or a walk, as he would.

Alongside them as they rode, their shadows were broad to the west, the breeze keeping the air cool around them, carrying the scent of the low country, green and grassy and damp, mixing it with the cooler, dryer air of the high country as they rode along, looking for strays, horses and cattle both.

Brody inhaled. He loved this smell, the freshness of it, the open sky above. Loved the exciting uncertainty of the land around them, the mix of wildflowers, purple and blue, bunching up from lichen-dotted rocks, the sudden curve of the land up on the left, down to the right.

And this morning, of all mornings, he felt easy in the saddle, his muscles relaxed, all tenseness gone, even from his shoulders where he usually held it. Usually a good, long ride like the one he and Quint were taking that morning would be enough, but last night with Kit in his arms, had transformed him, forever and for always, as he would not forget the sweetness they'd shared, the scent of Kit in his arms.

Kit had looked up at Brody with those big eyes, like Kit had before him everything he'd hoped for in the world. And Brody, touching Kit's face, had floated on those feelings right along with Kit.

"They think they've broken to freedom," said Brody, distracting himself with a small joke about the horses they were after as he urged Old Blue to catch up to Diablo, and when he and Quint rode side by side, he added, "Sometimes I just want to let them run wild, you know? To be free forever?"

"That'd be cruel," said Quint, ever practical. "Cruel to an animal who doesn't know that forty miles to the south and east of us is a big city with hard concrete and tall buildings."

"I know." Brody nodded, clucked to Old Blue and cantered ahead, all the while keeping his eye out for those strays. When he pulled Old Blue to a slow stop, he propped himself on the cantle, half turning around. "Say, Quint. I got a question for you."

"This about the orphan?" asked Quint, winking as he pulled up Diablo and adjusted the brim of his straw cowboy hat to shade his eyes.

"Don't call him that, he doesn't like it." Shifting to face front, his hands on the saddle horn, Brody looked out over the vastness of the landscape where it rolled and rolled away from them, a seemingly endless green sea that followed the foothills all the way north to Canada. "But yes, it's about him."

Which was putting it mildly as everything seemed to be about Kit that morning, the way Brody felt, the touch of Kit's hand on Brody's bare skin driven into his soul like a brand. How he was seeing the slopes of the foothills spread before him as if seeing them anew through Kit's eyes.

He wouldn't have it any other way. Wouldn't change his feelings for Kit, couldn't even try, for nothing would take the memory of Kit's sweet kisses, his eagerness, his willingness to trust Brody, even after all that had happened to him in his life before they'd met.

"Only teasing," said Quint, soothing Diablo with a pet, resting his hands on his own saddle horn, waiting, it seemed, until Brody was ready to ask what he wanted to ask.

In spite of the good memories of last night, shared with Kit, along with those memories of that morning, everything between them, all wrapped together, was starting to worry Brody ever since Kit had left Brody's side for his own tasks that day. The memory of how he and Kit had walked beneath the night-damp trees to the dining hall lingered. Kit had been so eager and happy to be with him, to be at his side. Kit was younger than his years in so many ways.

Was Brody taking advantage of a situation where whatever he did or said or even felt held sway over Kit's every waking action? And how was Kit to know whether or not this was a good thing for him?

It was up to Brody to make sure of Kit. To make sure he wasn't pulling Kit to him for his own sake, but also for Kit's.

When Brody had been with Quint, in the early days, freshly escaped from Daddy Frank's clutches, he'd been a raw-boned, still-growing seventeen year old. Quint's care of him had been of the utmost sweetness, never impatient, never rushed. And, except for Quint's night visitors, there'd never been a single overtone of sexual impulse or hint that Quint might want to take advantage of him.

"What's your question?" asked Quint. Still not impatient, still waiting for whatever it was that Brody wanted to know.

"When we were together, do you remember those days?"

"'Course I do," said Quint. "Just ask it, whatever it is."

"Okay." Brody had learned to trust Quint over the years, so this shouldn't be as hard as he was making it. Better just to ask than to hem and haw like he was ashamed, which he wasn't. He was only concerned. "Did you ever want to fuck me like one of your nighttime visitors?"

"You?" asked Quint, looking Brody up and down, like he was pulling out a mental record of their days together in the camper. He laughed gently and shook his head, showing his strong white teeth. "You were as pretty as a sunrise, still are, but no. You were too brittle-edged for me then, and you are too gentle a soul for me now."

"But you thought about it," said Brody. "You considered it."

"Sure, I did," said Quint, without the least bit of shame, his gaze on Brody steady and sure. "I think about it with everyone I meet, pretty much. I ask myself yes or no and then I ask myself why. You were a no, 'cause I wasn't what you needed."

"What do I need?" Brody leaned forward in the saddle, wiping the sweat from his forehead with a leather-gloved hand.

"You know the answer to that," said Quint. "I know you do, so why don't you tell me?"

Looking over the landscape, Brody had an impulse to take off galloping on Old Blue until he hit the far horizon, never stopping, never pausing beneath the blue blue sky until he found the source of it at the edge of the earth.

Maybe Quint would stop him before he got too far, or maybe Quint would watch him run until he himself decided to turn around and come home. Home to the ranch with the horses he loved and the job he was good at. Home to where Kit was, at least for a while.

If he spoke of his fears about Kit leaving, Quint would sagely reply, with a slow nod, that life was like that sometimes, and you couldn't hold on to some things, no matter how much you loved them.

In the meantime, Brody wanted to do right by Kit and to love on him till all that joy and affection soaked into those young bones, right down to his soul.

"I need Kit," said Brody, simply. "He fills my arms. He fills my spaces. When I look at him I see myself. See how I could have been had I not had you in my life."

"Doesn't seem like a problem to me, you put it that way," said Quint.

"Is it wrong to love someone who reminds you of yourself? Wrong to love someone who is so vulnerable, so easily influenced?"

"Not to mention the non-fraternization rule at the ranch." Quint laughed again, this time more harshly as he settled in the saddle, harshly because he didn't give a damn about most rules, only the ones he deemed worthy.

"Yeah, about that," said Brody, chuckling. At the beginning of the season, Leland broke that rule almost the first second Jamie Decker had drifted onto the ranch, ragged and sore and tired and homeless.

Brody remembered when Jamie had stepped out from beneath the dappled shade of the glade, a fey wind shifting his sunlight-tipped hair into his eyes.

Leland had looked a bit stunned, and Brody wished, oh, how he wished he'd made a money bet with someone as to how long it would take before the two of them got together. But he hadn't, and that was a shame because he could have made a fortune.

"So is it wrong, you ask?" asked Quint. For a long silent moment with only the rush of the wind across the grasses, he worked his jaw and looked out over the landscape with Brody. "I don't think so," he said finally. "You want good things for him, right?"

"Yes," said Brody.

"Then follow your heart," said Quint. "And tell him. Don't let the moment pass you by. Don't wait until sunset. Do it in the light of day. No regrets."

"No regrets," echoed Brody. And thought about why Quint had said what he said and what regrets were lingering in those spinel-colored eyes of his, dark gems dug up from the earth, carrying ancient secrets and old, old wisdom.

"Something about his mom in Vegas and maybe you think someday he'll light out?" asked Quint.

Nodding, Brody swallowed hard, realizing Quint must have heard this on the ranch's grapevine.

"Then he lights out and you can't stop him," said Quint. "But between then and today? You could have something sweet to take you through times so dark you can't even imagine them now. Build that light inside you now, while you can. Hear me?"

"Yes sir," said Brody, trying to smile at those last two words, the way Quint said them, like he was bossy and fierce and scary and Brody should be afraid. Afraid of big. scary Quint, which was the last thing he'd ever feel. All he'd ever received at Quint's hand had been loving and kind. All he wanted to do was to pass that experience along to Kit. "I hear you."

Quint took off his hat and wiped his forehead with the sleeve of his cotton shirt, then put his hat back on, firmly, as if to announce to Brody he was getting serious about the hunt for the lost animals.

"Let's head down into the valley," he said. "Follow Horse Creek and see what we find. Animals are bound to head back down to water from way up here, once they figure there isn't much."

Brody nodded, clucked to Old Blue and, staying close to Quint's side as they sped to a trot and then to a smooth canter as they headed down to greener pastures. There, tucked in the lee of a stone formation, were the horses and cows who'd determined their paths for themselves, once they'd found the gap in the fence.

They gathered up the animals and herded them back through the gap, then both of them passed through the gap, following behind, pausing to twist the heat-loosened barbed wire around the ragged and dry wooden posts.

"Send Clay up here with supplies to make this more secure," said Quint as he mounted Diablo, who, when Quint picked up the reins, danced and moved like he was pretty sure Quint had asked him to gallop in a round circle around those former strays to make sure they knew where they belonged.

"Settle down, old boy," said Quint, patting Diablo's sweaty neck, clucking to him softly. "We got 'em where we need 'em, so let's head back." Quint looked at Brody. "In the light of day, y'hear?"

"I hear," said Brody.

They cantered along the low slope, going through the gate for each line of barbed wire fence, till they got to the last one and, with that secured behind them, they dismounted, to walk their horses to the barn, rather than riding them, to let them relax and breathe, even to the point of loosening the girths.

Side by side in the afternoon's soft light, the breeze from the glassy river that provided the prized view over it to the grasses beyond, they reached the barn and tended to their horses in companionable silence.

This was, as Brody always thought, in moments like this, one of the best parts of being Quint's friend. You didn't always have to talk or keep up pleasant chatter. You could just do the work, share the burden, and just be silent in your own mind. *Quint's your friend*, Kit had said, and Brody knew he was one of the lucky ones to say yes, he was.

All around them as they'd ridden the front range, the ranch had come to life with an influx of guests. Staff was busy getting them settled into their lodgings for the week, in the fancy cabins over-looking the river, as well as the main lodge, over the dining hall, and the two bunkhouses. The sound of chatter, the energy of excitement, of newness happened every Sunday when guests arrived, but it always made Brody smile.

Guests came to play at being cowboy, to imagine that a cup of coffee on a wooden porch miles from anywhere somehow made the coffee taste better. As if being at this altitude, with trees and grass and hills all around, allowed them to tap into some unseen, almost phantom energy that they all declared they couldn't feel at home, at the places where they worked. And it always reminded Brody how lucky he was to be where he was, doing what he was doing.

"Can you finish?" asked Brody as he quickly groomed Old Blue. "I'll come back, 'cause I know the saddles still need to be prepped and checked for the week, but I want to, you know. While it's daylight."

"Never be ashamed to say how you feel," said Quint. He waggled a body brush at Brody. "Never. Now go along, scoot."

"Yes, sir."

Rolling up his shirt sleeves and taking off his straw cowboy hat to scrape his sweaty hair out of his face, Brody strode down the dirt road from the barn to the main dining lodge. Already it was the gathering place for the new set of guests, as if they couldn't bear it one more minute till they told other guests how beautiful it was up here, and how marvelous the sunset was going to be, and could those cabins be any cuter?

Tapping the brim of his hat, giving the guests a nod, Brody felt their eyes on him as he walked into the dining hall, scanning for Kit. Not just scanning, but searching, his stomach spinning, almost desperate to see Kit again, to make sure he was okay, that he was happy—just to see Kit's smile would have been enough, but Brody wanted more, he would always want more, now that they had shared their bodies and their hearts.

As it wasn't quite dinner time, the dining hall was mostly empty, except for a few staff setting up the buffet line, filling tubs with ice, or making sure the steamers were properly plugged in.

He could hear sounds from the kitchen, so he went through the tall double doors, swinging one open slowly, taking a peek inside. Levi was holding court by the stoves, quietly instructing his cooks about something, and at the back of that little gathering was Kit, dressed in cook's whites.

Which was a very good sign as to how well Kit was doing, because if you worked for Levi, only cooks wore that uniform, with its long white pants and the jacket and the double row of buttons. The outfit would be covered by an apron, but it was a display of Levi's professionalism.

Dishwashers and bus boys had their own outfit, their own symbol of work, and were treated with equal respect by Levi, but that Kit had been dressed the way he was, was special.

When Levi dismissed his special few, Kit, bouncing on his toes, looked around the kitchen as if searching for a friend to share his pleasure with. When he saw Brody, his eyes lit up as he waved and came over, all in a rush.

"I have to get back to the barn in a minute," said Brody, pointing his thumb over his shoulder, smiling so broadly in Kit's presence he was sure some passerby would remark upon it.

"And I have to bread the cod in a minute," said Kit in response to this, his face flushed, brightness dancing in his eyes. "Levi demoed and then had some of us show him what we learned, and I got picked."

"You've got a dab hand, then," said Brody, and at Kit's confusion, he added, "You're good at it, and I love the new uniform." It was a pretty big deal for Levi to assign someone so new to such a task, but Brody's throat was full of emotion he hardly knew how to express, and he was soaking in Kit's pleasure until it filled Brody to the top, threatening to spill over.

"I'll still wash dishes and other stuff," said Kit, with a blush, pleased as he tugged on the hem of his sparkling white tunic. "But that doesn't mean I still can't help you in the afternoon. I already checked with

Levi. And horse lessons, too, right? We can still do those? Just you and me?"

"Yes," said Brody, not even pausing to tease, because the earnest desire to be with him was plain and there on Kit's face for everyone to see. He wanted private lessons with Kit so he could spend more time with Kit, and so Kit could come riding with him along the low slopes of the foothills. "Private lessons, you and me."

As Kit smiled, Brody girded his loins and remembered what Quint had told him: *Never be ashamed of how you feel. Say it in the light of day.*

Brody could hardly focus on those words, but he knew they were true. He knew he needed to be brave right now, so he wouldn't regret not saying them, when the dark times came.

"Kit," said Brody, swallowing hard. "I wanted to tell you something."

"Yeah?"

"Come outside, into the breezeway." Brody signaled to Levi, who nodded quickly, then turned to a cook who'd come up to ask him a question. "Come outside with me."

His heart pounding, Brody led an eager Kit into the breezeway, and then, thinking about what Quint had said, drew Kit out of the shadows and into the sunlight, so they could share it together.

Overhead, the pine trees made dappled marks on the ground, and scented the air with their spicy warm smell. The breezeway was aptly named, as it pulled cool air through the roofed area, making a nice place for a break, or a place to unload cardboard boxes and other goods without exposing them directly to the weather. Except when deliveries were being made, it was a quiet, private place.

"I needed to tell you something," said Brody. He curled both of Kit's hands in his and watched as Kit blinked at him, his mouth falling open as though he knew, somehow knew, what Brody was going to say. "Which is this." He swallowed to moisten his mouth, to get some air in his lungs. "Since I met you, my life has been different."

"It has?" asked Kit, his eyes wide.

"Yes," said Brody. "Sweeter somehow, I don't quite know why, but that's how it is. And I'm falling—" He paused, his breath clicking in his throat, his heart hammering against his breastbone with hard jerks. "I'm falling in love with you. I don't know how long we have. How long before you find Katie, but until then—I will treasure every moment we share together."

"Me?" asked Kit, sounding very much as though the air felt too thin to breathe. "You love *me?*"

It almost broke Brody's heart to hear the surprise in Kit's voice, as if he'd never expected anyone to make a declaration like that to him. As if he was the last person on the planet whom anyone would find lovable.

But Brody did. Loved Kit's earnestness and his innocence and the way his energy kept his body from ever being still. There was something to love about every part of him, from the top of his dishwater blond hair to the tips of his well-booted toes, where they stuck out from beneath the hems of his cook's trousers.

"Yes," said Brody with a swallow. "I'm no good at this, but I wanted to tell you how I feel because it's important, you know. I don't want you to move out of our room and I don't want you to leave—you go if you have to, just know I don't want you to."

The sound Kit made as he flung his arms around Brody's neck and squeezed him tight tore at Brody's heart, the ragged edges moved to repair only when Brody wrapped his arms around Kit's waist and hugged him even tighter. Their bodies seemed to mesh into one body, so close they were, so ragged Brody's breaths, so heartfelt Kit's sigh in Brody's ear.

Maybe Kit was crying, or maybe he was only struggling to breathe, to gasp a breath to say something, but Brody knew that didn't matter. Words didn't matter when their heartbeats wove together as they were, in sync, so quickly, so easily, it was as if they'd been separated such a long long time and had now only found each other.

"I've got you, youngling," whispered Brody against Kit's neck. "I've got you."

He didn't want to ever let go and he sensed that Kit didn't ever want him to let go, but someone called from the breezeway, and there was work to be done so with great reluctance, Brody set Kit back on his feet. Scraped at his eyes. Touched Kit's shoulder as he swallowed hard.

"See you at dinner?" he asked, as casually as he could, as if nothing more remarkable had been exchanged between them other than a mid-afternoon hug.

"Yeah," said Kit, shining like he'd been lit up from within. Smiling with his whole body, eyes burning pewter blue. "Try the cod," he said, his laugh a little shaky. "I hear it's real good."

"I hear that too," said Brody, echoing Kit's laugh. "Go on now, scoot. Show 'em what you got."

Brody wiped his mouth as he watched Kit race off with his usual high energy, heard Kit's laugh from the breezeway as a co-worker greeted him, and waited till he was all alone before he placed his palms over his eyes and took several deep breaths.

He'd just declared himself to Kit, in the sunlight, as Quint had suggested, and he was scared, scared it could all go wrong. Or maybe he was scared it could all go right, and he'd just signed himself up for more love than he'd ever known before.

KIT

*K*it walked back into the large, busy kitchen, and though he remembered to wash his hands before going back to his station, he could hardly concentrate on what he was doing. Levi came over to him, tall in his cook's whites, looming over Kit when he was trying to get back to work.

"What's going on here?" he asked, ever polite. "We talked about this. It's egg, then breading, not the other way around."

"I remember," said Kit quickly, dusting his fingers on his apron, looking at the metal table with the metal bin of egg, all stirred up, and the other bin of flour and breadcrumbs and salt and pepper.

"Guests expect the food to taste good and look good," said Levi, patiently. "And it's their first night of a long-awaited vacation, so sharpen up and give them what they paid for."

"Yes, chef," said Kit.

He felt small and stupid, and while normally he might have kicked something or shoved the metal bins off the table and onto the floor, just to see them crash, just to make some noise, he stopped. And remembered. Brody loved him.

Nobody had ever told Kit that before, not even Katie. When the bronc rider had once ruffled Kit's hair and told him he was a pretty good kid, Kit had shied away from the touch, not trusting it, not understanding, at that time, why someone would say that about him.

Katie had just rolled her eyes and looked away as she tugged on the bronc rider's arm so she could get his attention back to where she felt it belonged, which was on her.

Maybe someone at the casino in Vegas had said *good job* to Kit, and maybe there'd been a gym teacher somewhere who told him he threw a good baseball, but other than that, Brody had been the first. The first to say something so tender and sweet, the first to touch him like that, the first person to ever give him a blow job—

Kit stopped, blinking fast, and tried to breathe slow. He was so hard beneath his apron, he wondered if anyone saw. Men got erections, they just did. Kit had taken health class, so he knew that much. And he'd been having erections for a good while now, and knew what to do, and loved the sensation that came with pleasuring himself. But to get all worked up thinking about one, single, special person, that was new.

It was sweet, and it felt good, and he wanted to keep that feeling forever. To keep it, to stay near Brody, he needed to keep his job, which meant he needed to concentrate on what he was doing, as Levi had asked him. So he did.

Egg mixture, breading mixture, cod on the tray. Repeat. The task soothed him, and the special feeling swirled all around him, and it might have been his imagination, but when he looked up, one of his co-workers was smiling at him.

"What?" asked Kit.

"You were whistling," said the co-worker.

"Oh. Sorry."

"No, man, it was nice. Sweet tune."

Bending to his task, Kit wondered what the song was, pursed his lips, but couldn't remember it. That didn't matter. Someone else would probably be bothered by him whistling and tell on him, go running to Levi to get Kit to stop. Only that thought didn't feel quite right, the way it might have only days ago.

Brody seemed to like Levi just fine, and that meant Levi was a good guy. And good guys didn't have assholes on their staff, either.

Kit finished up preparing the cod, then changed out of his cook's whites and washed his hands, hung his apron on a hook.

"You can go get your dinners, and then I need my dishwashers back because we are short staffed. That's you, Dale, Craig, and Kit."

Kit wanted to balk. If he had to work late, that would mean less time with Brody, and it felt so important that for a whole minute, while everyone bustled about, he just stood there and glowered.

But he realized the truth. Brody would know where he was, and wouldn't blame him for working late. Rather, there would be praise, and maybe a small kiss, and maybe Brody would say, in that way he did, his mouth saying Kit's name like it tasted good to him: *I'll wait for you, Kit.*

Hurrying into the main part of the dining hall, Kit got in the very short line for dinner, and felt, suddenly, a pair of hands on his shoulders. The hands were warm, and gentle, the pressure from those fingers very light, and the scent of Mennen swirled around him. Before he tipped his head back and looked over his shoulder, he knew it was Brody.

"Time to eat," said Brody, in such an ordinary way, as though he'd not just declared how he felt about Kit only hours before. "Then I have to go back to the barn for a bit."

"Me too," said Kit. He touched Brody's fingers, just before Brody's hands dropped away from his shoulders. "I mean, I have to work late in the kitchen, 'cause Levi is short staffed."

"It happens," said Brody, casually, like this was an everyday thing, which it probably was. "Sundays are like that. Lots of stuff, loose ends and all."

They got their trays and their cutlery rolled in paper napkins, and slid the trays down the buffet line, looking at all the offerings. Since it was Sunday, there was the breaded cod, fried up nice and crispy, and different vegetables and potatoes, and noodles, and Kit took some of everything, his mouth watering.

Katie never liked fish, and so Kit had never eaten much of it, but

Brody took two helpings and so Kit took the same. But when Brody took potatoes, Kit decided he wanted noodles, and Brody's nod, for no reason at all, made him feel good inside.

Sitting down together at a back table, Brody shook his head as he unrolled his napkin and laid his cutlery out.

"Leland likes it when we mingle," he said. "But I just can't do that right now, 'cause I'd rather be with you. Anyway, I get enough, you know." He pretended to hold a camera phone up to take a picture, and then laughed. "They'll find me soon enough, and then I'll mingle."

"Right," said Kit, and he was glad Brody didn't want to mingle, because it meant he had Brody all to himself.

All of this between them felt private and new and he wanted to keep it close, wanted not to share with anyone. But then along came Clay and Austin, laughing at some private joke between them as they sat across from Brody and Kit.

"Oh, man," said Clay, his mouth wide, eyes dancing. "It was just a bull snake, but I guess I jumped three feet, right?"

"At least three," said Austin, in a serious way, though it was obvious he was trying not to laugh. "But I would have wrestled that snake to a standstill, you know I would have."

"Can snakes stand?" asked Clay, but the words were cut off as he laughed hard, wiping his eyes.

"It's like this all the time," said Brody, not lowering his voice as he turned to Kit to get him to share the secret, smiling at Clay and Austin to let them know he was teasing. "They're so in love. Bah."

Brody's smile belied his mock-grumpiness, and in response, Clay blushed and Austin's gaze at Clay seemed like the two men were holding hands in the moonlight, or that Austin wished they were.

"Say," said Clay, waving his fork around. "I hear you're giving Kit private riding lessons, and thought we could tack Austin onto some of them. You know, kill two birds and all that. It's so Austin can come on more trail rides with me."

"Oh, sure," said Brody easily, like he wasn't handing over a grand gift, which was the time Kit was going to be able to spend alone with

Brody, on horseback, being with horses, which Brody loved. "I talked with Leland about it already, but that okay with you Kit?"

Kit's hands shook as he held his knife and fork, and the cod didn't look so appealing, and even the chocolate cake with the fine swirl of frosting Levi had insisted be put on the top of each slice didn't look so lush. He wanted to stand up and shove his tray and spill everything all over the place. He wanted to stomp out of the dining hall to show the three of them how much he *didn't* care.

But then he felt Austin looking at him, his face serious and still.

"Maybe not," said Austin. "Maybe we can just have separate lessons."

Austin seemed to know what Kit was thinking and that almost made it worse. His eyes grew hot, and he wanted to scrub at them, to fight the tears, and why was he like this?

"Oh," said Brody, his body going still. Then he dipped his arm to slip it around Kit's waist. "We can do it like we planned," he said, softly. "I think it'd be fun to do it together, but we can do it separate if you want."

Kit had to think hard about this, to think fast. People who worked at the ranch didn't pout or stomp, they talked things over, they said what they thought. Nobody got smacked for speaking their mind, nobody got told that the backtalk better stop or *else*. Maybe he should try to say what he thought and see what happened.

"What if we—" Kit stopped to take a sharp breath. "What if we did both, all of us together sometimes, and then just me an' Brody together sometimes."

His heart jumped up and down as he watched the three of them, Brody and Clay and Austin, exchange glances, their eyebrows going up as though they were communicating silently, like a trio of alien beings who weren't quite sure how to speak to humans.

"That sounds like a plan," said Clay, the first one to speak. "Then we can compare notes when we do the lesson together."

"Yeah," said Austin. He nodded. "I wouldn't want anyone watching me all the time, either. I'm like loose spaghetti in that saddle."

"I would never make fun of you," said Kit, feeling solemn about the promise.

"Nor I you," said Austin. "That's not how they do things here, anyway."

That was the truth of it, behind everything he'd experienced on the ranch since his arrival. Nobody pushed him around, or yelled at him, or shoved him, or even threatened to hit him.

He needed to get that through his head, but it was so different from his life before the ranch, that it was hard. He couldn't even explain to himself why it was hard, when life at the ranch was so nice, but it was.

Before the ranch, nobody had ever been nice to him, not really, except for the bronc rider, and he'd lasted one short week. Brody was nice to him all the time, and, really, everyone was. Nobody ever shoved or yelled or anything like that. The ranch was a different place, a better place. It was a good place to be, and he wanted to stay. With Brody.

"That's right," said Kit, nodding as he swallowed the thick fist in his throat, as if he'd been about to cry, but didn't want to. Nobody seemed to notice, or if they did, they didn't remark upon it. "I just want to. You know. Be with Brody."

There was a flurry of looks exchanged, from Clay to Austin, from Austin to Clay, and from Clay and Austin to Brody, and back again. He'd said it, right out loud, but other than those looks, everyone went back to eating and chatting about the weather, and if there'd be a storm later, which would be a shame, as it was the first night of the week for new guests.

"Nah." Clay shook his head and licked frosting from his fork. "A thunderstorm is romantic, romantic as *hell*. Guests'll eat it up."

"It'll mean a muddy ride on Monday, and what about the dance on Tuesday?" asked Austin.

"Boots, my good man, boots," said Quint as he sat down next to Austin, his big shoulders taking up space, his steady gaze on Kit somehow more bolstering than it was scary. "Guests love it when they think they're going through hardship. When they have to slog through mud to the dining hall or the barn and back, they get muddy. Then they take a hot shower and text their friends at home, *with* pictures, and say, *Oh, I got so muddy today! What an adventure!"* Quint laughed a little as he started to eat. "I'm telling you. They live for that shit."

"They do," said Clay. "That they do."

"It's like playacting, right?" asked Kit, feeling bold even as he asked it.

"That's right, Kit," said Quint, with a firm nod as though Kit had told the utmost truth. "They're coming here to act out a story in their heads. We create the environment and act as secondary characters in their little fantasies."

"There's nothing wrong with fantasy," said Austin stoutly.

"Never said there was, my dear accountant." Quint's smile at Austin was warm, and Kit sensed that Quint liked Austin, in spite of the fact they were nothing alike. "It's my bread and butter during the summer, and not a bad way to make a living. Not a bad way a'tall."

"What do you do in the winter?" asked Austin.

"I've got an Airstream in storage," said Quint. "I find a beach somewhere and carve things for the tourist trade. Foxes and ponies and suchlike. Keeps me busy, keeps me in groceries."

"Winter on the beach is nice," said Brody. "Remember Port Aransas?"

"Yes."

Quint's smile at Brody was like a secret they were sharing, and Kit made a mental note to ask him about it, to get Brody to tell him why there was a web of warmth between him and Quint as they shared that secret memory. He shouldn't be jealous, after all Brody had told Kit he loved him and whatever Quint and Brody had shared, Brody was with Kit now and he shouldn't be a big baby about it.

"Hey," said Brody, looking at Kit, dipping his chin. "You'd like it there," he said. "We could go sometime. Miles of beach. Miles of ocean."

"And that good salt smell," said Quint.

That was another secret shared between Brody and Quint as they smiled at each other. Kit had never been to the ocean, never seen it. Never smelled it. And he suddenly wanted to, oh, so very badly.

"That'd be cool," said Kit, trying to keep his voice light and failing, because every word wobbled as he said it. He swallowed and tried again. "That'd be cool."

"We'd probably stay with Quint," said Brody.

"Plenty of room," said Quint.

"Oh, can we come too?" asked Clay, though Kit couldn't tell if he meant it.

"Find your own place, lovebirds," said Quint, though his smile took the sting out of his words. "The Airstream is big, but not that big."

It took Kit a good, long minute to unravel everything in the conversation but, plain and simple, the end result was obvious. He and Brody were invited, and Clay and Austin were *not*. But it was hard to be left out, as Kit knew well, and he wanted to fix that.

"You could rent a little place up the beach from the Airstream. Like a cabin," said Kit.

"That's a good plan," said Austin, and he shrugged and ate some chocolate cake. "Though we have really no idea what we're doing this winter after the season ends."

"Nope," said Clay, agreeing, though the smile he exchanged with Austin said loud and clear that he'd like to spend a good long time alone with Austin figuring it out.

"Eat up, youngling," said Brody to Kit. "We've got work to get through this evening."

"Okay," said Kit, and never before had he ever felt more like he belonged than he did right at that moment. And never had he realized how much he'd wanted to belong. To someplace. To someone. Someone like Brody.

Somehow, being brave, he took one hand and laid it on Brody's thigh, and smiled with a sigh when Brody laid his hand on top of Kit's and squeezed gently, as though he wanted to keep Kit's hand there forever. It wasn't easy to finish his meal with the use of only one hand, but Kit managed it, managed just fine.

28

BRODY

*T*oward midweek, the afternoon shadows were long outside the barn as it threatened to rain, but then never did. That was fine by Brody as it made the air damp and sweet with the scent of wild grasses soaking up the rain. Guests enjoyed their lessons more when it wasn't baking hot, and the horses seemed to enjoy the break from summer temperatures.

"Thanks for your help, Kit," Clay was saying to Kit as the two of them trundled from the arena with wheelbarrows full of horse manure and bits of hay. "It's not glamorous, but it sure needs to get done all the time."

"I don't mind," said Kit, his voice bright, and when he looked over his shoulder at Brody, Brody was ready with a fond smile. Kit was making sure Brody was there, nearby and watching, as a shy horse coming out of its shell might, and that was fine by Brody. Eventually Kit wouldn't need that so much anymore, and that would be fine, too.

The surge of warmth inside of him, the sense of contentment, all of this mixed together and buoyed him up to crest a wave of happiness, and then after that, another wave, and another. It was odd to be this happy for such a long while, a good while, so he was soaking it up while he could. So he could bolster himself against the dark times surely to come.

Quint rode up on Diablo, who chomped his bit and stamped his iron-shod hooves, and generally made himself known. Guests walking from the arena on their way to the dining hall for dinner gave Diablo a wide berth, even as Quint dismounted and gave Diablo a hearty pat on his sweating neck.

Diablo dropped his head right away, and chuffed and sighed, as if he knew, which surely he did, that his saddle was going to come off, and the bridle, and someone was going to brush him down, put him in his comfortable box stall, and feed him sliced apples after giving him hay and making sure his water bowl was full.

"Hey," said Quint as he took off his hat and wiped the sweat from his brow with his sleeve. "Just checked the fence lines that Clay and Jamie repaired," he said. "They look good, but now I've got a meeting with Leland and Bill about those adventure rides. Would you be willing to groom Diablo for me? I'll owe you."

"Sure," said Brody, for it wasn't even a question that he'd help Quint out. "Good luck," he said to Quint's retreating back.

"I'll need it," said Quint with a gesture over his shoulder that looked like dismissal but was probably a thank you wave.

Absently petting Diablo's damp neck, Brody lifted his head and whistled for Kit as he went back past the barn with an empty wheelbarrow.

"Come and help me," said Brody. They'd not yet arranged a second riding lesson for Kit, but in the meantime, grooming Diablo, or any horse, would help Kit get used to the animals and how they behaved. And, besides, it was an excuse to have the two things he loved near to him, Kit on one side and a horse on the other.

Brody could see Clay nod before trundling off with his wheelbarrow and shovel, and after Kit parked his wheelbarrow by the door of the barn, he half-skipped inside, into the shadowy coolness, where Brody was cross-tying Diablo.

"Get the brushes and stuff while I undo Diablo's saddle." Brody jerked his thumb at the tack room, where the grooming supplies were kept.

"I want to do that." Kit came close, his shoulder brushing Brody's shoulder. Then he swallowed and seemed to rethink his words. "I mean, I'd like to learn how the girth and stuff works, so I can help you get the horses ready for riding lessons."

"Sure."

Brody waited till Kit came back with the grooming kit, and showed him how to loosen the girth, how to hook the far stirrup over the saddle horn so it wouldn't knock the horse's side, and then how to slide the saddle and saddle blanket off all at once.

"Put it like this," said Brody as he laid the gear over a saddle tree in the tack room. "We'll wipe it down later, but first we take care of Diablo."

"Okay."

Kit was close at his side, echoing each of Brody's movements, his use of the soft chamois to wipe the sweat from Diablo's body, rather than the sweat comb, and the gentle motions of the body brush, the metal comb for Diablo's mane and tail.

"Go slow," said Brody, bending to kiss the side of Kit's neck, in the shadow of privacy that Diablo's large form created. "Always slow."

Kit turned and wrapped his arms around Brody's neck and hugged him tight, and if there ever was a day that Kit didn't hold onto Brody like he was the last safety buoy before being pulled out to sea, today wasn't that day. Tomorrow didn't look good either, so Brody swept his arms around Kit's slender waist and just held on right back.

"Hey, now," whispered Brody into Kit's ear. He kissed Kit's cheek, and waited until Kit was ready to let go, and then side by side, they returned to their work, grooming Diablo, making him not just comfortable but presentable. Then Brody got an apple from one of the bins in the feed room and cored it and sliced it. "You give it to him."

Diablo seemed so sleepy and calm that Kit acted as though his fears of any horse were just a dream from yesterday as boldly he held the slices in the palm of his hand and one by one fed them to Diablo.

Who seemed grateful and sighed, slowing down from his morning's activity up in the high hills.

"He's so tame," said Kit. "Maybe I could ride him."

"I told you no," said Brody, stern. He didn't actually think Kit would take it in his head to saddle *any* horse on his own and go for a ride, let alone Diablo, but he needed to make it clear. "He's for advanced riders only. If you got on his back right now, he'd take off and we'd never see you again."

"I won't do that, then," said Kit with a low laugh as he leaned into Diablo's shoulder, lights dancing in his eyes as he showed Brody how bold he was, how brave. "But I'll hug him, like you hug horses all the time." Gently, but without any timidity, Kit looped his arm around Diablo's strong neck, and kissed the plane of his cheek, and jumped back a bit when Diablo snorted.

"Nicely done," said Brody. "Let's finish up and get cleaned up for dinner."

"They're going to show that movie tonight," Kit said as they hurried through the rest of Diablo's grooming and put him away in his box stall. "After dinner."

As they finished up in the barn and helped Clay finish cleaning the arena and the paddock, Brody didn't know how he felt about the viewing of the documentary film. He did know that he wouldn't care if his interview, his demo, or any piece of it that had him in it was cut from the final version. Leland had mentioned in the morning meeting that the documentary wasn't quite finished, that some parts had yet to be assembled, but for now there was forty-five minutes to be watched and he expected everyone to be there to support the filmmakers.

Guests were invited to the viewing but their attendance was not required, but Maddy had mentioned that Levi was making a new batch of homemade ice cream in several flavors, so Brody imagined that the dining hall would be full. He could sit in the back, and maybe sling his arm around Kit's shoulders, and just be close to him while he waited for the words *The End* to flash across the projector screen.

Dinner was ribs and cornbread, and they ate side by side in the very back of the room, using their fingers and more napkins than

264

usual. After, they got huge bowls of peach ice cream and went to the back table, away from the chatter and excitement as Finn and Artie set up their projector in the middle of the room, and the viewing screen in front of the buffet table. Clay and Austin sat up front, and Brody could tell Clay wanted to see himself on the big screen, as already his cheeks were rosy, his eyes bright with anticipation.

If Clay'd a childhood like Brody had, then all an interview would mean to him was Daddy Frank pinching his upper arm before the interview to get him to sit still, sit up straight, and to answer the questions the way Daddy Frank wanted him to. And then a whipping afterward, as there was no way Brody's performance would have come up to Daddy Frank's exacting standards.

Though, it wasn't fair, and Brody didn't really want to take away Clay's excitement, so when Clay looked around, Brody waved and gave him a thumb's up. Kit gave him a thumb's up too, and this seemed to settle Clay, who turned around and leaned into Austin's shoulder, as though preparing himself for the fact that his interview, and any clip with him in it, might ultimately be removed.

The lights were dimmed and the documentary started up just as Brody fed Kit a spoonful of peach ice cream, just to watch his eyes flutter with pleasure, and the glisten of his lips when he licked them. Then he put the empty bowl on the table and prepared himself to pay attention, as it would be rude not to.

The images in the documentary were crisp and clear, the voiceovers blending into the images and the points at which whoever was on screen talking, naturally, smoothly. The interviews, starting with Bill's and Leland's, were balanced, and didn't go on too long, and when Clay came on screen, he whooped and clapped, doing a little jig in his seat. Brody vowed to go up after the viewing and get his autograph, just for fun, just to make Clay's good feelings about himself and his five minutes of fame a little more real. It wouldn't hurt anyone, and he'd get Kit to do it as well.

When Kit came on screen, sitting up straight in the leather chair in Maddy's office, bravely talking, the crowd sighed, and why wouldn't they. He was so sweet-faced, so earnest in his answers that guests fell in love with him, and a few turned around to see Kit all the way in the back.

"Wave," whispered Brody.

Kit waved, and then giggled, and Brody was glad, for it meant that none of this was going to Kit's head. When Kit lowered his hand, he reached to hold Brody's hand, and that was a good thing, because Brody's interview came up before he was ready for it, even though he already knew the answers, knew what he looked like on screen.

It was what came after that he'd not been prepared for. Sure, he'd known that Artie was filming candid shots to give the documentary some humanity as well as veritas, but he'd not known Artie would be out by the arena, when Brody had been giving lessons and had, on impulse, hopped on Chiquita to demonstrate how to canter and turn without slowing down. The camera followed Brody and Chiquita as they went around the arena, and maybe Brody could say that he looked good, his shoulders steady, his seat low and solid in the saddle, if it didn't feel like he'd been filmed while naked in his room, where he expected his activities to be private.

"You're beautiful on horseback," said Kit, his voice warm and low as he leaned close.

That bit of candid film turned into him doing the trick roping demo, with the fairy lights of the dance floor glittering amidst the flair of his fringed chaps, white on white, sparkling like the lights were coming from inside of him. The rope became sheened and silky in the light, and his movements made him seem like the rope was part of him—and the guests oohed and ahhhed and Brody knew they'd be asking Leland for a demo of their very own that week. And Brody would have to do it, even though his skin crawled as the memories rose up from beneath his skin.

And then came the clip he'd least expected, which bared him to his soul.

As he'd dropped the rope, circling it around him like a snake rather than letting it spin out to the audience, he stepped off the dance floor. Kit, unaware that he was being filmed, raced up and threw his whole body into Brody's arms.

And there, in front of the guests and staff, and Leland, who was standing to the side of the dining hall, arms folded across his chest, watching the film and the audience both, saw everything. Saw the way Kit's head tilted back to look up at Brody, saw the way Brody tipped his head down to kiss Kit's temple, his arm slung around Kit's neck. Saw the flash of passion and the ribbon of love that flowed out of their eyes and that swirled around their bodies, tying them together and announcing to the world how much love there was between them.

Guests clapped, not knowing Brody had just crossed the non-fraternization line. However much Leland had already broken that rule, the rule still existed and surely Brody would be called to task for it. And for taking advantage of someone so young and impressionable. And yet, in spite of this worry, Brody wanted to ask Finn for a copy of that image, him and Kit together, so close and so happy, as he could keep it with him always and take it with him into the dark times when Kit joined Katie in Vegas, which surely he would someday.

Clay turned and gave Brody a thumbs up and a lascivious wink, making much of the moment, until Austin tugged on Clay's shirt and made him turn back around so they could focus on the rest of the documentary. But the evening was over for Brody, and even Levi's handsome serious face couldn't make him focus on the tall white screen.

When it was over, the lights came up and everyone stood up and chatted excitedly and Brody saw that Leland was making his way over to the back of the room where Brody and Kit were, holding their bowls, waiting until the guests were done bussing their tables of bowls and spoons and paper napkins. Brody knew that while he might not get fired on the spot, he was in the hot seat with Leland.

Except Quint, who'd been there watching the documentary, as well, only Brody'd not known it, stepped out from the shadow of the open doorway, and walked right up to Leland. There, he tapped Leland in the center of his chest as he talked. Brody could imagine that the tap was quite light, as the man brave enough to tap hard, the man with a death wish such as that, had not yet been born and likely never would be. Quint's voice would be low and earnest, getting to the heart of the matter like a sharp knife slipping between Leland's ribs.

When Leland lifted his head, his arms were still crossed over his chest, but he lifted one arm and crooked his finger at Brody. Quint stayed close as Brody and Kit approached. Brody's mouth went dry, but he didn't want to swallow and let Leland know how nervous he was, though Leland must know, as he always seemed to. Like he could see right into Brody's heart and just know.

"Quint's given me an earful, here," said Leland, smiling at guests as they went past, eager to walk beneath the shadowed trees and enjoy the evening air. "And I'm inclined to agree that mayhap the non-fraternization rule might need a bit of revising."

Jamie came up and curled his fingers around Leland's upper arm, as though he wanted him to soften his stance. "You know it does," he said, his green eyes bright, his words solid and sure. "It should be a guideline rather than anything solid, anyhow."

"Well, until that happens, here's my question," said Leland. "Do you love him?"

"Yes," said Brody, for he could not lie about this, nor dance around it, for it was too important to him.

"Yes," said Kit, piping up, his eyes wide as though he'd just realized what he'd said out loud.

"Have a care then," said Leland. "Don't be flashing it about, as this is a guest ranch and not a—not a—"

"Not a hoochie coochie show," said Quint, with a laugh and a gentle slap to Leland's back.

"A hoochie *what?*" asked Leland, and as Quint distracted Leland with his answer, he waved at Brody and Kit to make a quick departure.

And, hand in hand, this they did, slipping between the slower guests and around the faster ones, out to the darkness beneath the shadowed trees. And there, on the path to the staff quarters, Brody stopped and drew Kit further into the shadows. His arms were around Kit's shoulders, and their hips pressed together.

"We told 'im," said Kit, eyes wide, astonished. "I didn't know we were gonna."

"Well, we did," said Brody as he kissed Kit's cheek and cupped the back of his neck and inhaled the scent of pine needles, spicy and warm in the cooling air. "At least he knows now."

"Let the world know," said Kit, tilting his head back so Brody could kiss more of him. "Let the world know, I don't care."

Kit was too young to know that yes, sometimes, the world did care, and that a faraway mother might object to having her son's attention pulled from her. As each day passed with no call from Katie, Brody wanted to soothe himself with the idea that the call would never come. But it would. Some day. One day. But not today. At least not today.

"Let's get ready for bed," he said, his mouth moving along Kit's soft cheek as he spoke.

"A shower," said Kit, nodding. He turned to kiss Brody on the mouth, a tender pressure, but not a hesitant one.

"Yes," said Brody and he drew Kit out of the darkness once more, and along the path to the staff quarters.

No matter what Katie did or didn't do, he had this moment now. This moment, just him and Kit.

29

KIT

*A*s Kit went up to their room Friday afternoon to change into a clean shirt for the upcoming riding lessons, memories of that morning swirled all around him. He pulled out a pink and grey plaid snap-button shirt, and smiled at the neatly made bed, and wished the sun would hurry up and set so that it could be nighttime. So he and Brody could undress slowly and shower and crawl into bed, naked to their skins. And then he could practice on Brody what Brody had done to him that morning, sweetly kissing him all over and then between his legs, not touching his cock, quivering with hardness, until the last minute.

The build up of tension and expectation had sent Kit spinning over edges of himself he'd not known had existed. And afterward, the slow cuddles, the warmth of Brody's body as Brody held him. The slant of yellow sun through the blue morning sky, all of this had been amazing and perfect, and then short-lived, as Brody had hustled them out of bed, into their clothes and down the stairs. Work never waited and meetings were always too long but if he had Brody at his side, Kit knew everything would work out the way it ought.

Kit had bent his head to snap his buttons when his cell phone rang. He almost didn't recognize the sound, as it'd not rung in over two weeks. Looking over he saw it was Katie, so he yanked it up to his ear, eyes wide, almost panting with excitement.

"Katie?" he asked, his voice high-pitched that Katie had called him back.

"Kit, hi," said Katie, brightly, as if it hadn't been days and days *days* he'd been calling her, anxiously wanting word from her. "I've got great news! I'm getting married in Vegas on Sunday. The guy's name is Ralph, and he's got a double wide in San Lazaro trailer park, which is the nicest in all of Vegas."

"You're getting married?" Kit bit his lower lip as all kinds of feelings, his delight at finally hearing from her mixing with odd and squirmy ones he didn't know what to do with. "But what about—what about Eddie's money?"

"What money?" asked Katie, her voice growing faint and then loud again as if she'd lifted her chin away from the phone, like she was talking to someone standing quite close or that she was smiling at them. "Oh, that money. He'll never miss it anyway."

"Yes, he will." Clutching the phone with both hands, Kit nodded as though she could see him, and all the while his heart was racing. "He was pissed, Katie. He didn't like it that you took it and—" He gulped, not wanting to talk about it out loud, but he had to say it. Katie needed to know what had happened after she left. "He was rough with me and he threw me down the stairs—"

"You'll be okay," said Katie breezily. "I needed that money more than him, you know that. Anyway, you'll have your own room in that double-wide, just like I promised. And I *need* you to be my best man."

"Your best man?" asked Kit, his mind whirling with the idea of it, that he'd have his own room, that Katie sounded like she was finally settling down at last—except Katie didn't seem to care that Eddie had roughed him up. But then, had she ever been concerned when he was hurt? Kit knew the answer to that question was no, but long-ingrained impulsed allowed him to shove everything aside, all the hurts, all the confusion, so he could focus on what Katie was saying to him.

"Yes, I *need* you, Kit, I need you *with* me," said Katie. "I need you to be there 'cause it's such an emotional time for me. I can rent you a white tux, and you'll look so cute in it. I've wired money to the Greyhound station in Farthing, and a little extra money for snacks along the way."

"Greyhound?" asked Kit. All of this was happening so fast. His memories of the Greyhound bus station were tame next to his memories of the Rusty Nail, right across the street.

"Yes, Greyhound, 'cause I don't have the money for a plane ticket." Katie laughed that laugh she had when she figured her plan was best, and any problem the other person had was not her problem. "Anyway, don't miss that bus or you'll miss the wedding. We're staying at Sam's Town, so meet us there."

With a click, she hung up. But who was *us*, and what time was the wedding?

It was Friday. The bus left at three-thirty-two on the dot, and he needed to be packed and ready to go in less than five minutes, as he would need to walk the distance to town.

His stomach in knots, Kit went over to the closet and pulled out his worn backpack. He stuffed it full of his clothes, mostly his old ones, like his long-sleeved t-shirts, and some new ones, like his new underwear and socks. He grabbed two packets of Pop Tarts from beneath the plastic bin under the bed. Then he grabbed his cell phone and stuffed it in the side pocket of the backpack.

If Brody had his cell phone with him, Kit would have called, right then and there to tell him what was happening. But Brody, preferring to be out of touch sometimes, typically left it behind. It was sitting on top of the dresser, nicely plugged in and charging for Brody to use later.

Kit didn't pack his fancy new cowboy boots, and his cowboy hat, but he wouldn't need them—he was headed to Vegas where Katie was. Katie and her new beau, who was soon to be Kit's new step-dad.

His hands paused as he zipped the backpack closed. None of Katie's men, excluding the bronc rider, who'd not lasted that long anyway, had seemed to take a shine to Kit, preferring him out of the way as often as possible. And yes, he'd have his own room to hide in, but—

He closed his eyes and sighed and heard Katie's voice saying, *I need you Kit, I need you with me.*

It was a siren song he was unable to resist, so, in spite of the fact that his whole body felt like lead, he hefted his backpack on his shoulder and, taking a breath, opened the door. His legs trembled beneath him as he hurried down the stairs, where he nearly bumped into Stella who was standing at the bottom of the main stairs with a wicker laundry basket in her hands.

"Where you goin' in such a hurry?" she asked. "You nearly ran me over."

"Katie called and she's getting married," said Kit, moving around her, grateful for her question, which distracted him from doubts blooming in his head like a black cloud. "I'm headed to Vegas! She left me tickets at the Greyhound station and I gotta hustle or I'm going to miss the bus."

With a wave, he was out the door, like he was walking on autopilot, unable to stop himself. The dirt path thudded beneath his feet as he walked down the dirt road toward the green-painted gate at the entrance to the ranch.

If he didn't exactly hide the fact that he was walking quickly past the dining hall, he didn't exactly walk out in the open either. Instead, he stuck to the shadow of the trees on the far side side of the road and ran a little, trotted a little, and ran again, until he was across the parking lot and into the glade of trees without anyone seeing him. Or, at least without anyone seeing him who cared who he was or where he was going with a backpack full of clothes, and not wearing his straw cowboy hat.

He didn't stop at the arch of the stone bridge as it curved over the rushing water, but hurried all the way to the green-painted metal gate, being careful to close it behind him, lowering the latch with a metallic click.

Once out of range of any seeing eyes, and once out in the open, his heart started to slow. And then to ache.

Brody and he had just the day before announced their relationship to Leland Tate, the ranch's manager. Which in Kit's mind was the same as putting it in the newspaper or online, for anyone to see. Why was he leaving that behind? Did he not love Brody with all of his heart, or was his heart made of stone? What was wrong with him? Why couldn't he slow down?

He knew he loved Brody, he did, but Katie's siren call was hard to resist, screaming in his ear, drowning everything else out of his mind.

He kept walking to town, clutching at his shirt over his heart, dust rising from the road as the ranch disappeared behind him and the edges of the rooflines of Farthing appeared above the tall summer-brown prairie grasses.

Beyond Farthing, beyond the shimmer of the sun in the blue sky, something waited for him that he'd wanted since forever, since he was small. A home. A family. Katie being a mom. Some guy he'd not met who'd be his dad.

He'd be in Vegas inside of two days, with plenty of time to figure out where Sam's Town was. He vaguely remembered it as a nice small-scale hotel on the edge of town, but that the Greyhound station was in downtown Las Vegas. He'd need to hitch a ride or walk or, if he had enough money, take a taxi to get to Sam's Town.

As he approached the town, walking up Main Street, the sun was slanting slightly behind him. His steps went slower and slower as if his booted feet were heavier than he realized. Why hadn't he worn his new cowboy boots so he could show them off to Katie and her fiancé?

Because.

Those boots were a gift from Brody. They belonged to the ranch, they were part of who he was on the ranch.

And so who was he now that he no longer had them?

The question laced uncomfortably along his ribs, causing his heart to thud as he opened the glass door, spotty with bugs and grease, of the Greyhound station.

Up at the counter, he only had to wait a minute before asking the bored clerk about a ticket that Katie Foster had wired in that day. Sure enough. The clerk punched her keyboard, then handed him a printed ticket and five dollars change. The ticket was already smudged and the five dollars seemed to wilt as he held it in his hand.

"Bus is running late, so it'll only stand for a minute or two before heading out again," the clerk said. "Don't stray."

"Yes, ma'am." Kit slowly turned around, looked at the hard plastic seats along the window, and took a deep breath of the stale-smelling air. "I'll be outside," he said to her, to the empty waiting room, and pushed the door open to step onto the sidewalk.

His heart thudded painfully in his chest, and each breath seemed labored, like he was standing with his head just below the surface of a lake-full of bad water. What was he doing? Why was he leaving?

Across from the Greyhound station was the Rusty Nail, looking, with its plain-board, unpainted siding, and its sagging roof, as it always did in the middle of the afternoon, like a sleeping beast that would awaken come nighttime. Bars were like that. Busy at night, empty and dark in the day.

The Rusty Nail seemed so small and kind of ratty at the edges as he looked at it now, and he could hardly remember that he'd once thought it a nice place to stay when he and Katie had arrived, a kind of vacation location for the two of them.

The Greyhound pulled into the bay and chuffed for a moment, letting passengers off in a straggly line that extended from the open doors of the bus to the station, where the bathrooms were. Kit licked his lips and tried to cough away the diesel-smelling fumes that seemed to want to coat him from head to toe.

This was a bad idea, a *bad* one, all of it. But if Kit backed out now, Katie would be mad that she'd wasted bus fare on him. She'd call and holler about it and Kit already felt bad enough about the whole thing, so what should he do?

Across the street, Eddie Piggot came out of the Rusty Nail with a baseball bat in his hands. He held it like he imagined he was some kind of star slugger for the local team.

Kit watched Eddie march across the street, eyes focused on Kit, who was unable to bid his body to run and hide or even to move.

Uneasily, he tried to back into the shadows, though that was foolish, as Eddie already had Kit in his sights.

"Where's my fuckin' money, you little shit," said Eddie, growling. He swung the bat, hard, popping Kit on the shoulder. Kit stumbled back to land with a thud against the brick wall of the bus station, almost pinwheeling to stay upright. He almost dropped his backpack too, but hung on with both hands as Eddie swung again, striking Kit's hip, his thigh.

Nobody saw what Eddie had done, as they were both in the shadows. Kit's left side ached, blood thudding beneath his skin all up and down his body, and he was sure his cell phone was cracked, as he'd heard the snap of glass breaking.

As Eddie raised his bat again, Kit's only exit was the Greyhound bus, so Kit turned and sprinted for the door so he could slip through the waiting room and into the bay where the bus was parked.

Behind him, Kit heard the whistle of wood in the air as Eddie swung again, but Kit raced till he was climbing onto the bus, panting, his body aching, standing between the rows as the bus driver shouted for him to sit down as he had a schedule to keep.

Kit took a seat behind the bus driver and ducked his head, so he wouldn't have to look at Eddie and his snarling eyes. He curled over his backpack, sweat dripping into his eyes, a chill down his back as the bus took a hard right at the end of town.

He didn't know the name of the road they were on but they were headed south. The sun poured through the smoked glass along the windows on one side, and the low foothills were softened around the edges in the sun's glare.

Soon, toward sunset, as Kit well knew, those foothills would be touched with blue and purple and softened with rose. Soon, quite soon, within an hour perhaps, Brody would return from the upper fields. He and Quint would groom the horses they'd ridden, or maybe it would be Quint's turn and Brody would come up to their room to find Kit gone.

The bus chuffed. The edges of Kit's heart began to chip off, with each beat, growing more ragged, more sore. His leg and hip throbbed and his arm ached in time with the pulse of blood beneath his skin.

Too cool in the air conditioned bus, he felt ice grow along his back. There was no Advil in his backpack. No ice packs made with Brody's nimble fingers twisting a washcloth around ice brought from the ice machine next to the door of the laundry room in the basement of the staff quarters.

Blinking hard, Kit pulled out his phone to find the screen broken in two lightning-shaped jagged cracks. When he pushed the on/off button, nothing happened. The phone was dead, ruined by a swing from Eddie's bat. There was no way Kit could call Brody and tell him where he was.

There was no way—

There was no way this was a good idea, any of it. Of leaving without making sure Brody knew where he was. Of going to Katie and her mystery man, to a hurry-up wedding in a Las Vegas chapel, to promises that would never be honored.

Once Kit arrived in Vegas, his life would be as it always had been. Katie would expect Kit to bear the weight of her new life, to fit into the narrow spaces between her flares of activity, her bursts of promises.

Between her attention to her nails and whatever easy-money scam she had going on, her attention would be on her new husband, who surely would have a name like Ted or Bob or Jim. And who, no doubt, would figure out that while Katie might give good blow jobs, the best on the planet, as one of the Teds had candidly told him over beers while the three of them played a row of Triple Red Hot 7 slot machines, would also quickly find out that Katie was a lot like Vegas. All smoke and mirrors, empty promises, full of the excitement of the possibility of it all, but without the delivery of any promise made.

On the other hand—

Brody had promised Kit pretty much nothing, but had delivered on everything. Kit had new cowboy boots, new clothes, three meals a day, a soft pillow for his head. But, more than that, he'd felt Brody's gaze upon him, gentle and warm, as though Kit was Brody's pride and joy. He'd felt Brody's touches on his body, a gentle caress to his cheek, soft kisses. Being held in the night, Brody's arms around him, had made him feel safe, for the first time in his life.

On the ranch, his sleep had been interrupted by absolutely nothing, unless it was the song of the night, the whisper of star-lit breezes across the tops of the trees, the faraway howl of coyotes.

In Vegas, like the rest of his life, his head would no sooner hit the thin pillow than Katie would be shaking him awake, handing him some money, crumpled bills and old quarters scrounged from the carpet in some slot machine hall, to send him to the nearest bodega for chocolate-covered macadamia nuts or whatever it was her taste-buds wanted at three in the morning. But in the morning, while the package would be opened, only one or two would have been eaten, and the rest would start to freeze in the overly cool motel room.

The only thing that had woken Kit on the ranch were the warm touch of Brody's hands as he gently shook Kit awake. Or, lately, kisses along the back of his neck as Brody spooned him from behind. The first thing they would do was trade off in the bathroom—which Katie never did, she always went first and when it was Kit's turn, it was too late and they had to hurry out of the room or Katie would get fired—and then they would eat breakfast.

Always Brody would be watchful, making sure Kit had enough, encouraging him to eat things that were good for him. If Kit's buttons on his shirt were askew, Brody would pause and redo them. If Kit needed or wanted anything, Brody would get it for him.

Beyond that, those sweet gestures that Brody made daily, Kit knew he was the focus of Brody's attention, his love and caring. Being there, in the middle of Brody's world, Kit had begun to feel like he was shedding the skin of his old life and stepping into a new version of himself.

But now that he was on a Greyhound bus headed to Vegas, to Katie, it was as if he was trying to stuff himself into the shell of that old life. That old shell felt stiff, as though it no longer fit him. Which it didn't. It was an old life he'd left behind him as he'd walked into Brody's life, into Brody's arms, into his love.

Kit stood up, shoving his broken cell phone into his backpack, any old how. He didn't want to go to Vegas. He wanted to stay on a little ranch in nowheresville, Wyoming, that offered the best sunsets he'd ever seen. He wanted *Brody*.

"Hey, mister," said Kit, his voice shaking as he stood in the aisle right behind the bus driver, which he knew you weren't supposed to do or the bus driver would be pissed.

"Sit down, please, sir, while the bus is in motion," said the driver, half-bored, as though he'd said the same thing a million times already that day.

"Stop the bus," said Kit, as firmly as he knew how. He shifted his backpack on his shoulder, his heart pounding, his knees wobbling. "Stop the bus, I need to get off."

"I can't stop the bus while en route," said the bus driver. "I can only stop the bus at official stops or in cases of emergency. Now will you please sit down?"

Bending to the side, Kit pressed the Request for Stop button next to the outlet where he could charge his phone. Kit didn't know if the bus driver *had* to stop when that button was pressed, but maybe he did so maybe it was worth a try. Otherwise, Kit was going to have to bide his time till the next town, and then he'd have to get beg someone to borrow their cell phone so he could call Brody—

He pressed the button hard, two more times, and, amidst a hard chuff from the engine and a squeal of brakes, found himself falling forward to land in the aisle at the bus driver's feet. A pair of angry eyes glared down at him while the rest of the passengers started up a low angry chatter.

"Now what the fucking hell is that?" The bus driver pointed at Kit and then out the front window of the bus. "Where the hell did that come from?"

Scrambling to his feet, Kit bent low to look out the front window where the bus driver was pointing.

There, in the middle of the road, was the most beautiful thing he'd ever seen. Astride a sweaty and bit-chomping Diablo, was Brody, hatless, sleeves rolled up to his elbows, wind-chapped, his hair in his eyes as he held onto the saddle horn and tugged on Diablo's reins.

His lips moved as though he was talking to Diablo, begging him to be steady, to stay there in the middle of the road so that the bus could not continue.

As for Diablo, he was standing his ground, iron-shod hooves planted in the blacktop on either side of the dotted white line, like he was daring the bus to come at him.

With his breath stuck in his throat, his head whirling, Kit watched as Brody slowly managed to guide Diablo to the side of the road because of course not only did Brody know the bus driver had a schedule to keep, he wanted the choice to be Kit's. So Kit would have a chance to get off. If he wanted to. If he wanted to stay. With Brody.

"Sorry," said Kit to the bus driver, even though he wasn't. Even though he'd never been less sorry in his life.

He grabbed the straps of his backpack in one hand and held on to the steel handle alongside the steep steps with the other. "Open the door. Open the door please."

His heart was pounding as he got off to plant his feet alongside the road, looking at Brody as the bus pulled off with an angry snort, leaving greased air and dust to settle around him like a baptism.

Diablo spotted him just as Brody did, and the horse pranced to him, like Kit was a stray, which indeed he was. Diablo loomed large as he approached Kit, his mane tangled by the wind, bubbles of froth at the corners of his mouth.

"Let's go," said Brody, his voice sounding calm, like it was an everyday thing for him to be riding the toughest horse on the ranch, holding his hand out, one leg swinging free of the stirrup.

It was obvious that Diablo wouldn't hold for Brody to dismount so that he could help Kit astride. No, Kit was going to have to brave the dragon, even though half of him ached and the other half was crying, because Katie probably wouldn't even notice that the Greyhound bus would arrive in Vegas and then depart, and there'd be no Kit.

She wouldn't notice for days, even, and when she did notice, she might call to ask for her money back, or maybe she'd shrug and look at her nails and then it'd be her husband who'd be woken in the middle of the night to fetch whatever treat Katie had decided she needed right away.

But Katie really wouldn't care and maybe, quite possibly, she never had. And Kit knew he didn't care about her either, not anymore.

"Let's go, Kit," said Brody again, but though he sounded like he was in a hurry, maybe a little focused on keeping Diablo in check as he danced around, his iron-shod hooves striking sparks on the blacktop, the way he said Kit's name was just the same as it always was. Soft, loving, as though Brody liked the feel of Kit's name in his mouth.

"Here," said Kit, his heart juddering as he came close to those sharp hooves, alongside Diablo's shoulder as he handed up his backpack.

Brody took the backpack and slung it on the saddle horn so it draped on the other side of Diablo. Then he held out his hand again and Kit took it, his skin coming to life as he gripped Brody's forearm, feeling as though a charge of energy was surging through him.

It would have been easier to put his foot in the stirrup if he'd been wearing cowboy boots, but he managed it. Managed to sling his leg over Diablo's back to thump down behind the cantle of the leather saddle.

Right away, Diablo, making his own decisions as always, figured they were done being where they were and needed to be somewhere else right this minute. He trotted, half bucking, turning himself around to face the way back to the ranch and all the while Kit held on as best he could, Brody's waist a lifeline.

"Hang on," said Brody. "He wants the barn, and I can't hold him without tearing his mouth."

"Okay," Kit said, breathing the word as the wind snatched it from his mouth as Diablo took off, tearing through the high grasses, guiding himself, deciding for himself where he wanted to go, where he needed to be. Which was exactly where Kit wanted to be. Back at the ranch. In the barn, working side by side with Brody.

He would be there soon, and would be able to stay, that is, if Brody forgave him for leaving without a word. And if Brody understood how the impulse to be with Katie had become electric inside of him the second he heard her voice on the phone. How badly he had felt even merely putting things in his backpack, how confused he'd been with every step he too away from the ranch.

But as Diablo galloped down the long, jagged hillside into the valley, going around the back side of the ranch, cutting across wild country, the words jumbled inside of Kit and the only thing he could do was press close to Brody's back and hang on with everything he had.

30

BRODY

*T*he hills called to Brody to return even as he and Quint rode down the slope to the ranch, stopping in the shade of the barn. He planned on unsaddling and grooming both the horses they rode, Dusty and Diablo, but Quint was wordlessly making motions that it was his turn, and so Brody's plans began to change in his mind. He'd go back to the room to shower and change. He'd find Kit. They'd have an early dinner together and then—

Out of the shadows came Stella, dressed in her blue and red striped apron that covered her front and back, her white sneakers kicking up dust, the curls on her head dancing as she came right up to Dusty and tugged on Brody's hands.

"What is it, Stella?" he asked her, taking off his hat, leaning toward her.

"It's Kit. He's gone." She gripped his hand with both of hers and held on hard. "He's taking the bus to Vegas. Today."

"What bus?" asked Brody though he knew exactly what bus Kit might be on and that was the Friday afternoon bus, which pulled out of the Greyhound station three days a week at exactly three thirty two. "Today?"

"He got a phone call. Someone named Katie. Something about a

285

wedding." Stella's expression told Brody in no uncertain terms that she hated being the bearer of bad news, but that she would do it, out of her affection for him. "He packed his things and was gone not twenty minutes ago."

"That's enough time for him to get there," said Quint, coming up, leading Diablo by his reins. "Enough time to hop on that bus."

Slowly Brody dismounted, his heart pounding, the sweat beneath his shirt drying to a slick film on his skin. He could barely feel the dirt beneath the soles of his cowboy boots and only absently petted Dusty's neck. Though he could sense Quint looking at him quite hard, and knew that Stella had reached out to clasp his forearm, he was standing on the other side of a pane of glass that cut him off from everyone else.

He'd known this day would come. He'd known Katie would call, for how could she manage without her only boy-child being in attendance to make sure she was the center of everyone's world?

As for the fact that Kit had packed up and left inside of a heartbeat, Brody wasn't sure he was surprised. Though the messages Kit had left for Katie had begun to trickle off, they'd been mighty important to him. And maybe this was the darkness Quint had spoken of, the darkness Brody had needed to prepare for.

"Thank you, Stella, for letting us know," said Quint.

"I wished I'd stopped him." With a quick squeeze, Stella let Brody go. "I wish I had but it all happened so fast, and then he was gone down the road. If there's anything I can do, just let me know."

"Will do," said Quint, stepping in to speak for Brody's voice, which he seemed unable to use. "Brody."

Quint moved close, close enough for Brody to feel him there, his warmth, his steadiness. His hand on Brody's arm.

"You going after him?" asked Quint, his voice gruff and low.

"I have to let him go," said Brody. "I told myself I would let him go when he wanted to leave. I even told him that. So he knows—And besides you told me to get ready for the darkness to come. This is it. This is the darkness."

He was quite ready for that darkness to swallow him up. Quite ready to get dressed in his outfit of white suede and to demo his rope tricks to each week's batch of guests. Week after week, year after year. Forever until he died. After all, what else was there for him without Kit? Without those pewter blue eyes looking up at him, blazing with hope and adoration. Without that slender body rolling into his arms each morning, without Kit's laugh as he proposed that he was famous, so famous since being interviewed, only he didn't give a damn about that, he only cared about being close to Brody.

It was only when Quint cupped his cheek that Brody realized he was shaking.

"That first day," said Quint. "I would have said yes, let him go when the time came. Only now, I don't think so."

"But you can't keep people—" began Brody, his voice jagged in his throat, his thoughts slicing through his heart like knives. "You told me that."

"In this case—" began Quint, but he stopped and shook his head. "What's best for you? What's best for Kit? Right here and now. Today. Tell me. Just tell me. What does your heart say?"

Quint's hand stayed where it was, a warm curl of calloused fingers around Brody's neck. The feel of Quint's heartbeat through those fingers, Quint's spinel-colored eyes, his gaze, never wavering.

"It says go." Brody swallowed, hard. "Go and find him. Bring him back."

"If you take Diablo," said Quint, letting go of Brody, placing Diablo's reins in his hands. "You can ride over the hill by John Henton's cabin, and cut across that valley to the highway to Cheyenne. That's the route the bus takes. Diablo will know you're looking for Kit, and he'll take you there. You know how he is."

Indeed, Brody did know, for as he took those reins, he looked up at Diablo and Diablo lifted his head as if to ask, *Which direction? How fast?*

"We've got a stray, Diablo," said Brody as he mounted, his hat falling from his head to the dust. Beneath him, Diablo gathered, chuffing, his legs already churning in place as though he was impatient to go.

"Pace him," said Quint. "Don't let him boss you around."

With the slightest urging, the merest touch of Brody's heels, Diablo took off. And while normally nobody galloped at full speed along the dirt road that went through the middle of the ranch, Brody was prepared to break that rule and a thousand others like it, if it meant he could catch up to Kit and bring him home.

Diablo's hooves thudded on the road as they raced past the main lodge, beneath the trees to the parking lot, where Maddy stood on the shaded porch with her mouth open as she watched them barrel past her. Curving Diablo to the right, they raced up the faint track to the hillside where John Henton's rebuilt cabin was, and down along the steep slope to the wooded valley south of the ranch.

There was no road into the valley or out of it, only faint deer trails through the thick stands of pine trees. Brody had to crouch close, and hug Diablo's neck, and guide him gently, for Diablo had the bit in his teeth. And though Brody couldn't imagine Diablo knew they were chasing down a Greyhound bus, somehow, and very likely the horse was guided by the way Brody's body was leaning, Diablo raced through the valley, churned across the rough-edged sandy-banked river, and up the other side as though he did know that Kit was gone and needed to come home.

The trees thinned and the sunlight slanted on the grasses as they raced up the slope to the two-lane blacktop road that went between Farthing and Cheyenne, the next stop on the Greyhound's route.

There was nothing worse than the smell of diesel fumes, but inhaling that smell into his lungs was how Brody knew they could catch up. Diablo's legs, solid iron, tore up the dusty earth beside the road as Brody spotted the silver eyes of the bus, and pointed to it, as though Diablo was a sight hound and in his blood knew how to run a hare to earth.

With a fierce gallop, Diablo scrambled onto the blacktopped road to be ahead of the bus just as the bus was slowing down. It took Brody a minute as he tried to control Diablo, to keep him in place, to realize that someone was already standing up inside the bus and that the bus was stopping, even as Diablo's iron-shod hooves struck sparks on the asphalt.

The bus driver pointed at the pair of them as Brody held Diablo to a standstill in the middle of the road.

"We got him, boy," he said, his lips numb. "You were fast, so fast, but now you need to breathe and stand, breathe and stand. Don't let the bus go, we can't let Kit go, we *can't*—"

Kit tumbled off the bus, backpack in hand, his dishwater blond hair messy around his face as he steadied himself on his feet. Looking at Brody like he wasn't sure he should approach, like he wasn't sure he'd be allowed to.

However hard they might need to work to settle this between them, at least Kit had gotten off that bus under his own steam. He'd chosen to stay, and that was all that mattered.

"Let's go," said Brody, his heart pounding so hard he feared it might burst, his numb hands doing their best on the reins to hold Diablo still. Brody used the pressure of his legs on Diablo's side, urging him to stay in place, but he couldn't do it for much longer. "Let's *go*, Kit."

Coming up to Diablo as he chomped and sweated and danced, Kit's face was white, his eyes blazingly dark. And though afraid, he handed Brody his backpack and when Brody reached out his arm, Kit clasped it with icy fingers, and managed to swing himself astride Diablo, just as Diablo, rippling with sweat, determined his direction home.

"Hang on," said Brody. "He wants the barn, and I can't hold him without tearing his mouth."

"Okay," said Kit, his voice shaking over the word as he wrapped his arms around Brody's waist and tucked himself close to Brody's back as if preparing himself for the worst horseback ride of his life.

Diablo didn't go gently or kindly, he merely kept that bit in his teeth and tore down the slope to the wooded valley south of the ranch, going as fast as he pleased, in the direction he thought best. The only thing Brody could do was hold the reins so they didn't get caught in any pine trees. Hold onto the saddle horn, and clasp Kit's knee to be sure of him while Diablo galloped and slipped through the trees, the branches whipping back in their faces, the air filled with Diablo's hard breathing.

There was no fence line south of the ranch, which meant that there was no reason Diablo needed to slow down, but Brody knew he needed to get Diablo to slow, or everything would go to hell upon their return to the barn. It was one thing to have Diablo galloping in one direction, as that could be explained away, as Diablo was known for being headstrong. But both directions? There would be no way Leland would let that go.

Brody managed to get Diablo to slow down by the time they reached the parking lot, but he was lathered and breathing hard, and the fast trot was simply not fast enough for him, as he broke into a canter, then down to a trot, and up to a canter again, in spite of all of Brody's efforts to get him to just walk.

The faces of the people they passed along the road back to the barn told their own story. Diablo was a sight to behold, and word would get back to Leland soon enough.

By the time they reached the barn, Quint was waiting, and Clay, as well. Quint yanked Kit from Diablo's back, not in a mean way, but quickly so Diablo would know his mission was finished. Even as Brody was dismounting, Clay took off Diablo's bridle to replace it with a soft green halter, a simple rope lead clipped to the circle beneath Diablo's chin. Finally, Diablo's head went down and he chuffed, and sighed, still breathing hard, still covered in foam.

"Walk him," said Quint, handing the lead to Kit. "You owe it to him, to Brody, to walk him. I'll fetch soft cloths. Clay, can you get warm water?"

"What about me?" asked Brody.

"Get that saddle out of his sight, and the bridle, too."

Brody undid Diablo's girth, and hefted the saddle and bridle to his chest and hurried off to the tack room, there to place the gear on a rack so it could be cleaned before being put away. When he returned to the front of the barn, Kit, still white-faced, was walking Diablo slowly up and down in front of the barn, his head down, meek as a kitten. At each turning, Clay let the horse drink a bit of warm water from a shallow bucket, then pulled it away so Kit could walk him again.

"I've seen worse," said Quint to Brody. "He won't seize up if we walk him gentle and slow and then brush him down good."

Nodding, his face still numb, his body shaking, Brody did his best to breathe slowly to calm himself down. Except up came Leland in his silver F150. When Leland turned off the engine and got out of the truck, Brody felt Clay looking at him, and saw the question in his eyes: *Do you want me to go?*

Brody shook his head. Clay was already here, so they might as well get this over with, though when Brody kicked Kit's backpack out of sight, Clay saw but didn't say anything. He would owe Clay and then some, that is, if he got through the next five minutes with his hide and his job intact.

"Maddy called me," said Leland as he strode up to survey the tableaux in front of him. "Care to tell me what happened that we had a runaway in the middle of the ranch guests' last full day?"

"It was my fault—" began Quint, but Brody cut him off with a gesture of his hand.

"We came back from the field, and Diablo still had some energy to burn through, so I took him from Quint and thought—well, I thought I'd run him up to the pastures again, only Diablo decided different and I couldn't hold him. I'm sorry, Leland."

"Then why is Kit walking that horse instead of you?" asked Leland, his eyes glinting, his mouth a thin line.

"I wanted to help," said Kit, piping up, not stopping in his task of walking Diablo to cool him off.

"Me, too," said Clay, holding the bucket up, trying on a bright smile that didn't feel quite right to Brody, though he appreciated the effort just the same.

"Diablo's gentle enough without a bridle," said Quint.

Between the five of them the words fell to the ground, plopping like overripe fruit. Either Leland would believe the lie and let it go, or he'd ask more questions. Which would put Brody in the position of having to lie even more, so that he could keep his job. So that Kit could stay with him. So that Diablo's hard ride would not have been for nothing.

"A good wrangler," said Leland, quite slowly, his voice calm, but loud enough to be heard. "A good wrangler never puts guests or horses in danger, never asks them for more than they can give. But by the looks of Diablo, here, one of the toughest horses I know, you asked him for his best effort and he gave it to you. I certainly hope you appreciate that and the fact that I'm letting you keep your job when I should be asking you to step down. Now." Leland took a slow breath. "Get this horse seen to. It's already on the grapevine, but we'll tell guests it was what it looked like: a runaway horse, something that almost never happens, which is true. And get that backpack back where it belongs, Kit."

"Yes, sir," said Kit, meek as he stepped out of Diablo's shadow and into the light of Leland's glare.

"I'm going to dock your pay for skipping out of work this afternoon, understand?"

"Yes, sir," said Kit. He went back to walking Diablo slowly up and down, stopping to let Diablo drink from the shallow bucket. His shoulders curled forward, and his face was still white, but he seemed to sigh with a kind of relief.

Leland hadn't believe the lie, but then he didn't need to, as he seemed able to determine the truth, about the ride, about Kit, about everything. The thick fist in Brody's throat expanded as he tried to breathe around it as he watched Leland get back in the truck so Leland could park it where it belonged, behind the supply shed with the other vehicles.

"Dang," said Clay in the silence that fell in the truck's wake. The only sound was Diablo's breathing, which had slowed, and the slow, low clop clop of his hooves in the dust.

"You go on, Clay," said Quint, going over to Clay, his hands reaching out for the bucket. "We'll finish up."

"The hell you will," said Clay. He pulled the bucket out of reach and looked up at Quint, fearless, his blue eyes blazing. "We're going to do this together. We're going to fix Diablo up, brush him down, and oil his hooves. Then I'm going to braid his mane and tail, maybe with some columbine flowers in there so if guests come to see him, and you know they're gonna, he'll look so meek and mild they'll want to pet him and get their picture took with 'im. And they'll tell each other the story of him galloping down the road like he was something out of a fairy tale."

Brody blinked, and even Quint looked a little taken aback at being told what to do. But that's how Clay was, he was Leland's mini-me, and very skilled at organizing people and ideas. And his idea was a good one. They'd repaint the picture Diablo presented, and make a story out of it for guests, the way Quint was always talking about.

"An' Kit'll be the one holding Diablo's lead," said Quint, nodding, adding to the story. "Delicate Kit holding the lead of our own volcanic Diablo."

"I'm not delicate," said Kit, pouting, his face getting red as Clay brought back the box of grooming cloths, the needles for braiding, and a bunch of columbine stems, purple petals dripping over his wrist.

"Yes, you are, boy," said Quint, with a gruff laugh. "At least for the next while. You're as delicate as a butterfly's wing, hear?"

"Oh." Kit nodded and straightened his shirt, which was, thankfully, mostly clean.

As Brody and Quint and Clay began to wipe Diablo down, to neaten him up for any guest who might want to visit, Brody's heart began to slow down, his shoulders to relax. He wasn't alone and Kit wasn't alone. At least not any more. And they didn't just have each other, they had the ranch and its people all around them. Supporting them, helping them. That was how a family, a real family, should be.

"Here they come," said Quint, pointing his chin at the small collection of guests approaching the barn when they should be getting cleaned up for dinner. But, as Quint knew and Brody knew and the rest of them knew, this small event was organic, just the way Leland liked it, and something guests would take away with them and talk about for years to come.

Clay forced a laugh, but when Diablo farted gently in his face, the laugh was real, and he kept on braiding Diablo's lengthy tail as two women came up and started talking to him about Diablo's wild ride.

"Sometimes, ma'am," said Clay to the women as he tucked blooms amidst the twists of braid. "A horse just wants to run, that's all."

"He was going so fast," said one woman, timidly patting Diablo's hip. "In both directions."

"He's not wild," said Clay. "He just likes to run. Go on, pet his soft nose. Give Brody your phone and he'll take a picture of you two and Diablo."

Hurriedly, Clay snuck himself into the frame, braiding Diablo's mane as Quint rubbed Diablo all over with a cloth. Kit tried to get out of the frame, but Brody tugged on Diablo's lead to bring him close, and together with the two women, and Diablo's gentle stance, Kit was in the picture when Brody took it.

A few more groups came to have their picture taken with Diablo, who, when Clay handed out apple slices for guests to feed him with, seemed happy to chuff out a breath and cock his hoof to balance one leg on, and seemed happy to be petted by many pairs of inexperienced hands.

When the scent of cooking wafted through the air, Kit and Clay were both hunkered down to oil Diablo's hooves, and Diablo, merely ground tied, was looking in the direction of the barn as if he wanted all the excitement to settle down so he could have a nice long snooze in the stillness of his box stall.

"That's enough folks," said Quint. "You can come see him in the morning, if you like, and see what a mess he's made of his new hairdo. But it's dinner time now, so run along. Run along."

When Quint talked like that and gathered the lead to Diablo's halter from Kit, guests did as they were told. As Quint led Diablo into the barn, Clay picked up all the bits from Diablo's beauty treatment, the combs, the flower petals, the body brushes, the bottle of hoof oil, and took them to the tack room to be put away.

Which left Kit and Brody pretty much all alone, with only the shadow of Kit's backpack tucked just inside the open barn doors to remind them of how the crazy, un-ranchlike afternoon had started.

"Are you mad?" Kit asked, looking up at Brody, his eyes apprehensive, his shoulders tight.

"Yes," said Brody, for he knew he needed to be honest about it.

"I knew it was wrong the second I stepped foot off the ranch, but I couldn't seem to stop." Kit rubbed his mouth with the back of his hand, like he wanted to erase the words as soon as he spoke them.

"Why didn't you call me?" asked Brody, not moving from where he stood, unable, it seemed, to cover the short distance between them. "I would have driven you. I would have taken you."

"I wanted to, when I was on the bus," said Kit. "But my phone was broken. Eddie must have busted it when he hit me with his bat—"

"You ran into Eddie?" Brody took a step forward, his hands on Kit's shoulders, gently. "He *hit* you? Show me where."

"He must have seen me at the bus stop, and when he came for me it was him or the bus. So I got on the bus." Two hard tears streaked down Kit's grey-tinged face, tracking over his mouth, dripping from his chin. "I'm sorry I got on the bus. I'm sorry I left. But Katie called and said she was getting married and I kind of lost my m-mind."

Kit was not crying, but he looked just about destroyed, like he imagined Brody would consider this a betrayal. Though Kit knew by now, surely he did, that Brody wasn't going to smack him around, he looked just about resigned to the fact that Brody was going to ask him to pack up and head to Vegas. That Brody was going to insist on driving him to catch up with the bus he'd just gotten off of.

"Hey," said Brody, alarm rising in him that Kit had been hurt, and yet had ridden behind Brody as Diablo raced across the rough, untamed ground of the valley. "Hey, now. Let's get you inside, and I can take care of you."

That was the most sensible course of action, to focus on Kit, to take care of Kit. Yet, they were alone in the dusty area in front of the barn, and Brody's heart was still trembling as he moved forward and gathered Kit in his arms. He bent to kiss the top of Kit's head, and said, "Please don't leave me. Please don't ever leave me."

And it was he who was crying and Kit who was comforting him, his arms around Brody's waist, his head pressed to Brody's heaving chest.

"Never," said Kit. "Never *ever*."

Though Kit bent to grab his backpack, he did not let go of Brody as they headed beneath the trees to the staff quarters. There, Kit put his things away as Brody, bare-chested, washed in the sink and then used a damp washcloth to clean the streaks of Kit's tears, the stripes errant pine tree branches had left. To gently trace the hard lines across Kit's shoulders and thigh that Eddie's bat had left.

"Take this Advil," Brody said, holding out the bottle of pills. "I'll get you some ice from downstairs."

Kit swallowed the pills, using the little plastic cup that Levi had given them, and put on the clean shirt that Brody had pulled out for him to wear, just as Brody was putting on his clean shirt. So they'd be presentable. So nobody would know just how hard that ride had been.

"Maybe I can have the ice later," said Kit, his voice wobbling, his eyes shining as he looked at Brody. "Can we just go to dinner and pretend for a little while that I didn't actually pack up and leave you?"

"Yes," said Brody as he just about used too much force to close the closet door. "We can do that. You're my family now, not Katie's."

When Brody turned, he knew it was wrong to keep Kit apart from his mom, though he wanted to make it clear how much it meant to him that Kit was with him, rather than her.

"I mean, I want you to stay." Brody gulped as Kit came up and leaned against him, reaching up to cup Brody's face in his hands. "With me. Always. And not her."

"I will, I promise." Kit rose on his toes and kissed Brody on the mouth, gently, as though sealing the promise with his whole body. "Katie has always let me down. You never have. And I never want to let you down."

"But you will," said Brody, tucking a strand of hair behind Kit's ear, looking into those big pewter eyes that tracked his every move, the way a nervous horse will. "And I will. That's just how it goes."

"We'll do our best not to," said Kit, sounding solemn, nodding. "And that's the important thing."

"No," said Brody. He shook his head, and curled his arms around Kit's neck and hugged him to his chest. "You're the most important thing. The most important. To me."

Now Kit was crying, full out, his body shuddering against Brody's, his arms around Brody's waist. And Brody let him cry. There was time enough to put a brave face on it, time enough to wash their faces again and change shirts if need be before heading to the dining hall. To chat with guests and pose for pictures and remember the world, more often than not, was a better place than it seemed.

At least they wouldn't have to lie to Leland. And if someone caught them holding hands and kissing in the moonlight, they wouldn't have to hide that either. Wouldn't have to hide their love, not from anyone.

31

EPILOGUE

The first Sunday after their wild ride on Diablo, Kit was still a little rattled as he got ready for bed, watching Brody making sure the windows were open to catch the cool, evening breezes. He'd just gotten off a phone call, the first on his new cell phone, with Katie.

He'd managed to push into the conversation to tell Katie he wasn't going to make it to the wedding. She'd breezily told him it didn't matter because she'd found someone else to be her best man. Then she'd asked if Kit would arriving in Vegas on Monday because Ralph needed someone to pick up the slack in his snack machine business.

"No," he'd told her. "I'm settled here and I can't leave my job."

He'd been on the verge of telling her about Brody, but she'd raised her voice over his and kept on talking. Like she always did, spilling her anger about the fact that he wasn't coming to Vegas, along with her sadness, her needs, her wants, her desires, and to hell with what anybody else needed. To hell with what Kit had ever needed.

He guessed he'd known the truth about her for the longest time, only he'd never wanted to believe it, as the alternative, life without Katie, while it might have been potentially more peaceful, had felt so empty and uncertain. Now he had Brody in his life, now he had a place at Brody's side.

And though part of him, fearful, felt raw-edged about running off like he had, another part of him felt the balm of hope. Brody had forgiven him and seemed upset with himself at not doing more for Kit, which was completely different than how Katie would have acted. But as Brody would have said, enough about her.

"Hey," said Brody, coming out of the shadows of the bathroom, once he'd flicked the light off. "Want to come with me and do something magical?"

"Sure," said Kit instantly, his heart rising, expectant, full of love because Brody had asked him to do something special. "Which shoes?"

He pointed to his cowboy boots and his work boots, because on the ranch, different tasks required different footwear, an idea so new and novel, he was willing to change from cowboy boots to work boots and back again, all day long, as long as was required.

"Cowboy boots," said Brody. "We'll have to polish them later, but they're perfect for this. Perfect."

Kit slid into his cowboy boots, smoothed his blue jeans, and followed Brody out of the room and down the stairs, just about tiptoeing as they went out into the evening air, and stood beneath the rustle of tree branches as the wind started to kick up.

"It won't rain," said Brody, the words like a promise. "C'mon, let's go."

Brody led the way to the barn, and went into the tack room to pull out something that in the auto-light looked like a bridle, but without a bit.

"It's a hackamore," said Brody. "Only certain horses don't need a bit. You'll see."

Brody led them to the lower pasture, showing Kit how to slip between the barbed wire, how to walk among the grasses, how to use his night vision to not trip over rocks or stubs of horse-bitten grass. They went right up to the nearest herd, and Kit could just about see the pricked ears, the alert lift of their necks as the horses looked at them. All the horses seemed ghostlike in the darkness, like they were half in the field and half in another world.

"Gwen, I think," said Brody, half to himself. "If she's willing."

He clicked beneath the starlit sky, the darkness of the mountains to the west rising in a way that would have been threatening, scary, had Kit been alone. And had Brody given it the slightest bit of attention. But his attention was all on Kit, at his side, and on calling Gwen out of the darkness to greet them with a low nicker.

"Pet her neck," said Brody as he kissed Gwen's nose and slid the hackamore over her ears, looping the braided reins over her neck.

"What are we doing?" asked Kit. Of course he was all in with whatever Brody wanted to do, but he couldn't imagine they were going for a ride without a proper bridle, and without a saddle. In the dark.

All round them, the gentle slopes of the lower fields seemed to glow beneath the stars and the silver slice of moon that was just coming over the horizon to the east. The glow seemed to come from the grasses and low bunches of sage, as though the plants had gathered the light to themselves, enfolded it, and were now emitting it from the tips of their skinny green arms.

Kit had been out past bedtime, sure, in Vegas, or at the Rusty Nail, or anywhere, when Katie had wanted him out of the motel room. But there it had been lit by streetlights and traffic lights and the amber color of brake lights. It had not been like this, not silvered and green-shadowed, smelling sweet, the faint breeze bringing the scent of horse and field and mountain edges, all blended together.

"Up you get."

Kit focused. Brody was bent forward, making a cup out of his hands, the ends of the braided reins curled around his thumb.

"Up?" asked Kit.

"I figure you'd ride in front, and I'd ride behind with my arms around you." Brody looked up at Kit and in the semi-gloom, his eyes sparkled brightly. "That way I can keep you safe."

"Bareback," said Kit half to himself, but it was obvious to him that this was something special for Brody, so he swallowed his fear, put his booted foot gently in Brody's cupped palm, and let himself be hefted astride Gwen. "She's a buckskin," said Kit, being brave as he patted her neck. "A pretty buckskin like you."

"That's right," said Brody. He handed the reins to Kit and hopped astride Gwen, snugging close behind Kit, close enough so his strong thighs cupped the outside of Kit's thighs, and the inside of his thighs, all the way to his groin, made a safe space for Kit.

Brody's front was warm all along Kit's back, and when Brody curved his arms around Kit to take the reins, Kit felt himself relaxing. He was as safe as could be, there in Brody's arms, and no matter what happened, Brody wouldn't let any harm come to him.

"We'll start slow," said Brody, moving to urge Gwen to walk. "Until we get into the valley, where it's flat."

"Then what?" asked Kit, but maybe Brody didn't hear him, as he was concentrating on guiding Gwen as all the rest of the horses in the little herd folded in around them as if they too meant to go on a nighttime ride. They were surrounded by horses on all sides, by the click of hooves against loose stones, the swish of tail, the snort, curved necks, pricked ears.

But Kit forgot that as Brody leaned back as Gwen started down a steep slope, and instinctively, Kit leaned back against Brody, shifting when Brody shifted, feeling the hardness of Gwen's spine between his legs, rubbing against his balls, her broad back rubbing the inside of his thighs.

He was about to make a comment, to say something about how it would have been more comfortable riding with a saddle, when Brody clucked to Gwen and seemed to shift forward, pressing against Kit's back.

That's when Gwen sped up into a canter, and then a gallop, and all the horses in the herd sped up, too, and the sound of their hooves was loud, the whisper of wind in Kit's ears sinking into his soul as they flew through the darkness, galloping now. His head was in the stars, it felt like, and he was floating above the landscape, with Brody's arms secure around him, the wind lacing through his hair, his heart pounding at the speed, the joy of it, the magic of the night weaving into him, into his very being, tying him and Brody together.

"Faster," said Brody, whispering to Gwen, the sound tickling Kit's ear.

"Faster?" Kit asked, but the wind whipped away his question as Gwen picked up speed, turning the nighttime air to silver, lacing the surface of the river into streaks as they galloped along its banks. They rode farther into the night until Kit was sure they were halfway to Montana, when Gwen slowed and turned, the herd shifting around them, blowing air through their nostrils, dipping their heads to chomp on grass.

"That's her signal that she wants to go back," said Brody. He kissed Kit's ear. "You only have to listen to hear what a horse wants to tell you."

Kit nodded, leaned into Brody, rolling his hips forward as he tipped his head back to kiss beneath Brody's chin.

"Never ask 'em what they can't give you," said Brody. "And I never do. Never will. And I meant what I said when I told you I loved you. And I meant what I said yesterday, when I asked you never to leave. Maybe we should get married, or something, so nobody can separate us."

Kit sat a little straighter, almost knocking the top of his head on Brody's chin, but then he went quite still. The nighttime air was cool around them, and cooler as it came off the glassy, starlit river. Overhead, the sky was a blanket of softness, the mountains to the west, more blankets of darker grey.

He couldn't see Brody's expression, but he could feel Brody all around him, his body was tense as if he expected Kit to say no, to struggle for his freedom. But where could Kit go that would be better than where he was right at that moment? Nobody had loved him the way Brody did. And nobody ever would.

"Da dum de dum," hummed Kit, smiling as he pulled Brody's arms around his waist. "Da *dum* de dum—"

"Does that mean yes?" asked Brody, his voice rough-edged. "I shouldn't have asked. You're so young—"

"Not that young." Kit nodded firmly, and held onto Brody's hands at his belly button. "If I'm old enough to be at your side, then I'm old enough to stay at your side forever an' ever."

Brody reached to take one of Kit's hands, to lift it to kiss it, to clasp it to his face. Then, beneath them, Gwen shifted and snorted.

"She wants to go back to the field." Brody sighed, like he regretted the magic ride was over, only he didn't know the magic had settled in Kit's heart so firmly, it would never leave him.

"I liked this," said Kit. He leaned to pat Gwen's neck as Brody reached around Kit to pull her reins up, to get her going. "I was scared at first, and then. Then, it was like flying. Can we do it again?"

"Sure." There was a smile in Brody's voice as he clucked to Gwen to trot and then into a slow canter.

"On any horse but Diablo," said Kit over the rush of air as Gwen sped up down that dark road.

"Never fear, youngling," said Brody. "Never fear that."

Brody guided them back to the field, where they patted Gwen all over and let her go to roll in the dirt and chomp on nighttime grasses. On their way back to the barn, Brody showed Kit how to check the level in the water tanks and where the best spot to slip between strands of barbed wire was. And once back in their room, having dropped the hackamore back in the tack room, he stripped Kit to his skin and kissed him all over, pressing what felt like love into Kit's body with each kiss.

"I want more riding lessons," said Kit, softly.

"You got 'em," said Brody.

Kit pulled Brody into his arms, and when Brody's head was settled in the curve of Kit's shoulders, he added, "And I want you."

"You got me." Brody nodded, his hair a little scratchy against Kit's skin.

"Da dum de dum," hummed Kit and was pleased when Brody hid his face in Kit's neck, and that his face seemed warm, as though he'd grown a little shy. And that the curve of Brody's mouth was wide, and pleased, and content, which was all Kit would ever want, now and always.

WANT to read more about the sweet romance between Brody and Kit? Click here to get the bonus scene. (https://claims.prolificworks.com/free/iT4iHaJi)

WANT TO READ ABOUT LEVI, the ranch's head chef, and how he fell in love? Pre-order The Cook and the Gangster today! (https://readerlinks.com/l/1897450)

WANT TO READ AN M/M time travel romance? I have a whole series. Start with Heroes for Ghosts. (https://readerlinks.com/l/1568447)

You can stay up to date on upcoming releases and sales by joining my newsletter or my reader's group.

Newsletter: https://readerlinks.com/l/1775220
Reader Group: https://readerlinks.com/l/1776076

IF YOU ENJOYED *The Wrangler and the Orphan*, I would love it if you could let your friends know so they can experience the romance between Brody and Kit. Currently the book is available on Amazon, and is also listed on Goodreads.

JACKIE'S NEWSLETTER

Would you like to sign up for my newsletter?

Subscribers are alway the first to hear about my new books. You'll get behind the scenes information, sales and cover reveal updates, and giveaways.

As my gift for signing up, you will receive two short stories, one sweet, and one steamy!

It's completely free to sign up and you will never be spammed by me; you can opt out easily at any time.

To sign up, visit the following URL:

https://www.subscribepage.com/JackieNorthNewsletter

facebook.com/jackienorthMM
twitter.com/JackieNorthMM
pinterest.com/jackienorthauthor
bookbub.com/profile/jackie-north
amazon.com/author/jackienorth
goodreads.com/Jackie_North
instagram.com/jackienorth_author

AUTHOR'S NOTES ABOUT THE STORY

When I came up with the concept of doing a series of m/m romances set on a guest ranch, I already knew I wanted a brooding loner cowboy (Brody) who would find his one true love in the least likely of places. Brody's background is rough, full of scenes that were difficult to write—but his reward is the orphan, Kit, who loves Brody with all his heart and soul.

I have a thing about orphans, always have, as my own kidhoood was somewhat rugged. I know what it's like to have someone hold out their hand to pull you to your feet, to have someone care that maybe you didn't get enough to eat that day or perhaps for several days.

I was also inspired by the movie "Buck," which tells the story of Buck Brannaman, and how he came to be a horse whisperer.

Buck Brannaman was, in fact, part of the inspiration for the novel "The Horse Whisperer," by Nicholas Sparks, and main inspiration for the 1998 movie "The Horse Whisperer," directed by and starring Robert Redford. Buck Brannaman served as consultant for the movie.

I have not seen the movie or read the book, but just watched "Buck," almost moved to tears by him talking so levelly about his kidhood, which was far worse than mine.

I wanted to write a story about how someone with such a horrible, miserable time growing up could find love and happiness. You hold the result in your hands.

A LETTER FROM JACKIE

Hello, Reader!

Thank you for reading *The Wrangler and the Orphan,* the fourth book in my Farthingdale Ranch series.

If you enjoyed the book, I would love it if you would let your friends know so they can experience the romance between Brody and Kit.

If you leave a review, I'd love to read it! You can send the URL to: Jackienorthauthor@gmail.com

Jackie

facebook.com/jackienorthMM
twitter.com/JackieNorthMM
instagram.com/jackienorth_author
pinterest.com/jackienorthauthor
bookbub.com/profile/jackie-north
amazon.com/author/jackienorth
goodreads.com/Jackie_North

ABOUT THE AUTHOR

Jackie North has written since grade school and spent years absorbing mainstream romances. Her dream was to write full time and put her English degree to good use.

As fate would have it, she discovered m/m romance and decided that men falling in love with other men was exactly what she wanted to write about.

Her characters are a bit flawed and broken. Some find themselves on the edge of society, and others are lost. All of them deserve a happily ever after, and she makes sure they get it!

She likes long walks on the beach, the smell of lavender and rainstorms, and enjoys sleeping in on snowy mornings.

In her heart, there is peace to be found everywhere, but since in the real world this isn't always true, Jackie writes for love.

Connect with Jackie:

https://www.jackienorth.com/
jackie@jackienorth.com

facebook.com/jackienorthMM
twitter.com/JackieNorthMM
pinterest.com/jackienorthauthor
bookbub.com/profile/jackie-north
amazon.com/author/jackienorth
goodreads.com/Jackie_North
instagram.com/jackienorth_author